The Faces of Angels

The Faces of Angels

Lucretia Grindle

FELONY & MAYHEM PRESS • NEW YORK

All the characters and events portrayed in this work are fictitious.

THE FACES OF ANGELS

A Felony & Mayhem mystery

PRINTING HISTORY
First UK edition (Macmillan): 2006
Felony & Mayhem edition: 2011

ISBN: 978-1-934609-86-6
Manufactured in the United States of America

Printed on 100% recycled paper

Library of Congress Cataloging-in-Publication Data

Grindle, Lucretia W.
The faces of angels / Lucretia Grindle.
   p. cm.
ISBN 978-1-934609-86-6 (trade pbk. : alk. paper)
1. Serial murders--Italy--Florence--Fiction. 2. Americans--Italy--Fiction.
3. Florence (Italy)--Fiction. I. Title.
PS3557.R526F33 2011
813'.54--dc22
                          2011024339

The icon above says you're holding a copy of a book in the Felony & Mayhem "Foreign" category. These books may be offered in translation or may originally have been written in English, but always they will feature an intricately observed, richly atmospheric setting in a part of the world that is neither England nor the U.S.A. If you enjoy this book, you may well like other "Foreign" titles from Felony & Mayhem Press.

———◆———

For more about these books, and other Felony & Mayhem titles, or to place an order, please visit our website at:

www.FelonyAndMayhem.com

or contact us at:

Felony and Mayhem Press
156 Waverly Place
New York, NY 10014

Other "Foreign" titles from

FELONY&MAYHEM

The Faces of Angels

Chapter One

IT WAS HOT and there was a stone in my shoe. These are two of the things I remember, two of the things I think of when I think of the day my husband died. I understand that you might consider that strange. That you might reasonably expect something more momentous, a flash of insight, something large, or incomprehensibly moving. But in my experience it didn't work that way. That isn't what my memory hangs on to. What it grabs instead, what it salvages, are the small things, facts, details I can hold in the palm of my hand like so many grains of sand.

The stone, for instance. It had wedged itself between the flat sole of my new sandal and the bottom of the strap that crossed over my foot. They were typically Italian, those sandals, fancy and impractical, and not really like me at all. In fact, you could fairly say they were an aberration. And I would, except they matched the bag my lover had bought me, and the dress the salesgirl sold us afterwards.

They're ferociously good at that sort of thing, the salesgirls here in Florence, and they show no mercy. They spot you right away, as soon as you walk through the door of one of those fancy

1

little boutiques, and they recognize all the signs. The nonchalant fingering of price tags, the too-close attention to displays, the jumpy, irresponsible twitch at the edge of your smile and, if he's there, the man standing by, the one smiling indulgently and fingering the credit card—or, if he's married, the cash—in his pocket. The salesgirls see it all. Which is not surprising. After all it's virtually a genetic trait in this city, the making and selling of beautiful things, as is the talent that goes hand in hand with it: the special ability to sniff out your secret weaknesses, the holes in your heart that push you to buy, buy, buy. Handbags made entirely of seashells. Perfume distilled from iris kernels that cost more than gold. Engraved notes, and coloured sealing wax. Glass pens, beaded shoes. The salesgirls have them all to hand, all the beautiful, useless things you think you need when you're in love.

Which I was, at the time. And not with the man I was married to. I don't mean that as a confession, by the way. It's no *mea culpa*, that's not the spirit it's offered in. It's just a fact, that's all. Just one more grain of sand.

That wasn't how it seemed, though, on the day he bought me the dress, and the sandals, and the bright blue bag. On that day in early May when I looped my arm through his and he said, 'Wear it, and I'm touching you,' on that particular day, and on the days that followed, being in love seemed like everything. Everything you've ever been promised or dreamed or wanted. Nirvana. A bright shining light. Call it what you will. To me, that spring in Florence, it seemed like nothing less than that brass ring everyone talks about, the one that, just once in your life, you're supposed to reach out and grab. And I was ready to do that. In fact, in the days just before my husband died, I could almost see my hand moving through the air, almost feel my fingers making contact with the smooth, golden metal.

And then everything changes, and suddenly your life's a Scrabble game that's been knocked backhanded off a table so the letters no longer make up words you recognize. And though you don't fully understand it yet, you know, even before you try, that putting them back will not be possible; that some words will be missing. Holes will be left. There will be crevices and gaps that can never be filled, and things that won't make sense in quite the same way they used to.

So, while this happens, while the world slips, you cling to your strange little collection of facts, the ones you're absolutely sure of. The stone in your shoe. The sweat that slicked down your back and beaded across your chest. And the chalky white dust that was churned by the feet of running children and rose from the paths of the Boboli Gardens to hang on the still and languorous heat of a Sunday afternoon.

It was 25 May, that Sunday, and my husband and I were with other people. This was not unusual because, during the three months we were in Florence on what was effectively our honeymoon—if you can have a honeymoon with someone you've lived with for the better part of a decade—we were almost always with other people. Teachers, to be specific, and the occasional priest.

That was what my husband, Ty Warren, was, incidentally—a teacher, not a priest. Priests were part of the picture, though. They were part of the overall package, so to speak, because Ty was in an exchange programme teaching in religious schools, comparing the relative merits of the education systems. I'm Catholic, but I was just along for the ride, so I didn't really count. As far as the programme was concerned, Ty was the one who counted. He was the Quaker. There was a Baptist, a Methodist and a Lutheran too. Lance, Tricia and Melody, in that order, if my memory serves me right, which it does. And then, of course, there was Father Rinaldo.

Rinaldo joined us for lunch that afternoon, which was supposed to be a treat, a convivial splurge at a trattoria of the fancier kind, and afterwards he came with us to the Boboli Gardens. He waited, smiling, in the bright throng outside the gates while Ty ran off to buy tickets, and chatted amiably as we walked above the amphitheatre, then down by the orangery and made a visit to the grotto. But in the end he left early, most likely because of me.

Up until a week or so before, Rinaldo and I had been friends—if 'friends' is the right word for someone who hears your confession. During my first weeks in Florence, when I was alone for most of the time because Ty was teaching, and before I met Pierangelo, Rinaldo had taken me under his wing. He had spotted me one morning at San Miniato, standing awestruck in the vestry, and struck up a conversation. Rinaldo knew a lot about art. He was witty and spoke excellent English, and made a point of showing me some of his favourite places in the city. But by that Sunday afternoon at the end of May, our friendship was over. It ended because I made a mistake. A bad one. I told him the truth. All of it, naked and unvarnished.

Two weeks earlier, I had gotten down on my knees in the little black box of the confessional and whispered to Rinaldo that I didn't love my husband. And that I did love someone else. And that for the first time in my life I was happy—truly, wildly happy—and that what I wanted was God's permission to leave. Or, more precisely, to stay, since I understood even then that Pierangelo and Florence are inseparable.

I don't know, looking back, how I could have been so naive, and I wonder now what I had expected. Had I confused the Catholic Church with the Constitution? Did I really think my belief in it gave me a right to the pursuit of happiness? I don't know. The truth is, I would have settled for forgiveness, or even understanding. Compassion. Probably that's what I was really after. I mean, I thought that was the business Jesus was in. But apparently not. Rinaldo set me straight on that score. In the real church, he said, on the real path to God, rather than the byway I'd been wandering on, there was no room for weakness. We were all soldiers, and battles—nothing less than endless wars—had to be fought. In His Name's Sake. And I was blessed because my time had come. I had been presented with this chance to give up what I loved for Christ.

Of course, I demurred. I even went so far as to argue. But Rinaldo rose to the occasion. He insisted that the enemy was at hand. That it was, in fact, my own flesh, and if I did not engage, if I deserted the field and refused to fight—in short, if I didn't stop seeing Pierangelo immediately and dedicate myself, body and soul, to life with the man I had promised to love before God—well, then I might as well consider myself damned. Or at the very least cut off. Excommunicated. Out of the lottery in the stakes of grace.

Hearing those words was like leaning forward to receive a kiss and being slapped instead. And Rinaldo must have sensed it, because when he felt my shock, and heard my silence, he pushed the point home. There was, he said, no middle way. I must give up Pierangelo's love in order to accept Jesus'. My soul, he insisted, was in danger.

One has to admit the Catholic Church has always had an excellent sense of drama.

But despite the fact I knew full well about the histrionics favoured by certain kinds of priests, those words shook me to the core. Until that day I had lived my entire life as a Catholic, an obedient one, if not utterly committed, and so, shell-shocked by the strength of Rinaldo's conviction, I did what I was told. I remember walking back to our apartment from the church of San Miniato and feeling as though the lights had gone out, as though I was becoming slowly blind, and would be blind for ever. But still, I did try. That night I looked into my husband's handsome face, held his familiar hands, studied the flat, warm inflection of his words, and felt...nothing. Nothing but a horrible dulling hardness inside, as if my organs were slowly solidifying, ceasing to function and turning to stone.

When I told Pierangelo, which I did the next day before I lost my resolve completely, he tried to help. He assured me that he loved me, that he would always love me and that he would never forget, but he also assured me that he understood. Even if he didn't believe any more in the church himself, he too was married and, possibly more important, he was Italian. How could he ask me to choose between him and God? I suppose I could have hated him for that, but his response had the opposite effect. It didn't help, and it only made me love him more. Especially when he insisted that I had to do what I believed was right.

And so I did. But my heart was never in it. More than once I dialled his cell phone, just to hear his voice on the message, and occasionally I thought I saw him in a crowd, or on the street. I began to believe I was being followed, as though some other betrayed self, robbed of its chosen future, was dogging me down alleys and across squares. I was nearly run over by a motorcycle outside the apartment when I stepped, without looking, off the sidewalk, and I wondered if it was deliberate, if what I was really trying to do was kill myself fast, instead of ossifying slowly inside.

I did pray. In those awful leaden days, I begged God—I think it was God, or possibly the Virgin because I thought she'd be more sympathetic—that if I couldn't love Ty, could I at least feel something? Anything. But nothing touched the stones inside me, nothing relieved the conviction that I was dying by stages—heart, liver, spleen—and by the time we had lunch that Sunday and I sat there surrounded by the chattering teachers, wearing Pierangelo's dress and clutching the bag he had given me as if it were some sort of living memory, I think that by that time, I can safely say I hated Father Rinaldo.

He was aware of it, I'm sure, but I doubt he felt the same way about me. In fact, I'm sure he didn't, if only because hate implies a certain equality, and Rinaldo was an officer in the army of God whereas I was nothing more than cannon fodder caught on the brink of desertion. I'm quite certain, too, that he sensed the wavering of my resolve, knew where my dress had come from and why I wore it, and read the record of phone calls written on my soul. Every time he looked at me that Sunday a superior sort of pity lit his eyes, as if there was a private understanding between us of just how far I had fallen, and how the sad fact of it would only be offset by the thrill of my redemption, something I was certain he was planning even as he ate his ravioli and drank his wine. I could sense that like a mountaineer before a difficult climb, Rinaldo was getting ready, planning the route by which he would drag me back up the cliff of Faith before guiding me home through my own particular forest of thorns.

The assumption enraged me, which was at least a form of feeling, and therefore something of a relief, so I suppose I owe him that. Even now, about two years later, I can summon up the feeling of Rinaldo's eyes on my face that afternoon. They were like a physical touch, prodding and pushing. Soft, squishy fingers against my skin.

And yet. And yet. A lifetime of obedience, of hope, of Mother Church herself, cannot be so easily set aside. So, on that Sunday when Father Rinaldo finally turned and walked away from us, even as much as I hated him, I had to hold myself back. I had to physically stop myself from running after him, from dodging past the families and their children and the lovers who walked arm in arm, and throwing myself, right there in public, onto the gravel, and begging him—no, pleading with him—not to abandon me.

I remember how I stood there, feeling the need for absolution quivering inside me and tamping it down—one of Pavlov's dogs finally rebelling—and I wonder now if that's when the pieces started sliding. If it wasn't in that exact moment, the second when I did not run or plead, that the words that had made up my life until that day began to fall from the board, and if what came next wasn't just a kind of completion.

My husband was a natural leader. That's the kind of thing people used to say about Ty, and on that afternoon in the Boboli Gardens that's exactly what he was doing: leading. Up to the Belvedere fort and the Porcelain Museum, to be exact. The other three teachers had only been in the city a couple of weeks, and they all wore running shoes and carried water, big plastic one-litre bottles, as if they were expecting to cross the Sahara. They flocked around Ty as he read aloud from a guidebook, his voice ringing out, clear and flat amidst the babble of Italian, as he elaborated on the ruins of the mazes that had once been in the gardens, on the statuary and on the marvellous view they would see from the top of the hill. Then, when he was done, he opened his arms and made little flicking motions with his hands, herding them upwards, shepherd to sheep.

Ty excelled at shepherding, and in the normal course of things, he shepherded me. I think, deep down, he knew I was errant, and was convinced he had a duty of care to keep me on the straight and narrow. In Ty's book, love was vigilance, and while I'd given in to it passively before, once I met Pierangelo it drove me crazy. So I was alert for any opportunity to escape, and that afternoon he was distracted. He'd brought me to the Boboli before, but now he had a newer and bigger audience, one that wasn't already bored by descriptions of crumbling fountains and sculpted bushes, and as I stood there watching him, I realized that, for the first time in months, he wasn't paying any attention to me at all. No one was.

Below me the black column of Rinaldo's back grew smaller and smaller as he walked down the hill, while above me Ty herded the teachers away. Their chatter dissipated as they climbed, the words growing fainter, thinning like the vapour trails of planes. A bunch of children in their Sunday clothes ran down the wide avenue. The little girls wore dresses blotched with the white dust that rose from the gravel, and the boys wore navy-blue shorts and shirts with ties. Their parents pretended not to notice as they swatted each other with sticks, almost hitting me in the process so that I had to step away, which was when I felt the stone, and bent down to take my sandal off and get rid of it. I redid the buckle, then straightened up, looked around, and saw the tunnel.

Furry and disguised with new leaf, it opened like a mouth in the thick line of the trees. Thin branches laced overhead, their shadows throwing leopard spots on the path. I didn't know where it went, and I didn't particularly care. I could smell the damp undergrowth, and as I stepped off the avenue I was surrounded by a wavering light that was as inviting and green as the sea on a hot day.

At first, noises followed me; the sound of voices, barks of Sunday afternoon laughter, the clop of horses' hooves as the *carabinieri* rode up towards the fort, ramrod straight and two by two, like something from the ark. But they faded. As I walked on, the laughter fractured and died, and the horses passed. And then there was nothing, just the soft scrunching of my own footsteps and the slippery rustle of winter leaves no one had bothered to rake away.

I didn't know the Boboli Gardens all that well, but it was one of Ty's favourite places, and he'd told me quite a lot about it, so I thought that if I walked far enough I would eventually come out at the Mostaccini fountain.

The fountain is really a series of fountains, more like a little elevated canal. Before he showed it to me, Ty had described it in such glowing terms that when I actually saw it, it was a serious disappointment. Once, its grinning faces, every one different, spat water into a long stepped trough that had been designed to lure songbirds. But for years their mouths have been shut, stopped with leaves and clogged with gobbets of moss. Now their lips spit nothing but curlicues of vine, and the trough is dry and mottled with lichen. Like the ruins of the mazes the Medici built, the Mostaccini is nothing but a bone in the skeleton of the gardens, a fading line that marks the southern wall of the Boboli. Which was where I was heading, or so I thought, when I heard footsteps.

The truth is, I wasn't even sure they were there. I think I glanced back, half expecting to see Ty coming after me—which I was sure he would, eventually—but the path had gotten wilder and more overgrown, and I couldn't make anyone out. I turned a corner and leaves rustled. I thought I saw a shadow move. But I told myself that this was a public park and of course there were other people. I wouldn't be the only one who was drawn away from the glare and dust and noise of the main avenues. In fact, I was surprised I hadn't stumbled over lovers already, heard the snuffling sound of kisses in the bushes. I forced myself to smile at my attack of the willies, but, even so, something altered in my head and I walked a little faster, lengthened my stride and tried to calculate how much further I had to go. I heard the low hum of traffic, which meant I must be near the southern wall. And then a branch snapped, and I started to run.

The undergrowth got denser. The path itself almost disappeared a couple of times, and branches snagged my dress. They grabbed my purse and pulled it off my shoulder, but I didn't care. I was sure I could hear the sound of running feet and the quick huff-huff of breathing. Then I saw a change in the light. Just ahead of me sun glittered through the leaves, and I was sure that it was the avenue by the Mostaccini and that there would be people there, so I put in an extra burst of speed. I threw myself towards the greening light, and as I reached the end of the path I opened my mouth to scream.

But no sound ever came out. And just before he grabbed me, just before I fell, face down into the new spring grass, I understood. There was no long fountain. No pale grey vein of stone. There was no gravelled avenue ahead of me, and there were no people. I had made a mistake, and the path I'd followed had led me straight to the centre of one of the ruined mazes.

He brought me down from behind, one hand wound in my hair, grabbing me the way I have always imagined Perseus grabbed Medusa. The feral tastes of dirt and blood mingled in my mouth while his other hand moved all over me, caressed me with the soft inhuman skin of a leather glove, and finally pulled the sash off my dress. He tied my wrists together, and rolled me over, and that's when I saw the blade. It was bright and silver and very shiny, and he stabbed it into the grass so he could use both hands to prise my jaws open and stuff my underwear into my mouth. After that he took his time.

Black, that's what I remember. That's about all I could tell the police. A black hood pulled down over his head like something a kid would wear for Halloween. It had nothing but slits for his eyes, which didn't mean I couldn't feel them. I could, just as surely as I felt the touch of his hand. They slid down my body and back up. They stroked my skin and rested on my face, on my hair. Then they moved to the blade.

He cleaned it when he pulled it out of the earth, ran it between his thumb and forefinger, and brushed away tiny bits of dirt that fell on me. Then he reached down and slit the material of my dress. He peeled the flimsy silk back from across my breasts carefully, almost fastidiously, as if he were skinning a grape, and then he carved on my chest.

My breasts became his canvas as he worked his deliberate, intricate pattern; lifting and cutting, and cutting again. The pain was as bright and garish as Christmas lights, and finally I closed my eyes and felt as if we were spiralling through a night sky, just him and me and the blade. It went on for an hour or a minute. I don't know. The cuts flashed around me like blinking stars, and I lost sense of time. Then Ty called my name.

At first, I thought I was dreaming, or that this was death and he was calling me home. But his voice got louder. Bushes cracked and snapped, and I fell to earth, plummeted straight down out of my night sky, a bird with no wings. I could feel the ground, damp underneath me, smell grass and the sharp stink of sweat, and suddenly the possibility of living seemed real and urgent, something that I might be able to grab if I tried hard enough. So I did. I opened my eyes, and tried to scream. I tried to spit out my underwear. And when that didn't work, I kicked. I bucked and jerked like a bull calf, and the knife slipped, and he stabbed me.

There was a lot of weight behind it because I'd thrown him off balance, so the blade went in fast and deep. The man in the hood made a sound, not really a word, just a bitten-off noise, a grunt of anger, and when he pulled the knife out it sucked and slurped like a plug coming out of a bottle. Later, I understood that that's when he punctured my lung.

I could feel anger rising off him like heat, and when he stood up fast, still holding the knife, and stepped back, I was sure that this was it; that in the few seconds before Ty inevitably found us he'd kill me. I remember that I didn't know what to expect. A thrust? A draw across my throat? I had no idea how people were killed with knives, not really, and suddenly I wanted to see my body one last time. So I lifted my head and looked.

Blood swelled in ridges and lines. It ran down the mounds of my breasts where he had carved, and soaked the pieces of my dress. Bright red and strangely beautiful, I couldn't really believe it was mine. And I was watching it, staring at the rivulets and the little webs of pink froth that bubbled up where the knife had gone in, when Ty burst out of the bushes.

He threw himself into the clearing, breaking free of the branches, and his eyes locked on me. My husband had beautiful eyes. They were amber coloured, almost golden, and long lashed, and in that second, they widened, shocked, as if he had stumbled on me doing something obscene. Then, so fast it was like wind moving across water, his face filled with pity, and he froze, staring at me the way you stare at an animal that's been hit by a car, something still alive that's dying. And that's what cost him his life.

The man in the hood stepped forward and shoved the knife all the way up in one strong, fast thrust, and the bright blue purse, which Ty must have plucked from the undergrowth, fell to his feet. They told me later that the blade went straight through Ty's ribcage and into his heart. The man didn't bother to remove it. He left it there and stepped around the body, almost fastidiously, and came back to me. Kneeling, he took my chin in one hand while he lifted the hair off my forehead with the other, caressing, his gloves warm and sticky. Then he kissed me. I felt his lips through the thin fabric, and the tip of his tongue as it ran, damp and hard, across my cheek.

They got him, of course. The Italian police are really very efficient, and they picked him up in a matter of hours. He had our blood on his hands, literally, and under his nails, and on his clothes. His name was Karel Indrizzio, and he was a half-Albanian drifter from the Po Valley who'd been known to sleep rough in the gardens and had been in trouble with the police before, for purse snatching and fights outside bars, and once for exposing himself to a bunch of schoolkids who came across him in one of the grottoes. When they found him that evening, he was curled under a bush singing hymns to himself. Our wallets were in his back pocket. When the police questioned him, he pointed out that he didn't think we'd have minded him taking them since the last time he saw us he was pretty sure we were both dead.

Even taking into account its sensational nature, the attack on us might have been seen as nothing more than a potential rape and robbery gone wrong, except for one tiny detail, one thing the mounted *carabinieri* who finally found me almost missed in their eagerness to make sure I was still alive. At first glance, it was just a miniature papier-mâché mask, the kind of thing you buy in any souvenir shop in Venice for a euro. A cheap, nasty little face, it rested, hollowed-eyed and grinning, in the long grass beside me. To the investigating officer, however—a dour-faced man called Pallioti—it was manna from heaven. Once he established that it had never belonged to me, and that it wasn't from a key chain, or a cheap ornament one of Ty's students had given him, the tiny mask became the first break in a much publicized case involving the murders of two other women, a nun called Eleanora Darnelli and a nurse named Benedetta Lucchese.

The police had had nothing at all to go on for Eleanora, and in the absence of any other leads had fancied Benedetta's fiancé for her killing. But the mask changed all that. Both women had been killed with a knife almost identical to the one used on Ty and me, which was readily available in any kitchen shop, so that was not the cause for excitement. What excited Pallioti was what the police had kept to themselves: the fact that, like me, each of the other women had been left a souvenir. In Eleanora's case, a white ribbon tied around her left wrist, and in Benedetta's, a burnt-out candle folded into her hands.

They went to work tying Indrizzio to the two previous killings, and in the meantime charged him with Ty's murder and my assault. Despite the fact that he wiped it off, the blade that went into my lung must have been dirty, because the wound got infected. For a day or two they actually thought I might die, but eventually I recovered and was flown back to Philadelphia, where my husband's parents had delayed his funeral until I was well enough to attend. After that, I went back to the apartment Ty and I had bought in Philly and waited to return to Italy to testify at Indrizzio's trial.

Pallioti had told me it wouldn't be until the New Year. But in the end, I didn't have to wait that long, because just five months later the whole thing was over. Pierangelo gave me the news. A newspaper editor, he picked it up on the wire, and called me to say that Karel Indrizzio was dead. They'd been moving him to a high security prison outside Milan when a tractor-trailer had jumped the median on the *autostrada*. The driver of the prison van and one of the guards had survived. But the others, handcuffed inside, had died before the emergency services could get there.

So, that's how it ended. And now there's nothing left of that day but the grains of sand. The heat. The stone in my shoe. The knowledge that words slipped off the board.

I have made myself a promise I intend to keep: that what happened in the Boboli Gardens will not run my life, that I am a person beyond that, and I will not give Karel Indrizzio the power to rob me of the city and the man I love. And so I try not to think about it, what happened to Ty and to me, and Eleanora and Benedetta, and how Indrizzio himself must have died. And most of the time, I succeed. Or at least I did. Until I returned to Florence.

I'm not surprised by this. I expected it. But it is not, as you might think, because I've returned to 'the scene of the crime.' No matter what they say, you carry that inside you. So, no, it's not the physical proximity. It's not that at all. It's because memories breed here. In fact, sometimes I think that's all Florence is, layers and layers of the past. A city made not of stone and mortar, but of memories and secrets and the fevered imaginings of men, all of them piled like transparencies one on top of the other until they form the illusion of something solid. Golden buildings. Grey walls. Stone. In the early mornings, if you walk along the Lungarnos or stand on the misted spans of the bridges, you can almost believe the churches and piazzas and towers are nothing more or less than dreams. Of the Medici. And Michelangelo. And Dante. And Botticelli. And Galileo. And a million other more ordinary human souls who've passed through this place, shedding the shadows of their lives like the skins of snakes.

Chapter Two

I COULD SAY that coming back here was Pierangelo's idea, but that wouldn't be true. It was mine. All he did was what the best friends and lovers do: read your mind and give life—or, in this case, words—to the dreams already blossoming in your head. Even that didn't happen right away. It was a good six months after Karel Indrizzio was killed before Piero mentioned the possibility of my returning to Florence.

Once he did, it wasn't a hard sell. My marriage to Ty had been a mistake, and if I hadn't known it at the time, I realized soon after. We were bound by the years we'd spent together, and by dishes and books and wine glasses and an apartment, and by the fact that he loved me. All of which might have been enough, but wasn't. And yet that didn't make his death easier. If anything, it made it worse.

In those first awful months back in Philly I spent night after night with Father Rinaldo's words scrabbling through my head, running like rats on bare boards, whispering that I was damned. It is generally agreed that masks stand for deception, and when I looked in the mirror, I sometimes thought I saw an empty face. On occasion, when I dreamed, I traded presents with Eleanora Darnelli and Benedetta Lucchese—a candle and a ribbon. Sometimes I even spoke to them. Because they had been where I had been. We three in all the world had received Karel Indrizzio's kiss.

Our friends in Philadelphia assumed I was drowning in grief, but, try as they might, none of them could help because none of them knew the whole truth: that Ty was killed because of me but I had never loved him. The only person who knew that was Pierangelo, and when I finally heard his voice on the phone, it didn't sound like damnation. It sounded like someone throwing me a lifeline. Like being in prison and hearing rain against a window, then the rattle of a frame, and the first sweet shattering of glass.

Six months later, he had to come to the States, and we met in New York. During that week, Pierangelo told me that his twins, Graziella and Angelina, had moved out of the apartment in Florence, gone to university in Milan and Bologna to find their own lives. Shortly afterwards, about the time Indrizzio was killed, his wife, Monika, left too. Their marriage had been fracturing for years. They had never been happy, had stayed together for the same reason they were married in the first place, because of the girls, and Monika pointed out they'd soon be fifty. She said she, at least, still had a chance for a life.

Pierangelo loved me. He wanted me back. And now, we were both free. After he left, I returned to Philadelphia, which felt more and more like exile. That night, as Piero's plane arced across the Atlantic, I lay on the couch and watched his words flutter against the ceiling. Flying in and out of the light, they made shadow patterns, and in them I saw a map of the future.

Getting a chance at something you never thought you'd have is like a dare. It's like life throwing down the cards and saying: *OK, you finally got your winning hand, now can you play it?* The truth was, I didn't know, but I was certainly determined to try. And this time I decided not to make the mistakes I'd made before.

I make my living writing on design, for Sunday papers usually, and sometimes magazines, those glossy, heavy things with perfume inserts and endless lust articles on other people's terraces and bathrooms. Don't ask how I fell into it, I'm not sure myself, it was a detour that became a career, but it's not, so to speak, part of my long-term life plan. I used to paint. Drawings and watercolours of period buildings mostly, and I toyed for years with doing a graduate degree in art history. It wasn't Ty's fault, but while he was alive we couldn't afford it. Now, ironically, I could. He left me with a decent life insurance policy, and we owned our apartment. If I rented it out, I'd have plenty to pay for an art history course in Florence.

It didn't escape me that the death of his dreams was the beginning of mine, and the course wasn't just an excuse to be with Pierangelo. Having seen my mid-thirties come and go, I wanted to see if I could be a student again, just putting my toe in the water to start with, and even if I never slept a night in it, I knew I had to have a room of my own. Having been caught by the sheer force of domestic inevitability once, I wasn't about to let it happen again. For my sake and Pierangelo's. I can bear a lot, but I don't think I could bear to become something he'll regret. Which is why, tonight, while he's in Rome, I'm sitting on the balcony of my own apartment, roughly a stone's throw from Santo Spirito.

It's old, this building. I don't know how old for sure, but I'd guess four hundred, maybe five hundred years, which I confess I find comforting. Like a lot of Americans, I'm fascinated by the age of things. When you grow up in a place where two hundred years old is ancient, half a millennia of footsteps crossing your courtyard, five centuries of ghosts hanging around in the door-ways, either terrifies you or seduces you. Personally, I'm relieved to be reminded that nothing, nothing at all, dreams or fears, are new.

The balcony looks down on a courtyard. Tonight it's quiet, but often there's the sound of a piano from the apartment oppo-site, or the tinny voice of the radio news leaking up from the floor below. Signora Raguzza listens every evening, and sometimes I can hear her swearing at the prime minister or encouraging the Pope. I love that about Italy; the noise. In the States, silence is sacred. Success is your own quarter acre, a long driveway and a high wall. If you've really made it, an electronic gate. But not here. In this city lives are piled one on top of the other. You hear footsteps, singing, shouting. You know what the people downstairs are eating because the smell wafts up, and you know what their kitchen will look like because these palazzos are mostly the same; old, old shells inhabited by new lives.

The kitchen of this apartment, for instance, is beautiful and narrow and impractical. The ceiling is twenty feet high. The French windows that open on to the balcony do not bolt properly and rattle in the wind. The light is a Murano chandelier no one can reach to clean, and the cups and saucers in the dresser are as translucent as eggshells. Heels click on marble floors and the metal shutters that cover the windows run up and down like trains on ancient tracks. There is a silvered mirror in the hall that makes everyone who passes it look as if half their face is missing, and in the stairwell a tiny elevator no larger than a coffin creaks and winds from landing to landing.

In Milan, the capital of sleek, all this might be looked down on. But in Florence it is highly prestigious. So much so that Signora Bardino, who owns not only this apartment but also the art school I finally enrolled in, claims she doesn't normally rent it out at all. But one look at me and the woman I share it with, Billy Kalczeska, the signora said, and she felt sure we would appreciate the apartment's finer points. The ormolu desk. The Murano glass. She could tell just from looking at us that we had a sense of history. The comment made Billy, who was standing behind the signora at the time, roll her eyes and stick her finger down her throat.

The Florence Academy for Adult Education, where Billy and I are 'students,' is Signora Bardino's personal brainchild. Having come to Florence and fulfilled her own fantasies, she apparently decided to franchise the idea, and the result is an impressive web page that promises, though we may think it is too late, we can still Live Our Dreams of the Renaissance! For a hefty fee. Which explains why I have a room-mate. I hadn't planned on it, but the advantages, expense-wise at least, were obvious. The signora, whom Billy calls the SignEuro, charges what I will bluntly call 'a wack load' for us to exercise our sense of history, and splitting the rent, and the apartment, was actually her idea. She hadn't met Billy when she made the suggestion, but that didn't stop her from assuring me by email that Signora Kalczeska was 'delightful'. This was a few weeks before I arrived, and I looked Billy up on the academy webpage, where all of us were supposed to have posted a picture and a brief 'get to know you' biography, but there was nothing there.

This is appropriate in a strange way because the Florence Academy for Adult Education isn't really 'there' either. In fact, it isn't anywhere, except possibly in Signora Bardino's basement—a cavernous set of rooms in an equally cavernous palazzo near San Ambrogio. We meet there once a week for wine and cheese and slide shows presented by a retired professor called Signor Catarelli, who guides us through our adventures in the Renaissance, telling bad jokes along the way. For the rest of the week, we're free to indulge in a smorgasbord of 'activities'. For each three-month 'semester' Signora Bardino arranges for her 'students' to attend lectures on art history at the university, and the British Council, and anywhere else where someone might be talking about Massaccio or Pisanello, or 'The Development of Perspective' in English.

She also wangles discounted entry for us at the Uffizi and the Accademia, and a few stranger places like the Museum of Precious Stones, and the Specula, which features pickled body parts and a selection of perfectly preserved autopsies. In addition, we go on field trips once a week, in a minibus driven by one of her endless supply of nephews, outings that invariably end at a trattoria run by another nephew, where Signor Bardino—who is tall, lugubrious and very Italian—sometimes joins us. On these occasions, the signora's accent, which is impenetrable already, grows even thicker, something I have appreciated all the more since Piero told me that she comes from Westchester, New York. This fact alone makes her almost as much a product of her own imagination as her academy is.

I pointed this out to Billy the other night, and she laughed and blew smoke through her nose. 'Welcome to Florence,' she said. 'City of the Uncommon Delusion.'

Signora Bardino interests me, not only because of what she has morphed herself into, but because she's a friend of Pierangelo's soon-to-be ex-wife. Piero suggested her academy in the first place, and I've watched her to see if she has any inkling of my real connection to him. So far there's been no evidence, and it's certainly not something I feel inclined to reveal. To Signora Bardino or anyone else, for that matter.

It's not that I keep Pierangelo a secret, but I've been here almost a month now and I've noticed that none of us enrolled at the academy spend much time discussing who or what we are when we're not here. In my case the reasons for this are obvious—I don't talk about what happened to me with anyone—but generally I think we don't do it because it would ruin a vital part of what we're paying for: the illusion that this really is our life.

I don't know for sure what the others have done to increase the viability of their own particular dream worlds, but the first thing I did when I got here was change how I looked. I had my previously boring long blonde hair cut into a pageboy and dyed chestnut brown. Then, yesterday, I went a step further and had it striped. Now, I run my fingers through my metallic streaks, thinking what a fit the nuns at the convent summer camp I used to go to would have if they could see them, and watching the lights switch off in the apartment opposite. The sound of water burbling in our pipes tells me Billy's pulled the plug in her bath and is on her way to bed, which is a relief. Not because of her, but because, more and more, I think of this city the same way I think of Pierangelo; as an intimate, a lover. And I relish the time we spend alone together.

Florence knows things about me no one knows. These

narrow, hemmed-in streets, the blank grey faces of these buildings with their huge doors that conceal their secrets, in turn
know my secrets. This city knows where I was unfaithful—
where I held a hand, stole a kiss. It has heard my laughter, my
footsteps and my cruelty. Heard me tell Piero how Ty always
followed me, never left me alone, and how it drove me crazy. It
has listened to me complain that I was fettered by Ty's love, and
watched while I stood on street corners, or sketched a building.
It has seen me naked, standing at the window of a borrowed
apartment. And tied up. And gagged, lying in the grass, a paper
face laughing at nothing while consciousness flickered like a
firefly. Florence has seen all that, and the idea would be repellent
if stones judged. But they don't. They merely witness.

Love. Hate. Luck. I'm sure that's what the stones would tell
me if they could speak, that I was lucky, and caution me not to
forget it. And I don't because it's true. It was the first thing I
thought of this evening when Kirk mentioned the girl.

Kirk's Italian is not as good as he thinks it is, and he was
labouring over the paragraph in the evening paper when he
finally announced, 'It was a rower who found her.'

After that, he read on, his voice faltering over the longer
words, sounding out the syllables, and more often than not
getting the stresses wrong. But despite that, or maybe because of
it, that first phrase stuck in my mind—*It was a rower who found
her.* I closed my eyes and instead of Piazza Santo Spirito, where
we were sitting, I saw the muddy green band of the Arno. And
the boat. The oars rose and dipped and rose again, as the scull
flew across the water, fast and smooth as a skate on ice.

Sometimes, just after dawn, I go down to the bridges, so in
all likelihood I've seen him, the man who found this girl. He'll
be thin and agile, a water-borne greyhound, and I imagine him,
just as the sun is rising, glancing backwards, throwing a look
over his shoulder and not realizing what she was at first, because
by then she probably didn't look much like a person any more.
I imagine her putty white, mottled blue, her limbs heavy with
death, already something less than human. Maybe he thought

she was nothing but driftwood. Garbage that had been abandoned and left to rot in the neon green of the reed grass that grows below the ramparts of Ponte alle Grazie.

And it must have been a shock, spotting her like that. Hardly what you'd expect on an early spring morning. So I think the rower should be forgiven if the first thing he wanted to tell himself was that she was just a drunk, passed out. That's the natural reaction, to feel not fear, or even pity, but the pang of revulsion that sets the dead apart. I can't blame him if the first thing he did when he saw her was reach for the belief that the girl lying there in the grass could not be in any way like him. That she could never be his daughter, or his wife or sister, but must instead be a vagrant. A junky. One of the lost. Nothing but a broken rider of dreams who'd crashed to earth in Florence.

'Can I see?' I asked.

Kirk shrugged and handed me the paper. The picture of the girl was small and grainy and stared up at me as he reached for his wine glass.

'How much do you want to bet,' Kirk said, 'that somebody's picking them off? That it's the population protecting itself, fighting back against the Scourge of Art Students.'

'Does it say she was an art student?' asked Henry. Henry is a big bear-like creature of a man who refers to himself as 'A-psychologist-from-Baltimore-who's-on-sabbatical-maybe-permanently'. He has a beard and wears glasses and strange baggy trousers with oddly placed loops and pockets. It is not hard to imagine Henry as Baloo, the bear in *The Jungle Book*. Once, not long after we arrived, he entertained us all by drinking too much wine and singing, 'Get Happy.' Billy took a picture with one of the disposable cameras she loves and now it's taped to the door of our tiny refrigerator.

'Nope,' I replied. The paper didn't say anything about who she was. It didn't even give her a name, or age. The picture suggested 'young', and I held it up so the others could see. Henry grimaced, but Kirk ignored it.

Like Billy and I, they share an apartment, and Kirk is

Bagheera to Henry's Baloo. The only thing that isn't pantherish about him is his red hair. It's long, and when he tucks it behind his ears, as he does frequently, he reminds me powerfully of my Second Grade teacher, Mrs Cartwright, who was memorable mainly for her carroty hair, and for the fact that she once fainted in assembly. Kirk, however, is not a Second Grade teacher. According to his 'get to know you' note on the signora's website, he's a lawyer from Manhattan, but from the way he works a crowd, even one as small as the three of us, you'd be forgiven for thinking he's a stand-up comic. A sly smile snuck across his face.

'You know,' he said, 'the art students here. It's probably like the body fighting viruses. Or trees developing resistance to Dutch elm disease. Or maybe it's natural selection, the death of the weakest. The last into the Uffizi shall die.'

Kirk says his 'little sojourn at the Academy della Bardina' is a treat to himself for surviving three and a half glorious decades before he has to finally grow up for good and start a job in DC with the Justice Department, but I have to say that the idea of him going to work for the Feds strikes me as unlikely. Kind of like hiring Avril Levigne as a front woman for the Young Rotarians. On the other hand, Justice probably knows what it's doing, because if his performances in the bar are any indication, Kirk's a killer in court.

He leaned back in his little metal chair, his long black coat flapping on either side of him, and elaborated. 'In my opinion, it is distinctly possible,' he said, 'that the art students have started killing each other because things have gotten too crowded, like those animals—what are they, lemmings?'

'Rats,' Billy said. 'Lemmings jump over cliffs.'

Billy was watching the far side of the piazza as she spoke, spinning the stem of her wine glass between her thumb and forefinger, making the strip of lemon peel inside dance on a whirlpool of tepid Pinot Grigiot. 'Somewhere in Canada, I think,' she added. 'Or maybe Newfoundland.'

'Well, same idea.'

'Canada and Newfoundland?' Billy raised her eyebrows.
'Well, yes, as a matter of fact.' The intrusion of geography
made Kirk petulant. 'You cannot dispute,' he insisted, tapping
the table as though we might, 'you absolutely cannot dispute
that Florence has a superabundance of art students. Just think
about it. Just consider for a moment how many Junior Years
Abroad are passed in these poor, benighted streets. In fact,' he
added, 'I would guess that the population of Uffizi-goers toting
fanny packs and indulging in bad art theory is reaching something dangerously close to critical mass.'
    'What is "critical mass"?' Billy asked. 'I mean, exactly?'
    Henry put his beer bottle down and snorted. He likes to
drink Nastro Azzuro and peel the labels off the side. There are
usually little piles of shavings where he's been sitting. 'Are you
seriously suggesting,' he said, pushing his glasses up his nose,
'that this woman was killed because she said something stupid
about Botticelli? Does it even say she was killed?'
    'No,' I said, but everyone ignored me.
    Kirk grinned, his pale foxy face looking as if it had been
cracked with a cleaver. 'If she said it loud enough. And elaborated. Right in front of the *Primavera*.' There was a silence as
we considered this. 'I mean, who among us,' Kirk asked, 'who
among us can honestly say that they have not been tempted to
homicide when trapped in the Uffizi and forced to listen to some
halfwit reciting *Art 101*?'
    By this time Billy had stopped watching the piazza or,
presumably, wondering about critical mass, and she turned and
looked at us. Billy's six foot if she's an inch, her hair is long and
blonde and kinky, her eyes are the colour of sapphires. Of the
sky. A summer day reflected in deep, deep water. Billy's eyes are
the eyes little girls draw on the faces of princesses. 'In the bathroom,' she said suddenly. 'In the basement of the Accademia.
They brush their hair over the sinks.'
    'They always have long hair.' Henry was getting into the
spirit now. He pushed the too-long sleeves of his sweater up over
his wrists in a gesture that suggested he was getting serious, and

waved his big, blunt hands. About a week ago, Henry told me that he'd always wanted to be a sculptor, not a shrink, but sadly he had to make a living. I told him he looked like Michelangelo, which is actually true, and two little pink spots of pleasure appeared on his cheeks.

'It's tribal.' Kirk poured the last of his little bottle of Campari into his glass. 'The hair,' he announced, 'is a form of ritual identification, best known to twenty-year-olds. They signal by shaking their heads. Like horses, I believe. Studies have been done. In the case of the female, the long hair is absolutely essential for sitting in cafés and attracting Romeo. He pulls up on his Vespa and tells her she looks like a Renaissance angel, after which energetic, if largely uninspired, sex takes place.'

'I don't know,' Billy said. 'All I can tell you is, they hog the mirrors. And spend hours putting on lip gloss that's clear anyways. I never did get the point of that.' She tapped the last cigarette out of her pack and crumpled the paper in her fist. 'Clear lip gloss, I mean.'

'Smoochability,' Kirk said, leaning across to light her cigarette. 'All the heavenly legions wear lip gloss. And the Virgin Mary. They get a bulk discount. Like Sam's Club.'

'Well,' Billy said, 'I bet Mary Magdalene wears Chanel.'

Henry picked up his bottle and looked at it sadly when he realized it was empty. 'Lip gloss aside,' he said, 'the evidence would certainly seem to suggest that some thinning of the art student population is in order.'

And at that, we all turned and looked at the table where the Japanese girls were sitting, as though we didn't count.

Apart from the four of us and Ellen and Tony, a couple from Honolulu who have rented an apartment up in Fiesole and as a result almost never show up at the bar, the Japanese girls are the only other students presently enrolled at the academy. There are three of them, Ayako, Mikiko and, we think, Tamayo, although we're not sure on the last count. Kirk insists they're stewardesses from Cathay Pacific who got laid off during the SARS crisis, but Billy says she doesn't think this is true.

What is true is that, just like us, the Japanese girls come to the bar at Santo Spirito almost every evening but, unlike us, they almost never drink anything. Instead, they order one pot of tea between the three of them, which pisses the waitress off, a fact they don't seem to spend a lot of time worrying about. They don't spend a lot of time coming to lectures, either. In fact, as far as we can tell, the only thing they do seem to spend a lot of time doing is buying tiny pieces of designer leather. Key folders from Prada. Credit-card sleeves from Piero Guidi. Miniature coin purses covered with someone else's initials. The smaller the better, as if they are shopping for a colony of dwarfs.

Every afternoon the Japanese girls compare their purchases at a sandwich bar in Piazza della Repubblica, then they go to Vivoli and eat ice cream. After that, they usually show up at the bar.

Ayako and Mikiko and Tamayo come here and don't drink in much the same way they come to Signor Catarelli's lectures on 'The Rise of Perspective' and 'The Decline of the Byzantine' and don't talk. Instead, while the hapless signor mixes up his slides and babbles happily about Piero della Francesca, they watch us. Well, not us, exactly. Kirk. His translucent skin and lean neurotic looks appear to fascinate them. Or maybe it's his red mane, or the fact that he wears his black coat all the time, even indoors when the heat is on, like that guy in *The Matrix*. Whatever the reason, the Japanese girls are obviously far more impressed by Kirk than by Signor Catarelli. So much so, in fact, that we have noticed that whenever he writes anything down, they do too. It didn't take Billy long to suggest that Kirk scribble furiously whenever Signor Catarelli says goodbye or hello or makes a bad joke, just to see what would happen. We figure that in a few weeks the Japanese girls will have comprehensive notes on the words *ciao* and *arrivederci*, and the fact that that-fellow-Uccello-was-certainly-no-bird-brain.

'I'm hungry,' Henry said suddenly. And, as if on cue, the other three of us got to our feet, realizing we were hungry too. Then Henry went inside to use the bathroom, and Billy and Kirk indulged in their nightly ritual of haggling about the bill. The Japanese girls were whispering together, their heads bent, trying to decide whether or not they were hungry as well and should come with us, and as a result no one was watching me. So no one saw as I reached for the evening paper and slipped it into my shoulder bag.

That was several hours ago. Now all of the lights are out, and the arches of the portico are dark loops of shadow in the courtyard below. Over the rooftops I can just see the spine of Santo Spirito, lit up for the night. It is still too chilly for crowds, and the piazza will be empty, chairs piled on the tables of the bars, the branches of the trees nothing but black scribbles against the sulphurous grey of the sky. City cats will be prowling the base of the fountain, picking fights and looking for scraps, and all of it will be watched over by the giant Cyclops eye of the church window. Even in daylight, it's hard not to feel that eye looking down on you, and when we finally left the bar this evening, I was sure it was watching me, sure it saw as I picked up the paper, and stole the little picture of the dead girl.

I go back inside and close the French windows. In the kitchen, breadcrumbs are scattered across the polished wooden counter and there is a piece of tomato that will laminate itself onto the top of the stove if someone doesn't clean it off sometime soon. Two paper napkins are crumpled in a used glass, and a munchkin-sized ice tray has left a pool of milky water in a cereal bowl. The general effect is sluttish, which pleases me. Pierangelo's kitchen is virtually military in its order, and I have been neat all my life, so coming here and leaving dishes in the sink and clothes dropped on the floor feels like loosening a shoe lace.

I call goodnight to Billy as I pass her room, and then, even though I get no reply, I lock my door. I don't want to be interrupted. Hunkering down on the floor, I pull the paper out of my bag and spread the front page out. The print is a little smeared from being folded up and the picture's crumpled, so I can't see the girl very well, but I study her anyway. She has long dark hair and slightly slanted eyes. She could be Italian or French or Albanian, or, for that matter, anything. Anyone. It's impossible to tell. The article says she committed suicide, but it's not specific. I imagine she jumped from a bridge, or took an overdose and lay down beside the water to die.

I hold the paper up to the light, lean closer and look at her.

I shouldn't be doing this, I know, but I can't help myself. It's something I've acquired since the accident—that's how I think of it, incidentally, 'accident,' as if being chased and bound and cut was on a par with a car crash. Anyways, since then, I've acquired a heightened interest in dead people. It's not general, of course. I don't pay too much attention to the casualties of old age or disease. No. The ones who interest me are the ones who are like me but a little less lucky: the by-products of 'accidents.'

It started back in Philadelphia, in the months before Piero reappeared. During the nights I didn't sleep, when I couldn't reach Benedetta and Eleanora in my dreams, I searched Ty's 'accident' on the internet, and read about others. Perhaps it made me feel less alone, or maybe I believed that reading details in black and white could somehow make something up to him. I couldn't access what got published at the time here in Florence, which I never saw, thanks to being in hospital, so one of the first things I did after I arrived was go to the library and look up the newspaper articles from Monday, 26 May. I told myself I owed Ty that, and I was shocked to find an editorial by Pierangelo, which isn't really fair, given that it is his job. Still, it was strange to see myself written about as part of a phenomenon, an example of the breakdown of Italian society, and to know that my lover's hands had typed the words. At least he didn't refer to it as 'L'Assassinio della Luna Miele,' the Honeymoon Killing, like most of the other papers did.

I think about this as I get down on my knees, pull the

manila envelope from under the jeans in the bottom drawer of my dresser, and let the articles I've copied slither out onto the cold marble floor. The sheets rustle and whisper. I shuffle them around, put them in an order of my own, and think some day maybe I'll look up the other two women Karel Indrizzio kissed, just to make my collection complete.

The idea has a certain appeal, but I do realize that, like picking scabs, this little fixation is not particularly socially acceptable. I'm not even sure, exactly, why I do it any more.

It's a sort of crutch, I suppose, and I will give it up when I'm ready. In the meantime, however, I think it best to keep the manila envelope and its contents to myself. It's private. My harmless little secret. Perhaps the only one about me that even Pierangelo doesn't know.

Chapter Three

PIERANGELO CALLS EARLY the next morning to say he will be on the evening express from Rome. I offer to meet him and he laughs, but he doesn't tell me not to. This is one of the things I love about Piero, he understands tiny extravagances. A glass of wine in bed. A single flower. Meetings at train stations.

He has been in Rome for the last week because, even though he is now an editor, he still likes to do the occasional story, and the paper's upcoming feature on Florence's own pet cardinal, Massimo D'Erreti, is too important to be handed over to anyone else. D'Erreti is rumoured to be close to the Pope, and although St Peter's is hardly Pierangelo's natural stomping ground—he is at best agnostic and definitely a liberal 'small c' Communist—he covers the cardinal himself because he likes the challenge. D'Erreti is right-wing enough to have acquired the nickname Savonarola, and I think fair and balanced coverage requires every ounce of Pierangelo's professionalism. As a result, it's anyone's guess whether he'll come back from Rome in a fit of depression at the state of the nation, a black temper at the state of the church, or on an exhausted and slightly euphoric high, the kind runners get when they've just completed a marathon.

The six o'clock bells are ringing as I come into the station. People swirl around me, and finally I spot Piero halfway down the platform. He pauses to let a young woman pushing a baby stroller pass. To everyone else he's just one more tired businessman getting off the express from Rome, dark hair tousled, coat thrown over his shoulders, briefcase gripped in one hand and suit bag in the other. But not to me. To me he's the only person in this crowd. Which is precisely why I love meeting him in stations, or airports, or as he walks across a piazza or down a sidewalk; because in those few unconscious seconds, I own him entirely and don't have to share him with anyone, even himself.

On the way back to his apartment, we shop. Veal, *vitello*, already pounded wafer thin. Fresh asparagus. Tiny artichokes so young their outer leaves are soft and devoid of prickles so you eat them whole. A bottle of Brunello. But for all that, dinner has to wait. A week is a lifetime, and the dips and contours of another human body might somehow be forgotten. In time perhaps this desire to consume each other will wear down like a tired clock, but not now and lying on the faintly rough linen of his sheets I let Pierangelo read my scars. He walks his fingers across the angry red lines and pale risen welts. Sometimes he bends down to kiss one of the ridges, as if it's a landmark on a map he loves.

With the exception of doctors and nurses, whom I could not avoid, no one else has ever been permitted to even see the secret calligraphy embossed on my skin, much less touch it. Most of the time I wear turtlenecks, and when I don't, I keep collars buttoned. Sometimes I wind scarves over and over around my neck. And on the very rare occasions when I slip up, or when I'm forced into a position where someone gets a glimpse, I mumble about an accident. I give the distinct impression of twisted metal and shattered glass.

'You changed your hair.' We are finally getting out of bed, driven by hunger of the more banal kind, and I watch in the bedroom mirror as he runs his hands through my tiger stripes. They're bronze and copper, with one deep pink streak on the left side. Our eyes meet in the glass, mine an intermediate hazel, his the peculiar pale bluish-green one sees occasionally in this part of Italy, bits of luminous glass set in the severe, almost hawk-like cast of his features. 'It looks great,' he says. 'I love it, Mrs Warren.'

'Who's she?' I ask. 'Your other lover?'

'Yeah,' Piero replies, 'a lady I knew once. No one you need to worry about. You don't even look like her.'

In the kitchen, I lean on the counter, rolling a lemon back and forth across the bright stainless-steel surface while Pierangelo pulls the cork on the Brunello and pours us each a glass. His apartment is almost directly across the river from Billy's and mine, and although it's also in an old palazzo, the similarities end there. From our leprous gilded mirrors to the silk counterpanes and massive beds it's clear, to me at least, that Signora Bardino's eye for design comes pretty much directly from *The Garden of the Finzi-Continis* and *The Leopard*. Pierangelo and, I assume, Monika, on the other hand, are distinctly 'New Europe.'

The ceilings here are as high and the windows as symmetrical as those of the apartment Billy and I live in, but instead of marble, Piero's floors are stripped pale wood. Natural-linen blinds hang in place of our armour-plated ones, and the lighting is so recessed it's virtually invisible. Large Rothko-like canvases cover bright white walls whose plaster is smooth and silky. Even the lemon pots on the roof terrace are not the regulation terracotta, but cylinders of stainless steel. The trees themselves are studded with tiny lights that glitter in the leaves like Dante's stars.

Pierangelo cooks to relax and his kitchen is outfitted with glass-fronted cabinets, magnetic racks of knives, and gadgets. Centre stage is a six-burner gas range I've seen him stroke as lovingly as other middle-aged men stroke sports cars. The results of his meticulous preparations are almost disturbingly perfect, which I tease him about. I've threatened to get a measuring tape and make sure his cubes of zucchini are exactly symmetrical, or, worse, to make dinner myself, which would almost certainly involve spilling things.

At the moment, he's concentrating completely on slivering the tiniest carrots I have ever seen. The tip of his knife flashes up and down, and I know better than to interrupt. Instead, I occupy myself with a game I play called *How many traces of Monika are left here?* I've yet to find anything as concrete as a piece of clothing—an old bra at the back of a laundry basket, or a shoe. Not even a half-used lipstick. If I didn't know better, I'd sometimes think she never existed. Now, I slide open the drawer that holds the phone books to see if there's anything lurking, and hit gold dust almost right away. Underneath a set of manuals for the dishwasher and the dryer, there's an old Catholic calendar, one of those gory ones with all the saints and martyrs and how they died. I give myself a ten for the find and another ten for speed, and roll the lemon absently as I read that today is the anniversary of three guys called Felix, Fortunas and Achilleus, who were scourged and broken on the wheel somewhere in ancient Gaul. The names sound like brands of men's cologne, and why people would want to remember things like this is beyond me. Pierangelo finishes with the carrots, heaping them on a plate and setting it aside, which means I can talk to him.

'How was Savonarola?' I put the calendar back, and slide the drawer closed, thinking D'Erreti would probably approve of some scourging and breaking himself.

'It was OK.' Piero grabs the lemon in mid-roll and replaces it with the glass of wine. 'In fact,' he adds, 'I would say His Eminence is thriving. This Vatican suits him. All they need to do is bring back the Holy Inquisition and he'll be in seventh heaven.'

We both laugh, but the truth is that, despite his posing, or probably because of it, Florence's cardinal is popular. Very. He did some time in Africa and the U.S., where he apparently picked up some tricks from Evangelists, and when he's in town D'Erreti's appearances at the Duomo are as packed as rock concerts. I haven't actually heard him preach, but I gather that on occasion he's borrowed a page from his namesake's book and even evoked a black cross hanging over Florence. Personally, I never was too into fire and brimstone, even back in the days when I went to Mass. But I realize I'm in the minority.

'The odd thing about D'Erreti,' Pierangelo says, picking up his glass and shaking his head, 'is that despite the fact I disagree with him about basically everything, I know why people admire him. I even feel myself doing it sometimes. Whatever else he may be, he's not a hypocrite. And then there's the whole power trip. And the history.'

Pierangelo told me once that he was an altar boy. It just slipped out, and it surprised me at the time, both because of how he feels now, and because his parents were university professors, one a mathematician, the other a historian. He doesn't talk about them much, or about his brother, who lives in Milan and is some kind of big shot at Fiat, but as far as I know, they weren't particularly religious. As he puts his glass down and turns back to the cutting board, I realize that while I know what drove me away from the church, I've never asked him what made him change his mind, or drew him in the first place, for that matter. And now I wonder if it's some residual love, or revulsion, or a combination of the two that draws him to D'Erreti.

'What's this piece on, I mean, exactly?'

'Our fiftieth birthday.' Pierangelo glances over his shoulder at me as he says this and bursts out laughing. 'You should see your face,' he says. 'Don't panic, *cara*, Savonarola is not my long-lost twin. The paper's just doing a profile in honour of his half-century.' He shakes his head, grinning, and checks the contents of a bright copper pan. A spout of steam erupts like a mini-Vesuvius. 'You know the kind of thing,' he adds, 'modern man —goes to the gym—rides a motorcycle—but radical reformer—and beloved of the people—Is This the New Future of Mother Church?'

'And is it?'

'Well, maybe. But I certainly hope not.' Pierangelo begins dropping the baby artichokes one by one into the boiling water. 'For a start,' he says, 'D'Erreti would probably like to do things like have all homosexuals forced to publicly recant. Or, if they refuse, have them rounded up and shipped to God knows where. Some island somewhere, along with all the other undesirables. You know, women who want to be priests, men who think women should be priests, women who need abortions, doctors who perform abortions, NGO workers who don't believe starvation offers a neat opportunity for conversion. Oh yeah, and anybody who believes that condoms might actually stop people from dying of AIDS and that you aren't necessarily criminal if you want a divorce or use birth control.' He stops and looks at me. 'But the fact is,' he says, 'a lot of people think that's just what the church needs. To stand like a rock. Be firm hand on the tiller in this sea of moral relativism. And provide an apartment for every child molester in Vatican City.'

'It won't work,' I point out. 'It will only alienate more people. Besides, it's mean.'

'Right,' Pierangelo agrees. 'But I am not in the college of cardinals, and neither are you. So, when it comes to one of the most powerful institutions on earth, we don't get a vote. Instead it's in the safe hands of the men in red, the little gremlins the Pope appoints in the first place.' I'm surprised by the anger in his voice.

'So, you think this is real?' I ask. 'You really think D'Erreti's in some vanguard, that this is where it's going?'

Pierangelo shrugs. 'I think it would be a tragedy, but I don't see why not.' He sweeps a pile of chopped parsley onto a saucer and reaches for his glass again. 'D'Erreti's backed by Opus Dei, for what that tells you. They think he's great.'

The Opus, the Work, as they call themselves, was founded in the 1930s by a Spaniard, a big admirer of Franco's who's since been canonized, some think with unseemly haste. It operates like a free radical in the body of the Catholic Church, unanswerable to most of the usual channels, and awash in money, how much, nobody really knows. Rumour says a justice of the Supreme Court, at least one United States senator, a British cabinet minister, and God knows how many other political movers and shakers are members. In point of fact, God may not even know. The Opus like to call themselves discreet, but most people would probably use the word 'secretive'. Some mutter 'sect.'

There's a school of thought that says they're deeply sinister, but I have to admit I find them kind of silly. Fanatics, especially when they think they're being subtle, tend to overdo it like cops in old movies. I discovered after I'd known him for a while that Rinaldo was Opus, and once, back when we were bosom buddies, he introduced me to some members of a prayer group he led up at San Miniato. The whole episode was like a bad satire on religious cults. Rinaldo primed me by talking about how 'we're all alone in the world and need real friends' and when I met them his disciples murmured and fluttered around me with such extreme godliness that it was positively cloying. Even if I hadn't already been seeing Pierangelo, they would have been enough to send me straight out into the streets to do some serious sinning.

As it was, Piero and I laughed about it in bed the next afternoon, and he still teases that if he hadn't bought me a Martini one rainy day maybe I'd be sleeping on a board in an Opus Dei house right now. Doing the Work. Turning my pay cheque over to Rinaldo for His Bank Account's Sake, and greeting every morning by kissing the floor and wrapping barbed wire around my thighs for fun.

It's on the tip of my tongue to ask Pierangelo if he's come across the good father lately, but I don't. It's bad enough that suddenly I swear I can feel the soft pressure of Rinaldo's hand on my shoulder. The puff of his breath in my ear. Any minute now, I'll hear him whispering his recipe for salvation. I reach for one of the olives on the counter and bite into the bitter green flesh.

The veal is perfect, tender enough to cut with a fork and crispy on the outside. Asparagus was a serious treat when I was growing up, something we ate only at Easter, and I can still remember my aunt scolding me one year for cutting all the tips off and leaving a large serving plate of nothing but stalks. The idea of repeating the trick is tempting, but I content myself instead with slicing my artichokes and pairing them off with what's left of my veal while I listen to Pierangelo talking about his daughters.

Angelina is at Bologna and wants to be a lawyer, although that's probably just because she's dating one, while Graziella, on the other hand, takes after her mother, and is mainly interested in shopping. Frankly, Piero says, he might just as well have handed her a credit card, sent her to Milan, and forgotten about the university altogether.

I have never met either of the twins, but I have seen their pictures in his study. Unidentical, they are still obviously a pair, as lean and fragile as gazelles, with wide eyes, their father's height and their mother's golden hair. Both of them were still living here when I first met Pierangelo—Monika waited to leave until they had gone off to college—but now their rooms are like empty boxes.

Pierangelo gets up, takes my plate, and ruffles my hair. 'I bought you strawberries,' he says, 'from Sicily. The first ones. They were in the market at Campo dei Fiori, but I forgot the bag on the train. Senility setting in. How about I take you for *gelato* instead?'

'Only if I get a double.' As he pretends to consider this, the intercom buzzes.

Piero's building doesn't have anything as vulgar as keys. Instead, all of the doors are controlled by security numbers that you punch into little pads. I stand up and take the dishes from him as he goes to the door. A moment later I hear another urgent buzz.

'*Pronto.*' Pierangelo releases the locks, and just for a second I am absolutely convinced it's Monika, that she's standing down in the street, has come to tell him she's changed her mind, grown tried of her toy boy, and still loves him. Wants him back. But I'm wrong. I didn't hear what was said through the intercom, but I know from the sound of his voice, which has become flat and quick, that whatever this is, it has to do with work.

Our visitor turns out to be a motorcycle courier. As I come into the room, he's already on his way back into the open elevator in the vestibule.

'Important?'

Pierangelo shrugs, studying the envelope he's just been handed. 'Stuff on a story they want me to check before tomorrow.'

'I'll get my jacket.'

He nods, OK, but he's concentrating on the envelope, not me, and as I walk past he spills the contents out onto the dining-room table. Piero runs his hand across the pages. On top is a blow-up of the photo I studied last night, a grainy eight-by-ten of the girl they found by the river.

'Are you going to write about her?'

Pierangelo shrugs and licks his ice-cream cone as we wander across Piazza della Signoria. The rain didn't materialize, just a drizzle which has left the paving stones slick and bright. Rising from the middle of his fountain, Neptune glows in the floodlights, and the bronze circle marking the spot where Savonarola burnt is surrounded by tiny puddles that shine like fragments of a broken mirror.

'We're thinking about a piece. More on the university, than the girl specifically. Profile of students today, that sort of thing.'

'She was a student?' I try to keep my voice nonchalant, as though this doesn't really interest me, but I can't help feeling that somehow Pierangelo knows, that he's magically gotten inside my brain, and even as we walk here he can see me folding last night's newspaper into my bag and, later, ogling the contents of the manila envelope I keep hidden in my bottom drawer like porn.

'Yup,' he says eventually, 'in her final year at the university. She was pretty well known. Some kind of activist.'

'And does she have a name?'

Piero knows this is a pet peeve of mine, the fact that the dead, and even the victims of crimes who manage to survive, are usually referred to as objects. In most of the pieces I've collected, for instance, Ty is called simply 'her dead husband' and I'm usually 'the woman who was attacked', as if any other identity we might have had became irrelevant the second Karel Indrizzio got out his knife.

'Sorry. Ginevra Montelleone. Twenty-one years old. From Impruneta.' It's a village on the outskirts of the city, known mainly for producing huge pieces of pottery, urns so big you could hide in them, outsize copies of the Venus de Milo, that sort of thing.

'I'm just not sure what the story is here,' he adds. 'Or even, really, if there is one. You, know, if it's bigger than she fell off the bridge, or jumped, or whatever.' He takes a lick of his cone, his tongue as fast and agile as a cat's. 'So she killed herself.' He shrugs. 'You know how college students are.'

He smiles as if we're sharing a joke, the full, sensuous curves of his lips at odds with his tone of voice, and I start to reply that, no, I don't. At least, not if he's suggesting that jumping off bridges is some sort of adolescent rite of passage, something that maybe Angelina or Graziella might do, when they get sick of dating lawyers and shopping. But then I stop. I don't feel like arguing and, besides, I know it isn't fair. I know I'm hearing the newspaper editor, not the lover, or the father. A cold gust of wind comes up and riffles my hair, blowing it into the top of my ice cream.

'*Bella!*' Pierangelo picks the strands that are plastered in *frutta de bosco* out of the cone with his free hand. 'Very good,' he says, and hands me a napkin. 'Almost matches your other stripes!'

'Don't be a smart ass.' I take the napkin he's offering, and can't help laughing myself because suddenly I am hit with a splash of pure happiness, just at the miracle of being here with him.

After that, we wander slowly, zigzagging and window shopping, and when we get back to the apartment, it's late. The courier's envelope is still on the table. Piero scoops the papers up and takes them down to his study, and by the time he comes back, I'm already in bed. He sits beside me with his hands behind his back. A sneaky smile lights his green eyes. I know what this means. Pierangelo loves giving presents, usually clothes. A peacock-coloured robe from Loretta Capponi. A watered-silk shawl from Como. Silly-looking army pants that tie in bows at the ankle. Sometimes I joke that I'm nothing but the giant Barbie doll he must have secretly yearned for as a kid.

'Della sinistra? O della destra?' he asks.

'Sinistra.' I tap his left elbow three times, as if I'm summoning a genie, and Pierangelo whips his hand out.

'I forgot earlier. Senility, I'm telling you.'

This time it's not silly pants or a pair of shoes, or even stockings or a bracelet. It's a cell phone. He drops the tiny silver lozenge into my hand. 'Now I can keep track of you,' he says. 'You can even send me pictures of yourself. Punch "one,"' he adds, 'and it dials my number.'

I thank him, of course I do. But the truth is, I hate these things. I hate their stupid ring tones. And I hate the way people grapple through their pockets for them, as though they're so important that any call they miss might precipitate disaster. Most of all, though, I hate being with someone when they get a call and leave you on a sort of metaphysical hold with no idea where to look or what to do while they answer and then proceed to chat animatedly. In my book it's as absurd and rude as being in mid-conversation and suddenly saying, 'Oh wait a sec, I'm just going to pull out a pen and jot down a letter to someone else.' All of which is a very roundabout way of saying that Pierangelo and I might never have gotten together at all, because the very first time I ever met him, about five seconds after we sat down at the bar where he'd suggested we have a drink, his cell phone rang.

It was the Culture editor of a paper I sometimes wrote for in Philadelphia who gave me Pierangelo's name. 'He's an arrogant prick,' she said. 'But he knows absolutely everybody.' And since I wanted to do a piece on a private villa in Florence I had no way of getting into, I eventually called him.

It was March, and cold and very wet, and I ordered a Martini, dry with an olive because, silly as it is, drinking them makes me feel like I'm a grown-up. I think I even mentioned that to Piero, because I remember he laughed, and ordered a scotch. Then his phone made a cheeping sound like a baby bird begging for food and he mumbled something about a story, and turned his head away as he answered, leaving me staring into the mirror behind the bar, reading the labels on the backs of the rows of bottles, and watching the made-up women who drifted by behind us like tropical fish swimming in a tank.

Pierangelo didn't say a word when he finished the call and closed his phone. Instead, he downed the scotch that had arrived and signalled to the waiter for another almost in one gesture, and when I finally looked away from the mirror and back at him, there was no trace of a smile, no sign of the slick Italian bad boy I'd sat down with, in his face. 'I'm sorry about that. It's a story I'm working on,' he said without my asking. 'A follow-up. Eleanora Darnelli.' He laughed, but it was more of a half-hearted bark, and I realized he was genuinely upset. 'I hate this fucking story,' he said. 'But it'll do well because of the religious angle, seeing how it's almost Easter.' The bartender placed a second glass in front of him, and he took a quick sip and looked at me. Then he saw that I didn't understand.

I remember what happened next because it was the first time he ever touched me. Piero reached out and placed the tips of his fingers on the back of my hand, his skin cold from the ice in his drink. 'It's been a big deal here,' he said. 'But of course, you wouldn't know.' I shook my head, intensely aware of the pressure of those four cold points and the swimming green of his eyes. 'It happened before you arrived,' he explained. 'She was murdered. Up in Fiesole. In January. Before that,' he added, the corner of his mouth twitching as though the words themselves were distasteful, 'she was a nun.'

The memory comes back so swift and clear that I wonder if it's somehow contained in the little silver lozenge I hold in my palm. I know he did the piece, but I didn't hear Eleanora Darnelli's name again until I was in the hospital, where Ispettore Pallioti told me she'd probably been killed by Karel Indrizzio. He said the words carefully, as if they might hurt, and I remember thinking, in my drugged-up state, that they were nice. That this fact made me not so alone. Eleanora Darnelli and me, we were in this together. Soul sisters. At the time I thought we could practically be each other.

Now, the idea leaves a sharp taste in my mouth, as if I've bitten glass.

Chapter Four

PIERANGELO'S A NIGHT prowler, one of those people who almost always gets up and works for a couple of hours at two or three a.m. before coming back to bed. The result is usually a deep sleep until the alarm, followed by a chaotic rush, and the next morning is no exception. I leave him searching for a tie, and walk back across the river to buy the morning paper and the bitter marmalade-filled croissants that Billy and I have become addicted to.

The shop just down from our building is always crowded in the morning. The bakery trays arrive early and sell out fast, and the papers arrive at about the same time, tied in bundles, which makes it an acquired art to pull one out without ripping it in half. In the normal course of things, the large barrel-shaped signora rushes here and there, her dyed red hair bouncing up and down in a solid helmet of curls as she throws pastries into paper bags, works the till, and keeps a hand free to tug down her very short skirt and swat at children who are fingering the fruit.

For the last few mornings, however, the shop has been less chaotic than usual. I figure that this must be due to the fact that the 'Help Wanted' sign that's been in the window since I arrived is gone, so now the signora has time to join her customers, most of whom hang around before and after they've shopped to chat about the weather and the prime minister and the shocking price of housing. When I come in, she's in rapid-fire conversation with a wizened old man whose dachshund is lifting his leg on a crate of wine bottles. She nods when she sees me eyeing the pastry tray and shouts, '*Allora*, Marcello!' without taking so much as an extra breath.

Marcello is presumably the result of the sign. He appears from behind the beaded curtain at the back and shuffles to the counter, eyes lowered and shoulders hunched. A solid young man in a dark sweater, there's something oddly insubstantial about him, as if he wishes he could disappear. Taking my coins, he almost drops them, but when he mumbles '*dispiace*' and suddenly looks me in the eye, I'm struck by how sweet his face is, oval and almost childlike, although he must be in his early twenties. His eyes drop, long lashes brushing the rising pink on his cheeks. The poor guy's so painfully shy that his hands actually tremble as he gives me my bag.

When I get home it turns out there are six croissants in the bag instead of the four I paid for. Maybe a mistake, I think, and then flatter myself with the idea of maybe not. Silly as it is, this gives me a little flush of pleasure. It's the hair, I guess. Or perhaps there's truth in the old saw after all, that being in love makes you beautiful. I lay the croissants on a plate, almost tenderly, proof positive as they are of the new me. Then I spread the paper to see if there's anything in it about Ginevra Montelleone.

There isn't a word. It looks like Piero's right. This isn't his paper, but she isn't a story for this editor either. At least not today. Most of the headlines are taken up by arguments about immigration and the economy, and by a piece on Vatican politics. So I'm not surprised to find Massimo D'Erreti staring out at me from the bottom of the page. I study him, looking to see if he really does look like those paintings of Richelieu, and have just about decided he doesn't, not even a little bit, when Billy comes up behind me.

'Who's the hunk?' she asks, making me jump so badly I almost choke on my coffee.

'Jesus, I wish you wouldn't do that!' I wipe my chin with the back of my hand, and she grins and reaches over me for a croissant.

'Jumpy? Didn't get much sleep last night?'

A shower of crumbs falls onto the cardinal's face, and as Billy brushes them away with the back of her hand, I realize she's right, he is handsome. It's something of a revelation. I never thought of him that way before. Billy smirks and glides out of the kitchen without making a sound. This is something I've learned in the month I've lived with her, for a very tall person, Billy is unusually silent.

It's disconcerting. Last week, for instance, I was slicing a red pepper, making neat thin strips with the very sharp carving knife I'd bought the day before, when she announced, 'I never even saw a red pepper until after I was divorced,' from so close behind me that she could have been sitting on my shoulder. When I whirled around and damn near gutted her, she didn't even blink. She just picked up one of the pepper strips, and bit it in half. 'I thought all peppers were green,' she said. 'And I never did see a romaine lettuce until I was twenty-one. Imagine.'

The absence of romaine and red peppers. Divorce. Billy drops these clues about her former life like Hansel and Gretel leaving breadcrumbs. When I asked her once, by way of conversation, how she made a living, she shrugged and replied, 'Oh you know, stuff.' Then, a second later, she added, 'For a while I used to be a nurse,' like it was something she'd just remembered.

Now she reappears in the kitchen and pours herself the last of the coffee. Then she opens the French windows so she can have a cigarette, which would probably give Signora Bardino a seizure if she knew about it. Despite her Sophia Loren accent and liberal use of the word *bambina*, Signora Bardino is still American enough that she wanted to know we didn't smoke before she rented to us. We assured her, of course, in unison, that we didn't. In my case it's true. But in Billy's it's a downright lie.

I've told her cigarettes will kill her. A few days after we moved in, I pointed out that they'll strike her dead sure as a bullet or a speeding car. But Billy just smiled and pulled out her pink Elvis lighter. 'My ex-husband bought this for me in Vegas,' she said. 'As a wedding present. A week after we graduated High School.'

Now smoke hovers above Billy's head and hangs in the damp morning air, mingling with the faint smell of diesel and mud that rises from the river a block away.

'Listen.' She cocks her head and gestures to the apartment opposite, and I hear it too, the high-pitched whine of a child crying.

We've heard it before, more than once. In fact, it's become something of a feature of living here. In the mornings it's usually a petulant shriek, the bratty yell of a second pastry denied, or toast thrown on the floor. But at night it's different. At night the crying is deep and breathless, the jagged, frantic scream of nightmares.

'They fight,' Billy says. 'That's what's wrong with that kid.'

She nods her head like an old woman as she speaks, punctuating the words with certainty, because we've heard that too. Along with the child's howling, we've heard the ring of adult voices, the rising rhythms of sarcasm, and trills of matrimonial gripe that are so universal they don't need translation. Walking across the courtyard, or sitting out on the balcony, we can even figure out, more or less, which names they call each other.

The wail reaches a crescendo, and Billy stubs her cigarette out in the green tin ashtray she stole from the bar. 'Kids,' she says. 'I tell you. They're cute, but you know, whenever I felt tempted, I just thought what it would be like to have a vampire hanging from my tits.' Then she goes to get dressed for a lecture on Perugino she doesn't want to miss.

A few minutes later, I stand on the balcony and watch as she comes out of our side of the building and walks across the courtyard. Halfway, she stops and looks up. Her hair ripples around her face, and from up here the baggy tweed coat she bought in the market at San Ambrogio looks like a tent. 'Bar?' she mouths, and I nod. Pierangelo has already told me he'll be late tonight so there's no reason not to join the others for a drink. I wave, and Billy waves back. Then she hoists her leather pack, skirts the skeletal lemon trees in their enormous pots, and disappears, the yellow crown of her hair turning suddenly dark as she steps into the shadow of the archway that leads to the street.

The crying winds down to whimpers, thin shreds of sound that slip from the apartment opposite and drift away like smoke. A window opens, and against the background noise of the city, I can hear the murmur of a woman's voice, low and soothing. I imagine her bending to pick up the dropped toast, moving to get the pastry after all or refill the glass of juice, and I wonder what it must be like to be that child, and to grow up in that apartment in a city like this, so surrounded by beautiful things you don't even know where to look.

Beautiful things were in pretty short supply where I grew up. Going to Mass on Sunday mornings, to the Rotary Social on Saturday nights, sneaking cigarettes behind the High School auditorium and coming home to fall asleep and dream you were from somewhere else—somewhere like this, maybe, except you didn't know it existed—that was about it for Acadia, Pennsylvania. Billy grew up in Indiana, somewhere outside Fort Wayne, which her mother called Fort Pain. In certain parts of Indiana, Billy says, that passes for a joke.

When she told me where she came from, I laughed, and then, embarrassed, explained that I'd never actually met anybody who grew up outside Fort Wayne before. At that, Billy looked at me over the rims of the granny glasses she sometimes wears, and said, 'Don't be such a snot, Mary Thorcroft. I bet you don't come from anywhere so special.' And she's right, of course. I don't.

Coal and quarries. *Deer Hunter* country. A town that lived, thrived only moderately, and finally died at the hands of the mining industry. The land around Acadia was too scrappy to farm, and the town too far from anything to be much use once the mines closed, so by the time the sixties rolled around most of the men, like my uncles and my dad, ended up first unemployed, then in Vietnam.

Afterwards, the ones who made it home bought hunting rifles and collected disability and got mean on their own bitterness. And I guess that might have happened to my father too, and probably would have, if he'd lived long enough to find out exactly what things like napalm and Agent Orange really do to the inside of your head. But he didn't. Instead, he made it all the way through the war and came home to get himself killed, drunk as a skunk one Christmas, driving my mother back from a party at the veterans' club.

Not that I understood that too clearly at the time. I was seven, and on the night my parents died, my aunt Rose, who was married to my daddy's older brother Frank, just told me they couldn't come home for a while but that they loved me more than anything in the world. I can remember her, in her party dress, kneeling by the edge of my bed. Her perfume smelled like air freshener, and the light that fell in a shaft from the hall made the red sparkles on her sleeves and earrings twinkle like stars. She had a big Santa Claus pin on her shoulder, and if you pulled the white cotton ball on top of his hat he sang the first bar of 'God Rest Ye Merry, Gentlemen.'

Aunt Rose was crying. Her nose ran and she kept wiping it on the back of her hand and muttering 'damn,' then she unpinned the Santa and gave him to me. And since I didn't really want to listen to what she was saying, I pulled the ball on his hat, once, then twice, and then over and over again. 'God rest ye merry, gentlemen, God rest ye merry, gentlemen, let nothing you dismay,' Santa sang. And long after Aunt Rose stood up, and kissed my forehead and tiptoed out, he kept singing. Over and over he sang his single phrase until the high tinny notes drowned out the noises of grown-ups downstairs, of crying and the clinking of glasses, and the opening and closing of the door, and the stray words—'drunk' and 'shame' and 'speed'—that drifted up the stairs along with the blasts of cold air and the noise of cars coming in and out of the driveway.

I told Billy that story mostly to make up for laughing about Indiana, and when I finished, she lit a cigarette and looked at me for a second. Then she said, 'That's sad.' But I shook my head. That wasn't why I told it. And besides, I explained, really, it isn't. All it is is proof of what I found out early: that the Good Lord giveth and he taketh away. Mainly because he feels like it. All of which may or may not go some way towards explaining why I have always hated Christmas.

Billy frowned through the smoke. Then she asked, 'What happened next?' So I told her how I went to live with Mamaw.

Mamaw was my mother's aunt, and her only living relative. Her real name was Mary Margaret Tulliver, and she ran a book-keeping business called Tulliver Accounting out of her den. She kept the books for most of the not very many businesses in town, so we always knew exactly how bad or good it was for Dave's Hardware, where we bought nails and duct tape, and for Real Brite Dry Cleaners, and for the Pig Stand that sold corkscrew fries and soft ice cream in the summer.

Mamaw wore navy-blue nylon pants suits five days a week, dresses on Sundays, and lipstick every day that left bright red bands on the filters of her Lucky Strikes. She didn't believe in walking under ladders or stepping on cracks, and she taught me how to say 'good morning' to single crows in case they brought bad luck, and how to throw spilled salt over my left shoulder to blind the devil's eye, and how to be Catholic. 'There's no sin in being alone,' Mamaw told me once, in a voice so hushed she sounded like she was sharing a secret. 'But if you are, and you belong to the church, then you'll always belong to something, and no matter what happens, even if nobody else loves you, Jesus will.'

Mamaw's daddy had been a miner and a rock hound, and when he died all he had to leave her was his collection of polished rocks and the house she was born in. She was still living there when I moved in. Mamaw's house had a steep gable roof, ugly black shutters and a front porch nobody ever sat on, and it didn't look an awful lot different from my parents' house, which had been all of three streets away. There was the same maple tree in the yard and the rooms were even laid out the same, so I didn't get lost. Kitchen and den at the back, dining room and living room at the front, three bedrooms and a bathroom with liver-coloured shower tiles upstairs, all of it covered in avocado-green shag carpet that smelled like cigarettes.

There was a front walk, a lawn, and a back yard with a Webber grill and picnic table too, just like my parents'. But Mamaw's house had theirs beat flat on one count. At Mamaw's, I could lie in bed on winter nights and look straight out of my bedroom window through the bare branches of the maples to the flying horse on the gas station sign down the street.

I loved that horse. As far as I was concerned, he was the most beautiful thing in our town, and over time he became more important to me than anything else, even Jesus. For a start, the horse stayed lit up all night long, so no matter when I woke up, if I had bad dreams, or heard the tinny notes of the Santa Claus song, there he'd be, flying through the winter trees with his bright hooves and his snow-white wings.

I dreamed of those wings, as big and strong as an angel's. And of the whooshing sound they made, and of his hooves, which were as black as patent leather and threw sparks that turned into stars as we galloped down the streets. I dreamed of my hands wound in his mane as we went, faster and faster, until finally we left the ground, and rose through the shredded night clouds, and flew.

I told Pierangelo about my horse not long after we met, and he put his arms around me and asked, 'Where, *cara*? Where did you fly to?' But I told him that back then I didn't know, and I didn't care. Anywhere. Just anywhere at all where there weren't liver-coloured tiles and shag carpets. 'Closed' signs nailed to downtown windows. Mountains of frozen slush that lasted till Easter. And Santa Claus pins that sang in the dark.

'That's her! That's the woman from the apartment!' Billy tweaks my sleeve, but I'm not paying attention. Instead, I'm leaning as far as I can over the parapet of the Ponte Vecchio watching the fish.

Centuries ago, before the gold merchants who are here today moved in, butchers lined this bridge. Carcasses hung here, and there were those who believed the future could be read in the entrails of the slaughtered animals. For a penny or two you could have intestines thrown down onto the blood-slicked cobbles, and love, death, fortune—your whole life—would be divined by those who knew how to read the patterns. Then, every night at sunset, the offal would be swept up and dumped into the Arno to feed the ancestors of these same fish which, four centuries later, still come and hang just below the clouded green surface of the water, driven by ancient hunger.

I love the fish. I admire them for gobbling up the future, but Billy, who is definitely more interested in gold than prophecy, thinks my fixation with them is stupid. More than once I've told her I'm sorry for them, and that I think they should somehow be rewarded for their persistence. Secretly, I've contemplated bringing them a steak. I've imagined pulling the pink slab from a bag, allowing it to slither out of its wrapping, and hearing the splash as it hits the water below.

Billy tweaks me again. 'It is her!' she hisses, and I pull myself back from the parapet and turn to see where she's pointing.

It's marginally warmer this evening, and the *passeggiata* is in full swing. At least half of Florence must be out here, promenading up and down, moving along the box-like fronts of the jewellery stores, inspecting the rows of gold bangles and rings and charms displayed in the brightly lit windows. This is serious business, the viewing and comparing of merchandise, and on a nice night the bridge and the avenue all the way up to the Duomo will be packed solid, full of couples holding hands, tourists and students, and pairs of squat middle-aged ladies in suits and expensive shoes, all of them eating ice cream and examining displays of jewellery and handbags and gloves.

A woman pushing a bicycle with a little white dog in the basket weaves through the crowd in front of us, momentarily blocking our view, then Billy pulls at the elbow of my sweater.

'There,' she hisses, 'over there. I swear that's her.'

And she's right, it is the woman from the apartment opposite. I know, because I've seen her too. In fact, I saw her just yesterday. She was attempting to manoeuvre her way through the security gate under the archway of our building, her child's empty stroller in one hand and a shopping bag in the other, and she nearly fell down the steps. Standing nearby, I leaned out to help, grabbing the bottom rung of the stroller and lifting it to the sidewalk, and afterwards, as I stepped up and took the edge of the gate before it could swing closed, she thanked me, murmuring the way strangers do. Our eyes met, and I saw the telltale red rims and pink blotches on her cheeks, and knew she'd been crying. Now, she's pushing the stroller again, but this time her child is in it. A man in an overcoat walks beside her, his hands dug in his pockets.

The man is handsome, in a saturnine sort of way. He has dark hair and a beaky nose. It's a face you would call 'horsey' if they were poor, but is 'patrician' because they're obviously not.

'Phew,' Billy whispers, 'get the cut of that cashmere. Overcoats like that mean serious real estate.'

I nod, but the truth is, neither the man nor his overcoat interest me. It's her I keep looking at. Everything about the woman from the apartment opposite is curved, from the ample rise of her chest, to her hips, to the curls of pale colourless hair that fall over the black collar of her coat. Her cheeks are round and still slightly flushed, as if she has been crying since yesterday, and the child she pushes looks way too old to be in a stroller. Six or seven at least and dark like his father, the little boy sits staring straight ahead. Wrapped in a scarf and coat and hat, as if this is the Arctic winter instead of spring in Florence, he looks like a large doll, a boy made of wax. To be honest, he looks not quite human.

'The kid looks kind of retarded,' Billy whispers.

We watch as they draw parallel to us, fascinated and slightly guilty because we know something about them the rest of the world doesn't. Out here, they're a nice young family; handsome, prosperous father and plump, pink-cheeked mother taking their little doll boy for a stroll. But behind the walls of our palazzo, we've heard them shriek and call each other names.

'She's pretty,' Billy murmurs, 'but she's fat. I never noticed before that she was fat. I bet he's having an affair,' she adds. 'I bet that's it.'

Billy lowers her voice, even though there's no earthly way they could hear us. 'I think it's the kid,' she says. 'I mean, look at him. I bet he's one of those guys who just can't stand kids that have something wrong with them—you know, perfection freaks. Or,' she whispers, 'maybe he doesn't like fat. If she got her act together, fixed her hair and lost fifteen pounds, he probably wouldn't screw around.' She shrugs, losing interest. 'I mean, with a body like that,' she says, 'what do you expect? Guys like perfection, or at least something close to it, you know?'

'Yeah? Well, not everyone can be as perfect as you! Some people don't have that choice!'

The words come out before I even realize I've said them, fast and harsh, and I feel myself blush, feel the colour rising up under my turtleneck and flooding into my face. The couple and the child have passed us by now, but I watch resolutely until they're swallowed in the crowd, and finally I have no alternative but to look back at Billy.

I don't know what I expect to see. Shame? Some token effort to be contrite? It isn't there. Instead, her eyes are glittering. A tiny smile twitches at the corner of her mouth. The way she's looking at me reminds me uncomfortably of a child who has just lifted up a rock and seen something pale and naked wriggling underneath. Billy opens her mouth and closes it again, silently, like one of the fish. Then she says suddenly, 'I have always wanted one of these.' She turns towards the jeweller's window immediately beside us. 'Look.' Billy taps her nail on the glass, pointing to a tray of rings. 'Don't you think they're absolutely gorgeous?' she asks.

The rings are thin gold bands, intertwined to hold a pair of gemstone hearts, each a different colour. The stones sparkle under the lights, aquamarine and topaz, fire opal and amethyst, garnet and citrine.

'They're beautiful.' I mumble. And I try to look as if I'm seriously studying the heart rings, instead of watching Billy's reflection in the glass, and the tiny knowing smile that flutters across her lips.

Chapter Five

By THE TIME we arrive at the bar the big mushroom heaters have been turned on. Fairy lights lace through the trees and floodlights hit the blank façade of the church. I comment on how beautiful it is with its Cyclops eye, but Billy just looks at me sideways. A gust of wind comes up as we sit down.

'The weather,' Kirk announces when he and Henry join us a few minutes later, 'is supposed to get better.'

'Oh right! When? In the next millennium? After the current ice age ends?'

The wind has gotten stronger and now, despite the heaters, it is cold. Billy hunches down into her coat, reaches for her wine glass, and shakes her head in disgust. In the half-hour since we left the bridge, she has become progressively snarkier.

I don't know Billy that well, in fact, I barely know her at all, but I'm beginning to suspect she likes a little excitement. Prefers things spiced up. Mixed and stirred. And I think she hoped that after I'd snapped at her on the Ponte Vecchio, I'd wind myself into a real temper tantrum. Perhaps attack her in a wild and illogical fashion for being six foot tall. Maybe she thought I'd burst into tears and declare my unbridled jealousy for her perfect body. Announce that I lusted for her. Or for the woman next door. Who knows? I don't actually think Billy would be picky. But I do think, as I watch her toying with the edge of the ashtray that, for just a second, under that rock, she thought she saw something interesting. Something she might poke with a stick. She was hoping, I think, for some fireworks to light up the night, and now she's sulking because I've really let her down.

The breeze gusts, making the fairy lights dance, and I put my gloves on. One's bright blue and one's bright green, and when he sees them, Henry winks. He has a gigantic scarf wrapped twice around his neck and the end of his nose is red, as though he's either drunk or getting a cold. We could move inside, of course, but there's an unspoken agreement that that would be seriously wimpish, so instead we brave it out. Only Kirk doesn't seem to care about the weather. Wrapped in his black overcoat, his body temperature is apparently static.

'The clocks go forward next week,' he says, reaching for the bottle of Chianti we've ordered and filling his own glass, then mine and Henry's. 'So I think we should have a celebration. To mark the official start of summer. Regardless. On Sunday.'

'What? Put roses in our hair and dance around a maypole?' Billy's drinking white wine, as usual, but she places her hand over the rim of her glass anyways, as if she's afraid Kirk will turn it into rosé.

'I think Mary would look very fetching with roses in her hair,' Henry says.

'I'm allergic to roses. They make me sneeze.'

'Mary, Mary. Quite contrary.' Billy takes out a cigarette, making a big deal of fiddling with the package. Then she says suddenly, 'Oh I forgot. Something happened today.'

'What?' Henry asks. 'The sun rose in the west?'

Billy smiles. She slides her eyes around the table. 'A priest came to the door,' she says. 'Of our apartment.'

Kirk raises his eyebrows. 'And?'

'Well,' Billy shrugs, lights the cigarette and cups it with her hand. 'Since he was already inside, I thought he had to be looking for the old lady downstairs.'

Kirk stares at her, waiting. 'Don't tell me,' he says finally, 'he wasn't? This sure is a cliffhanger, Bill.'

Billy ignores him. 'He said he was looking for a Mrs Warren,' she announces.

I have never told Billy my married name, and, suddenly, my mouth feels uncomfortably dry. I reach for my glass and start to ask when this happened, exactly, but I don't get the chance, because Henry is being witty again.

'That Mrs Warren,' he asks, 'doesn't she have a profession?'

'Oh I wouldn't be so Shaw,' Kirk says.

Billy waggles her cigarette at him. 'I told him I only knew a Mrs Dall-o-way, so he went a-way.'

'Oh very good. Touche-ay.' Henry raises his glass in a toast.

I don't know what they talk about after that, but I don't talk about anything. I'm too busy wondering how on earth Rinaldo could have figured out where I was. Because it was him. I can feel it. It's as if thinking about him last night conjured him out of thin air and how I practically expect to look up and see him sitting across the square from us, watching me. Smiling. His smooth round face creased like a baby's, sure in the knowledge that at any moment I will get up and come towards him, propelled like a sleepwalker, one of those ladies in Bram Stoker's *Dracula*, pale and driven and begging for forgiveness.

By the time we leave the bar, an hour later, I've worked myself up into a state of barely suppressed fury. I'm convinced that Rinaldo is following us through the streets, and that at any minute he'll pop up like some dreadful priest-in-the-box, and I'll have to explain him to Billy.

She doesn't actually say anything as we walk back, but more than once I catch her watching me out of the corner of her eye. When we finally get in, she makes a big deal of asking me what

I want to eat, and ignoring me when I say I'm not hungry. She takes her coat off, flings it down and rootles through the fridge, sighing loudly as she takes things out and puts them back again. I was going to ask her more about Rinaldo, but this performance is driving me crazy, so instead I slip into my room and use my new phone to call Pierangelo.

'Pronto,' he says before it even rings. 'I was about to call you. I'm on my way home in just a minute.'

'I knew that,' I say. 'I'm psychic.'

I have never seen his office at the paper, but I imagine him now, leaning back in his chair, one arm behind his head as he talks, and suddenly Rinaldo and Billy and everything else seem ridiculous.

'What?' He asks.

I settle for, 'I'm hungry.' Which is actually true, I just didn't want to give Billy the satisfaction of feeding me.

Pierangelo laughs. 'So you pick up the Chinese. I'll be home in fifteen minutes. I have to go back to Rome in the morning, early. But,' he adds, 'that doesn't mean we can't watch the football.'

Football is something of a joke between us. I'm no big fan, admittedly, but Monika banned the watching of matches altogether. No matter how great the club, Real Madrid, Barcelona, even, God forbid, Milan, she decreed it vulgar. As a result, Pierangelo was forced out of the apartment and into the homes of friends, to sports bars, or sometimes even to a hotel, to watch his beloved clubs. Now, he celebrates the absence of *La Tiranna*, the Tyrant, as he calls her, with orgies of Chinese takeout, beer straight from the can and a lot of obscene cheering. We take it in turns to buy the chow mein and egg rolls.

A half-hour later, when I arrive and buzz the intercom, nobody answers, so I figure the match has already started and punch in the security code myself. Piero has never actually given me permission to do this, or explicitly told me what it is, but I'm sure he knows I know it. One of the talents you acquire if you grow up around an accountant is an excellent memory for numbers. Mamaw taught me how to read columns of figures the same way she taught me to read books, and all I have to do is look at a sequence once. I still feel a little funny, though, letting myself into his building like this, so to make up for it, when I get out of the elevator on the top floor, I knock on his apartment door.

There's no answer, and I don't hear fans screaming and frantic Italian commentary, or the sound of Piero's footsteps coming across the living room. Which is weird. Maybe he's in the bathroom. Maybe he isn't even back yet, and I should wait out here. But the food's getting cold and the bags aren't that great. They already feel like the bottom might drop out of them, and I don't want to be stuck with a pile of noodles at my feet, so I figure *What the hell?* And punch myself into the apartment too.

The lights are on, and the first thing I notice is Pierangelo's overcoat thrown across the sofa. So he is here, somewhere. Probably in the shower. I go into the kitchen, study the Ferrari-like stove, turn the oven on to warm, and stick the food in. Then I listen. At first I think I'm hearing the radio, but no, it's Pierangelo's voice, raised and angry and coming from the study.

The apartment is L-shaped, the master bedroom, bathroom and living room in the long front wing, kitchen in the corner, a utility room and hallway leading down the short arm, where the girls' bedrooms look onto the side alley, and, opposite them, Piero's study looks over the inner courtyard. Good manners demand I should go find a magazine, or hang around humming and pretending I can't hear, but I've literally never heard Pierangelo angry before, and I'm curious, so I sidle into the utility room and hover beside the washing machine and linen closet. Then I step into the hall. The study door's ajar, and now I can hear Piero clearly. My Italian has improved, and I get that he's arguing, hard. Something about the police. Then I hear the word *mostro*, monster. There's no answering voice, so he must be on the phone.

'What do we start if we start this?' he says. 'This girl, and then after her, how many? I don't know how long you want to cover their asses.'

There's a pause, and I'm not aware of it, but I must have stepped forward, because I can see Piero's shoulders, the back of his head. He senses me, swings his desk chair around, and pulls the door open.

'Yeah, yeah,' Pierangelo says to whoever he's talking to. His eyes meet mine. 'I get that,' he adds. 'I just think it's a lousy idea. We're not in the business of covering up. For anyone.' He listens again for a second and then nods. 'OK. OK. I do see the point. I just don't agree.' His voice drops, indicating either acquiescence or defeat. 'Well, fine. But you know what I think,' he adds. 'Certo. Ciao.'

Pierangelo puts the phone down and sighs. His eyes are on me, but mine are on the long, polished expanse of his desk. Photos of the girl they found by the Arno, Ginevra Montelleone, are splayed across it like playing cards.

'She didn't commit suicide, did she?' I ask.

'No,' he says. 'No, she did not.'

Pierangelo looks at me for a second. Then he begins to gather up the photos and slide them into an envelope. I feel a sudden wave of irritation.

'For Christ's sake, Pierangelo! I won't go to pieces, you know!'

He stops, his hands in mid-motion. 'I know,' he says, 'it's just—'

He doesn't like talking about this kind of thing with me, and he's not alone. I've noticed this in other people, too. Back home in the States, the ones who didn't want me to write or talk endlessly about what happened to me seemed to feel they couldn't mention the words death, attack, kill, or murder in my presence. Some even struggled over saying knife. I know it was well intended but, frankly, it really pissed me off, just like this is pissing me off now. Between Billy's pop-up priests and Pierangelo suddenly treating me as if I'm made of glass, it's turning out to be a really crappy evening.

'Look,' I say with more force than is probably strictly necessary, 'I was attacked two years ago. And it was terrible. But every awful thing that happens to someone else does not threaten my sanity.'

I'm probably glaring at him because he sighs, runs his hands through his hair, and leaves the photos where they are. 'I'm sorry,' he says. 'She was murdered.' He waves his hand over the desk. 'Of course, you can see for yourself.'

And so I do. I step forward, look down at what are obviously copies of Ginevra Montelleone's crime-scene pictures, and see that she wasn't just murdered. She was butchered.

She looks unusually clean, as though she's been washed, which makes the wounds, if you can call them that, even more graphic. Strips of skin have been peeled back from her ribcage. And despite my determination not to, I feel sick.

'Here,' Pierangelo jumps up from the chair and starts to take my shoulders, but I push him away. I can't stop looking at her.

'What's that?' I point towards Ginevra's white naked shoulder, which is partially covered by her hair. Long and dark, it looks as if it's been combed, and in the midst of it, above her naked breast, there is a lump, something bulging. Pierangelo picks up the photograph.

'*Una borsa di seta rossa.*' His voice sounds flat and tired.

'A bag of red silk?' I think I must have misheard him, but he looks at the photo and nods.

'*Si, signora,*' he says. 'A bag of red silk, stuffed with birdseed. It was pinned to her shoulder with a giant safety pin. You know, one of those things they use in upholstery shops.'

We don't watch the football. Instead, we take the food out of the oven, open a bottle of wine, and eat sitting at the shiny kitchen counter.

'We've been asked not to run the story.' Piero dips his egg

roll in the hot Chinese mustard and takes a big bite, as though this will make him feel better.

'Because?'

He shakes his head and swallows. 'Because of the "public good".' So this is what he was fighting about on the phone. 'Because it will cause panic. Because there is an ongoing investigation. Because blah, blah, blah,' he mutters, picking up his wine glass. 'They're scared shitless,' he adds, 'because, to use your colourful American phrase, they haven't got jack shit, and they're wetting themselves because they can't blame Indrizzio any more. Shit!' He fans his mouth and swallows more wine, 'That mustard's hot!'

Piero gets up and pours himself a glass of water. 'Do you think they make it like that so you can't taste the food?' he asks. 'Boiled dog, or whatever the hell it is the Chinese eat? Although we should talk.' He turns the tap off and a smile flashes across his face, the first one I've seen tonight. 'In the twenties,' he says, 'restaurants in Florence were fined for serving cat.'

'Oh yuck! And yeah,' I agree, 'they probably use the mustard to mask taste, like the English used curry in India.'

'India? They should use it in England.' Pierangelo's faith in the supremacy of the Italian *cucina* is unshakeable. He sits down again and pours us more wine. 'Listen,' he says, 'here's the really weird thing. You saw her, right? So you know how she died?'

'Well.' A vivid picture of the strips of flesh hanging off Ginevra Montelleone's torso flashes in front of me, and I put my fork down. I'm not so certain I'm hungry any more. 'Sure.' I nod. 'Yes.'

'No.'

'What do you mean, no?'

Piero shakes his head and watches me for a second. Then he says, 'She drowned.'

I look at him as though he's crazy, but he nods. 'I didn't believe it either. But the paper has "friends" in the morgue, that's how we got the pictures. I thought they were crazy. Just plain wrong. Wrong girl, you know, wrong body. Some idiot making a mix-up. So I called a friend of my own, at the Questura.'

As far as I can figure, Pierangelo knows half of Florence through his family or Monika's, and the other half from his days as a reporter. His contact at the police headquarters could equally be some obscure cousin or a tame cop. Maybe both.

'She really drowned?'

This sounds so goofy to me that I can't keep the incredulity out of my voice. Pierangelo raises his eyebrows, inviting me to think about it. I picture Ginevra's body, how it looked unnaturally clean.

'You mean, they found her in the river?' I ask.

He shakes his head. Nuh-uh,' he says, his mouth half full of egg roll. 'That's it. They didn't. Her lungs were full of water, but the guy, the rower who found her, he says she was lying there on the river bank, cut to shreds, naked, on her back, her hands folded across her chest as if she was asleep.'

It's still dark when Pierangelo leaves in the morning. He bends down to kiss me and I smell the lemony scent of his cologne and the minty tang of toothpaste. 'Sleep,' he says. 'I'll call you.'

I hear him pick up his bag. His footsteps cross the living room and the front door of the apartment opens and closes. I don't really go back to sleep afterwards, but doze, aware that I'm alone in this bed that isn't mine, and finally decide to get up and have a bath. Pierangelo's bathroom is vast. It has a sunken tiled pool set into the floor with steps down into it, like the ones I imagine in those Japanese bathing houses, and as the water starts to gush in I stand watching it, and thinking about Ginevra Montelleone.

Pierangelo's 'friend' at the Questura says the medical examiners are sure she died, by drowning, after the cuts were made. In other words, whoever did it flayed her alive.

Then drowned her.

Then brushed her hair, and laid her out on the river bank. And pinned a red silk bag stuffed with birdseed to her shoulder.

I think of my little mask, which seems like nothing in comparison. The nun, Eleanora Darnelli, and Benedetta, they had things left too, souvenirs like mine. But as I lower myself into the water and think about it, I realize that, beyond the fact that they were knifed, I don't know exactly how they were killed.

It's odd, but I was too embarrassed to ask. Ispettore Pallioti told me about the other women, but after I didn't bleed to death, and my lung was reinflated, and the infection went away, and everyone kept telling me how lucky I was to be alive, it seemed like enquiring for details about the less fortunate victims of Karel Indrizzio would be somehow ungrateful. More than that, unseemly. Almost pornographic. So, although I wanted to know, I never asked. And I still have no idea.

Pierangelo does, though, because he wrote the newspaper stories. I lean back, turn off the taps, and consider this. He keeps files here, in his desk in the study. I know because he's pulled them out occasionally to show me something he's worked on in the past. And he won't be back until late Monday. Or maybe Tuesday. He's spending the weekend following D'Erreti around the Vatican City. I pour some of the special bath salts Piero buys for me into the tub. Acacia. He orders body oil for me too. For my scars, or so he says. He has it made up specially. And perfume. He loves acacia. He even likes to taste it on my skin. I swirl the water back and forth, making the sea-green tiles shimmer. Did Ginevra wear perfume, I wonder. Did the others?

It's an hour later when I stand in the doorway of his study. I've washed up the dishes from last night, made the bed, and even done a little sweeping, as if that can make up for what I'm about to do. At best, I'm about to abuse his hospitality, and at worst, his trust. But I want to know. I have to. The murder of Ginevra Montelleone has ignited the need like an itch.

I pull open the flush wooden filing cabinet, and tell myself that all I'm doing is saving myself a session in the library. I'm sure I could look up there all the same things Pierangelo has here. After all, it's public information. Then I tell myself that if what I'm looking for is in the safe, even though I know the combination, I won't open it. I'll only look if the file is right here in front of me.

It's the third one under D, fat and bulky, and I take just a second to peek inside and check it's what I want. Then, before I can think any more about what I'm doing, I pull it out and slip the whole thing into my shoulder bag. I slide the drawer closed with a click, my heart giving a little flicker of excitement because I know this is bad. Then, as I turn to go, I see the pictures of Ginevra, right where we left them last night, and before I can stop myself, I reach out and take one of those too.

Now that I have the damn thing, I feel bad about taking it. Which is typical. Somebody once said guilt is how us Catholics get what we want; we do bad stuff then feel bad about it, which makes it OK. Sort of.

I decide I'll return it, right now. Then I decide that's really stupid. Pierangelo won't be back until Monday night at the earliest. I'll keep the file for a day and see how I feel about it. I'll test it out. He'd let me read it, if I asked. I know he would, so there doesn't seem to be much point wasting time doing research he's already done and that won't be as good anyways. I reassure myself that this is perfectly reasonable, but as I walk towards Santa Maria Novella, where I am going to a lecture on the Spanish Chapel, I can feel the file weighing me down, dragging on my shoulder as if the words written in it are made of lead.

The frescoes in the Spanish Chapel are an allegory on the philosophy of the Dominicans, the Dominus Cane, Dogs of God, bent on protecting the church. On the walls around us, the good brothers arrange the redemption and salvation of man, ushering the chosen up the path into paradise, while below, the dogs, who are also them, stand watch, ready to attack the wolves of temptation and sin. At the gates of hell devils dance in rage and cover their hairy faces in distress, curling their claw toes and whipping their spiked tails as the friars hold them back, protecting Florence and all the souls within her.

The colours are vivid, even after six hundred years, and when I come out of the church the city seems monochrome in comparison, as if the struggle depicted inside is somehow more real than the people who surround me. A languid drizzle, half mist, half rain, hangs in the air, unable to summon up the energy to actually fall. Moisture beads on my cheeks and the backs of my bare hands. A bevy of pale grey nuns appears out of nowhere and sweeps across the wet paving stones, causing the pigeons to rise in a cloud, and groups of students hurry past me, their excited voices rising in a crescendo as they cross the street.

The apartment Ty and I were assigned by the exchange programme is near here. It was a small, cramped, ugly place, my marriage home, furnished with a green tweed sofa and mustard-coloured curtains. And although I used to walk here almost every day, this is not a part of the city I like. In medieval times, the streets of Florence were so narrow and the buildings so tall that even during daylight the passages had to be lit with torches. These days, they're clogged with traffic and lined with cheap hotels that cater for the hordes of newly arrived tourists. Three of them are bearing down on me now, in close formation, dragging their wheeled suitcases behind them like reluctant pets, and I step out into the traffic in order to avoid being trampled. A taxi driver swears at me, telling me I'll meet God sooner than I might have planned and, as if in agreement, the bells of Santa Maria Novella begin to ring in a low lugubrious boom.

By the time I weave my way out of there, down Via Belle Donne, the street of beautiful women, and Via Tornabuoni, the street of very expensive shops, the tourists have thinned and the drizzle has thickened. Fat grey drops fall straight down out of the sky and splat on the sidewalk as I walk back across the river and into the warren of alleys that lead to our building.

Despite the undeniable fact that I'm getting wet, I dawdle, walking almost in circles, exactly the same way I used to when I was a kid trying to delay the inevitability of going home after school. I tell myself that this is because, after last night, I don't know what kind of mood Billy will be in, and I don't feel like summoning the energy to deal with her. But that's not the truth. The truth is that I'm putting off being alone in my room with Pierangelo's file. I don't want to have to see whether, when left to my own devices, I'll succumb to the wolves of temptation, and read it.

I make another turn, and another, and end up in a narrow walled alley where suddenly I'm hit by a high-pitched wave of laughter. Ahead of me, the gates of a school fly open, tipping a squadron of children out onto the street, and I realize it's past noon already, and that there are parents, smart-suited men, some of them with briefcases, and mothers in overcoats and leather boots, leaning against the wall opposite, chatting or reading newspapers. The children surge towards their parents, who fold their papers and open their arms.

And that's when I see her, the woman from the apartment opposite. Almost directly in front of me, she's wearing a red coat with a red velvet collar. Her pale hair is pulled back in a pony-tail, which does not suit her, and her face splits into a grin as the little boy we saw on the bridge last night comes running towards her. She grabs him and lifts him straight into the air. 'Paolo!' she exclaims. 'Paolo!' And his small, peaked face opens like a flower as he looks down at his mother.

The boys are already in the shorts of their summer uniform, and when she puts him down, her son bends to pull up his knee socks, exposing the soft crown of his head. She tousles it with one hand, reaching with the other for the shopping bag she has left leaning against the wall. As she does, Paolo giggles and bats at her, and steps sideways. His foot hits the edge of the sidewalk, and suddenly two things happen at once: I see him begin to fall, to topple in slow motion like a statue tipping, and I hear the loud roar of a motorcycle.

Before I know what I'm doing, I drop my bag and lunge. There is the sound of my own voice, shouting, of his mother's cry of alarm, and the huge black BMW hurtles past us as I grab the little bird-like shoulders.

In truth, I don't think it was that close. But it was coming the wrong way down a one-way street, and when I look at him, the boy's face is white and beginning to crumple. His mother's face is white too, a bright pale moon with two livid, red cherry spots on her cheeks.

'*Signora, grazie! Grazie!*' she says, as she folds Paolo into her, pressing his head to her stomach. The other parents buzz and hum around us. 'Those goddam motorcycles,' they say. 'They should be banned!' 'No respect for others! For children!' 'It's a school, for God's sake.' 'He was going the wrong way on a one-way street!' Another mother bends down to pick up my bag from the sidewalk, and I thank her, moving quickly to get there before she does. But the file has not fallen out and, much to my relief, Ginevra Montelleone's dead face is not staring up at us from the gutter.

'Oh your bag. It's wet. It's ruined! I'm sorry.' The woman from the apartment opposite is mopping at my old leather shoulder bag with a red gloved hand, but I tell her it's fine, that this bag has seen a lot worse, and besides, if the damage is bad, it will give me an excuse to buy a new one. We are speaking in Italian, and she laughs. After all the crying and swearing we've heard flying across the courtyard, it's an unexpected sound.

'Your Italian is better than most Americans',' she says suddenly. Then she adds, in English, 'I'm from London, but I've lived here for eleven years. My husband calls me Sophia, but my name is Sophie.' She laughs again. 'Sophie-Sophia Sassinelli. What's that like for a name?'

She extends her hand, and when I take it her shake is soft and a little squishy. Up close, her face is younger than I thought. She can't be much more than thirty, and still with puppy fat.

Everything about Sophie-Sophia reminds me of an overripe fruit.

'Mary,' I say. 'Mary Thorcroft.'

'I've seen you.'

I let go of her hand suddenly, remembering the bridge last night and all the other times Billy and I have lingered in the kitchen, hiding behind the linen panels in the French window, listening to her almost nightly fights with her husband. But it turns out that's not what she's talking about, or if it is, she's too gracious to say so.

'You helped me,' she says, smiling. 'The other day, when I was coming to get Paolo and couldn't get the stroller through the gate.' She doesn't have the stroller with her today, and she looks down at the little boy, who has begun to fidget and tug at her hand. 'He shouldn't even ride in the buggy any more, really,' she says. 'He's too big. But I guess I just can't let go of my baby.'

I don't know if Paolo speaks English, but I suspect he does because he scowls when she says this.

'Do you have children?' she asks. She looks into my face, her brown eyes as round and guileless as a rabbit's, and as I shake my head I understand that Sophie-Sophia Sassinelli is almost unbearably lonely.

We walk together out of the high-walled alley that houses the school and turn down towards Santo Spirito. Paolo is silent now, scuffing the toes of his polished shoes on the sidewalk, probably embarrassed, both by the fact that I grabbed him and that I'm still here. He drags on his mother's hand, twisting it sideways so it looks as though her arm must be rotating in its socket. She doesn't seem to notice, but it might explain why she's so keen on strapping him down and wheeling him around.

'Your Italian is good,' Sophie says again. 'Have you worked here?'

I shake my head. 'Nope. I've studied it. And I have a friend who's fluent. I'm here on an art history course,' I add, answering the question she hasn't asked.

'Me too,' she says. 'I mean, that's how I came here. To do art history. You know, one of those things where you get to live in a *pensione* and wear black all the time.' There's the laugh again, high and unexpected, like a carillon of bells. I look at her out of the corner of my eye. I cannot begin to imagine her wearing black. Her rounded figure and baby-doll eyes summon up Laura Ashley. Flowered smocks and matching cardigans. Possibly headbands. School uniforms for children who have grown too big.

'I was just a schoolgirl, really,' she says, as if confirming this diagnosis. 'My parents weren't sure what to do with me after I didn't get into Oxford, so Mummy arranged for me to come here. Then I met Big Paolo, it's my husband's name too, you know how Italian families are, and, well, the rest is history, as they say. They say that in the States, don't they?' she asks. '"The rest is history"? I've always thought it was an odd expression.'

The laugh is nervous now, and there is no corresponding smile on her face. In her bright red coat, she reminds me of a plumped-up robin, or a sad Christmas elf. 'But I like it,' she adds, 'really, I do. I love living in Florence.'

We have crossed the piazza by this time, skirted the fountain and turned into the street that houses our building. At the bottom of the steps I grope for my keys, but I'm spared the effort of finding them when Marcello from the grocery store suddenly appears in the archway and pushes the security gate open, holding it for me. The signora has delivered to the old lady below us before, but now I notice a Vespa with a delivery box on the back propped against the wall, paintings of vegetables, carrots mainly, and a few tomatoes and peas, emblazoned across its mudguard. It's obviously brand new. Now she has Marcello she's branching out.

'Very smart,' Sophie says.

Marcello mumbles something as he gets on the scooter, and I tell him it looks pretty sharp, which causes him to blush so badly that for an awful second I'm not even sure he's going to be able to start the thing. It farts and sputters before he finally roars away, the signora's phone number glowing in bright red letters across the back of his helmet.

'Oh dear,' Sophie says, watching him. 'How awful. To have to ride around Florence as a moving advertisement for carrots.' I am standing on the steps, but she has stopped on the sidewalk. 'We have to go on to the bakery,' she adds. 'That's what Paolo and I do, don't we? Have a pastry every day after school.' She looks down at the little boy and smiles, but he is staring at the sidewalk, looking almost as mortified as Marcello, his shoulders hunched inside his school jacket as if he wishes he could turn it into a snail's shell.

'Well, thank you again.' Sophie smiles up at me hopefully, and all at once I feel as if I'm looking into the memory of my own face. Her miserable marriage, her loneliness, it's all written there in not-so-secret code, the meaning plainly visible to the initiated.

From the entry at the bottom of our stairs, I can hear the claustrophobic little elevator, whirring and grinding, lowering itself inch by inch to the ground floor. And as I climb up, passing it, I wonder if maybe it's Father Rinaldo, come like a determined door-to-door salesman, pushing salvation again. Maybe if I hang over the stair rail, I'll see the pink bald spot on the top of his head when he gets out of the little wire cage. But when I hear the elevator hit bottom, the footsteps that echo across the vestibule are definitely a woman's. There's the unmistakable click of high heels. Probably the companion who lives with the old lady below us. I've met her before, said *buongiorno* when crossing the courtyard, but I have no idea of her name.

I open the apartment door, feeling the key pull back the heavy locks, and call for Billy. Since I've done something bad in my borrow-stealing from Piero, I decide I'll make up for it by being especially nice to her. Another Catholic trick: a good act on one side of the scales equals a bad one on the other. It's pretty simple really, all this redemption stuff, even dummies can get it.

But my goodness is destined to be denied. There's utter silence. Admittedly that's not unusual, but when I see that her old tweed coat is gone from the hall closet, I realize Billy's definitely not here. Well, I think, every coin has two sides. I don't get to do a good deed, admitted, but I'm cold and damp, and can have a cup of coffee in peace, maybe even make myself a grilled cheese sandwich. Then I'll think about the contents of my bag, and how to handle meddlesome priests.

Twenty-four hours after the fact I have to admit that Rinaldo doesn't seem so important. I was just hungry and grumpy, and I consider the idea that Billy was not winding me up deliberately and instead just misunderstood. Her Italian is lousy, so maybe 'Warren' was just a coincidence. A lot of things could sound like Warren, with an accent.

'War-hen. Warreen. Warrensi. Warrensini,' I say out loud.

Or maybe it was Billy's idea of a joke. Maybe telling someone a priest came looking for them is a real hoot back in Fort Pain. Either way, I forget about it as soon as I walk into my room.

The place reeks of my perfume. My foundation and brushes have been moved. And my two new compacts. I may leave dishes in the sink and clothes on the floor, but I am fastidious about my make-up. I don't have much of it, and no matter where I am, I always line it up in the same order on top of my bureau. Always.

Now, everything is messed up. My eye shadows are not in neat piles of two. My lipsticks have been rearranged. My earring box is open, and the top has been left off my hair 'glistener'. It even looks as if she sat on my bed. I can see the indent of her behind on the cover. And the pillow's mushed down.

'Goddam it!' I swear. 'Billy's been in my stuff.'

Chapter Six

ITʼS SATURDAY BEFORE I open the folder.

Billy came back later on Friday, after I'd eaten and called Pierangelo, but I didn't feel like talking to her so I went to a movie. As Piero pointed out, the incursion into my room was so flagrant that she virtually has to be picking a fight, so the best revenge is to ignore her. He said that always worked with his teenage daughters. I believe his exact words were: 'Don't let the enemy draw you into the conflict of their choice.' Or something like that. Anyway, it sounded pleasingly adult, which suited me fine. I don't like conflict, and what, exactly, was I planning to say? *I know you moved my lipstick! And touched my eye shadow!* Was I going to accuse her of looking at my earrings? The more I thought about it, the more I thought I ran the real risk of looking and sounding like an idiot.

So I waited until she went to a lecture on Caravaggio this morning, then made myself coffee, went into my bedroom, and locked the door, just like I used to when I was in High School and reading something I knew Mamaw wouldn't approve of. Barbara Cartland novels. *The Story of O.* The battered copy of

The Joy of Sex that did the rounds the spring I was in Eighth Grade, rented out for a dollar by a girl called Sandy Skivling who stole it from the adult section of the Book Mobile. These stories don't compare, though. These stories are worse than anything I've ever read. Eleanora Darnelli was indeed a nun, but only just. She was on the verge of leaving the convent when she was killed two years ago, sometime during the evening of 21 January, and I guess her story might be romantic, if it wasn't so awful.

Originally from somewhere in Calabria, Eleanora was sent to Florence by her parents to live with a family friend so she could go to better schools. She started out as a pupil at the convent she later joined in Fiesole, in the hills above the city, where eventually she taught in a day-care centre. Apparently she was happy there, and a good sister, a proper handmaiden of Christ. Or so everyone thought. Until the summer before she died, when an artist called Gabriel Fabbiacelli came to do some restoration work on the chapel.

Within weeks they had fallen in love, and by the end of the summer Eleanora had informed the Mother Superior that she could no longer honour her vocation, and she wanted to leave. The convent did everything it could to dissuade her. Pierangelo's notes don't go into details, but just reading this gives me the creeps. It's more than Karel Indrizzio's blade we share.

But despite the inevitable whispering in the confessional, the threats of damnation, the cold shouldering and general pressure I am absolutely certain she endured, Eleanora apparently stuck to her guns, because by January the Mother Superior had finally given permission for her to move in with a friend in Fiesole, a lay teacher from the day-care centre, so she could think over her final decision.

A better Catholic than I ever was, Eleanora continued to go to Mass every day, and the afternoon of the twenty-first was no exception. The last time anyone admitted to seeing her was in the cathedral in Fiesole where, after the service, she had a conversation with the local priest about helping with the flowers for Lent. According to him, she was in good spirits and optimistic about the future, whatever it held, when she walked out into the piazza shortly after six p.m. By that time the hazy sun would have been long gone, the winter night dropping like a blanket over the hills.

When she didn't come home for supper, her friend went looking for her. By nine p.m., she had called the local *carabinieri*, who advised her that Eleanora had probably gone into the city, maybe to do some late shopping. After all, they suggested, the sales were on. It was possible, the friend thought. Eleanora had talked about needing clothes for her new life. But still she was uneasy, and she was right to be, because Eleanora Darnelli had gone no further than the Roman Ruins. She was found the next morning behind the amphitheatre, not five hundred yards from where she had heard Mass, her throat cut, a white satin ribbon tied in a bow around her left wrist.

Benedetta Lucchese, a nurse at one of the big city hospitals, disappeared about two weeks later, on the night of 4 February. She lived north of Fortezza da Basso with her fiancé, a Moroccan contractor called André Dupin, and at six p.m. that evening they quarrelled. Loudly. Several of the neighbours heard them. André was leaving to visit his aunt and uncle in Tangier early the next morning, and her sister, Isabella, later said he was pressing Benedetta to set a date for the wedding so he could make plans with them, something she was apparently reluctant to do. André eventually stormed out and went to drown his sorrows in the local bar, where several people saw him.

While André was drinking himself silly, Benedetta went to see her sister, who still lived in the family house on the other side of the city, on Via San Leonardo, a beautiful road that winds through the hills beyond the Belvedere fort. She didn't get there, however, until just before nine p.m. According to Isabella Lucchese, Benedetta went to a late Mass first.

By eleven p.m., Benedetta decided she was ready to go. Her sister urged her to spend the night, but Benedetta insisted she ought to go home and make things up with André since he was leaving very early the next morning. She refused a ride, saying she'd rather walk the five minutes to the main road, the Viale Galileo, and catch the last bus. Her sister kissed her goodbye shortly before eleven-fifteen, and watched her walk down the drive and out through the front gate. It was the last time anyone saw her alive. Except Karel Indrizzio.

Her fiancé assumed she'd stayed with her sister, so he left on schedule the next morning, planning to call Benedetta and make it up when he arrived in Tangier. But he never got the chance. She was found late the next day in the olive groves below the walls of the Belvedere fort, a burnt-out candle clutched in her folded hands. Until 25 May, when Indrizzio chased me into the maze in the Boboli Gardens, a place he probably knew well since he frequently slept rough in the area, André Dupin was the prime suspect in Benedetta's killing, and still fighting extradition from Morocco.

I put the file down, feeling as if something cold has brushed very close to me. Billy comes home, and shouts through the door that she's going to the movies with Kirk and Henry, and do I want to come? It's Nicole Kidman wearing a fake nose in *The Hours*, and I shout, 'No thanks.' Even if I hadn't seen it last night, I can't imagine sitting still in the dark. She hovers a little, and finally asks if I'm OK. I say, 'Sure,' mumble something about how maybe I have a cold, and she leaves again.

The pictures are the hardest part. Sometime during the day, I got back into bed, as if snuggling under a pink duvet would make reading this stuff easier, and now I finally force myself out, pull up the covers and lay the photos on Signora Bardino's embroidered silk counterpane. Then I make myself study the faces and bodies of Eleanora Darnelli and Benedetta Lucchese.

Both of them were found fully clothed, and in Benedetta's case the extent of her injuries isn't even apparent in the crime-scene photos. She just looks dead. Not asleep; dead. You can tell because, even on film, there's nothing in her face. Lying in the frosted grass, holding her candle, she's utterly empty, like one of those awful Victorian monuments, an angel or a praying virgin, knocked over in a graveyard.

It wasn't until they got Benedetta back to the morgue and undressed her that it became clear she had been savagely beaten, tortured really, burnt, and cut. Her breasts had been carved up, a similarity that—along with the souvenir and the type of knife— added to Pallioti's conviction that Karel Indrizzio had attacked us both. Like me, Benedetta had been tied up. Marks on her arms and legs showed that she'd struggled hard. The patholo-gist thought she'd been dead for somewhere between twelve to fifteen hours when she was found, and that the single stab wound that killed her had been delivered last, after the other injuries had been inflicted.

Indrizzio kidnapped her, tortured her, finally killed her, and then dressed her up again, like a doll. He washed her before he put everything back on: underwear, socks, boots, blouse, skirt. Even her overcoat. He cleaned her hands and face, and combed her hair. The only thing he forgot was her wristwatch. According to Pierangelo's notes, the police thought that that was probably calculation rather than carelessness because every-thing else was obviously so meticulously planned.

Eleanora, on the other hand, does not look doll-like. She is lying on a large slab of grey stone, also fully dressed, wearing everything except one shoe, which makes her stockinged foot look oddly vulnerable. But although her injuries were nowhere near as horrific as Benedetta's—if you can apply that kind of sliding scale of horror—she looks much worse. Because there is a lot of blood. Everywhere. Eleanora Darnelli was not washed and she had no other injuries, but the pathologist said Indrizzio cut her throat with a stroke that was so clean, he nearly severed her head.

I have not nearly finished reading and examining everything in the file yet, but I keep seeing him. I feel his hands on my body, his tongue on my cheek. Finally I have to get up and walk around the room, chafing my palms as if I'm cold, because at last, and maybe fully for the first time, I understand now what Ty saved me from. To look at Eleanora and Benedetta is to see what I would have been.

I knew this before, of course. But now I feel it in my gut. The lamb to my Isaac, Ty sated whatever terrible thing it was that turned and writhed in the void of Karel Indrizzio's soul. By accident or not, he gave his life for mine. The blunt truth is I am only here because he did the thing that had always annoyed me most; he refused to leave me alone.

I feel as though cold water has just been dumped all over me and, suddenly weepy and light-headed, I long to talk to someone. I am not sure what I need to say, but I want to spill words out. Offer them up. But to who? If I call Pierangelo, he'll want to know what's wrong with me, why I have suddenly come to this realization, and I can't tell him without confessing to rifling his desk. Besides, he doesn't like to talk about Ty. I could call a friend in the States, but then the word would get out that I was finally cracking up, and I have a feeling that that is what most of the people I know have been expecting, and they would shimmer with self-satisfaction, possibly even volunteer to fly over here and bring me home 'where I belong', tutting at me all along that coming back was a bad idea. I even consider going and knocking on Sophie's door. Consider the idea, and dismiss it. I ran into her in the shop when I ducked out earlier today to buy a sandwich, but beyond the two conversations we've now had, I don't know her, and what I want desperately is to be with someone I know well. Or, more importantly, to be with someone who knows me. For the first time in a long time, I miss Mamaw.

Finally, after washing my face and making myself a large, bitter espresso, I decide what I am going to do. I will read through Pierangelo's file, every single word of it, then I will return it to his apartment. After that, I will know everything there is to know and move on.

Determined, I go back into my room, sit down by the photos on my bed, and run my fingers over the faces of the two women. Then I select one picture of each, and add them to the collection in my bottom drawer. Pierangelo won't miss them. And I tell myself that, although I plan to seal the envelope, I need them more than he does. I can't afford to forget what they looked like, what I would have looked like, if not for Ty. I didn't give him much while he was alive, but I can give him at least that much now.

There are a few more things in the file, some clippings, a note remarking that Eleanora Darnelli's left shoe was missing and never recovered—possibly taken by local dogs? Results of the pathologist's toxicology screenings, both of which came back clean, and some indecisive DNA—not the silver bullet it's cracked up to be, as everyone now knows—and one more manila envelope. I assume this has copies of Piero's finished article, or articles, and although I've already read the rough drafts, in the interests of thoroughness, I open it and tip the contents onto the bed.

But it's not copies, it's more pictures. There are about six of them, all obviously from a crime scene, and it takes me a moment to understand that they are of a woman I have never seen before. I hold one up to the light, just in case I'm making a mistake. But I'm not. She looks a little like the others, in that she has long dark hair, but she's a total stranger.

This woman is lying on what appears to be scrub grass. I can see pieces of a bush or shrub, and some twigs. Like Eleanor and Benedetta, she has the forensics unit's little markers laid alongside her for scale, so there is no question she's anything but a murder victim. Her hair is fanned out around her face, which is bruised and cut. Her nose is broken, even I can tell that. A little trickle of dried blood is caked on her upper lip. Blood has soaked her pale-coloured T-shirt too, covered it in blotches so it looks like some hideous Rorschach test, and her hands are on her stomach, holding something. I find a close-up. Her nails are long and painted a dark colour, plum or black. One thumb nail is broken, and her fingers are wrapped around a tiny dead bird, its head lolled sideways in her hands.

Pierangelo is usually extremely thorough, keeping both handwritten stuff and printed write-ups, but the notes with these photos are thin at best. They don't tell me much of anything. Only that the bird is a goldfinch, her bag was missing, and she was a hooker called Caterina Fusarno.

I sit down on the edge of the bed, not knowing what to think. The only explanation is that there must have been a third woman, one I was never told about. Maybe the police weren't sure they could tie Indrizzio to her murder so they never mentioned her. Or maybe they just didn't want me to know, thought somehow three would be that much worse than two, and that my brain was overloaded enough as it was. It's possible. Thanks to the punctured lung and the fact that it got infected, I did nearly die.

I decide that has to be it. She must be Indrizzio's third victim, another one of us. So I get down on my knees and put her picture where it belongs, with the others. Then I shove the manila envelope as far back into my bottom drawer as it will go and think: *Enough.*

It takes me less than five minutes to stuff everything in the file, pull my jeans and boots on, and get out the door. By the time I cross Ponte di Santa Trinita, I'm almost running, desperate to get back to Pierangelo's and dump this awful archive where it belongs, in his desk, with his records of the past.

It's seven o'clock on a Saturday evening and not raining, so things are crowded. Stores don't close for another half-hour, and rather than going up Porta Rossa, where half the world will be out shopping, I stay on the Lungarno and cut through the tiny Piazzetta del Limbo, where eight centuries ago the city's unbaptized infants were left for burial. The cemetery is gone now, but the place is still strangely hushed, like a bubble, a tiny pocket of air in the centre of Florence where the twelfth century is still alive. My heels echo on the paving stones as I pass the church of Santi Apostoli and hear the flutter of wings, birds nesting under the eaves, or the whispering of tiny souls begging to be let out of purgatory.

I slip up a side alley so narrow I can touch both sides, hop over rain dribbling down a gutter, and by the time I reach Pierangelo's street I'm breathless, probably more with relief than anything else. I pat my bag and think *Mission almost accomplished.* Then I stop dead in my tracks. Standing across from his building, I look up and see lights in the living-room windows.

I was sure I turned them off when I left. I know I did. I couldn't have made that big a mistake. So, he must be home. He must have cut short his time in Rome and come back early. Probably he's about to call me. Maybe he's doing that now. I left the phone on my bureau, charging.

Pierangelo being back presents a few problems, all outweighed by how happy I am. My goody-goody side announces that I'll definitely tell him what I've done, while the more pragmatic part of my brain points out that, just in case I don't, it will be easy enough to slip into the study and replace the file without him noticing. Then that will be that. As I cross the street and ring the bell, I wish I'd worn something a little nicer, or even brushed my hair.

The intercom light goes on, and I'm about to say something mature like, *Trick or Treat!* or *Are you the guy who ordered the Kung Pao chicken?* when a woman's voice, loud and very clear, says, 'Pronto?'

My finger moves off the bell as though I've been burnt, and I check it's his, that I haven't rung the wrong apartment by mistake.

'Pronto?' she says again, louder this time, and a little annoyed. Then she mutters something in Italian, and I'm not sure, but I think I hear a man's voice in the background.

I can't believe this. Even as I step away, I tell myself to calm down. That it is perfectly possible that there's a very logical explanation for the undisputable fact that there is a woman who is not me in Pierangelo's apartment. He has a brother. Perhaps the brother from Milan, Frederico, and his wife are using Pierangelo's place for the weekend.

I like the sound of that. It's reassuringly banal. And if Piero didn't tell me, well, why should he? I'm not his wife. I don't even live there. My choice: he did offer. Reminding myself of this—that he wanted me to move in lock, stock and barrel, and that it was me who didn't—makes me feel infinitely better, and I tell myself not to be so silly. After all, as the folder in my bag proves, I have a lot to be thankful for.

The bravado sticks with me all the way back to the apartment, but the second I get there I go straight into my room, grab my phone, and call Pierangelo. He doesn't answer, something else I immediately tell myself is not unusual. Even so I try again. Just in case I punched the wrong number or got a crossed line. It happens. When he doesn't answer again, I leave a message. Cheerful. And loving. And not the least bit possessive or jealous or suspicious. As a result I sound disturbingly like Marcia in late-night reruns of *The Brady Bunch*.

'I didn't know you have a cell phone.'

I whip round to see Billy standing in my doorway, a book in her hand.

She must have come in from the movie while I was out. She considers me for a moment, peering over the top of her granny glasses. 'Mary Thorcroft,' she says finally. 'International Woman of Mystery.'

If Billy had any hard feelings about my behaviour over the last few days, she seems to have forgotten them, because when I wake up the next morning she is bouncing around my room shouting, 'Spring! Spring!' She grabs the cord of the metal shutter on my window and yanks it so the panels rattle like stones in a tin can, which makes my head hurt.

A doctor in Philadelphia gave me a bunch of sleeping pills right after I got back, and although I don't like using them, I took one last night. I blink like an owl in the unexpected sunshine, and when I finally focus on Billy, I see she's wearing a pinafore dress and a pair of pale blue high-topped sneakers that have flowers painted on them. She looks like a funky Alice in Wonderland.

'Wake up, sleepy head!' she sings. 'Rub your eyes, get out of bed!'

She puts her hands on her hips, looking suddenly stern. 'The clocks went forward,' she announces. 'You have to get up, Mary, Mary. We're meeting Kirk and Henry in half an hour. For the picnic.'

Between Pierangelo's grisly file, which is now stuffed in the bottom of my wardrobe, and the mystery woman in his apartment last night, I admit I haven't really given much thought to Kirk's picnic. In fact, I'd completely forgotten about it. But not Billy. She must have spent most of yesterday at the market, because when I come into the kitchen the table is covered with plastic containers of olives and stuffed peppers, and wax-paper packages of sandwiches. It looks like there's enough food here to feed a small army, and she's busy packing it all into a big straw basket I haven't seen before.

I'm still annoyed with her for messing with my make-up, I haven't heard back from Pierangelo, and the pill has made my head feel like an inflated balloon, all of which makes me inclined to hate pretty much everyone and everything, especially picnics. Grass always gets in your food. Stuff's stale and warm, and things spill. And besides, I remember now that we're supposed to be going up to Bellosguardo, and I've been there about a hundred times. I don't even think they let you have picnics in Caruso's garden, but I'm in such a mean temper, I don't say so. Let them get all the way up there and find out for themselves. When Billy asks me if I want mortadella or ham, I ignore her and go out onto the balcony. I know I'm behaving like a bratty child, but I don't seem to have the energy to stop.

It's about half past eleven, the sun is all the way up and the difference between today and yesterday is so pronounced it feels as if someone's turned on a celestial heat lamp. I lean on the iron railings and look down into the courtyard while in the kitchen Billy sings, 'Ding dong, the witch is dead.'

Warmth seeps through my shirt, and for the first time the shadows under the portico look potentially cool and inviting instead of just damp. Even the sad, bony lemon trees have perked up. I hear voices, then the clang of the security gate, and little Paolo bursts from under the archway and runs across the paving stones.

He's wearing grey trousers, shiny black shoes and a miniature blue blazer, and from where I'm standing he looks more like a foreshortened adult than a child. A second later, Sophie-Sophia and her husband appear. They're dressed up too. She is wearing a green suit and high heels and carrying a small beret-type hat, and despite the warmth he has on the same fancy camel-coloured overcoat and shiny brown shoes. Watching them, it occurs to me that they have just come back from Mass. As if to confirm this, a priest appears a second later from our side of the building. He stops to talk to the Sassinellis, and I wonder if this is who came to our door. When we met in the shop yesterday, Sophie told me he comes regularly to hear confession and serve Mass for Signora Raguzza and her companion downstairs, who, Sophie whispered, is an illegal immigrant called Dinya.

Signora Raguzza is an invalid, and she is dying. Slowly. Which is driving her son crazy. I also know this because Sophie told me. She pointed out the son, who was scurrying down the street ahead of us as we walked back. Sophie says the son and his wife and children are living with his wife's family in Pozzilatico while they wait for his mother to die so they can move into the apartment, and the whole thing's costing him a fortune. He pays for the companion—even though he does get her on the cheap—and for the doctor's visits, and for the donations to the church the priest comes from so he'll come and say Mass, and for everything else that his mother insists she has to have because she can't walk. Or so she says. According to Sophie, the son occasionally comes over for a grappa with the Sassinellis to recover from visiting his mama, and after a couple he's prone to suggesting she can walk pretty well. If she has to. He even confessed that once, when his in-laws were driving him really buggy, he considered proving the point by, say, setting a fire. Just a little one. Just enough to get the old bat on her feet. Sophie sympathizes, but both she and Big Paolo urged him to reconsider. Now the priest gives a little bow. The long black skirt of his soutane swishes across the paving stones as he merges into the shadows and disappears under the archway.

Little Paolo has been entertaining himself by pulling leaves off one of the lemon trees and dropping them into the wide mouth of the pot. His father says something I can't catch to his son, and guides him towards their door, his large man's hand flat against the little boy's back. Sophie walks a few steps behind. Then, just before they disappear into their entryway, she turns and looks up. Her eyes squint in the sun, and she waves, her hand rising in a little half circle of recognition, as if she has known the whole time that I have been up here, watching.

Ten minutes later Billy yells it's time to leave. I still don't want to go on a picnic, but I can't think of a good excuse to get out of it, so I'm sticky as molasses, deliberately slow. I literally drag my feet as I go to get my phone in case Piero rings, and fuss with my shoulder bag. Out on the landing, Billy opens the elevator doors and sends her basket, which takes up just about all the room there is, down by itself. Then she runs down the stairs to meet it, yelling over her shoulder about the Japanese girls, and how she told Kirk and Henry to invite them, and ignoring the fact that I'm ignoring her.

People are still spilling out of Santo Spirito as we round the corner and come into the piazza. They congregate on the wide apron of the church terrace and on the steps, talking in little groups, commenting on the sermon and the unexpected sunshine. I walk behind Billy, lollygagging, looking in windows I'm not interested in and examining menus I already know by heart while she marches ahead with her basket, using it like a battering ram. In no hurry to join the others, I detour to the church steps where a little black and white pirate dog with a blotch around one eye is giving anyone who passes his best smile. I'm a sucker for dogs, especially mutts, so I give him a pat. 'Hey, dog,' I say, and he doesn't seem to mind it's in English.

As I rub behind his ears, the dog widens his grin to show me his pink tongue and his snaggle teeth. His fur is silky, and he's wearing a nice leather collar. The boy who obviously belongs to him is sitting on the steps above with his back to us, and I can see that his clothes are clean, but ragged. His blue shirt is fraying, and so are the hems of his jeans, but as much as anything else it's his scuffed trainers that mark him as one of Florence's street people. His shoulders give him away too. Their curled slope is more like an old man's than a young one's.

Half turned from me, he's watching the front of Santo Spirito, so I can't see his face, just a thatch of dirty blond hair, the same colour as Ty's was, and the nubbly, exposed bones at the top of his spine. For a second, the shape of him, the thin shoulders and bent back, reminds me of an El Greco, of one of his emaciated saints with their too large hands and sandalled feet. Then he turns round.

He's not a boy, but the boyishness is still there in his face, which is unmistakably Italian. More than that, it's Florentine. You can see it in any fresco with its wide cheekbones, pronounced, slightly bullish nose, and full, almost flushed lips. But that's not what startles me. What startles me are his eyes. They're golden. Amber coloured, like a lion's. I have only ever seen one pair like them before in my life, and they belonged to my husband.

We stare at each other. Then I step backwards suddenly and trip. The dog gives a startled yip and jumps up, and someone exclaims as I bump in to them.

'Scusi, signora. Scusi! Dispiace!' I turn to steady the elderly woman I've almost knocked over.

'Non fa niente.' She takes my hand and smiles, saying it's nothing, forgiving me my clumsiness, because, after all, it's Sunday and she has just come out of church. I smile back, apologize again, then turn to look for the dog and the tall thin man.

They should be right above me on the steps, but a couple are standing there now, arguing about where to go for lunch. I have to have been wrong, I think. It's the sleeping pill. No one but Ty ever had eyes like that. I imagined it. I know I did. But, suddenly, I desperately need to check. To prove I'm not going completely nuts.

I climb up to the terrace, stepping over people and past them, and look again. But I can't see a faded blue shirt, or a patch of black and white anywhere. They're not on the terrace, or in the piazza below. They've vanished, been swallowed into the crowd, and the only person I do recognize is Billy, waving to me from under the white umbrellas at the bar.

'See,' Kirk says, as I finally join them, 'I told you it would be spring today. Oh, ye of little faith, I told you so!' He spreads his arms and his overcoat flaps at his sides like wings.

'Where are the Japanese girls?' Billy is looking around at the outside tables as if she expects to see them sitting there with their pot of tea. 'Didn't you ask them?' She turns on Kirk. 'I brought them sandwiches,' she says, and the indignation in her voice suggests that this fact alone, the mere presence of prosciutto and Gorgonzola with their names on it, should be enough to make Ayako and Mikiko and Tamayo materialize out of thin air.

Kirk shakes his head. 'They are otherwise engaged. La Bardino, or, as it should be, La Bardina, has whisked them away.'

'Away?' Billy asks as though she envisions a dungeon, or at the very least an impossibly tall tower.

'To fair Verona.' Kirk presses his hands together and bows like something out of *The Mikado*. 'They are going to bisit Womeo and Juriet!'

'Bad!' Billy slaps his shoulder, but she's laughing too.

'Oh yes,' Kirk says, 'and after that they are hieing themselves hence to Mantua, which, if you ask me, is actually prettier.'

'How do you know?'

He shrugs. 'I was there a few years ago. It was fab. Great ducal palace.'

'I never knew that.'

'That I was a duke? I was, in my former life. You should see my last duchess.'

'I don't know,' Henry says. 'Sounds to me like you're waving, not Browning.'

'Oh, boo,' Billy groans. 'That is definitely one less sandwich for you.'

She loops her arm through Kirk's and takes his hand, their fingers intertwining, and for the first time I notice she has a new ring, one of the ones she pointed out on the bridge. The little heart stones, pink and green, sparkle in the sunlight. I glance at Henry, who raises his eyebrows. Clearly he's as surprised by this development as I am.

Kirk lifts the basket off the bar table with his free hand and groans at the weight. 'So,' he asks, 'have we got the tickets?'

'There's a *tabaccaio* right beside the bus stop,' I point out, suddenly relieved that at least we don't have to walk up to Bellosguardo dragging Billy's huge picnic basket.

'Bus stop, bah,' Henry says. 'On a day like this we have to be at one with nature.' My heart sinks again. It's a steep hill. Then Henry says, '*Voilà!*'

He bows like a magician and holds up four tickets. 'Change of plans,' he announces. 'We're going to the Boboli Gardens!'

Chapter Seven

I COULD THINK of a hundred things. I could say I'm sick, or that I have allergies, or that I've just remembered my grandmother's going to die today. For that matter, I could just leave, but what would that prove? I have to go back to the Boboli Gardens sometime, so I might as well get it over with while I'm already in a bad mood. After all, just yesterday I was all excited about 'moving on.' As we come out of the alley opposite the main entrance, I try to remember who the clever clogs was who warned about getting what you wish for.

The Pitti Palace glows dirty yellow in the sun, the huge façade looking as though it's been blasted by a sand storm. The apron in front is crowded with people sitting on the pebbled cement, reading newspapers, talking on cell phones, lounging, as if they're on the beach instead of slap in the middle of the city with traffic streaming by.

'Weird,' Billy says.

As she leads us through the sea of bodies, we catch snatches of conversation in so many languages it sounds like Sunday at the Tower of Babel. There are a lot of foreign students and backpackers sitting out here, probably because some guidebook told them it was an authentic thing to do, but there are Italian kids too, and when we reach the entrance, I find myself scanning the crowd, not sure whether I want to catch sight of the blue-jeaned El Greco and the black and white dog again, or not, or what, exactly, it would mean if I did. That my epiphany last night summoned him up, and now Ty's ghost is following me around Florence? The idea is less than appealing, no matter what I owe him.

'And one for you, Miss Little Lamb.' Kirk slaps a ticket into my palm, and for half a second I see him with a hood over his face, with gloves on his pale, long-fingered hands, and eyes that stare out at me through slits. If I look as though I'm about to shriek, he doesn't appear to notice.

Henry hefts the basket. He's taken his jacket off and spread it over the top in a not very convincing disguise, and we walk right by the sign that says No Picnicking, and pass under the archway into the courtyard.

The entrance to the gardens is on the far side of the Pitti, up a tunnel that passes under the hill behind the palace. As we make our way towards it, hundreds of rows of windows look down on us. Several tour groups are gathering by the flights of stairs that go up to the museums, but the courtyard still feels empty, as if so much history has spilled out of here that it can never be filled up again. I give my ticket to the man who sits at the tunnel entrance and tuck my hands under my arms, as if it's winter and I should be wearing mittens.

'Where should we go?' Kirk stops at the top of the steps as we come out into the sunshine. The hill rises in front of us, the amphitheatre, where the first opera performance in the world took place, scooped out of its centre. I'd forgotten I even knew things like that, about the opera. For an uncomfortable moment, Ty's voice comes back to me, reading aloud from a guidebook, and I wonder what else I'm about to remember. Gravel paths lead left and right.

'This way.' I step past Kirk. 'Up here.' My voice sounds weird, even to me. 'Up here are the best views.'

'How do you know?' Billy stops and looks at me.

'Because,' I mutter, 'I used to come here with my husband.' Then I turn my back on them, still chaffing my arms, and begin to climb the steps that lead away from the crowds and off towards the abandoned vineyards and the derelict coffee house where the terraces crumble in the long grass and you can see all the way to Fiesole.

I am deliberately heading in the opposite direction from the long gravel walk with its white dust, as far as I can get from the green tunnel of trees, and skeleton of the Medici maze, but, even so, I'm surprised to find out how much I don't like being here. I feel queasy, and I have the bizarre sensation that I might turn around and see Ty or, worse, Father Rinaldo standing behind me.

We finally reach the best spot, below the coffee house, spread out the rug Billy's brought, and lie down in the sun. Very few people come over to this side of the garden, so it's quiet. You can hear birds. Someone starts pouring wine, and I close my eyes. But instead of blotches of sunlight and shadows and leaves, I see the statues on the long walk above the round pond that Ty made such a big deal of that last afternoon. They're dwarves and grotesques, blindfolded boys who beat each other with sticks. It was so hot that the stones seemed to move, undulate in the heat, as if they were coming alive. The children run down the hill. Their mouths open in silent scream, they melt in the crowd where Rinaldo walks like a black crow amidst the bright summer shirts and dresses.

'Earth to Mary.'

The picture vanishes abruptly and I open my eyes to see Henry, smiling and handing me an apricot. Velvety and round, it looks like a perfect golden egg in the palm of his hand.

'Did you know,' he says, 'that this place used to be full of weird stuff like mazes?'

This is not addressed particularly to me, or at least I don't think it is, so I ignore it and bite into the sweet fruit, the juice dribbling down my chin. Kirk looks at him through a sleepy eye. He has actually taken his coat off and rolled up his sleeves, exposing the fine red hairs on his white freckled arms. 'Mazes?' he asks.

'Yeah,' Henry says. 'You know, like the Minotaur.'

Henry is wearing sandals, with socks. He reaches into the basket for another bottle of wine, and I watch him struggling with Signora Bardino's very fancy corkscrew, which is complicated and shaped like a fish. He stuffs the top of the bottle into its mouth and twirls its tail ineffectively. 'Mazes were very popular,' he says. 'Incredibly ornate. You could be lost for days.' He adjusts his glasses, gripping the corkscrew by the tail as if it might escape. 'Presumably,' he adds, 'every time you went into your own back yard you had to carry a ball of string. Or would it be breadcrumbs? I forget.'

'The breadcrumbs were Hansel and Gretel.' Kirk leans over and takes the bottle and corkscrew fish out of Henry's hands.

'The Medici, being the Medici, had three.' Henry does not seem to be at all worried by the loss of the bottle. 'Mazes,' he adds. 'In these gardens.'

'How do you know all this?' Billy asks. Now that we've polished off one bottle of wine she's decreed we should eat, and she's handing out sandwiches, peeking into the white paper packages to be sure of what's what, and announcing, '*Prosciutto! Asiago e ruccola! Pomodoro e mortadella!*' like a barker at a fun fair.

Henry shrugs. 'I read a book thing.'

'A book thing?'

'Yeah. You know, with pages that have words on them. Anyways, I guess you can still find the outlines of the mazes, if you know where to look. The paths, and the centre.'

'The room.' Henry looks up at me when I speak. 'The room,' I say again, louder. 'The centre of a maze is called "the room."'

Already, it feels like we've been drinking too much, and my voice is slipping away from me like a dog on an extendable leash. Kirk opens one of the white paper packages. The butter in the sandwich is melting, running in little rivulets down the brown flaky edges of the crusts.

'Usually they used yew, or box hedge,' my voice says. 'But one of the mazes here was planted in trees.'

Henry picks up one of Signora Bardino's wine glasses and flicks a bug out of the bottom of it. 'Trees?' he asks.

'Uh-huh. When they grew up,' I hear myself say, 'the trunks got so close together they became a wall. So once you got in, there was no way out.'

'Spooky-wooky.' Kirk is holding the bottle. When he pours the wine it leaves little fizzing bubbles on the edge of my glass. A bird starts to sing. It's a high trilling sound from the trees behind us, and Billy rolls over as if the sound is a cue and starts fanning her arms like she's making a snow angel.

'Do you think that's a nightingale?' she asks. 'Wouldn't that just be too cool if that was a nightingale?'

Henry takes the bottle back. '"Thou wast not born for death, immortal bird! No hungry generations tread thee down."'

'Keats,' Kirk says. 'Tuberculosis. Dead. Spanish Steps.'

Henry shrugs and starts to laugh. 'When I was little,' he says, 'my uncle told me, he honestly told me, that there were no songbirds in Italy because the Italians were so crazy they shot them all.' He picks up a sandwich and takes a bite. 'I can remember it perfectly. He seriously said, my uncle said, people in Rome stood on their balconies and shot birds with pistols. I think he'd been in the war. Anzio or something.'

'Shit.' Billy starts to laugh. She sits up and holds her glass out. 'That's a great story.' She lies back on the grass, balancing the wine on her chest. 'Let's all tell stories,' she says. 'Let's just stay here and lay around for days, eating and telling stories.'

'It's been done, darlin'.' Kirk reaches out and pulls her hair. 'It's called *The Decameron*.'

'Oh, fuck you,' Billy bats his hand away. 'You are such a prick. I'm not going to talk to you.'

'Ever again?' Kirk asks.

'Ever again!' Billy's voice is suddenly edgy with sun and

alcohol and not enough food. 'I want Mary to tell a story,' she demands.

'I don't know any.'

'Yes, you do.' Billy sits up again. She looks like an angry angel now, one that has pieces of grass in its hair.

'I don't,' I insist. But I can feel words rising in my throat, feel them slipping into my mouth and pushing at my lips, determined to get out, like smoke curling under a door.

'There are no more birds,' I say suddenly. 'Or, at least, there shouldn't be. Because Henry's right, they did kill them. They used to kill them all. But not with guns. They did it with nets. They stretched nets called *rangaie* between the trees. That's what this whole garden was designed for. To begin with, anyways. Killing birds. They built the fountains to attract them, then they drove them into the nets and killed them.'

I pause for breath, and I can feel Kirk staring at me, a sandwich halfway to his mouth. 'They liked killing things,' I say. 'Especially in gardens. As a matter of fact, there's a story about it in *The Decameron*.' My voice is gathering speed now, running away like a ball rolling downhill.

'A young man falls in love with a woman, but she doesn't love him, so he kills himself. Then she dies. And since suicide is a mortal sin, and she was so hard-hearted because she didn't love him, both of them are punished. For eternity. His punishment is to chase her through this beautiful wood, and her punishment is to run away from him. But, every time, he sets his hounds on her and catches her, and kills her and cuts her heart out. Then, as soon as he does, after just a few seconds, she jumps up again, runs off again and he has to chase her again. And they go around and around like that in the beautiful wood, him killing her because she didn't love him, and her being killed because she was so cruel, over and over and over. For ever. Amen.'

'Jesus.'

I don't look at Billy, but I can sense her eyes on me. I can feel her parted lips and see the bright white line of her teeth just the same way I can see the birds flying into the nets, and the running woman, and the hounds. The man wielding his knife. The shower of feathers landing on the trampled grass. I reach for my wine and it spills, running down the inside of my wrist.

Henry touches my arm. His hand feels hot through the sleeve of my shirt. 'Mary?' he asks. 'Are you OK?'

'Oh, just leave her alone!' Billy stands up suddenly, pieces of grass clinging to her hair and dress. 'For Christ's sake,' she says, 'just leave her alone.' Then she turns and stalks up the slope towards the ruins of the coffee house.

'I'm sorry.' It's a few minutes later when I say this to Henry.

Kirk has followed Billy up the hill, his coat a dark pile, like a skin some animal has shed, lying on the edge of the rug. From where we are sitting we can see them standing by the red plastic tape that's stretched across the entrance of the little rococo coffee house. Billy runs her hand down the ornate crumbling stone, her fingers plucking at clumps of carved grapes and the worn edges of leaves. Then she ducks under the tape and disappears. Kirk follows her.

'For what?' Henry asks.

I look at him stretched out in the sun, his head resting on his balled-up sweater. He smiles, and I think again that he looks like a curly-haired bear. It's easy to imagine Henry swiping honey from a pot, or plucking ripe fruit from the branch of a tree.

'I don't know.' The strange fuggy feeling that has enveloped me all afternoon is slipping away, as if a fog inside my head is clearing, and I wonder how crazy, exactly, I sounded. 'It's an ugly story,' I add. 'I guess it upset Billy. Anyways, I'm sorry if I ruined the picnic.'

'Picnic shmicnic,' Henry shrugs. 'And don't worry about Billy. She's fine. You want my bet?' he asks. 'In my professional capacity, that is? I'd say Miss Billy's just not too thrilled when anyone else is the centre of attention.' He grins at me. 'Especially,' he adds, 'if they're talking about dead birds.'

In the end, it's Henry and I who pack up the picnic.

Billy and Kirk eventually reappear, holding hands like teenagers, and announce they're going to the Porcelain Museum, an expedition it's clear we're not really invited to join, which is no big deal, since neither of us want to go anyway. Henry says he's not interested in soup tureens and china monkeys playing violins, and I've seen them already. So we volunteer to throw the remains of the sandwiches into the bushes, and wrap up Signora Bardino's sticky glasses, and carry the big basket back to the apartment, where I finally get a call from Pierangelo. He'll be back from Rome tomorrow night and he wants to take me out to dinner.

All day, I have been trying not to fantasize about him pretending to be in the Vatican City with the cardinal while in fact hiding in his apartment with some strange woman, probably Monika, who, in my mind, is now a combination of Angelina Jolie and Sophia Loren, so this cheers me up considerably. Or at least enough to agree when Henry suggests we 'abandon the lovebirds' and go off for an early meal by ourselves.

We dither for a while over where to go, but our minds are finally made up for us because so few places are open on Sunday evening. We eventually find a tiny trattoria over in San Frediano and have to stand in line, our backs smushed into the coat rack as we hover over the jammed-in tables where couples drink wine out of pitchers and devour the Florentine version of the Blue Plate Special, which usually turns out to be tripe.

'God,' Henry says when we finally sit down, 'I am starving. You know what,' he adds as the waiter flings two menus in our direction, 'I really hate picnics.' He raises his eyebrows when I start to laugh.

'I'm sorry,' he insists, 'but I do. There's always way too

much food, and you never eat it, because it's all stuff like olives. I mean, I like olives, in moderation. But to tell you the truth, I think sandwiches are really overrated.'

'I don't know.' I am remembering the deli around the corner from our apartment in Philadelphia. 'I never went for cheese steaks,' I confess. 'But I have a serious weakness for Ruebens.'

'Well, that's different! A Rueben isn't a sandwich. It's an institution. With a pickle.' We raise our glasses to this idea as the waiter comes to take our order, which in neither case is tripe. I have pasta, and Henry has a good old-fashioned steak.

The food arrives and we eat for a few minutes in companionable silence. Then Henry says, 'Tell me about your husband.'

He is cutting his steak as he says this, concentrating on the pink slab of meat, and for a second I stop chewing. In the normal course of things I would probably demur, or change the subject, or maybe even flatly refuse. But Ty has been so on my mind in the last twenty-four hours that I don't.

'What do you want to know?'

Henry shrugs. 'I don't know. Whatever you want to tell me. I mean, what was he like?'

I consider this for a second, then pour myself some more wine. The truth is, I don't know how to answer. I had known Ty for so long by the time we got married, since our senior year at Penn, that I can't remember when I last thought about 'what he was like'. He just 'was.' Which, I suppose, means I took him for granted. 'He was a teacher,' I say finally. 'And a good person. Some people thought he was virtually a saint.'

Henry glances at me. 'Saints don't exist.'

I smile. 'What about angels?'

'*Oy Vey!* Mary, I'm Jewish, the jury's out.' Henry waves his fork in the air. 'How about we settle for human beings?' he asks, and for some reason we both find this funny. Our laughter mingles with the cloud of conversation that fills the little room. Then I tell Henry about Ty.

I tell him about the Warren family, who were nice, philanthropic Philadelphia Quakers, and about how we met, unremarkably, in a seminar on 'William Faulkner and the Genesis of the American Novel' in the fall of our senior year. I tell him how Ty asked me out, picking me from the hundreds of other girls he could have chosen, which to this day puzzles me, because he didn't know me at the time, and now I think the truth is, he never knew me. Not that it seemed to matter to him. Ty claimed he loved me. From the very beginning. Sometimes he'd sing a little song that went, 'No, honestly, you know you belong to me.' And eventually it became true because Ty decided it was.

'Sometimes,' I find myself saying, 'I felt as if I was standing outside the whole thing, watching a movie about two people, one of whom bore a passing resemblance to me. I think I was sleepwalking, for the better part of a decade. Which is kind of scary. But I did it.'

Henry does not watch me too closely while I say all this. He eats, and nods, orders more wine and smiles occasionally. And I understand now why he probably has an awful lot of clients who pay him enough so he can afford to take three months off to learn bad jokes about Brunelleschi's dome. In the end, I even tell him about my parents and Mamaw.

'Your great-aunt sounds like she was just that,' he says, when I finally stop to attend to my pasta. 'Great.'

'Yeah,' I say. 'She was.' And then without really intending to, I explain how Mamaw died, and how afterwards it really did feel as if Ty might be the only person in the world.

I describe how she called, and her voice had a new huskiness underneath it, and a cough that wouldn't quit. I thought it was a cold, but Mamaw said, 'I have to talk to you, honey. I have bad news.'

As I tell it, the house in Pennsylvania swims up like something in a dream. Leaves collect on the lawn, drift against the maple tree, and skitter like birds across the frozen grass while I hold the car door open and Ty helps Mamaw into the back seat. He adjusts a pillow under her feet, tucks a blanket over her knees because, even though we have put her parka and lined jeans on, she's cold now all the time. The engine turns over, roaring in the chilly air, and Ty reaches out and squeezes my hand. His wide, tanned fingers close over mine, and both of us try not to look, not to intrude as Mamaw presses her face to the glass of the car window so she can keep looking and looking, so she can hold on to the white clapboard and ugly black shutters until the last possible moment, until we round the corner by the gas station and the house her daddy left her slips out of sight, lost amid the bare branches and scraggly untrimmed hedges of November.

There are poinsettias at her funeral because it's Christmas. And gold-coloured chrysanthemums, which Mamaw loved but I still think are ugly. Ty's parents drive up from Philadelphia, meaning well, but are too sleek and smooth-edged for Mamaw's avocado carpet and the smell of cigarette smoke. His mother asks and asks if there is anything she can do, but it is Ty who shakes hands and talks. He is the one who listens to people cry, who pays the caterers and thanks the priest. And it is Ty who drives back up with me one Sunday in January to pack woollen blankets in plastic bags and mothballs, and pour antifreeze down the drains, and check that the storm windows are locked.

And it is Ty who, a week after that, picks a dog out of the city pound to make me feel better. He brings it home on a red leash and we call it Leo, and when it gets hit by a car one afternoon the next summer both of us cry. Then, one rainy day in December when Mamaw has been dead for almost exactly two years, Ty comes home early and tells me that someone has dropped out of a teaching exchange programme sponsored by his school. It's a comparative study, teaching in other religious education systems, and they've offered him the space. Italy. Six months in a school in Florence. There's an apartment and everything, and he can take a spouse.

Rain pours down the window above my desk making wormy shadows crawl across the piles of paper stacked on the sill. 'Marry me,' Ty says. It is not the first time he's asked, but now he gets down on one knee. He produces a diamond ring in a velvet box. 'Come on, Mary,' he says. 'Marry me and come to Florence.'

When I stop talking, my half-eaten pasta is cold and the waiter is glaring at us because he wants us to order dessert. Henry is mopping bread around the edge of his empty plate, his brow furrowed as if this is very important work.

'So what happened?' he asks. 'I mean with the two of you?'

I shrug, surprised I've said all this. 'I fell in love with someone else.'

'So, you got divorced.' It wasn't a question, but I shake my head.

'No. He died.'

Henry doesn't look up. 'I'm sorry,' he says. 'That must have been awful.'

'Yeah.'

He swallows his bread, and the waiter pounces on our plates. Do we want crème caramel? Tiramisù? A pear with Gorgonzola? We both ask instead for coffee.

'I did too,' Henry says suddenly. 'Fall in love with someone else, I mean. She didn't love me, but it didn't particularly matter. I couldn't go back to my wife afterwards. Not 'cause she threw me out. I mean, she wanted me to come back, said she still loved me. But I couldn't. It just wasn't possible.'

He shakes his head and stirs the thimbleful of espresso that has just been put down in front of him. 'People are different.' Henry shrugs. 'It doesn't work the same way for everybody,' he says. 'But, personally, I don't think it's fair to ask a bird to fly back into a cage.'

By the time we leave, there is no longer a line. The dessert display is pretty much empty. Couples are scraping spoons around the inside of glass dishes and pouring the last of their wine while the waiter snuffs out candles and strips red and white cloths off of the tables. Out on the street, people walk arm in arm, savouring the memory of the first warm day.

'Sure you don't want me to walk you home?' Henry asks. But I tell him, no, I'm fine.

He kisses me on the cheek before we part, splitting in opposite directions. Henry shuffles off towards the apartment he shares with Kirk in Torquato Tasso, his big bear figure merging into the shadows.

I don't know this part of town that well, but I'm not concerned. If I head in the right direction, I'll hit the Carmine or Santo Spirito sooner or later. A couple drifts past me, languid and leaning into each other. Their whispers hang in the dark and the woman's perfume trails behind her like smoke. Looking at them makes me miss Pierangelo, suddenly, like a pain in my stomach. The city seems bigger than it is, and strange, without him in it.

I cut down a side street that I'm pretty sure is leading the right way, and find myself in a tiny piazza. There are dozens and dozens of these in Florence. Like this one, they are often just a widening of an alley fronted by a forgotten church. The space is almost entirely filled by municipal garbage bins, and by the empty deck of a wine bar, its windows thick with condensation. Lights from inside glint off the stainless-steel chairs stacked and chained to the outdoor tables. I am skirting around them when a hissing sound comes from behind me. I didn't notice them before, but when I look into the shadows I see a pair of young men, both in tight jeans and leather jackets, lounging in the portico of the church.

'*Ciao, ciao, bella,*' they mew, sounding like the hungry feral cats that slink across the rooftops and drop into the sleeping streets.

I shrug off a tinge of unease, telling myself this isn't a threat, just a pastime so routine it doesn't even qualify as a compliment. Then I realize I'm wrong. One of them detaches himself from the wall and saunters towards me, his shape gaining bulk as he comes into the light.

'*Ciao, ciao,*' he mews. '*Mi chiamo Gianni, dimmi chi sei.*' Tell me who you are.

I feel a throb of panic and start to step backwards when I realize that the other one has circled around behind me. The railing of the wine-bar deck is at my side, hemming me in, and suddenly my bag seems huge and ostentatious and obviously filled with money. Shit, I think, I'm about to get mugged.

I open my mouth to scream, but before I do there's a burst of noise, people talking. A wedge of light streams into the piazza, and Gianni falters. Confusion flashes across the weaselly features of his face, and I realize something's happening behind me. Turning round I see his friend staggering unnaturally backwards. Unnaturally because someone has hooked an arm around his neck and is tipping him sideways as though he's a life-sized wooden doll.

'Get the hell out of here, scumbag,' my saviour says in Italian. Two other guys who have just appeared are looking on and they start to clap. Gianni flashes them the finger and says something unsavoury about their mothers, but the bravado's fake. Already, he and his pal are slithering into the shadows of the alley. My heart thumps as I watch them melt away, then I feel a hand on my shoulder and a voice says: 'Signora Maria, are you OK?'

I realize with a shock that my saviour is Marcello from the grocery store. He looks older and suddenly more substantial in the requisite leather jacket. There's no hunch to his shoulders now, and if he's blushing, it's lost in the dark.

'I'm fine.' It takes me a second to find my voice. 'Really,' I add, nodding. 'Thank you. I'm fine. They didn't even touch me.' Relief and nerves mingle in the words. 'They didn't have a chance,' I add.

The door of the wine bar bursts open again, and now there's a small crowd coming and going. People nudge past us. The sound of laughter shoots up and bounces off the high walls of the piazza. A lighter flares in the dark and there's the smell of cigarette smoke. Marcello takes his hand off my shoulder, some of the awkwardness returning. 'Look,' he says, 'are you going home? I'll walk you.'

I start to insist, as usual, that I'm perfectly OK alone, but when I look at the alley I can almost feel the slithering shadows. Marcello must see the hesitation in my face because he adds, 'Really. I'm going that way.'.

The people around us, mostly young men, indistinguishable in a uniform of jeans and leathers, are dispersing. They move off in groups down the alley. The owner pulls down the blind on the wine bar's door as Marcello and I follow them. He has his hands dug deep in his pockets, his head ducked. His shyness grows with every step we take away from the piazza. I can feel it walling him in. It's practically a physical disability, and it makes me ache for him.

'Thanks,' I say again, trying to crack the silence. 'Really. That was pretty impressive.'

I feel rather than see him shrug. 'They taught us in the academy. I was going to be in the police.'

'Wow.' I glance at him sideways. We've just come out onto Santo Spirito, and the fine lines of his face, the round cheeks and soft boyish curve of his chin, are caught in the wash of the church floodlights. 'What happened?' I ask. 'You change your mind?'

He shakes his head, a lock of hair coming loose, and I hope I haven't put my foot in it and embarrassed him further because he was kicked out or something.

'An accident,' he says. 'On a scooter. I broke my leg. There are four pins in it.' He looks down as he speaks, as if we might see the pins through his jeans, and I notice for the first time that he walks with a slight limp. 'I was in hospital a long time,' he adds. 'The police gave me disability. Now I'm trying to figure out what to do.'

Damn, I think. No wonder he's embarrassed to be riding around on a Vespa covered in vegetables.

'Well, hey, you've got lots of choices, right? Whole new start.' I try to sound as though this is really great, and it looks as if maybe I succeed, because Marcello actually glances at me and smiles.

'I've tried some other jobs,' he shrugs. 'I was a gardener for a while, but that isn't a career.'

'Any other ideas yet?'

'You'll laugh.'

'I won't.' I hold two fingers up. 'Swear on my mother's grave.'

'I want to do something good.' He shrugs again. 'There's a lot of crap in the world. I think we all have to fight against it, do what we can.' He glances at me sideways. 'That's why I wanted to be a cop. I thought about the lay ministry, but, I don't know.'

'You mean, like social work?'

He shakes his head. 'It didn't work out. I volunteer for stuff, though.' I can feel the effort it costs him to say this much, and my heart goes out to him again.

'Not a lot of young guys think that way.' This comes out horribly. Patronizing and icky. Not at all what I'd intended. 'You've got all the time in the world,' I say quickly. 'You'll think of something, and it'll work out because, obviously, your mother raised you right. That's the expression we use in America,' I add. 'You know, when somebody does good.'

'I'd like to have a family,' he says. Then he asks abruptly, 'You're married?'

'Not any more,' I say. 'I was. My husband died.'

I don't know if this makes Marcello blush again or not, because it's dark. 'I'm sorry,' he says quickly. And then oddly, 'He must miss you.'

It's the sort of inappropriate remark really shy people often make, and it makes me smile in the dark.

'I don't know about that,' I say. 'He was a much better person than I am. He tried to do good in this life too.'

'What did he do?'

'He was a teacher. Little kids. He taught in religious schools, mostly.'

'I'd like to do that.'

'You'd be good at it.'

I don't know why I say this, really. Ty's ghost, I guess, egging me on, getting me to recruit for the cause. Even so, walking along like this, I can imagine Marcello doing what Ty did. Kids probably wouldn't embarrass him as much as everyone else seems to. They usually like shy people.

We round the corner and in a few seconds we've reached the front of my building. He waits while I grope for my keys, fit them into the lock.

'Well, listen,' I say, 'forget kids, you're my hero. Really.'

This time he does blush, I can see it in the security light that blinks on under the archway as I push open the gate. Marcello shrugs as I start to step inside, then his face turns serious. All of a sudden I can see him in uniform, the young knight out protecting damsels in distress.

'You should be careful, signora,' he says. 'Really. You never know who's on the streets. There are Roma around, gypsies. Not all of them are so good.' He gives a little bow and turns away as the security gate clicks shut, locking me in.

The night has turned damper and colder, and as I cross the courtyard I realize the mist has come down because I'm leaving footprints on the sidewalk. Inside our entryway the elevator cage is open, and the smell of cooking, of some kind of roasted meat and something tangy, hovers in the stairwell. As a rule, I don't use the elevator, but tonight I make an exception. The cage slides closed with a bang, the ancient gears grind and whimper, and a few seconds later I step out onto our landing, and slip my key into the heavy locks.

It feels good to be back inside, back in my own lair, safe from slithery shadows and the Giannis of this world. I don't think the two of them would have hurt me, it was too close to the wine bar, probably what they had in mind was nothing more than a quick theft of opportunity. But, nonetheless, I'm glad Marcello appeared, and I realize I hope he gets his life straightened out, and that the vegetable signora is nice to him.

Our unlit hallway is so still that I assume Billy must have

stayed with Kirk over in Torquato Tasso, but I call her name anyways to check. There's no answer, just a faint glow from the kitchen, so she must have been back and left the little table lamp on for me. My boots sound unnaturally loud on Signora Bardino's inky-green marble floor as I go down the hallway to turn it off.

Ahead of me the linen panels on the French windows are bright white against the night and as I get closer, I see that the latch hasn't caught again. I'll buy some string tomorrow, or find a shoe lace to tie them up. I should tell Signora Bardino, but that would make her come over, and I have to do something about the state of the apartment before that happens. I run my fingers along the half moon of the little hall table and across the top of the absurdly delicate rococo chair outside Billy's door, leaving tracks in the dust.

Night air hits me as I come into the kitchen, and I'm all the way across the room, actually reaching for the handle of the French windows, before I sense Billy.

She's sitting at the table, a book open in front of her. Her hair looks wild in the halo of light from the tiny lamp, and although she's still wearing her pinafore dress she now has a baggy brown cardigan thrown over her shoulders. The effect is disturbing, as if she's an old lady pretending to be a child.

'Hey. I didn't know you were here.'

I try not to sound resentful, but she's rattled me. I can't figure out why she didn't answer when I called. 'What's up?' I ask, trying to keep the pissed-off sound out of my voice.

Billy has an unlit cigarette in her hand. She picks her Elvis lighter up off the table, flicks it and takes a deep drag. 'I thought I should wait up,' she says. 'To make sure you were OK.'

Her voice is completely flat. She's not joking. A prickle of irritation runs down my back. I feel like a teenager caught sneaking in from a date. Maybe I should check that I don't have bite marks on my neck, or my lipstick smeared across my face.

'I'm fine.' I go to the sink and pour myself a glass of water, more to disguise how annoyed I am than because I want it.

'So, you went to dinner with Mystery Man?' This is how Billy refers to Pierangelo, which annoys me even more.

'Henry, actually.'

She takes another pull on the cigarette. 'You could have left a note,' she says, and something inside me snaps.

'You're right.' Now I'm not even trying to mask my irritation. 'You're absolutely right,' I say. 'I could have. But since I'm almost forty years old and you're not my mother, I didn't.' Billy stares at me impassively and I stare back. Then, I slam the glass down, turn on my heel, and march out of the room.

Chapter Eight

I HAVE WEIRD fragmented dreams about Gianni's weasel face and devils hissing in the Spanish Chapel and finally, at three a.m., and despite my earlier resolutions not to use them any more, I get up and take a sleeping pill. And leave a note—right in the middle of the kitchen table where she can't miss it—asking Billy not to wake me for the morning field trip.

As I'd hoped, she's gone by the time I eventually get up, and as I make myself coffee the events of last night—Gianni and Marcello and pretty much everything else—recede like an outgoing rip tide at the prospect of dinner with Pierangelo. I blow off even the idea of lectures and spend the day shopping.

My appearance isn't something I've traditionally put an awful lot of effort into, but tonight I want to look as good as I possibly can. *Pierangelo went to Rome*, I tell myself over and over again. *He loves you.* But all day long, as I pick through dresses and try on shoes, I hear that woman in his apartment. '*Pronto. Pronto. Pronto*,' she says. As if she owns the place. As if she belongs there. By five, when I get home, Pierangelo's intercom might as well be in my head.

I have a long bath, wash my hair, and even go to the trouble of blow-drying it, rolling it out with my round brush so my pageboy falls just right, rounds up under my chin exactly the way the stylist promised it would. Then I spray gloss on my stripes so they shimmer. The woman who did them put a pink one down the left side, promising it would be 'very fashionable, a surprise,' and in my desire to get rid of the old boring Mary, I let her. Now I swing my profile back and forth, trying to figure out how surprising I look.

I fuss and primp until seven-thirty, when finally, with Piero's wretched folder trapped safely in my shoulder bag, I set out, walking so I have time to compose myself in case of a possible 'worst.' I need to remember that Florence is beautiful, with or without Pierangelo. It sounds good, but I'm not sure I believe it.

Above the river, the swallows dip and swirl. Tiny acrobatic jet fighters, they swoop down to kiss the water, and zoom up again to lose themselves in the darkening sky. A pink tinge kisses the façades of the buildings on the opposite bank and, as I watch, the floodlights come on and Santa Croce glows above the rooftops. I cross the street into Piazza Demidoff, a tiny park fringed by gravel walkways, and pass old men who have come out in the warm evening to sit on benches and read the papers and smoke cigars.

I eventually bought a new skirt and blouse and little matching half-jacket that I've been eyeing in the window of my favourite boutique. I did my nails and put on earrings, long dangly glass ones that I found in a tiny shop behind the Bargello. My shoes are new too, and they pinch. It's been a while since I've worn high heels. I stop and check myself out in the darkened window of a shop, smiling unconvincingly. High above my head on the yellow stucco wall, a bronze plaque marks the flood level from 1966.

Pierangelo drove to Rome this time, and a few minutes later, I spot his car parked opposite the restaurant. When I come in he's already at our table, and he sees me right away.

'Very nice, *cara!*' Piero gets to his feet. He pivots me around, like a ballerina, complimenting me on my new outfit, so I can't study his face, look for what I really don't want to see. 'It really suits you,' he says. 'Clearly, I should go away more often.'

While we finish our aperitifs and peruse the menu, Pierangelo talks about D'Erreti, the politics in the Vatican, and the fact that he's finished now with his interviews.

'All that's left is checking the background and getting the damn thing written before Easter week. It's coming out on Palm Sunday.'

I'd forgotten about Easter pretty much completely, but Pierangelo points out that it's coming up fast, which is a pain, because the city shuts down and tourists arrive, or, rather, more tourists than usual. 'D'Erreti will be here to do his thing in the cathedral,' he says. 'Big hoo-ha.'

The waitress, a thin girl with hair cropped so short it's almost a crew cut, finally takes our order and brings a bottle of wine. After she pours us each a glass, he raises his and smiles. 'I hope this is all right. And I have to warn you,' he adds, 'before we get home, I stopped to change and the apartment's a mess. It looks like a bomb hit it.'

I put my glass down and look at him, my stomach contracting. This is the lead-up, I can tell. Pierangelo is going to say he wasn't really in Rome. I'm quite certain now that if I had let myself into the building and gone down to the basement on Saturday night, I would have seen his car sitting there in the underground garage. Maybe Monika's would have been there too, in the space next to Piero's, which is usually empty. What will it be, I wonder. A Ferrari? An Alfa? A silver Porsche?

'I don't know.' Pierangelo is still talking and shaking his head. 'Graziella's impossible at the moment. It's this boyfriend, this Tommaso, he's a disaster. A complete horse's ass. But if I say anything, she'll probably marry him. So I guess there's nothing to do but wait, and hope he passes, like the flu.'

'Graziella?' I have no idea what he's talking about.

'I could kill her,' he says, 'frankly. She's just behaving like a little slut. They left dishes in the sink, the bed unmade, everything. Who do they think I am, Dada the Maid?'

'In your apartment?'

Pierangelo looks at me. 'Yes,' he says. 'Of course in my apartment. Where else, a hotel? Tommaso the Magnificent would have had to pay for that. There was some conference they wanted to go to, so good old Dada said *certo*. But I really didn't expect—' He stops talking, bemused, because I have begun to laugh. 'What? You think I'd look cute in a frilly uniform? With a feather duster?' Pierangelo asks.

I have to put my glass down again. 'Yes. Of course!' I say. 'You'd be darling.' Then I add, 'Oh God, Piero, I am sorry. Really. I have been such an idiot. You have no idea.'

I have no choice now but to tell him how I was outside on Saturday evening and saw the light, then rang the bell and heard the woman's voice on the intercom.

'I'm sorry. I'm sorry,' I say, 'but I thought—'

'You thought, once a philanderer, always a philanderer?' Pierangelo looks at me, his face suddenly serious. Then he puts his hand over mine. 'You thought,' he says, 'that because I was unfaithful with you, I'd be unfaithful to you.'

I don't know what to say because that's exactly what I thought, and he knows it. I feel an awful hot blush creeping up my face.

'*Cara*,' Pierangelo says softly, 'I married Monika because I had to. She was pregnant with the twins. But I didn't choose her. I never chose her. I did, however, choose you. Because I love you.'

The room seems to recede. The rest of the world has grown tiny. Pierangelo smiles and squeezes my hand. 'Look,' he says, 'I've brought you something.'

He doesn't ask for left or right this time, just reaches into his pocket and puts a blue velvet box on the table. Now he's grinning.

'Go ahead, open it.' He nods as I lift the little hinged lid, and there, lying in a black satin nest, is a necklace. It's a spun cocoon of gold with a stone imprisoned inside.

'Do you like it?' he asks.

'I love it.'

'It's a blood agate. They're supposed to bring good luck.' Pierangelo kisses the tips of my fingers, and fastens the chain round my neck.

We eat our meal and have ordered grappa, when I reach into my bag and pull out the folder. I know I don't need to do this, that I could sneak it back without him knowing, but I want the slate wiped clean.

'I'm sorry.' I place the folder on the table in front of him. 'I took this out of your desk, on Friday morning, after you left.'

Pierangelo looks at it for a second as though he doesn't recognize it, then flips open the cover and closes it again quickly as the waitress puts our grappa down.

'I'm sorry,' I say again. 'I just wanted to know what happened. It was this whole thing with the girl by the river, I guess.' This is not, of course, entirely true, given the manila envelope that rests in my bottom drawer, but I've already decided never to open that again. 'I wanted to know about the other women.' It sounds so lame now, sitting here. Its only virtue is that it's true.

Piero thinks about what I've just said for a second, his hand resting on the cover of the folder. The place where his wedding band sat for twenty years is white against his olive skin, and I can feel my stomach sinking. It's on the tip of my tongue to tell him everything, to confess the way I confessed to Henry, but this time include the clippings I've been keeping, and my trip to the library, the pictures I took. I want to explain this need I had to know the other women.

'You see,' I start, 'I feel as if we're—' My words stumble and I realize I probably sound like one of his daughters when they were kids, making excuses for something bad they'd done. 'I wasn't going to mention it,' I say. 'I was just going to put it back in your desk, but—'

Pierangelo shakes his head. 'I'm glad you told me. It's better. It's my fault,' he adds, 'that you didn't feel you could ask me. I would have told you, *cara*. Anything you wanted to know.'

This only makes me feel worse.

'I just didn't think you liked talking about this. I mean, with me.'

Piero laughs. 'Well, I don't really like talking about it with anyone. Murdered women is hardly my favourite subject.'

The tension between us vanishes. I raise my glass. 'Here's to that.' Then I add, 'If you mean it, though, there is one thing.'

If I'm really going put this behind me, I might as well do it, once and for all.

Pierangelo sips his grappa. 'Which is?' he asks.

'The third woman, who was she? Caterina something.'

'Tusarno.'

It may be my imagination, but it feels as though the room gets very still. Pierangelo puts his glass down. At first, I think he's not going to say anything more, then he says, 'She was a prostitute. Thirty-two years old. Single mother. One child. Found in the Cascine.' He names the park that runs along the river in the west of the city. It's a huge place, site of the notorious squat that's been there for something like twenty years, and parts of it are pretty unsavoury, certainly after dark. Pierangelo looks at me. 'You've seen the pictures, I guess,' he says. 'Of the crime scene. When they found her.'

'They found a bird? She was holding—' We both look at the folder, as if we can see through the paper covers to Caterina Fusarno's broken black fingernail and the tiny ball of feathers cradled in her palms.

Pierangelo knocks his grappa back and signals for another one. 'A goldfinch,' he says. 'She'd been attacked with a knife. Rather brutally, as a matter of fact. After that her hair had been brushed.'

I ask for another drink too. 'So,' I ask finally, 'was she the first? Before Eleanora? Or in between? Or after Benedetta?' He shakes his head. 'After.'

I look at him. 'Well, when?' Benedetta was killed in February. We arrived pretty soon after, and I don't remember anything in the papers.

The grappa arrives and Pierangelo looks at the folder as if he hopes it will suddenly speak for itself. 'They found her on New Year's Day,' he says at last.

'But you just said she was killed after Benedetta Lucchese.'

'That's right.' He looks at me, but I still don't get it. 'She was found in the Cascine on January first. Of this year.'

I don't know what to say. Surely I've misheard. 'This year? You mean, four months ago?'

He nods.

'Then she couldn't have been killed by Karel Indrizzio.'

'No,' Pierangelo says. 'She couldn't.'

We leave shortly after that, drive back with the headlights flooding the streets, turning the city black and white. Neither of us says anything, but when we cross the Ponte alle Grazie, I know we are both thinking about Ginevra Montelleone.

'What do the police think?' I ask finally. 'About Caterina Fusarno? I mean, there are similarities, right? Her hair. She was knifed. She was laid out. The bird.'

Piero shrugs, not taking his eyes off the traffic light in front of us that has abruptly decided to turn red. Pedestrians walk by. A boy pushing a bicycle, two girls, arm in arm, laughing.

'They don't know,' he says. 'I think that's why they're asking the papers not to say anything about this girl they found by the river. At first, they thought Caterina was just another dead whore. Or hoped she was. Now it looks a little different.'

'Is that what you thought? That she was just another dead whore?'

'No.' He shakes his head. 'No, I didn't think that.' He glances at me. 'You saw how she was holding the bird. Like Benedetta Lucchese's candle. And her hair. The grooming.'

'So why didn't you tell me?'

The light changes and Pierangelo shifts gears. 'Because,' he says as the big car shoots forward, 'I was afraid you wouldn't come back.'

We don't talk any more about Caterina Fusarno or Ginevra Montelleone, or much of anything else that night, and the next morning we sleep late and have breakfast on the roof terrace, eggs and orange juice with the swallows wheeling overhead. Piero's going to be working pretty hard to get his piece whipped into shape, so we take our time, even going back to bed after we've eaten, as if the mere fact of making love can somehow push away the idea of women's dead bodies, bows and masks and red silk bags. Then we take a long shower. In the end, it's well past noon before I let myself into Signora Bardino's apartment and find the postcards on the living-room rug.

There are about thirty of them, all of paintings, arranged in some arcane pattern, which is clear, presumably, only to Billy. The three Graces hold hands and dance. Benozzo Gozzoli's Magi ride up and down jewelled hills. San Sebastian drips with blood. All of Lorenzo's villas are here, and Caravaggio's Medusa, and even Botticelli's *Calumny*. In the centre, Savonarola burns at the stake while tiny people raise their hands and run from Piazza della Signoria. The theme, if there is one, seems half Florence pastoral and half Renaissance gore. I flop down on the couch. Maybe, I think, if I rub my eyes, or stare long enough, I'll see Gianni's weaselly face, or the golden-eyed man and his black and white dog staring back at me. But I don't. Instead, I see Billy.

The photograph of her, a three-quarters shot of her head and shoulders looking demurely away from the camera in the style of the late Renaissance, is disturbingly like one of Lippi's angels or Perugino's sweet-faced, curly-haired Madonnas. So much for truth in portraiture, I think. But it makes me smile anyways, and then I realize I get it. This is Billy's little commentary on the confusion between beauty and virtue; the dichotomy between what we see in front of us and what actually exists.

After a few minutes, the whole thing makes me feel a little dizzy and finally I haul myself up off the sofa and go into the kitchen. The fridge is full of leftovers from the picnic, curling pieces of salami and stale rolls, which is fine, because, although it's lunchtime, I'm not really hungry anyways. The French windows aren't latched properly, again, and when I push them open and step onto the balcony, a breeze hits me in the face. It feels good, and suddenly I think that instead of actually cleaning the apartment, which is what I'd planned to do, I'll go for a walk. Maybe it will help get rid of this scratchy feeling that I can't quite shake.

Now I'm alone, I'm increasingly annoyed with Pierangelo for not telling me about the woman in the Cascine. Not because the fact of her murder scares me especially, but because it brings up the old resentment at being sheltered, babied. If I really 'fess up, I think as I wait for traffic at Porta Romana, I'm also annoyed that he would have thought I'd baulk at coming back here. We didn't ever say it out loud, but I understand that the two killings that have happened this year may mean there's an Indrizzio copycat running around. Admittedly it's not a particularly heart-warming thought, but it doesn't affect me any more than it affects any other woman in Florence, and I'm irritated Pierangelo would think I'd change my life because of it.

The light changes, and I start up Viale Macchiavelli. The boulevard snakes its way through the hills to the south-east of the city and cars cruise by in both directions. Occasionally I pass someone walking a dog. I've ridden up here on the bus, but I've never come on foot. Hedges and walls hide the gardens of big, old-fashioned villas and I get glimpses of bright blue swimming pools, green swathes of lawn. If I go on long enough, this will turn into Viale Galileo and then I'll come to San Miniato, which, I realize, is not something I want to do. The way things are going just at the moment it would be my luck to run smack into Rinaldo and his little band of heavenly followers.

I turn down a lane on my left that leads sharply downhill, back towards the Boboli Gardens. Within minutes it turns to cobble, transforming itself into one of the pockets of Florence that look and feel as if they're a Tuscan village. This is what I love about this city, the sense that it's made of magic boxes, that not only does time slide back and forth—suggesting you might turn a corner and run into Beatrice, or Byron, or the ancient Botticelli, raving, with spittle in his beard and God in his eyes—but that the place plays tricks too. One second you're standing in front of a wild baroque altar, the next you're on a medieval battlement, or wandering in an olive grove. Add Fiesole, and you'll get a Roman bath or an Etruscan shrine.

I stop by a break in a high wall to my right where a potholed drive winds into the olive groves that stretch between the Belvedere and San Miniato. The gate is closed, the old-fashioned latch heavy and rusted, and the sign, which reads 'La Casa degli Uccelli,' the House of the Birds, is half hidden by ivy. Tall spires of cypress rise on either side of the drive. The façade of the villa glows ochre pink in the afternoon sun. On the slope above it is a similar building, called Villa Magnolia, and across the street is the Casa della Maschera, the House of the Mask, a baroque folly with strange leering faces looking down from its gates.

The buzz of traffic rises behind me, but standing here it seems as if this is the real world, and cars and buses and scooters belong to some other, and infinitely inferior, dream.

Down the hill, the lane opens out into a small village-like square. To the north, the huge star-shaped fort of the Belvedere rises out of the olives, and behind the little square is what I realize must be the back wall of the Boboli. The buildings radiate from a central piazza, each of their façades imprinted with a bumblebee, suggesting they're a remnant of one or another of the assorted Napoleons who set up shop in Italy. It's a settlement of doll's houses with glossy front doors painted in red or navy blue. Neat front walks cut perfect straight lines through tiny front gardens. The place feels oddly deserted, like one of those villages in science-fiction books and fairy tales where everyone vanishes or falls asleep. My running shoes squeak on the warm sidewalk as I wander down past the window boxes already filled with tight-budded petunias and the bright, upturned faces of pansies. Then I reach the bottom of the street, and the charm turns sour.

A huge old villa sits in the shadow of the Boboli wall. Its side faces a little piazza, and I suspect the bumblebee houses sit in what was once its garden. Tear tracks of soot run down either side of its boarded-up windows. The pale plaster is dirty and the wide front doors, their paint flaking, are riddled with woodworm. A rusted chain with a shiny new padlock twists through the iron handles, and two squat towers crouch on the roof. What once might have been a portico running between them is now nothing but an empty balcony with a jagged, broken rail.

The sidewalk dead-ends here, falls away abruptly and turns wild with weeds that converge on a tall fence that runs from the wall of the Boboli, dividing the bumblebee houses and the villa from the broad avenue beyond like the demarcation line of another world. There is a gate, which was once probably magnificent, but it too is now looped through with a chain. Not, I realize, that this stops the inhabitants from coming and going. As I sit down on the villa's steps, a well-dressed woman, sleek with prosperous middle age, passes me, picks her way down the worn path in the weeds and ducks through a gap in the fence where a couple of railings have been removed.

The sight is vaguely surreal, and made more so when she stops on the far side, reaches into her large leather shoulder bag, and deposits a tiny dog in a plaid coat on the grass at her feet. The dog scampers off to lift his leg against a bush, then trots after her as she walks along the edge of the Boboli wall and stops to chat with the man who sits just inside a cottage at the garden's exit. I watch her for a moment before I realize with something of a shock that this must be where they brought me out.

If I am right, and I'm sure I am, the Mostaccini fountain is directly behind this wall. The ambulances probably pulled up not twenty yards from where I am sitting now. They would have screamed up the avenue beside the Art Institute, wheeled around the dozens of parked cars, and jerked to a halt on the scrub grass where the woman is standing chatting. Did people gather, I wonder. Was there a crowd of onlookers as they carried me out? And where was Indrizzio? Was he among them, reaching into his pocket and fingering the thin, dark fabric of his hood as he watched? Or was he sitting right here, on these very steps?

The thought makes me get up faster than I mean to, and I almost collide with a tiny old man and his dog. The dog is an ancient grey poodle, and she peers up at me with clouded eyes and wags her stumpy tail. The old man touches his hat and jerks on the dog's leash, then he says, 'Out of the way, Perla! Out of the way for the Madonna of the Steps!' And bursts into a cackle of laughter.

An hour later, when I get back and walk into the kitchen of our apartment, a huge bouquet of overblown pink roses, which Pierangelo knows are my favourite, are sitting in a vase in the centre of the table. Propped against them is a florist's card which simply reads, 'I'll miss you this week.' Billy has stuck a yellow Post-it note on the vase's rim that says: 'Handsome man brought these by for you! Meet us at Flavio later?'

I push my face down into the blossoms and inhale the sweet, heavy scent. When we first met, Pierangelo used to buy me these all the time. He swears they are the very same roses Catherine de Medici had distilled and sent to Paris when she was miserable, a balm for homesickness that started the craze for what the world now calls perfume. They're better than any walk, and I call Piero and thank him. Then decide I will go to Flavio. I haven't been very pleasant lately, at least to Billy, and I should make up for it.

Flavio, however, isn't cheap, and I decide I'll earn all this living high off the hog by spending what's left of the day cleaning the apartment. The kitchen is still a mess and so is the living room, although the postcards have vanished. In the bathroom, I notice my toothbrush has vanished too. This causes me a momentary pang of severe irritation, and a quick trip to the pharmacy down the street for a new one, but the flowers make up for pretty much everything. I remind myself of that when I get to my room and find Billy's 'borrowed' my make-up again. This time, though, it at least looks as if she tried to disguise it. But she can't fool me. The lipsticks have been put back in the wrong order.

Chapter Nine

By THE TIME I reach Flavio, the rough face of Santa Maria del Carmine is bathed in faint golden light and the last pigeons circle the sky. The trattoria is in the corner of the piazza, which tends to serve as a giant parking lot, and as I weave through the rows of tiny Fiats and motorcycles that are as big as cars themselves, I can see that tables have been set up outside. A few of them are occupied, but not by anyone I recognize, so I go inside and right away spot Kirk's red hair and hear Billy's laugh.

'Mary,' Henry says as I edge through the tables towards them, 'glad you could join us.'

'Hey,' Kirk says, 'have a pew.' He pats the seat of the chair between him and Henry.

Billy peeks out at me from behind her menu as I sit down, and winks. 'New necklace,' she says. 'Very *bella*! And flowers, gentlemen. Both from Lover Boy, and all in one day!'

Henry whistles, and I feel myself blush.

'Mary has a boyfriend,' Kirk sings.

The teasing is cut off by the arrival of a large plate of anti-pasto, which immediately leads to a discussion of black olives versus green ones, and the menu. When I finally ask about the field trip, which was to one of the Medici villas, Billy shrugs. 'You didn't miss much,' she says. 'If you want to go sometime, it'll probably still be there.'

'Well, it has been for five hundred years,' Kirk points out. 'Along with most of that lunch we had.' He runs his hands through his hair and shakes his head to dispel the horror. 'You should have seen the place she dug up this time. A veritable stable, my dear, replete with wheelbarrows, harnesses and straw-covered Chianti bottles.'

Kirk is convinced that Signora Bardino arranges most of her field trips for days when restaurants in Florence are closed, forcing her further afield for lunch. Some of her choices have been distinctly more 'miss' than 'hit.' We've begun to learn we're in trouble when she announces that whatever out-of-the-way *locanda* we're destined for is owned by 'a very talented young chef' who just happens to be one more of her husband's nephews.

For the next half-hour, I listen while they relate the general awfulness of the experience. Then Henry reports that the Japanese girls are in love with Verona, and Kirk adds that they've come back sporting matching accessories, in this case strange-looking bright green hats. Billy wonders out loud if Tony and Ellen from Honolulu are actually brother and sister instead of husband and wife. Or maybe both.

'They are exactly the same height, and they look alike,' she says, when we express our scepticism. 'Exactly alike. Their earlobes are the same shape. I promise you. It's a dead giveaway. And they sound just like each other too.'

Kirk snorts as he stabs at one of his ravioli. 'That's just what happens when you're married. It's creepy, but normal, like *Invasion of the Body Snatchers*, or those people who start looking like their dogs. Right, Henry?'

'Oh right,' Henry agrees. 'Of course. Shortly after we got married my wife grew a beard.'

'I am serious.' Billy waves her fork at us. 'I am deadly serious. I bet you they're, like, one of those pairs of twins that marry each other and then go off somewhere so nobody knows them. Just like that book, *The Secret of the Villa*—whatever it's called.'

'Oh yeah, I really liked that one,' Kirk says. *The Secret of the Villa Whatever It's Called*. By Who's His Name. Didn't it win the Pulitzer?'

'*Villa Golitsyn*,' I say. 'By Piers Paul Reid.'

'How do you know?'

I shrug. In fact it was another product of Sandy Skivling's from the Book Mobile, but she didn't get as much for it because word got out it wasn't as racy as she promised.

'Mary,' Billy announces, 'is a fount of information.'

'Absolutely,' says Kirk. 'Mary is a walking version of the Dewey decimal system. In fact, she's a robot with a computerized brain. The Three Little Maids from school are actually clones. Tony and Ellen are in fact their own parents. And you're insane.'

'Well.' Billy humphs. 'If you don't like that idea, try this one. Ginevra Montelleone was about to get kicked out of the university.'

'Who's she?' Kirk asks.

'The girl they found by the river,' Henry says. She was named by the papers a couple of days ago, but it still seems odd to hear her brought up like this. Henry abandons his *bollito misto* and looks at us. 'Right?' he asks.

'Right.' Billy shrugs.

She is eating a veal escalope and impales a piece of meat on her fork, lowers it to her plate and fussily cuts it in half. 'At least I guess so,' she says. 'I mean, yeah, she's the girl. And it looks like she committed suicide because she was being kicked out. I mean, that's what I heard.'

'Where?'

I put my knife and fork down. I haven't actually read the papers in the last few days, and I guess Piero's editors and everyone else have decided to keep toeing the police line. Billy is cutting her meat into tinier and tinier perfect squares. She's so absorbed, she doesn't answer me. 'Did it say that in the paper?' I ask finally. 'That she killed herself?'

'I don't know. I heard it in the cafeteria.' She pops a piece of the veal into her mouth. 'I stopped in for a cup of tea, on my way to the library, and everybody was talking about it. I guess she'd been kicked out of the university a few weeks ago or something. Oh yeah,' she adds, 'and there's a candlelight vigil thing. We should go. Pay our respects.'

'No, thank you.' Kirk shakes his head. 'You can keep the Sylvia Plath Brigade to yourself.'

'Why?' Henry asks. 'I mean, why was she being kicked out?'

'Abortion.'

Billy begins to chew, her jaw working in small, methodical motions that remind me of a guinea pig. I push my plate away. I can't get the pictures of Ginevra out of my head, and as a result I don't feel hungry any more.

'She led a pro-choice rally a few months ago, I guess,' Billy says. 'Threw eggs and things at some right-wing politician and got arrested. In fact, it sounds like she was quite the activist, Miss Ginevra Theodosia Montelleone. How's that for a handle? You should be glad,' she adds, nodding at me, 'that you're just plain old Mary.'

After that, the conversation devolves into stories about names, and by the time we come out of the trattoria a thin veil of fog has dropped over the piazza, and it's dark. The squat façade of the church looms above the sea of cars, the people winding amongst them faint ghostly shapes picked out by nothing more than the shrill ring of their voices and the occasional smatter of laughter. Billy loops her arm through mine. 'I'm taking Mary home,' she says. 'She needs a good night's sleep so she'll be bright-eyed and bushy-tailed in the morning.'

'Right in time for the Pazzi Chapel.' Henry leans forward and kisses my cheek. There's an early lecture tomorrow on 'Proportion and Design in the Italian Renaissance' that he apparently has high hopes for.

'We'll be there at nine. Sharp.' Billy is already dragging on my arm and as we move off, I glance back to see Henry and Kirk going in the opposite direction. Kirk reaches out and raps his knuckles on the roof of one car, then another. The sound is hollow, like gunfire far away.

'What the hell was that all about?' I mutter. The rapping sounds get fainter and fainter. 'Bright-eyed and bushy-tailed?'

'Well, I'm sorry,' Billy says. 'But you look exhausted. Lover Boy is wearing you out.'

'Don't call him that.' I don't really like being dragged and I take my arm away.

'Well, what should I call him?'

'Pierangelo, that's his name.' My resolutions about goodwill seem to be dissolving.

'How picturesque,' Billy says. 'Did he come along before, after, or with your husband?' She stands back and looks at me. 'I mean, is that what happened?' she asks. 'Archangel, or whatever his name is, appeared, and "poof", your husband vanished?' Her hair is pinned up and the foggy glow of the street light catches it, forming a nimbus of light around the shadows on her face.

The spectre of Ty, with his smile and his golden eyes and his kindness, materializes, as though her words have conjured him. If I look down maybe I'll see a gold ring, a chip of a diamond on my left hand. Billy has pulled a chiffon scarf out of her pocket and is tying it under her chin, but I don't really see her. Instead I see a cowl. Damned, I hear Rinaldo's voice whisper. Damned. Billy blinks. Her mouth opens. Then I hear my own voice.

'It's none of your damned business.' Tears blur, soft and mushy, at the rims of my eyes. 'What happened to me,' I say again, 'is none of your damned business.' Then I turn and walk off.

We have reached the tangle of narrow alleys on the far side of the piazza. Laundry lines stretch from window sill to window sill on the upper floors of the buildings and the clothes that hang from them are strange dangling shapes above our heads. I start down it, leaving Billy behind, wiping away the tears that run down my cheeks, and angry at suddenly feeling this way. There are no street lights. About halfway up the block a single window is lit, high up, but other than that it's so dark I can't see the gutters, or dog shit, or even the bumpy ridges of the cobbles beneath my feet.

In a few seconds, I hear Billy's footsteps behind me and, as pissed off as I am with her, I slow down so she can catch up. Thinking of Gianni and his friend, I remember that she doesn't know this part of town that well, and it's easy to get lost. The rhythmic sound of her steps echoes behind me, bouncing off the walls of the buildings that seem so close I swear if I spread my arms I could touch both sides.

It occurs to me that I should ask Signora Bardino if I can move. Or I could just move in with Pierangelo. He all but suggested it again last night. But at virtually the same time I think this, I realize I don't really want to do either of these things. Moving out would create insufferable tension, so I'd probably have to quit the course too. Which would leave me with nothing to do. Besides I don't want to. Billy's been bugging me, but she's also right, I am tired. And we've been drinking a lot. Probably too much. And Ginevra Montelleone and Caterina Fusarno have upset me more than I care to admit, and she hit the nail on the head about Pierangelo, which is not exactly her fault.

'I'm sorry,' I say it without looking back. My voice floats up into the night, but Billy doesn't reply.

We continue like this for perhaps a block, her footsteps beating out a counterpoint to mine. 'I'm sorry,' I say again, louder, but she still doesn't say anything.

A breeze comes up. A couple of towels hanging from a line ripple in the wind. Up ahead there's an intersection, and a car rushes by on the bigger road, its headlamps hitting the ochre façade of the corner building, flashing a streak of orange in the dark. The sound of the engine fades away and the silence afterwards is too quiet, like a river that's stopped running.

I turn round. The glow from the single window is far back now, nothing more that a muzzy yellowish smear in the dark and at first I can't see anything. Then I spot Billy. She's just a shape, standing in the middle of the street, about half a block behind me.

"Bill,' I call. 'Come on, I'm sorry.'

She doesn't answer, and I start to call again, but something stops me. I stare into the dark, and feel Billy staring back. A nasty feeling prickles behind my neck. It skitters across my scars like a mouse, as we stand there, neither of us moving.

Then the shrill wail of a horn splits the night, and a moped veers round the corner so fast it almost hits me.

The scooter swerves, and although I can't see the driver's face or make out what he shouts, his hand gesture is universal. A second bike follows hard on his heels, and they zoom up the alley, filling it with noise and light. The beams of the headlights sweep down the dark buildings, picking out nothing but worn mouldings of grey stone and the damp shine of the cobbles. Billy's gone. Vanished as though I imagined her.

The whole thing leaves me peculiarly rattled, and I'm glad to get on to Via dei Serragli where there are lights and a sidewalk. Eager to get home, I almost trot, and when I reach our building about five minutes later the lights are on in the courtyard. The lemon trees throw shadows that look like pickup sticks and I can hear music, Vivaldi. A shrill staccato burst of voices comes from Sophie's apartment, sharp and clear before they're swallowed in the high notes of a violin. I look up and see that our apartment lights are on, too.

Staring up at our windows, I have the horrible thought that the only person who has a set of keys, other than me and Billy, is Signora Bardino. She, or, worse, her husband, has probably dropped by to check out the condition of their precious apartment. I have picked up my room and the living room, but, between going out for a new toothbrush and generally messing around, I didn't do as much as I'd planned this afternoon and the kitchen is still a tip. I'm sure Billy's ashtray's on the table, and it looks like the French windows are loose again. La Bardina's probably having a conniption fit even as I stand here. Or, better yet, maybe she's found out I'm sleeping with her best friend's husband.

I seriously consider running away and hiding in the bar. Then I figure it's pointless. If she knows, I'll have to deal with it sometime. Even so, I climb the empty stairs slowly, instead of taking the elevator, to buy myself time. I figure the best thing to do is say I knew Piero professionally, which has the benefit of being at least sort of true. When I get to the landing, I plaster a smile on, prepare to be charming, or at least contrite, and push the door open to find myself face to face with Billy.

Her coat and scarf are in her hand and she is standing in her socks, the clogs she was wearing at dinner tipped over in front of the hall closet. 'Mary, I'm sorry,' she says immediately. 'I was really out of line. You're right, it's none of my business, I—'

'How did you get here?'

She looks at me. Then she smiles, but half-heartedly. It's the first time I've ever seen Billy look uncertain. 'I live here,' she says. 'I have a key.'

'No.' My voice is suddenly high and insistent. 'No, I mean, how did you get here. Back here. So fast. Before me?'

'I—by the river.'

It's just not possible.

'You were behind me,' I insist. 'You followed me in the street. I heard you. I saw you.'

I'm getting shriller and shriller, the same way Mamaw used to when I did something dangerous, like diving off the old quarry walls, jackknifing twenty feet into dark water, and making her angry and scared at the same time.

'I saw you,' I say again. 'I apologized. I yelled at you. Then I turned round and I saw you. Standing in the street. Behind me. So how did you get here first?'

Billy has stopped smiling and is shaking her head. Her curls come loose and fall on her shoulders.

'When you walked off,' she says, 'I just decided to go the way I knew. I can't find my way out of a paper bag, you know that. So, I went to the bottom of the piazza, to the river, and came that way. I—' She stops. 'Look, Mary,' she says, 'about before, what I said. I'm sorry, really. I—'

But I don't let her finish. My heart is jackhammering. I hear Marcello, telling me about dark streets. See Gianni's weasel face. 'It's fine,' I say. 'Forget it.' I step past Billy and pull at the glass knob of my bedroom door so hard it almost comes off in my hand.

Somebody followed me. Someone stopped when I stopped, and stared at me in the dark. Or maybe they didn't.

I sit on my bed, then I put my head in my hands and close my eyes. I'm losing it. It must be post-traumatic stress syndrome or something, but I'm falling apart. Flying into a hundred tiny pieces. First my ranting in the Boboli Gardens, now this. A guy tries to take my wallet, and I convince myself I'm being followed in the streets. I see my dead husband's eyes in the faces of homeless people. I hear priests whispering in my ear. I can't even find my toothbrush. I squeeze my eyes shut, screw them up, press my palms to my temples and realize my hands are shaking.

The door opens, and for once I hear Billy come in. She kneels in front of me and takes my wrists, firmly and gently, and holds them until I open my eyes and look at her.

'Mary,' she whispers, 'I want to help. Tell me what happened to you? Please tell me. Please.'

And for a second, I almost do. The words rise up and bubble in my mouth, ready to pop out, drop like pebbles into Billy's lap. Then I remember how much I hated being treated like an invalid in Philadelphia: *You have to rest. We'll take care of you.* Or worse, as a curiosity: *That's the woman whose husband was knifed.* I'd hear them say it at the parties I was invited to, or as I walked by at the office.

I clear my throat. Billy is still holding my hands. Her face is creased with concern, even compassion. She's good at this. She was a nurse. I try to smile.

'I'm sorry,' I say finally. I parse my words, carefully. 'I'm OK, really. It's just that, when I was here before, my husband was killed.'

Billy's face blanches. The normally pink spots on her cheeks go pale. 'I am so, so sorry,' she says. 'Oh, Christ, Mary, I'm so sorry for what I said back there. What happened?'

I look at her for a second, and then I give a distinct impression, not of hoods and blades, but of speed and twisted metal and shattered glass. I close my eyes and mutter: 'We were in an accident.'

Chapter Ten

OVER THE NEXT few days, the tension between Billy and me evaporates almost completely, which is fortunate, because we spend a great deal of time together due to the fact that I have misplaced my keys. Note that I use the word 'misplaced' not 'lost'. That's because I do this on a fairly regular basis—this is the second set since I arrived—and although the first time I just went ahead and had Signora Bardino's originals copied, I don't want to do it again. At least not yet, because they'll turn up. They always do, in the laundry or, once, in the ripped lining of a purse. All I have to do is wait them out. In the meantime, Billy and I coordinate our schedules. We arrange to come and go together, like Tweedledum and Tweedledee.

I barely see Pierangelo, barricaded as he is in his office at the paper, but he's taken to texting me, and the little messages that appear on my screen—*What R U doing? I love U*—are almost as good as the touch of his hand. But not quite.

I see him only once, when I go to the apartment late and cook him dinner. What I produce is nothing like as good as the food he prepares for me, but he doesn't seem to mind. The weather is suddenly warm, it flips between cold rain and almost summer these days, and we eat up on the roof terrace. As we watch the pigeons strut and squabble across the red chipped tiles, Piero tells me that the more he writes about Massimo D'Erreti, the more he likes him as a man, even feels close to him sometimes, and admires what he's achieved and how far he's come in his life. However, they can never agree about God, especially when the church has an agenda Pierangelo sees as increasingly, even dangerously, right-wing. The cardinal does good work with hospitals, with the homeless, with education. That's all true, Piero says. Even with drug rehabilitation, as long as it's tied to accepting doctrine. But how can you claim to fight AIDS and tell people using condoms is a sin? And refuse to help prostitutes at all? How can you call women equal, then deny them the right to control their own bodies? Make them have babies they don't want? And insist they're not fit to baptize other babies in your church, or give the final sacrament to the dying? How can you tell people who are gay that they're damned, and cannot raise children or serve your God, who is also their God? Who, or what, gives you the right to judge one man or woman more fit for salvation than another? Where is the love and compassion in that? Pierangelo asks.

And I have no answers.

These are not the sort of things Billy and I talk about. We talk about ourselves. Our original reticence becomes almost completely reversed, and now we peel back the facts of each other's lives, comparing notes at every stage. With the same kind of surface intimacy that springs up on planes, or in hairdressers' or between kids at camp, we discuss how we are both only children and don't want our own children, and confess that we hate our names: Mary, which I think is boring, and Anthea, which is why she calls herself 'Billy.' Her mother said she was as stubborn as a billy goat, and it stuck. Billy tells me about her childhood, and her cousin Floyd, and her aunt Irene, who could always tell when the phone was going to ring because she had 'the gift.' We talk about where we'd like to travel next—India and France—and which paintings and buildings we like best here: Botticelli, Filippo Lippi, Bronzino, the Pazzi Chapel. Both of us want to visit Urbino and Ravenna, and go to Mantua to see Palazzo del Te and the Sala dei Giganti, the room of giants. We even bring home train schedules. Sitting on the balcony one night, I tell Billy I have always wanted to be an architect and she eggs me on. You have to have dreams, Billy says. It's required. The bigger the better. Birth isn't destiny, she insists. It can't be, or else what's the point?

Billy lights a cigarette and grins. 'Hell, look at me,' she adds, 'I've been trying to turn myself into something else my whole goddam life. If I didn't believe I could, I'd probably still be living in a trailer park somewhere in the back ass of Fort Pain.'

She tells me she became a nurse because they needed the money and it was the only thing her husband would let her do. It was OK for women to be in 'the caring professions', although he really didn't think they should work at all. The fact that he apparently didn't think he should work either made things kind of tough.

Billy shakes her head and blows smoke through her nose. 'That's what you get for getting married at seventeen. The fact I liked nursing just turned out to be a coincidence.' Someday, she says, maybe she'll go to medical school. You never know.

The day after this conversation there's a trip to Siena. The university and the other schools are closing down for the Easter holidays, so Signora Bardino has laid this on as a special treat. In the end, though, Billy doesn't go. She has a sore throat. She gets them, she says, ever since she had strep real bad as a kid, and she knows the only thing to do with them is hit them hard and fast with too many drugs. When I offer to stay with her, or help her find a doctor, she pooh-poohs the idea. She says she carries a pharmacy with her, and in twenty-four hours she'll be 'right as rain.' The fact that I don't comment on the possible relationship between the state of her throat and the number of cigarettes she smokes a day must be testament to the growing friendship between us. Instead, I just leave her a cup of mint tea early in the morning, which is all she says she needs.

In the event, she turns out to be right. Being a nurse, I guess she does know what she's talking about. When she buzzes me in that night and I finally climb the stairs and flop down in the living room, slightly damp because it rained again and we got thoroughly soaked, Billy's lying on the couch reading *Gombrich on the Renaissance*, surrounded by teacups and insisting the fever she had this morning is history. She points to a little fancy-wrapped package on the ormolu desk.

'Arrived by special delivery,' she says, 'and we know what that means.'

She rolls her eyes, teasing me, as I rip the paper off like a kid. It's a purse, a pretty bright blue one with a zip and a little gold-embossed M on the side. Pierangelo has been complaining recently that my old one is ratty, and that I should have a zip one so I don't spend my whole time digging for euros in the depths of my bag, and I call and thank him. Then I open a can of soup and make Billy eat it while I tell her about the Pinacoteca, and the Piccolomini library, and the completely fantastic meal the Bardinos laid on at Lorenza de Medici's restaurant at Coultobono.

Billy says it all sounds great, and that she'll have to go by herself sometime. Or maybe we could blow the bank and go together. But forget the art and the food, what she really wants to know is if Tony and Ellen held hands all day, even while they were eating, and what the Japanese girls wore. This week the green hats have been accompanied by identical itty-bitty shoulder bags with butterflies on them. And I tell her that for Siena, Ayako, Mikiko and Tamayo sported bright pink leopard-spot sunglasses, and they didn't take them off even when it rained.

Billy likes the idea of the sunglasses, and the next morning, when she's well and truly back up on her feet, she suggests we make a trip to Rinascente, the big department store on Piazza della Repubblica and try to find some matching ones of our own, in a different colour, of course. Blue maybe, or green. Billy says we're too old for bubblegum pink, we need to go for something more dignified. Possibly a pastel.

We agree to meet up in the afternoon because I want go to a last lecture before the break and Billy wants to go to the Bargello. When I leave, she's fussing around in her room, turning things over and swearing because she's lost her favourite eye shadow. 'Use mine,' I hear myself yell as I go out of the door. 'Use anything you want!' And marvel at the fact that things can change so fast.

Now, as we consider racks of sunglasses and hair do-dads on the ground floor of Florence's biggest department store, I listen to her talking about a dog she had when she was a kid, and then about something Ellen told her about wanting to get pregnant.

'So, Ellen said they really wanted a baby, and I said that was nice, but you've got to wonder, when people say, "I want a baby." I mean, what do they think they're going to have? Kittens?' Billy shakes her head. 'Do you realize,' she says, 'that if Ellen gets pregnant, there is, statistically, a one in five chance her kid'll be Chinese?'

Billy's conversations are like this. The topics have no apparent connection and replying is optional. It has been pouring on and off all day, and she's dressed for the weather, carrying an umbrella and wearing a long mauve slicker and a pair of pale pink gloves that I realize look familiar because they're mine. She plugs the sunglasses she's been playing with back into the display, and gives it a half-hearted twirl. 'Come on,' she says, 'I'm tired of this. Let's get out of here.'

Outside, the rain alternates between sudden bursts and misty drizzle. We pick our way towards Piazza della Signoria, heading for Rivoire where we have decided we need a treat. In the market, where the traders sell fake pashminas and knockoff watches, knots of people gather under the deep roof of the loggia. A few tourists rub the wild boar's nose and throw coins into his fountain, but, despite the numbers, there's a hush. It's something to do with the buildings themselves, with the way they crowd up to the thick cottony sky, and with the rain that drops like grey beads. And with time, as if centuries and centuries have silted up in these streets, muffling voices and causing footsteps to fade away.

A juggler throws soggy red and blue balls into the air, and someone begins to play a saxophone. The low mournful notes trail after us as we come into the piazza, where the cartoonists lean their sketches of big-mouthed women and giant-headed men under a canopy beside Palazzo Vecchio. In the Loggia dei Lanzi the white men stand on their pedestals.

I don't know if the white men are unique to Italy, but I have never seen them anywhere else. They're out-of-work actors, or drama students, I guess, who cover themselves in chalky makeup and long white gowns so they look like snow-frosted Petrarchs or whitewashed models of Dante. And, although they are mute, like mimes, the white men don't do much of anything.

There's something perverse and Italian in their refusal to pretend to push walls apart or walk against the wind. Instead, they stand in public squares, under loggias or outside buildings, hands outstretched, feet poised, their eyes locked on some distant point. If they're good, the crowds gather around them, half entranced by the suggestion that they really are watching a human being turn to stone, and wait, like Leontes in *The Winter's Tale*, to see the statue move.

Three of them are here today. Billy and I climb the steps and join the quiet press of bodies. The figure closest to me is turned away, the starched white sheets he wears falling in columns from his thin, sloping shoulders to his feet. His neck emerges from the stiff collar, elongated and powder white beneath the fold of his turban. Billy is not as entranced by the white men as I am and she plucks my sleeve.

'Do you think,' she whispers, 'that I should make a reservation for tomorrow, since there's a bunch of us?' We are going up to Fiesole for lunch, and I nod, and dig in my bag for my phone. Then the white man begins to move.

He turns his left palm up, in a gesture of supplication, the fingers of his wide hands spread open. His arm straightens, and the crowd shifts, swaying with him as he pivots, so slowly he looks barely human. I see the broad ridge of his cheekbone and the flat strong nose, and my stomach contracts.

'I have the number,' Billy whispers. 'It's local from here, right?' People glance at us, annoyed, as I shove the phone into her hand and the white man turns to face me.

The extraordinary amber-coloured eyes lock on mine, just as they did at Santo Spirito, and this time I feel as if I'm falling, as if I am shedding time, sliding out of days and months until I am lying on deep spring grass, bound and gagged, as Ty pauses, hovers in the air, and falls.

'Come on!' I grab Billy's arm, shoving someone in the process and not even apologizing as I elbow our way towards the steps, desperate to get out of here, down into the piazza where people will be scurrying to cafés and jostling at the postcard kiosk. Or into Via Calzaiuoli where crowds will be window shopping, even if it means getting wet. Anywhere where I'm not going to come face to face with ghosts.

I drag Billy across the loggia, the phone still pressed to her ear. 'Wait,' she says finally, pushing my hand away, 'it's ringing. It's really raining again,' she adds, apparently unperturbed by my behaviour as she waits for an answer. And she's right, it is. A curtain of drops falls off the loggia roof, hemming us in.

I take a deep breath and don't look behind me, while Billy makes our reservation for tomorrow in Fiesole. Then she hands me back the phone and starts to fuss around with her umbrella. Rivulets dribble down the steps in tiny waterfalls and I wish I'd worn rubber boots. But I don't even have a pair. I should buy some, I think. I saw some green striped ones in Rinascente. I could go back there now.

'Come on,' Billy says. 'Let's make a run for Rivoire. This rain sucks.'

She hops down a few steps, pushing her umbrella open as she goes. It's kelly green with little white flowers all over it. I haven't seen it before. The wooden handle looks expensive, and I feel a little pang of covetous lust, which is a relief. Ogling umbrellas is reassuringly normal. I make a deliberate effort not to glance behind me, and say instead, 'That's nice.'

Billy bats her eyelashes and steps down into the rain, dainty on tippy-toes in her lace-up boots. Drops spangle around her as she twirls. 'It is a gift from a gentleman friend,' she says. Now she's Melanie from *Gone with the Wind*, and come to think of it Kirk actually does look a little like Ashley Wilkes. I follow her, glad to get away, and feeling foolish for it, as she skips into the piazza. If I went back and looked at the white man's eyes, I tell myself, they'd be perfectly normal. Blue or brown. It was just my imagination. The fact I didn't eat lunch. The light playing tricks.

Rivoire is full, so we find a free table under an awning at one of the other cafés. The horses and carriages have gone but a few damp tourists still run out and pose in front of the Neptune statue, spray rising behind them and glittering in the rain. The waiter comes and Billy orders a bottle of Prosecco. 'We deserve a treat,' she announces. 'Just because.'

'L'chaim,' she says after her glass is filled. 'I'm Jewish too. Didn't I tell you?'

'Uh-huh,' I say.

'I am!'

'And I have a one in five chance of being Chinese. Statistically speaking.'

So far Billy has informed me, at various times, that she was raised as an Episcopalian, a Unitarian and a Druid, and that her mother's other sister, Eloise, was born with six toes, which definitely makes her a witch.

Now she laughs and knocks back half of her wine in one gulp. Then she turns to me, her face suddenly serious. 'Your husband,' she says. 'Is it OK if I ask about him, or would you rather I didn't?'

'Sure.' I shrug. 'I mean, I don't mind.' It seems unfair that Ty can't even be mentioned, like killing him twice.

'Well, what did he do?' Billy asks. 'Unless you don't want to say.'

The way she puts it makes it sound as if he was a spy, or some peripheral member of an organized crime family. The Warrenzittis, perhaps. The idea is so absurd it makes me laugh out loud.

'He was a teacher.' I sip my Prosecco and feel the bubbles exploding on the back of my tongue. I only had half a croissant this morning, and if I'm not careful this is going to go straight to my head. 'That's why we were here,' I add. 'He was teaching in a cultural exchange programme for religious schools.'

She raises her eyebrows, as if this is fascinating, or at least unexpected. 'So he was a Catholic too?' A little smile sneaks across Billy's face. 'Don't you guys mate for life, or something, like swans?'

'No. No swans, no geese, and no again, he wasn't a Catholic. He was a Quaker.' I start to tell her that it didn't much matter anyways because our marriage was over pretty much by the time we got here—in fact by the time we got married—but this seems unfair too, so I swallow the words with another drink, which means my glass is already almost empty.

'Quakers. They're the ones who say thee and thou, like that guy who kept microfilm in the pumpkin.'

'Yup. And they don't say anything at funerals.' I reach for the bottle to pour myself more.

'Did that bother you?' Billy asks.

'That they don't talk at funerals?'

'No. I mean, with the way you were brought up and all, didn't you want a nice Catholic? An altar boy or something?'

'No, Bill.' I'm now definitely beginning to feel light-headed. 'I didn't go shopping for altar boys.'

I start to add that I didn't go shopping at all, as far as husbands were concerned, but before I can Billy begins to giggle. She reaches for the tiny dish of nuts on our table and throws one into her mouth, catching it like a trained seal. 'I learned how to do that specially to annoy my mother,' she says. 'She thought I'd choke.'

'She might have had a point.'

'Yeah, I guess.' Billy shrugs. 'She was kind of sensitive about it because one of her friends choked on a brazil nut. In a Chinese restaurant. OK,' she adds, 'so, no altar boys. But what about those priests? I mean, they're the guys with the wine, right? I bet you had a crush on your priest. You had to have. All you Catholic girls did.'

I shake my head. 'Hate to disappoint you, but I don't think our virtue was ever in too much danger at St Andrews, even if we'd wanted it to be.'

'Well, they are human, Mary,' Billy says. 'I mean, they have sex. We all know that now, after Boston.' She widens her eyes, being wicked. 'I bet they do it all the time,' she says. 'In the confessional. It's kind of like a phone box.'

'Right.' I think of doddering old Father Perseus who probably slept through the catalogues of made-up sins we competed so hard over when I was a kid. Or of Rinaldo, with his white hands and his baby face. Somehow, I don't think it's the physical side of things that turns him on, but you never know.

'It's the simplicity of it,' Billy adds. 'The classic quality. Just give me a man in a little black dress. Better any day than a hunky labourer. Speaking of which,' she says suddenly, 'that kid in the grocery store has the hots for you.'

'Oh please.'

'Uh-huh.' Billy rolls her eyes. 'He's pretty cute too. I told him so. Maybe I'll snatch him up myself, since you're so preoccupied with Signor Rose Petal.' This is her new name for Pierangelo, adopted since his roses, which I still won't throw out, have disintegrated all over the kitchen table. 'Or actually,' she says, reaching for her glass again, 'maybe not.'

'No?' I feel a brief pang of regret for Marcello. A fling with Billy would probably be the highlight of his life.

'No.' She shakes her head. 'Vegetable boy's definitely a virgin, and I don't do virgins. They are waaay too much trouble.'

'Well, then better stick to lusty clerics.'

'Been there, done that.'

'You are so full of crap!'

'Well, true,' Billy says. 'True. Actually, an undeniable fact of life.'

We are both getting loaded now. The waiter brings us more nuts, takes our empty bottle away, and without asking brings us another one. Around us, tables are filling up with people leaving work and I am suddenly convinced that at least half the faces are familiar. Behind us a group of Germans press themselves together, and a flash goes off. Men in suits stop to buy the evening paper at the kiosk and women in bright clothes flit across the cobbles and come in out of the rain, dropping down onto the frail café chairs like butterflies. Drops patter on the canopy making it sound like we're camping out, and despite the weather a line forms at the *gelateria* on the far side of the square. As we watch, the lights go on at the Palazzo Vecchio, catching the tips of Neptune's trident and the dark solid lines of David's torso, and the slight, sad tilt of his head.

'Shall we get those people to take our picture?' Billy whips out one of her disposable cameras and waggles it at me. She loves the things, says they're cheaper than digital, and have the element of surprise when you get stuff developed.

'No.' I hate having my picture taken.

'Grump.' She drops it on the table. 'What time is it, any-ways?' Billy asks this all the time; along with the picture taking, it drives everybody crazy.

'About six.' I glance at my own watch. 'Ten past, to be exact. Why don't you buy a watch? I'm sure there are plenty in the market.'

She shrugs. 'I had one once. I lost it. Besides,' she points out, 'there are the bells. That's what they're for anyways.'

'Yeah. Until you leave Florence. They're not exactly handy to pack.'

'Maybe I'll stay for ever,' she announces. 'Well, why not?' she asks when I raise my eyebrows. 'From what I hear some people do. Besides,' she says, 'you just never know. Maybe I'll meet Mr Perfect too. You're not the only one. Maybe I already have, and I just haven't recognized him. Mr Perfects can be like that,' Billy adds. 'They often travel in disguise and jump out at you when you least expect it.'

We sit in silence for a minute, sipping our Prosecco. Then Billy turns to me, a sly conspiratorial smile creeping across her face, and, despite myself, I feel a twinge of both anticipation and anxiety. I was essentially a goody-goody as a kid, more from lack of inspiration than desire, and just for a second I can imagine Billy as my sister, my bad alter ego, leading me into all the dangerous places I secretly want to go. I can see her wrestling me to the ground, sitting on my stomach and tickling me until I agree with whatever she proposes or, at least, say 'Uncle'.

'Let's blow the bank and stay for dinner.'

Meals at places like this are crazy expensive, but right now I don't care. It occurs to me that if Billy suggested we run up to the top of the Palazzo Vecchio and jump off to see if we could fly, I'd probably go along with that too.

'Don't you have plans?' I ask. I know perfectly well that Kirk called the apartment this morning and asked her out.

'Oh, I guess,' she giggles. 'But Kirk'll chew me out for drinking too much, and besides he wants to go somewhere incredibly minimalist. He was talking about a sushi bar. I mean, what's the point of that, being here and pretending we're in Tokyo?'

'Well, do you want to use my phone to call him at least?'

She shakes her head. 'Neh,' Billy says. 'He'll live. He'll be fine. I'll tell him I was sick,' she adds, and raises a pink-gloved hand like Marie Antoinette, beckoning the waiter to bring us a couple of menus.

He obliges, sniffing a tip, and when it arrives I open mine, suddenly starving after my missed lunch.

'What looks good?' Billy's flicking the heavy pages.

'Not sure yet.'

I glance up. She's tugging my gloves off, finger by finger. 'Yum!' She picks her menu up again, and peers over the top of the fake-leather folder. 'What?' she asks.

But I can't answer. My mouth has gone dry and I feel cold. I see her nose broken, a rime of blood crusting her upper lip. She should have a broken thumbnail. And if I look long enough, be holding a goldfinch.

'What?' Billy asks again. She narrows her eyes. 'Mary, why are you looking at me that way?'

'I'm not,' I flounder, and blink hard to make the image go away, to drive the picture back into the sealed envelope in the bottom drawer of my bureau where it belongs. Finally I ask, 'Where did you get that nail polish?'

Billy looks at her hands. 'It is a little dominatrix, maybe. Not very "you," but cool.'

'Me?'

'I thought it was yours,' she says. 'It was in the bathroom.'

I shake my head, wondering if I'm really going crazy now, but Billy just shrugs and vanishes again behind her menu, leaving me watching her fingers on the fake leatherette, studying her perfectly shaped nails that are painted black, just like Caterina Fusarno's.

Kirk does live. But he isn't fine, and now he and Billy are standing in the piazza at Fiesole, fighting. She shakes her head as he digs his hands into the pockets of his black coat and presses his lips in a thin hard line. Billy has only spent one night in the apartment at Torquato Tasso this week, and that, along with her blowing him off for dinner last night, is what this fight is about. And maybe, I think, something more. Kirk knows the dynamic in our group has changed, and he's started looking at me strangely.

Billy's voice is shrill. I can't make out the words exactly, but lovers' quarrels are essentially the same, so we all get the gist.

She chops her hands through the air as Henry and I and the Japanese girls try not to pay attention, which is difficult, because this whole outing was her idea.

Due to the Bardinos' elaborate Easter festivities, Signora Bardino is not able to accompany us on field trips for the next two weeks, and with Signor Catarelli away, visiting his family in Genoa, we have been left to our own devices. Signora Bardino explained this in a handwritten note of apology she sent to each apartment. She could not be with us, she said, because her husband's family had 'traditions'. Our note—stuffed into the downstairs letter box along with circulars from a Dominican charity and a city flyer concerning garbage collection—prompted Billy to wonder out loud what sort of traditions? Perhaps, she speculated, Signor Bardino dressed up as a rabbit? When I pointed out that I didn't think they had the Easter Bunny here, she shrugged and suggested we all come up to Fiesole for lunch.

So because she suggested and arranged it, Billy's the hostess. She's the one who looked up the bus and booked the table. Fiesole would be perfect, she pronounced at the bar a few days ago. It was meant to be beautiful and, personally, she was just dying to see the Roman amphitheatre and the Etruscan ruins.

Finally Ayako and Mikiko and Tamayo, and Henry and I get sick of looking at our feet and commenting on whether or not it will rain again, and Henry takes charge and leads us to the trattoria that fronts Fiesole's main square, where we find a table reserved for 'Signora Billy' under the outside awning. Henry orders drinks while we wait for Billy and Kirk to stop fighting, and for Ellen and Tony from Honolulu, who live just down the hill and are supposed to be joining us. Ellen has volunteered to act as our guide because she says she now knows absolutely every little last thing about Fiesole.

The Japanese girls chatter. Their voices rise and drop like a smattering of high-pitched music as they talk about their trip to Verona and to Mantua, and about Juliet's balcony and how they are planning to go back later in the summer to see *Aida* in the amphitheatre, with live horses. The carafes arrive, and Henry turns our glasses over one by one and pours our wine while we all try not to watch Billy yanking her arm out of Kirk's hand and marching across the piazza towards us.

'Warning,' Henry mutters, 'incoming.' And the Japanese girls squeal with delight. Today they have abandoned their hats, but they're still wearing their sunglasses. As Billy sits down, they turn towards her in tandem, like three baby birds.

Ellen and Tony arrive a few minutes later, on bicycles, and by the time we actually finish eating, a thin spit of rain has begun to fall. It's been threatening all day. Kirk insisted during lunch that he felt drops on his head, which Billy said wasn't possible, given his hair and the awning. Their argument is apparently over but, like cracks under wallpaper, you can see the fault lines between them. During the meal they snark at each other, or smile and finger each other's hands, both of which make the rest of us uncomfortable, so we are glad, finally, to dive away, even if it means getting wet.

In Fiesole, one ticket gets you into the little art museum, the archaeological collection and the ruins themselves, which are only a few steps from the cathedral and the piazza where we have just had lunch. It is Henry who suggests we go and look at the pictures first in the hope that it might stop drizzling by the time we come out, and Ellen agrees and immediately volunteers to lead the way. She crosses the street, making for the tiny museum without even pausing for breath as she describes the contents in detail.

The Japanese girls follow her reluctantly. They feel like they shouldn't because they have been watching Kirk for cues, and every time Ellen opens her mouth he rolls his eyes as though he's on the verge of an epileptic fit. Finally he says he won't go into the picture museum at all, which leaves them in a quandary. Kirk has the status of at least a demigod in their book, but the Japanese girls also like to pick off pictures the way hunters pick off birds, and there is a very famous pregnant Madonna here. For a few seconds they actually dart back and forth in the road like squirrels in front of a car, but eventually culture wins out, and they trail behind Ellen into the Pinacoteca like sulky children.

'Pregnant Madonnas,' Ellen announces in her loud flat voice as she reaches the top of the stairs, 'are extremely rare in Italian art. The most famous example is Piero della Francesca's *Madonna del Parto* in Monterchi. The pregnant Madonna here is generally considered inferior.'

'Well, she's certainly gotten her money's worth,' Billy mutters. 'She's now fully qualified to drive anyone in any museum in the world completely nuts.' We sidle away from them into the next room and come face to face with a painting of St Agatha holding her breasts on a plate.

'Look,' Billy says, 'that's interesting—' She points at the painting of the slant-eyed saint, but before she can finish her sentence, an alarm goes off.

'Attenzione! Restare indietro della linea rossa!' a mechanical voice shouts, and Billy jumps back behind the faded red line on the floor as if she's been burnt. She tries again, but virtually as soon as she raises her arm the voice yells again. This time a young woman in black Lycra pants and mean-looking glasses comes to the doorway and glares at us, so we abandon the saints and move to the other end of the room where there are three extremely strange panels entitled *The Triumph of Love*, *Modesty* and *Eternity*.

Eternity is pretty straightforward, a conglomeration of angels, deities and adoring civilians, but the other two are downright weird. In the first, Love drives a triumphal carriage with degenerate types dancing around it, while in the second, he's come a cropper and is tied up as one angel kicks him and another breaks his bow across her knee.

'Mean old angels,' Billy mutters.

I don't even want to think about what Ellen will have to say about this, so we move on to a few pallid 'school of Botticelli' Madonnas before she descends on the room. By the time she does, braying about the Sienese school and the evolution of the Virgin's depiction in medieval art, even the Japanese girls have begun to fidget. Ayako looks at us, positively begging for salvation.

'Come on,' Billy hisses, 'let's get out of here.' She grabs me with one hand, and Ayako with the other. 'If the lions are too much for you,' she says, 'head for the Romans.'

'The Roman theatre is meant to be very beautiful,' Ayako announces. 'Very complete.'

'You bet.' Billy virtually pushes us down the stairs. 'And I am just dying,' she announces, 'to see what it looks like.'

What it looks like is a pile of rubble.

Chunks of grey stone are strewn everywhere as if a giant, possibly Vulcan himself, lost his temper with a sledgehammer. To be fair, this is not true of the whole site. Ayako is right, the theatre itself, and some of the Roman baths, are largely intact. But in this far corner where I am standing behind a scrim of ragged cypress trees, walls have fallen and what might have been an altar has cracked in half. There is nothing either beautiful or complete about the place where Eleanora Darnelli died.

I waited until the others had gone down into the amphitheatre, then picked my way here, climbing over stones and slipping more than once on the livid green patches of moss, the soles of my loafers sinking and squelching in the mud that oozes through a thin layer of grass. Three naked, empty archways tower against the sky behind me, and when I look back I see the heads of the others, Kirk, Henry and Ayako, bobbing against a background of grey and green.

They are moving through the Roman baths, walking along the furred paving stones that once made up ancient streets, and the arches make it feel as if I am looking backwards through a one-way mirror, watching them framed in another world. Somewhere in the town a dog begins to bark, then another joins it, and another. The baying rises up to the mottled grey sky and drifts like smoke through the broken columns.

I step over the low cornice of a wall that might have been the entrance to a Roman house, to a couple's bedroom or their kitchen, and find myself standing in a semicircle of stones. I know I have found the right place, because the first day I met Pierangelo, in the bar where the ladies swam in the mirror like fish, he showed me pictures. After he told me about Eleanora, he pulled them out of his wallet, snapshots he'd taken himself and carried around in his pocket like talismans. They were sans body, of course, but he pointed out where she'd been found. He said the first time he came here there were still traces of her blood.

They weren't obvious. There were no great streaks or spatters dashed across the worn lumps of granite or dribbling down the sharp edges of the shattered marble. Those had been cleaned away by the police. But if you knew how to look, Pierangelo said, if you adjusted your eye, you could see small ochre spots, like lichen, or the speckles on a bird's egg.

Pierangelo told me he had closed his eyes and run his fingers across them because that was all there was to touch; all that was left of Eleanora Darnelli in this world. And now I do the same. I can't help it. I crouch down and put my hand on the rock, close my eyes, and think I see her.

'This is where she died, isn't it? The nun?'

Billy's voice comes out of nowhere, and I feel as though I should be surprised, but I'm not.

'How long have you known?' I open my eyes and see tiny cold specks of granite clinging to my palm.

Billy's standing a little behind me so I can't see her. But I feel her shrug. Sense her shoulders moving in the huge tent of her old tweed coat. 'A few days,' she says. 'A week or so. I guess.'

I take this in without any real sense of shock. The manila envelope floats in front of me, and I imagine the contents, tipped out on my bed, or hers, see her long pale-fingered hands with their black nails picking through the articles and the pictures I've amassed and stolen.

'I knew there had to be something,' she says. She's too nice to accuse me outright of lying.

When I don't reply, she goes on. 'After that day in the gardens, when you were behaving so strangely, and then, when you finally told me you'd had an accident...I'm sorry,' her voice falters, 'I ran a Google search on you. After that priest came. I used "Mary Warren" and "Florence." Then I looked up the articles in the library.'

It might be true. She might not have gone through my drawers.

'Look, Mary, I shouldn't have, I guess, but—' Billy's voice runs out, and I feel her take a step towards me. 'Please don't be mad,' she says. 'I haven't told anyone. I never would. I promise.'

I stand up slowly, so I'm not crouching like a supplicant in the mud at her feet. 'Why didn't you say something?'

Billy moves closer and drapes her arm around my shoulder. She's so much taller than me that it lands there naturally. 'Because I wanted you to tell me. I hoped you would.' She squeezes the top of my arm, her fingers firm and strong through the fabric of my jacket. 'Please,' she says again. 'Don't be mad.'

'I'm not mad.' It's true. I don't care. It doesn't bother me that Billy knows. In fact, it's almost a relief. It's as if a heavy bird, a vulture or a crow that has been perched on my chest has suddenly lifted up and flapped away.

'Honestly, Mary, I can't imagine—' Billy's voice fades. Then she adds, almost sadly, 'I want to be—I'm your friend.'

I reach up and take her hand, which is cold in the drizzle. 'I know,' I say. 'I know you are.'

The dogs have stopped barking and our breath makes little clouds in the damp air.

'Really?' she asks.

'Really.' I squeeze her hand.

'I can see why you don't want to talk about it,' she says after a second. 'It must be scary. And incredibly painful—' I shake my head, cutting her off.

'It's not that. I don't care about that. It's that I don't want to be a freak show.'

I look at Billy. The rain has matted her hair down. Tendrils cling to her forehead, leaving her face strangely naked. 'They caught the guy who did it. Karel Indrizzio. He's dead. It's over,' I explain. 'I don't talk about it because it's over.'

'Is that why you came back? To prove that?'

I consider this for less than a second. 'No. I came back for Pierangelo. And because Florence is the most beautiful place I've ever seen and I dreamed of living here. What happened with Indrizzio doesn't matter, it's done. He doesn't make decisions for me.'

Billy nods. She opens her mouth and closes it, and I wonder again if she did go through my room and, if so, if she saw the pictures of Benedetta Lucchese and Caterina Fusarno and Ginevra, and that was what she was about to mention. But whatever it was, she thinks better of it, and instead lets out a little huff of breath, unspoken words that hang between us.

We stand there for a minute or two, looking down at the place where Eleanora Darnelli died, then Billy lets go of my shoulder and looks around, at the bell tower we can see through the empty arches, at the monastery of San Francesco on the hill above, and the dark damp screen of the trees. She rubs her hands as if she's cold, and shoves them deep into her pockets.

'What the hell was she doing here?' she asks. 'In January? Is it even open?'

'Yeah.' I am still looking at the stone, trying to find the dots. 'It's open all year, but it closes earlier then. Three or four o'clock, probably. She went to an afternoon Mass in the cathedral,' I add. 'Nobody saw her again after that.'

'What's-his-name did.'

'Indrizzio.'

'Right.' Billy glances at the high chain-link fence behind us and the tall crumbling wall that runs along the road. 'No matter what time it was,' she says, 'I bet there are plenty of ways into a place like this. I bet the locals never buy tickets.'

'No, probably not.'

'I don't know. She was going to leave, right? I mean, the article in the paper I read said she had a guy and everything.' She steps away, her shoulders hunched. 'To be that close, and then just get cut off.'

A thin slick of rain pools on the stones around us and slithers through the dark spongy patches of moss. Even Billy is cowed by the atmosphere of this place, by all the centuries piled up and ruined here.

'I'm going back,' she says. She looks at me for a second. 'Don't stay too long.'

'I won't.'

She half smiles, as if this satisfies her, then I watch as she walks away, as she climbs over the stones, drops down and disappears for a second into the Roman baths, and rises again, the crown of her head golden in the dull afternoon.

No one talks on the bus ride back. Henry and Kirk stare out of the window and the Japanese girls huddle together on the back seat looking cold. We part with muffled goodbyes at the bus stop, and when Billy and I get to our building, I still reach for my keys. My hand gropes in the bottom of my shoulder bag, pushing aside the folds of my old pashmina, and my date book and wallet. Billy gets hers out instead and opens the security gate.

'If we cleaned up,' she says, 'you'd probably find them.' And both of us nod, as if this is something we might actually do.

As I trail behind her across the courtyard, I realize things have changed. Billy has finally pried away the shell I have built so carefully, and I have let her. I didn't even struggle. A light is on under the portico, and from Sophie-Sophia's apartment we can hear someone playing the piano. I don't recognize the piece, but whoever it is stops and starts and stops again, sounding like a record that's stuck. Our shadows stretch across the wet stones, and when we get inside we leave dark footprints in the vestibule.

Above us, the gate of the elevator clangs shut and we hear it creaking downwards, passing as we climb the stairs. Billy opens our door and flicks on the hall light. She takes her coat off as I go into my room and switch on the lamps. A second later, when I turn round, she's standing in the doorway.

Even in her stockinged feet, Billy is so much taller than I am that when she walks towards me she makes me feel like a child. Her figure throws a shadow across the bare marble floor and the lamps light the side of her face and catch the tips of her curls. A soft fuzz of rain still glows on her cheeks.

'You're not a freak show.'

Billy takes my shoulders and turns me around. Her eyes watch mine in the blotchy silver mirror, and before I am even aware of it, her hands are moving. She pulls my wet jacket off my shoulders. It falls with a sigh at my feet, and her fingers brush the buttons on my blouse. They are small, mother of pearl, and as translucent as fish eggs against her black nails. She unbuttons one. Then a second. And a third.

Billy parts the damp material, peeling it from my skin, and gasps. It's nothing but a faint intake of breath, a tiny whooshing noise in the stillness of the room. The stones of her heart ring wink in the light and her fingers are cold as she traces them down the road map of my scars.

Chapter Eleven

I COULD HAVE asked her. At any minute, I could have said: 'Did you go through my drawers? Dig out my secrets?' But I didn't. And now I'll never know, because last night I told Billy everything.

I told her about Ty and me, and Pierangelo, and Father Rinaldo, and the heat that Sunday afternoon in the Boboli, and the stone in my shoe, and how Karel Indrizzio died, and how I came back and found out about Caterina Fusarno and Ginevra Montelleone. I told her all that, and everything I know about the other women. But I didn't show her the pictures. I didn't even get the envelope out.

Telling was one thing. That was letting a whole flock of birds rise up and fly off my chest. But to show her, to display the dead women's faces and hands, the cuts on their bodies, and dribbles and patches of their drying blood, that would have been betrayal. We're members of a club, initiated and bonded by Karel Indrizzio's knife. We have received his private kiss, and I can't put them up for public display, even to Billy. I can't show her that sacred glimpse of what I might have been.

A minute ago, my door locked, body shielding the drawer as if Billy might slip through the keyhole like Nosferatu and look over my shoulder, I pulled the envelope out and tested the flap. I tried to remember if the gum felt less sticky, or if the corner crimped differently from the way it is now. But I couldn't. So I put it away again, and chose to believe Billy's version of her story, that she relied on Google and the library.

In the kitchen, she sits at the table, smoking and picking at a pastry, reducing it to an unrecognizable pile of flakes. Finally she pushes the plate aside, gets up and opens the French windows. A gust of morning air blows in and stirs her fug of smoke into a cloud.

'I don't think you should go,' she says, her back turned to me. 'I just don't.'

I am standing in the doorway holding a laundry bag, on my way to Pierangelo's to use his washing machine, but that's not what she's talking about. She doesn't object to my having clean socks. What she objects to is that I plan to go to tonight's candlelight vigil for Ginevra Montelleone. 'I'm serious,' Billy says again. 'I really don't think it's a good idea.'

'Oh come on. I'm not Laura in *The Glass Menagerie*.'

Billy refuses to look at me. It's not news that she doesn't like being crossed, and her forehead is creased, her mouth dangerously close to a pout. I can imagine her in scrubs behaving like a temperamental Amazon when a patient refused to have their temperature taken or eat what was put in front of them, and I can't resist a prod. 'What do you think's going to happen?' I ask. 'That I'll fall down in a heap and faint? Treat you to a psychotic episode?'

Billy shrugs, turns round and sits down again. 'Why upset yourself?' she asks. 'Won't it just make you remember?'

'You think I forget?'

We stare at each other for a second, then she looks away. 'I'm sorry,' she says. 'That was stupid.'

'It's a vigil, Bill. We're supposed to remember. That's the point. Besides,' I add, feeling stubbornness building up inside me, 'I'd like to pay my respects. I mean, if this guy is copying Indrizzio, then this girl and I have something in common. It seems like the least I can do.'

'He might be there, you know.'

'Who?'

'Whoever did it.' Exasperation creeps into her voice and she waves a hand in the air. 'Whoever killed that girl. They do that sometimes,' she adds. 'Turn up at, like, funerals and stuff. They get a buzz out of it.'

'Only in the movies.'

'Mary, from what you told me about what he did to those women—'

'Billy,' I say, 'I know what he did. Believe me. And I know I'm lucky to be alive. But I told you, Karel Indrizzio is dead. He doesn't make decisions for me from beyond the grave. And neither does whoever this creep is. If I start letting him, I'll turn into a basket case. I won't be able to walk down the street. I might as well leave Florence. And every other major city on the face of the earth and live in a cabin surrounded by barbed wire. Besides,' I add, 'there's no reason to think this guy even knows who I am, or that he's any more interested in me than in any other woman in this city.'

This doesn't cut much ice with her, I can tell. 'Come on,' I flick my hair, trying to get her to smile. 'I'm Sally Skunk Stripe now. I don't even look like me any more.'

This does finally make her smile, sort of. She sighs theatrically and pulls off another piece of pastry. 'OK,' she says. 'I give up. Oh, by the way, here.' She pushes something across the table towards me, but I can't see what it is because of the clutter, a pile of books, the vase of dead flowers, a couple of glasses. 'Your keys, madam. I found them behind the sugar canister. So, now you can let yourself in and out.'

Billy stands up and stretches like a cat. 'I guess this thing is at eight,' she says, 'right? So, we'll be there or be square.'

Out in the street, I shoulder my bag, feeling like Santa Claus. As I turn the corner and dodge past a delivery van, I see Marcello ahead of me, stacking tomatoes outside the grocery store. I haven't spoken to him since the other night when he walked me home, and now, in the daylight, it's hard to believe he's the same boy. His shoulders are sloped over again, as if he's trying to curl into himself and disappear, so much so that he reminds me of Little Paolo, and I wonder if maybe he grows in the dark, blossoms like those flowers—what are they called? Queen of the Night? Or maybe he just really hates this job, which would be understandable given the new apron the signora has him wearing. It's bright red and almost ankle length. When he straightens up I'm glad to see that at least it hasn't got her phone number printed all over it like the Vespa helmet.

'Ciao.' I stop in front of him, nodding at the tomato tower. 'That looks nice. Very skilled. Maybe you could build pyramids for your next career? Be an architect.'

As I speak, Marcello trips slightly on one of the ridiculously long apron strings and bumps the display. Several tomatoes start to topple, and I drop my bag to help him catch them. The familiar pink stain crawls up his neck and blossoms on his cheeks as our hands collide. I should have known better than to try to joke with him; now I've embarrassed him and made him klutzy.

'It was a joke,' I say. 'Really. I wanted to be an architect, so I now want all my friends to be one too. Then I won't be lonely.'

'It's OK. They're better if you roll them in the street,' he mutters. Another tomato falls from the pile and when he dives for it, catching it just before it hits the gutter, I see for a second the same fast, self-confident kid who wrapped his arm around a mugger's neck and tipped him over like a doll. Marcello lands back on what must be his bad leg and winces.

'Does it hurt a lot?'

He shakes his head. 'Only when I pinch it wrong. Like then. One of the pins isn't right,' he adds. 'It's hard to crouch down.' He shrugs and places the fruit back on the pyramid. 'Jesus says pain is good for you.'

'Mmm. And battling devils and walking on water, but I don't think I'll try it. Listen,' I say, 'I want to thank you again.

For the other night. If you hadn't been there, outside that wine bar I—'

Marcello is facing the shop door, retying his apron strings as I speak, and suddenly his hands freeze and a look of something like panic flashes across his face. I glance over my shoulder and see the signora hovering, fiddling with a bucket of flowers. Her skirt looks even shorter than usual today, and in the sun her bright red hair has a distinctly purplish tinge. She's clearly been trying to hear what we're saying. A flash of complicity passes between us, as if we're kids with an adult on the prowl, and I point to a box of tangerines. Covering fast was one of my better skills in grade school.

'And six of those,' I say, louder than necessary. 'They look good.'

The signora retreats back inside as Marcello grabs a bag, picks them out and hands it to me. Underneath the tangerines I see he's put some tomatoes in too. I dig my change out and pay him, and when I drop the coins into his palm, I can't help myself, I wink. To my amazement, he winks back.

By the time I jostle down the street and get onto the bridge, it's all I can do not to break into a trot. Pierangelo has been bugging me to get a bicycle, and now I wish I'd taken his advice, then I could cross the Lungarno and zoom down a side alley, flying towards him faster than my feet can carry me. I haven't seen him for three whole days, and suddenly I'm desperate for him. For his voice, the colour of his eyes, the feel of his hands.

He said he didn't have to be at the paper until after lunch, and I count the seconds between the floors in the elevator. When the doors ping open at the top, I dart out, and practically start peeling my clothes off right here in the vestibule. Then I stop. There's an envelope stuck to the apartment door and I know what that means. Excitement fizzles out of me like wine going flat. He's had to go to the office. The note reads, '*Cara*, I'm really sorry, couldn't wait. Tried to call, but your phone off. Make yourself at home with laundry!' Underneath he's added, '*PS: They've given Ginevra M. to Pallioti.*'

Pallioti, the detective who handled Ty's murder. This doesn't surprise me at all. It's natural that the same man who got Indrizzio should hunt his copycat.

Ispettore Pallioti came to my room every day while I was in the hospital, and sat by my bed, watching me. As the infection in my lung subsided and I became more aware of what was going on around me, I sensed him as a presence in the room, more solid than a shadow, but just as still. Sometimes I'd feel his eyes on my face even before I woke up.

When I was well enough to talk, it was Pallioti who asked me what happened. Pallioti who made me repeat every detail, over and over. Sometimes he'd raise his hand, stop me, and wind me back as if I were a machine and he was learning what I recited, committing every second of it to memory so it would be etched in his brain exactly the same way it was in mine, there for him to examine and re-examine after I was gone. Oddly enough, when I got back to Philadelphia, I missed him.

I think of this while I am putting the laundry in, and wonder if he still looks the same. Once, waking up and seeing him sitting there on his plastic hospital chair, I thought he looked like a lizard, alert but immobile, his grey eyes clear and unblinking. Later that morning when he opened his mouth, I half expected his tongue to dart out and flick towards me, pink and thin, grabbing one more tiny fact as if it were a fly.

That was the drugs, I think, as I stuff shirts into the drum, the beautiful drugs the doctors drip-drip-dripped down that plastic tube into my veins. They made me dream and dream, those drugs. Sometimes I rode my flying horse. Sometimes I heard Mamaw's voice. Once I even dreamed I was dying and that Rinaldo was there, giving me extreme unction, dripping oil on my forehead and rubbing the soft pad of his thumb against the soles of my feet. It makes me smile now, remembering how totally out of it I was. When Ty's mother arrived, I thought at first she was the Virgin Mary. It was the blue coat she was wearing that did it.

I set the dials on the washer and wander down the hall to Pierangelo's study. The door is ajar, the cushion on his chair still dented, and the room seems forlorn without him. In fact the whole apartment seems forlorn. Maybe, I think, I'll take myself out for lunch in a café to make up for the disappointment of not seeing him. Read the newspaper while my clothes spin.

Pulling the door closed, I turn back in to the hall and stop. There's the whoosh and slap of the machine, a car in the street, and something else; the hollow clack of heels on wood. Someone is walking across the living room. Pierangelo must have come home early. He's in the kitchen, I can hear him now, opening cabinets. He probably brought lunch. I start up the hall but, even as I do, I know something's wrong. The noises aren't his noises. They're lighter, more tentative. Doors open and click closed. Someone is looking for something.

I stop in the doorway and stare. The woman is crouched down, rummaging. The straight line of her back. The blonde hair in a ponytail. Long legs. Impossibly slender thighs. Expensive high-heeled boots. I can smell her perfume from where I'm standing, and almost feel the heavy expensive silk of the scarf that's slung so easily across her shoulder. She can't be anyone but Monika.

When she swings round to face me, both of us gasp. She recovers first, and her English is perfect, only slightly accented. 'You must be Mary,' she says, standing up. 'I'm so sorry if I startled you.'

The hand she stretches towards me is tanned, the skin toasted a soft golden colour, and her eyes are faintly slanted, greenish-grey. They could be her father's. This is not Pierangelo's wife I have come face to face with. It's one of his daughters. 'I'm Graziella,' she says. 'It's really nice to meet you.'

When she takes my hand, her grip is warm and firm. 'Daddy's told me all about you,' she says. 'I didn't know you were here, or I would have rung the bell.'

Graziella laughs and shrugs, catching the scarf before it slithers off her shoulder and onto the floor. 'With Dada you never know whether he's in or out, so I just let myself in. Actually, I wanted to borrow his big paella dish. The yellow one.'

She talking fast, and I realize suddenly that I've unnerved her as much as she startled me. 'Tommaso and me,' Graziella nods towards the street, 'we're on our way to Monte Lupo for a few days. We have a bunch of friends coming, and I don't have any big serving dishes.'

Monte Lupo is the family's country house down near Pienza.

'It must be beautiful,' I say, sounding idiotic. 'At this time of year.'

Graziella smiles. Her teeth are white and even and perfect, like everything else about her. 'It is,' she says. 'I'm sure you'll see it, sometime.'

She fiddles with her scarf, rolling the edge of it around her finger, and then she says suddenly: 'Mama and Dada are fighting over it. Dada doesn't like Tommaso, and he doesn't exactly know we're—' She looks at me hopefully. Tommaso's the boyfriend Pierangelo thinks is a jerk, and she's asked her mother, not her father, if they can use the house. Graziella is so perfect-looking, so sophisticated and put together, that it would be easy to forget how young she is, not much more than a teenager.

I smile. 'Your secret's safe with me.'

She looks visibly relieved. I've just made my first foray into currying favour with Pierangelo's children.

We beam at each other pointlessly for a couple more seconds until finally Graziella asks me if I actually know where the dish is. 'It's just,' she adds, 'Tommaso's waiting in the car.'

I have been so busy staring at her and wanting her to like me, generally behaving as if I have just found a unicorn in the middle of the kitchen instead of a young woman, that now I burst into frenetic motion. I do know where the dish is, or at least I think I do. But I turn out to be wrong, and when I eventually locate it I insist on washing and drying it before I hand it to her, as though it's mine and she'll think I'm grubby if I don't.

'Thanks.' Graziella puts the dish on the counter and shakes her head. 'Dada should get it.' She's adjusting the knot of her scarf as she speaks, and it takes me a second to realize she's talking about the farmhouse, Monte Lupo, and not the paella dish. 'Mama is just being a bitch.' She doesn't add the 'as usual.' but I hear it loud and clear. 'It's only right since it belonged to Dada's mother anyways, his real mother, I mean,' she adds. 'So Mama has no right to it. It really is his.' She stops when she sees me staring at her. 'Oh didn't you know?' She looks slightly stricken.

'His real mother?'

I repeat her words, and Graziella colours slightly. The blush suits her.

'Yeah.' She shrugs. 'Her sister, well, my aunt, brought Dada up, from when he was little. His mother—well...' She laughs, the way people do when something ought to be funny and isn't. 'She gave him to her sister. She was a little wild, a hippy, you know, except they didn't have them then. I don't think she could cope with a baby. She's dead now. He never really knew her. He'll tell you, I'm sure,' she adds quickly. 'He's just a little strange about it. Embarrassed.'

More like hurt, I think. 'What about his father?' It's probably not fair to put her on the spot by asking her like this, but I can't help myself. I'm fascinated by this nugget of information.

Graziella shakes her head. 'I don't know. I don't think he does, either. My uncle was father to him. I think Dada was pretty happy and everything, but Monte Lupo, it was his real mother's. She died there and left it to him, and now Mama wants it, which I don't think is fair. Mama just wants everything.' Graziella looks at me for a second. 'She says he owes her,' she says. 'She just blames him for everything. Like he's God, and he made everything happen. It's not fair on him.'

Graziella shakes her head like a frisky horse. She knows she's said too much, and now she tries to skate over it, flick it away like a fly. 'I just want Dada to be happy,' she adds. 'So, I'm glad you're here. He is too, you know.' She grins, and I see the ghost of a naughty child flit across her features. Then she asks, 'Have you met Lina yet?'

Lina is the family name for Angelina, her sister.

'No.' I shake my head and Graziella nods, as if this is no surprise.

'She's really angry with Dada. It's funny, isn't it? How family's split? I'm his girl and Angelina's Mama's.'

I can imagine this, good twin, bad twin. It's not too hard to see the messy charming flirt in Graziella, the little girl who could wind her dada around her little finger, and probably play her parents off against each other in the process. She's obviously delightful, but I don't know how much fun she'd be as a sister. A picture of Angelina forms in my mind, beautiful, dutiful, serious, and perennially pissed off. There are a hundred questions I'd like to ask, but I'm half afraid to breathe in case this window into Pierangelo's marriage gets slammed in my face.

'Lina'll come around,' Graziella announces with such certainty that I doubt she actually believes it. 'Just don't let her bother you,' she adds. 'Mama's—'

Mama's what? I think. What? But a horn honks outside in the street and cuts her off. Tommaso. The mood shatters.

Graziella grabs the dish and glances at her watch, which is big and gold. 'Listen,' she says, 'I really do have to go. But next time, maybe we can have coffee, OK? *Ciao*, Maria!' She leans forward and kisses my cheek, the touch of her lips nothing more than the brush of a moth's wing.

'*Vino e Olio*.' Billy stops and looks at directions she's scribbled on the back of an envelope. 'How many wine bars do you think there are in this city called *Vino e Olio*? Twenty at least, I'll bet.' She looks around for a street marker. 'Up here,' she says, and takes my arm and pulls me into an alley that leads towards San Niccolo gate.

According to the posters up around the university, the candlelight vigil for Ginevra Montelleone will leave from the wine bar we are headed for at nine p.m. and process to Ponte San Niccolo, to the exact spot she is supposed to have jumped from. How anyone knows where this is, is open to question, since the wine bar was the last place she was seen alive and, besides, she didn't jump. I point this out, but Billy says, 'Don't be nit-picky.' She pinches my arm through my jacket. 'You get all hung up on details.'

'Anyways,' she adds a few seconds later, as we come out into another street, 'this has nothing to do with facts. It's about drama. Don't you know anything? College students don't care what happened, they just love this kind of stuff.' She draws 'love' out so it sounds like a train whistling through a station. 'Loooove.'

'They all get to wear black,' she's whispering now because we've arrived, 'and act tragic.' Billy winks as she pushes the door open, and I follow her into the crowd. 'You sure you're OK?' she asks over her shoulder.

'Don't worry about me, Nurse Ratched,' I assure her. 'Never been better.'

I've worn jeans, my leather jacket and sneakers. With the addition of an unattractive shade of violet lipstick and a lot more mascara than usual, I'm hoping I can at least blend in, if not pass for being a good deal younger than I am. It's not supposed to be a disguise, exactly, but now that we're standing here Billy's earlier suggestion that we might be rubbing shoulders with Karel Indrizzio's Number One Fan is not something I feel as blasé about as I'd like. I wonder if the police have had the same thought she did, and if they're here too, peppered through the crowd, pretending to be students. Maybe I'll see Pallioti sitting in a corner, his tongue flicking for flies.

Billy shoves a glass of red wine into my hand. 'Oh,' she says, looking around, 'there's—' I put a hand on her back and push her away.

'Get outta here. Don't babysit me.'

Billy spends much more time at the university than the rest of us, and a second later I catch a glimpse of her back as she bobs and weaves through the throng of people, already waving to someone she's recognized.

Kirk and Henry stuck to their word and gave this a miss, so

now I'm alone, surrounded by a steady stream of people pushing their way through the big wooden doors, letting in gusts of evening air and staccato rattles of traffic. Eventually I end up against the bar, like driftwood pushed to the bank of a river, and turn round to find myself face to face with a framed picture of Ginevra Montelleone. The effect is startling, as if I'd bumped into the woman herself.

This picture is different from both the one I stole from Piero and the one in the paper, and for a second I feel betrayed, as if she's deliberately disguised herself and come here pretending to be somebody different. Mottled blue clouds float in the background behind her head, suggesting that maybe she's in heaven. She's wearing a white blouse and a demure little gold crucifix and her dark hair is brushed loose. Her face has the strange plastic look of studio portraits, the eye shadow's too blue, her lips too pink. A couple of votives have been placed around the portrait. The bartender leans over and lights them, and the touched-up colour ripples and twitches in the candlelight. For an awful second, I swear I see Ginevra blink. She looks as though she's just come to life and is struggling to escape. After a couple of drinks, her lips might move.

Someone knocks my shoulder and a babble of voices explode behind me. *Let me out*, Ginevra whispers. *Let me go!* Jesus, I think, maybe Billy was right after all; I shouldn't have come.

I turn and shoulder my way past a clutch of older people—probably professors, or cops, who knows?—struggling like a fish swimming upstream, out onto the terrace where tight little knots of students bunch around picnic tables. Some of them wear black armbands, and every once in a while there's a bark of laughter that's cut off abruptly because tonight is not meant to be funny. I perch on the edge of the terrace wall, and sip my wine, relieved to be out of the bar, but still fighting a growing case of the creeps.

'Ciao.' The voice startles me so much I jump and spill my wine.

'Oh no! I'm sorry, I'm sorry.' The guy who spoke laughs and pulls out a paper napkin. 'Let me get you another!' he says.

He wipes at my jacket and takes my glass out of my hand, and dark and very handsome as he is, once he'd definitely have set my pulse fluttering. But now I want him gone, and it's all I can do not to bat his hand away. The spill was tiny, and he probably means to be nice, but when he vanishes through the doorway with my glass, smiling at me over his shoulder, I realize that if I'm still here when he comes back I'll have to make coy conversation, talk about what I'm doing in Florence, and how tragic this is, and how I knew, or didn't know, Ginevra.

The idea's unbearable, because what's most tragic about tonight is what no one knows: that Ginevra was probably doing fine until some son of a bitch cut her to pieces and drowned her in the Arno. My skin starts to crawl. All at once I'm certain Billy's right. He's here. He's watching me. Maybe he just took my wine glass.

Before I really know what I'm doing, I'm on my feet and edging my way down the terrace, looking for Billy to tell her I'm leaving.

The wine bar is made up of two large dark rooms joined by an archway, and I make for the back one which, mercifully, has no portrait and no votive candles. Instead, there are tables and a couple of harassed-looking waitresses. I don't see anyone I recognize, though, and I'm about to give up and leave, when I hear her voice. 'It's from Las Vegas,' Billy's saying. 'Isn't it great?'

I turn round and see her holding court at a table with four or five people who are obviously students from the university. The guys appear completely enthralled. The girls are sulking.

'You can't even buy them at Graceland. They're a limited edition.'

She reaches over and plucks her pink Elvis lighter out of one of the boys' hands before he can pocket it, then she waves at me. 'Mary!' she calls. '*Ciao!* This is my friend Mary,' she announces, as I edge towards them. 'Maria.'

Five faces look up at me. The two girls are very pretty, and as I come over they breathe a sigh of relief, as if I offer some hope of stopping Billy from seducing their boyfriends, leading them away like the Pied Piper with her Elvis lighter.

One of the boys jumps up and pulls out a chair, and although I'm intending to leave I find myself sitting in it.

'I'm very sorry about what happened to your friend.' It's sort of a stupid statement, but I can't think of anything else, and I feel I ought to say something.

One of the girls pours me a glass of wine from a pitcher on the table. 'We didn't know her that well,' she says. 'It just sucks, you know, when anyone feels that bad about their life.'

There's an awkward silence while Billy plays with Elvis. After a few seconds, to fill it, I say, 'Your English is excellent.'

The girl smiles at me and shrugs. 'I did an exchange year. The University of Chicago. We all did,' she gestures at the table. 'Ginevra was going in the fall, post-grad, I guess. Before they kicked her out. My name's Elena, by the way.' She stretches out her hand, which is long and fine boned and has bright green nails. The other girl introduces herself as Elissa and I don't catch the boys' names.

'Why were they going to kick her out, exactly?' Billy is watching me out of the corner of her eye as I sip my wine, which is true student grade, essentially paint stripper. Normally just smelling it would give me a headache, but I'm feeling a little desperate.

'Eggs,' Elena says. 'She was in a protest, to get more funding for a clinic at the university, and she threw eggs at Savonarola.'

'At Savonarola?' I put my glass down. My estimation of Ginevra, whatever it was before, goes up.

Elissa shrugs. 'It wasn't really that big a deal,' she says. 'Lots of people threw eggs. And other stuff. Ginevra's problem was, she didn't miss.'

One of the boys laughs, then covers his mouth with his hand.

'Isn't Savonarola dead?' Billy looks from one to the other of us, and before I can explain, another of the boys says, 'It's what we call His Eminence, the Cardinal.' You know, on account of his left-wing views.'

Elena lights a cigarette. Using a match. 'The university didn't think it was so funny.' She lets the flame burn down almost to her fingertips before she drops it in the ashtray. 'Since they invited him to come. Although God knows why,' she adds. 'He's an asshole.'

'He's a good speaker.' This comes from the third boy. He looks younger than the others, and more intense. But maybe I just think that because he's skinny. 'I'm sorry,' he says. 'But he is.' He looks around the table, bracing himself for argument. 'I don't agree with him,' he adds. 'But at least he believes in something. And he has the balls to say so.'

'Yeah,' says Elissa. 'That we all love God his way or go to hell.'

'When did this happen?' I'm wondering where Pierangelo was at the time, if maybe he was standing too close to D'Erreti and got caught by one of Ginevra Montelleone's eggs.

'A few weeks ago,' Elissa says. 'The beginning of Lent. That's why he was speaking, you know, about what we were all supposed to give up and sacrifice and shit. In his opinion, incidentally, that included most of our rights. Anyway,' she adds, 'nothing really happened at the time and everybody thought it had been forgotten. But there was a picture in the paper. So, sure enough, they hauled Ginni up in front of a disciplinary board. I guess she heard a few days ago, and that's what did it.'

'I suppose there's no question she committed suicide?' Billy doesn't look at me as she asks this.

Elena picks up her glass and drains it. 'Well, that's what it's usually called,' she says, 'when you jump off a bridge.'

Her voice is so matter-of-fact she might have just suggested we all go for a pizza, and I stand up faster than I mean to, mumbling something about a headache and a glass of water. My bag snags on the back of my chair, and Billy starts to stand up too. She asks if I'm OK, but I say I'm fine, I just need to get something at the bar.

Outside, I lean against the terrace wall. I did get something, but it wasn't water, and after that wretched Chianti, this Brunello's like silk against my tongue. It was expensive, but I don't care. I roll it around my mouth, trying to take the bad taste away, and tell myself that in a minute, when I calm down, I'll get the hell out of here and call Pierangelo.

I shouldn't have let Elena's tone of voice upset me, but it did. It made me want to reach across the table and slap her. And now I can't stop my own picture of Ginevra from hanging in my head like a poster, can't stop thinking about the strips of her flesh, and the fact that he brushed her hair. And pinned a goddam bag of birdseed to her shoulder. I look around for something else to focus on, and that's when I notice the girl.

It's getting chilly now, and people have begun to filter back inside, so she has one of the picnic tables to herself. But that's not what sets her apart, the fact that she is virtually alone out here. Nor is it her blonde hair, so pale it's almost white, or the vivid clashing stripes of her sweater. What makes this girl different aren't her dreadful clothes or her outdated punky haircut, it's the listless, dull hunch of her shoulders, and the way she hardly seems to be aware of the fact that she's crying, that tears are welling up and running down her cheeks and blotching the backs of her hands as she half-heartedly wipes them away. What sets her apart is that she's the first person I've seen here who's genuinely upset.

'Have some of this.'

The glass of Brunello is huge and I slide it across the table towards her as I slip onto the opposite bench. She hesitates, then grabs it without looking at me and takes a greedy sip. Like a lot of very blonde people, she's frail, almost bird-like. The skin on the backs of her hands reminds me of waxed paper. Her fingers wrap around the globe of the wine glass and I see her nails are bitten to the quick. They're ragged, with angry red rims. When she finally looks up at me, her eyes are almost black, two holes in the pasty white dish of her face. 'Thanks,' she says. 'I'm sorry. I keep crying.'

'It's a terrible thing. Why shouldn't you?'

She glances around and shrugs. 'No one else is.'

We're speaking Italian, and even I can tell her accent is no more authentic than mine.

'I can't believe it,' she says. 'What? Two weeks ago we were sitting right here. Just like this. And now—' Her voice trails off, and she begins to drift away again, into some sealed-up world of her own.

'Where are you from?' I ask it fast, as if I'm throwing out a baited line, trying to hook a fish before it slips back under the water.

She thinks for a second, as though this is difficult. Then she says, 'Norway. Well, my father is, anyways. My mother's Italian. That's why I came to the university.'

This evokes another thin stream of tears, and before she can wipe her nose on the sleeve of her sweater I dig in my bag for a Kleenex.

'Ginevra lived across the hall from me the first year I was here,' she says. 'We agreed about everything. You know how it is when you're just the same as someone?' She takes the Kleenex out of my hand, looks at it as though she has forgotten what it might be for, then blows her nose. 'My name is Annika,' she adds.

'Mary.'

'How did you know Ginevra?'

'I didn't. I'm studying at the university too, kind of,' I say. 'Art history. Of course.' Annika smiles weakly. 'I heard her speak, though, once.' This is obviously completely untrue, but I want to say something nice about Ginevra, if only to make this poor girl feel better. 'I thought she was very powerful.'

Now I'm gilding the lily, and Annika's grief is so naked I feel bad lying to her, even about this. But if I think she'll notice, I'm wrong. She's so completely absorbed in her own pain that I could tell her I was Yogi Bear and she wouldn't bat an eyelid. 'It seems unfair she was going to be thrown out,' I add, more for something to say than anything else.

Annika shrugs, her thin shoulders rising in bony points under her sweater, and smiles. Well, not really. Actually what she does is bare her teeth, which are very white, and unpleasantly pointed. 'She was depressed.'

'Well, it would be depressing. To be asked to leave so close to graduating.'

'She didn't give a shit about that.' Annika reaches for my wine glass and laughs as she says it. It's a high shrill sound, like breaking glass, and for the first time it occurs to me that she's totally wasted.

'Hey! Are you ready?' A boy holding a sack has materialized beside our table.

Annika sucks on the rim of the glass as though she is contemplating biting through it. Then she drains the wine and reaches into the sack. 'Sure,' she says, pulling out a candle. 'Come on, let's go.' There is a faint purple moustache on her upper lip. She stands up, slightly unsteady, and grabs the edge of the table.

People are pouring onto the street now, and I see Billy, still flanked by the boys. She's looking for me, twisting her head back and forth so her hair bounces like a slinky.

'Come on,' Annika grabs at my jacket, half to steady herself and half to drag me along with her, and before I can protest she's pulled me into the crowd.

People are milling everywhere, handing around lighters and matches. Someone shoves a candle into my hand and lights it, but the flame sputters and goes out, and when I look around, Annika's disappeared. The crowd swells and moves like an amoeba, inching towards the city gate where floodlights have been turned on, catching the pale stone walls and the huge iron brackets. As they pass under the cavernous archway, people's jackets and the crowns of their heads are lit up, bleached in bright white light. And that's when I see him.

This time, there's no chalky make-up, and no sign of the pirate mutt dog either, but I'm still sure. I'm absolutely certain it's the same guy, the El Greco saint from Santo Spirito, the white man from the Loggia dei Lanzi. If he looked at me, I know he'd have my husband's eyes, tawny and golden. I start forward to chase him, find out who he is. But then I stop. Because walking right beside him is Father Rinaldo.

Chapter Twelve

'MARIA. MARIA, MY CHILD.' That's what Rinaldo used to call me.

Sometimes he said it with reproach, as if he had looked into my soul and seen for himself what a sorry mess it was. And sometimes he said it with his hands outstretched, welcoming, as if God's love really did flow through them and the embrace they promised was salvation itself, something he could deliver personally, right here in San Miniato.

Seeing him last night was almost surreal, the way seeing someone in the flesh is, after they've been existing so completely in your head, and now standing outside of what I'll always think of as Rinaldo's church, I remember the last time I came here, almost two years ago. Just like this morning, it was particularly beautiful. The sky was clear, an almost translucent blue, and when I turned and looked back from the top of the pilgrims' steps, I saw the city so pristine it could have been etched on glass: the brown-red patchwork of the roofs, the creamy stucco of the villas, scattered like sugar cubes on the hills, the pale grey spans of the bridges.

San Miniato itself is just as I remember it. Still and time-less, with its ornate front and wide doors, and its Byzantine Jesus staring down, his face a little jaded, as if he's bored with the centuries of human folly he's been forced to witness from up here on his hill. Nothing has changed. Except me. Or so I tell myself. I say: *I am not who I was.* Then, *I'm not really even Catholic any more.* And, *I have nothing to be afraid of.* When that doesn't work, I try: *I have not done anything wrong, I have not sinned.* I mutter the words like a crazy person as I climb the steps and walk inside, where I know I will find Father Rinaldo.

I don't know if he saw me at Ginevra's vigil last night or not, but I do know he's expecting me. I can sense him like a vapour, a shadow drifting around behind me, coming to my apartment, following me in the streets, willing me up here, as if I am a stray dog that will return to a place where it once found food. I realize now that I should have come right away, as soon as I got back to Florence, and put an end to this.

Inside, the floor is cold, I can feel the chill reaching up to finger my body, as if the stones themselves are hungry for the warmth of human flesh. The nave is empty, the walls shadowed by Uccello's faded saints. Nothing moves but the dust motes spiralling down the thin shafts of light that fall through the high windows and pick out the painted rafters, the dragons and the griffins that creep along the green and crimson beams.

Shadows drift in the corners, and for half a second I think I see Ty's unhappy wife there, my own reflection bouncing back through time. I reach automatically for the edge of the font, as if I'm confronting vampires instead of myself, and need holy water to ward them off, but it's empty. There's nothing but a greenish rime halfway down the bowl. Still, I dip my knee and make the sign of the cross. Call it superstition. Or habit. I like to think I do it for Mamaw's sake; touch my forehead, my chest, my shoulders. Mutter God's name before I turn away from the altar, skirt the pews and move towards the steps that lead to the sacristy.

This is the room I need to see again, the place where the Opus members gathered to pray. It's odd, this laying of ghosts, but I am discovering that it has rituals, certain steps that must be observed. At the door I rest my hand on the iron handle and listen, certain that this is where I'll find him, but when I push it open the room is empty. There is not so much as the whisper of a prayer. Arentino's scenes from the life of St Benedict float on the walls above me. The saint stands barefoot in a translucent stream. Devils tumble the church, crushing a monk under stones, and Benedict builds it up again. In one corner angels and demons fly across the sky, interchangeable as they battle for the realms of heaven.

Back in the main church, I feel slightly foolish. What did I expect to see? The shadow of myself again, that girl with her blonde hair and pretty summer dresses? The El Greco saint? Rinaldo's angels? Ty himself? I turn and start down the steps. I don't know what time it is, but I'm sure the bells will ring soon for early Mass and that, even before that, the women who make up most of the congregation here will begin to arrive. Young and old, tall and bent, they'll cross the line of light in the nave, their shoes making squeaking sounds on the stone as they come down to the crypt, where Rinaldo must be waiting to hear confession before the morning services.

The steps down are broad and worn, and the crypt below nothing but a hollowed circle of dark. At evensong, the monks chant plainsong here, hands folded in their sleeves, heads bowed in their cowls. The echo of their voices hangs in the damp cold air, the litany as much a part of this place as the stones themselves.

When my eyes adjust to the gloom, I make out lines of pews. A stack of canvas chairs is piled beside one of the columns. I used to know this place well, and now I breathe in the familiar chilly smell and feel time fall away like petals drifting from a dead flower. One red candle flutters beside the altar as the air stirs, a sigh coming from deep within the church.

My eyes wander back and forth across the dark space. They touch the coffin-like confessionals and brush the well of shadows behind the statue of the Virgin and the offering boxes, skim over the altar with its dull gold cross, and stop, drawn to the semicircle of monks' chairs carved into the back wall. The shadows are deepest back there, as if they've been accumulating for centuries, so it takes a second before I see him. His cowl is raised, and he's sitting so still he's just a thickening of the darkness.

As she begins to rise, his black cassock looks like one of the columns that has come loose and now moves of its own accord. Without a sound he detaches himself from the darkness and glides to the front of the altar. Transfixed, I watch as he kneels to perform obedience, then turns to face me.

'Maria. My child. I hoped you would come.'

The words sound like wind whistling in the vault, and at first I'm not even sure I've heard them. Then the red flicker of the votive candle dances over white skin, and a hand, as round and soft as a baby's, emerges from the long sleeve.

Rinaldo glides towards me and, although the features of his face are hidden, I can feel his eyes on me, sense that pitying, half-excited look: the shepherd who's found a wandering lamb.

I open my mouth. *Just say what you have to say,* I think. *Don't let him start. Just say it, and get out.*

'How did you know where my apartment was? What do you want?'

I find it harder to speak to him than I'd expected, and my voice sounds disturbingly childish.

'I want you to leave me alone. I've left the church, so it doesn't mean anything to me any more. Do you understand?' I ask. 'I want you to leave me alone!'

Rinaldo's hands are still outstretched, he's still beckoning me into his arms, but my words seem to make him sad. I've been a big disappointment. Again.

'One cannot leave one's children, Mary,' he says in his low whispery voice.

This is classic priest-speak—never dignify a question with an answer, or address a point, especially one from a potentially hysterical woman—and I have to resist the temptation to shriek at him, to shatter this still air by screaming that he has no children, and that even if he does I was never one, and certainly am not one now. I feel myself quivering with anger, a rage I've stored up for over two years.

'Ginevra Montelleone,' I spit. 'Was she one of your children? Is that why you were there last night? Or were you following me? Again?'

Now Rinaldo does drop his hands. He turns them palm up, pink and pudgy, in the eternal profession of innocence.

'Ginevra worshipped here when she was a baby,' he says, shaking his head. 'With her family, before they moved out of the city. Her mother is distraught, naturally. The loss is terrible. Although,' Rinaldo adds, his voice heavy with its familiar disappointment, 'they feared Ginevra was already lost to them.'

'Because of her politics?'

Rinaldo ignores the question, but I have the distinct impression he's smiling.

'I have missed you, Maria,' he says. 'I always knew you would come back. God's love is like that. We think we have left it, but that is only because we are deluded into believing we have that choice.'

I have no desire to discuss theology with Rinaldo, and I clamp my lips together. Otherwise I am going to scream.

'Your pain is my pain, Mary,' he says. 'It always has been. That is the true meaning of God's love, if only you can surrender yourself to it.'

His hand is beckoning me again, obscene and pink. The pale fingers look like maggots, things that grow fat on the dead, and I feel my stomach heave. I back up and bang against the stack of canvas chairs. Rinaldo steps towards me. He's droning on in his low sticky voice, about love and God and salvation, and suddenly I think this was a very bad idea.

'Leave me alone. For ever.'

The words seem an incredible effort, and if Rinaldo hears, he doesn't take any notice. Maybe I didn't say them after all. Maybe they never got out of my mouth. He steps forward again, and for the first time it occurs to me that Father Rinaldo is a big man.

Sweat breaks out across my chest, in my hairline. Rinaldo's voice is low and heavy, his words bricking me in. He's nothing but a dark shape moving towards me, and I am stepping backwards, wiggling around chairs, trying to avoid the touch of his hand as he drives me towards the heavy arched columns and the line of pews.

'Father, *buongiorno!*'

'We hoped to find you!'

The voices crack into the crypt like gunfire, and Rinaldo and I both spin round, shocked and guilty as discovered lovers.

Two women are standing on the stairs. One has what looks like a basket of flowers in her hand, the other is holding a vase.

Rinaldo recovers first. 'Signore, *buongiorno,*' he says, his voice drippy with welcome. And as the women begin to come down the steps, talking about flowers, I flee.

I catch one glimpse of their startled faces as I skinny through the line of pews, dodge past a confessional booth and bound up the right-hand set of steps. Then, as if I'm going for sprinting record, I run down the long corridor of the nave, bolting for the shaft of sunlight that falls through the open door.

Outside on the terrace, I stop and lean my hands on my knees as though I've just run a three-minute mile. Rinaldo's words bat around my head, and I wish there was a water cooler up here because I have a very bad taste in my mouth.

The bells have not started yet, but people are beginning to arrive for Mass, climbing up the stairs from the road in twos and threes. At the top they pause to catch their breath and admire the view, then they head towards the church doors, skirting me as if I'm an awkwardly placed piece of furniture. By the time the third pair almost bump into me I decide it's time to go, so I straighten up, look around, and see Billy.

She's on the far side of the terrace, perched on the edge of the parapet above the cemetery, watching me. As I walk towards her, I wonder how long she's been here.

'Hey,' she says as I get up close.

'Hey yourself.' My breathing has almost come back to normal, but I'm still not sure my voice sounds quite right.

Billy smiles, but her eyes are skimming over my body as if she's checking it out for signs of something, looking straight through my jeans and jacket to the beads of sweat I can still feel curdling on my skin. Two spots of colour bloom on my cheeks, and to my horror I realize I'm embarrassed, as though I've just been caught in the act with a lover. Rinaldo never did actually touch me, but all of a sudden it feels like his soft white hands have travelled all over my body. I don't want Billy to see, so I rest my elbows on the parapet and lean out, pretending to drink in the view.

'What are you doing here?' I ask.

'I was coming to Mass,' Billy says.

'Bullshit.'

'Bullshit yourself. I'm Irish Polish, why shouldn't I be Catholic?'

I snort, and Billy jumps off the wall. 'OK,' she says. 'I saw you go out, and I followed you. I thought I'd be discreet and wait out here until you were done. There's something I want to show you.' She's already walking away as she speaks, and I find myself trailing after her. She waits for me at the top of the steps and grabs at my hand as I catch up. 'Come on,' she says, 'it's almost eight-thirty. We can have coffee up there.'

'Up where?' I have no idea what she's talking about, and all I really want is to go home and have a shower, scrub even the hint of Rinaldo's maggoty fingers off my body. But apparently it's not to be.

'The fort.' Billy looks at me as though I'm dense. 'They reopened it yesterday.'

She points to the Belvedere fort that sits on the crown of the hill straight across like a giant starfish beached, high and dry, above the city. Apparently the views from up there are spectacular, but it's hard to know for sure since the site's been closed for as long as anyone can remember. Like ageing movie stars, the fort and the Medici villa in the centre of it have been permanently '*in restauro*'.

That is, until yesterday, when the site was suddenly opened up in time for Easter week. There's a new installation of modern sculpture, some of which apparently features neon. I know this because Piero mentioned it, and also because, like San Miniato, you can see the Medici villa from almost anywhere in the city. Normally it just fades discreetly into the dark. But alas, no longer. Walking home from the vigil last night, we looked up and saw its porticos lurid with streaks of red and blue. If we'd been in the States, Billy commented, they would have spelled out an ad for pizza, or for a bar with a name like the *Dew Drop Inn*, but since we're in Italy it's Art.

Now she drops my arm. 'Come on,' she says again. 'There's something I want to show you.' Billy smiles at me, making me feel like a selfish rat. After all, she's followed me all the way up here, and it's practically on our way home. 'Really, I promise,' she adds. 'It's cool. You'll like it.'

The bells start to ring as we come down the steps and walk along Viale Galileo, and a few seconds later my phone cheeps in my pocket like a baby bird. When I pull it out, the screen is dark. This happens occasionally. Pierangelo will start to either text or call and get interrupted. *Hi Love U*, I punch in and send.

Where R U? comes back on the screen a second later. Piero does this, asks me where I am all the time, and I imagine him with a big map of the city, sticking pins in it to track me, reaching out with his fingertip to touch the piazza or street corner that I am standing on. Billy has stopped to tie one of her Converse All Stars. *Risposta?* my phone asks, and I reply, *San Min on wA2 Bel4tere.*

Luv U2, Pierangelo says, and Billy straightens up and looks over my shoulder as the tiny screen goes black.

'You guys!' She rolls her eyes. 'You're worse than teenagers!'

A second later we turn off the big road onto Via San

Leonardo, a lane that runs straight across the ridge of the hills to the city gate and the fort's entrance. This is the road Benedetta Lucchese's sister lives on, and I can't help thinking that we're tracing the path she took the night she died.

When we reach number forty-five, Billy slows and looks at the gate. I can't remember whether or not I told her about Isabella Lucchese, but she must have figured it out somehow, because she hasn't picked this place by chance.

'This is it, isn't it?' she asks, confirming my suspicion. 'The sister's house?'

I nod. The gate's iron, like all the other gates around here, and the black paint is flaking, which doesn't mean a thing. Florence is one of those places where a certain amount of rot implies status. The requisite wisteria spills over the villa's walls, the buds puckered tight as purple beans. There's a battered red sign wired to the railings, with a bad drawing of a German shepherd on it and the words 'Attenti Al Cane.' All the gates around here have them, whether or not they have dogs. You buy them in the hardware store for five euros. Billy peers in, then shrugs and turns away.

'You know,' she says, 'all that stuff, Indrizzio's little presents? It's all to do with the church. White for purity. The goldfinch for Christ's passion. Candles mean transubstantiation.'

'How do you know?'

She smirks. 'I looked it up in *The Dictionary of the Italian Renaissance.*'

'Smarty-pants. And there I was thinking you were Catholic.'

'Was Indrizzio?'

'I guess so.'

'But not a mask. That's weird.'

'What is?'

Billy shrugs again. 'I couldn't find anything churchy about masks. All I could find was distinctly un-churchy.' Despite myself, I feel an unwelcome clench in my stomach at the thought of the tiny grinning face.

'Deception,' Billy is saying. 'At least that's what it stands for in Renaissance art.' I don't tell her I already know this. Not really a toughie, I guess,' she adds. 'If you think about it. But I drew a blank on the red bag. Wasn't that what he left with her? Ginevra?'

I nod, but I really don't want to dwell on all this, so I try changing the subject. 'These houses, what do you think it would really be like to live in one? I mean, it might be great, or it might be really creepy.' Billy can usually be distracted by this sort of stuff, but not this morning.

'Mary,' she says. 'I wish you would take this more seriously.'

She faces me, exasperated, and I feel stubbornness rising between us, my refusal to dwell on the murders colliding with Billy's apparent desire to make me. Telling her everything was a mistake, I think, suddenly. It was relief for me in the short run, sure, to get those black birds off my chest, but a mistake if she's going to keep this up.

'Billy,' I say, finally, 'I do take it seriously. But I told you, I can't live in a state of permanent alert. I won't. Besides, for me, it's over. And I don't know what you want me to do, anyways. Leave? Hire a bodyguard? Not have a life? Give up Pierangelo and go live in purdah somewhere? What?'

We stand there facing each other. Billy opens her mouth, but before she can say anything there's a sound like the rumbling of an oncoming train. She grabs my arm and yanks me to the side of the narrow lane just as a huge black motorcycle comes barrelling round the corner doing at least fifty miles an hour. Despite the fact that we're flattened against the wall, it almost sideswipes us.

'Slow down, asshole!' Billy yells, but there's no sign the driver hears her, covered in black leather and helmeted as he is.

'Jesus!' She steps back into the street, genuinely rattled, something I haven't seen before. 'I hate those things,' she says. 'I mean, what is it with guys and bikes? Even normal guys?'

The sound tunnels away from us. It buzzes up towards

the fort, and we stand there on the cobbles outside Isabella Lucchese's house, neither of us saying anything, waiting until it fades completely and we have the morning to ourselves again.

We don't discuss anything more to do with the murders, and the momentary tension between us dissipates as the sun gets warmer and we walk on. As we come around the last corner, we see that despite the early hour we're not going to be the first people to arrive at the Belvedere. We've been beaten, if only just, by a group of Japanese tourists. Their leader holds what looks like a broken TV antenna with a plastic rose taped to the top of it and waves it in the air as she barks at them in a high staccato voice. The couples, all of them in raincoats despite the sun, line up behind her with the orderliness of well-behaved school children. Most of them look sad. Frowning and clutching their cameras they stare up at the fort as if they're about to be imprisoned in it.

A minibus, probably theirs, and a couple of cars are pulled up by the fort's walls. Suddenly Billy stops. Beside the bus is a motorcycle, a big black one, about the size of the Smart car on the other side of it. A helmet is padlocked to the handlebars and the engine is still warm, we can hear it ticking.

Billy drops my arm, walks over to it and kicks the front tyre, hard. 'Fucker!' she says. Several of the Japanese people start to laugh. Billy glances at the line. 'Shit,' she mutters to me, 'maybe we should go through the other place.'

'The other place' is a way into the fort that we discovered on one of our previous walks, when the Belvedere was still closed to the public. It's nothing more than a tear in the chicken-wire fence that fronts the wide grassy skirt at the base of the walls. The trampled grass and scrub on either side suggest it's the entrance of choice for junkies and amorous teenagers. I'm sure it's used mainly at night, and the idea of us sneaking up there in broad daylight and getting caught breaking and entering into cultural monuments—and exactly how we would explain it to Signora Bardino after we got arrested—is enough to make me laugh out loud, which makes Billy cross.

'Well,' she points out, as we step into the line that is snaking towards the ticket booth, 'you have to admit, it would save four euros. And that buys you breakfast. If you don't eat much.'

I have no idea why, exactly, Billy was so anxious to come here, but I'm pretty sure it's not for the art. The first thing we see as we climb up through the tunnel that leads to the top of the ramparts is what looks like a big pile of smashed-up cars. The Duomo floats behind it. In the distance we can see the mossy green hills of Fiesole, while below all of Florence is at our feet. The Medici knew a good building site when they saw one.

On closer inspection, the smashed-up cars turn out to be old plane parts, created, if that's the word, by someone from Texas. I guess the juxtaposition is supposed to tell us something about the human condition, but I'm not sure what. The other installations are equally weird. There's a grid of aluminium bars set out on a triangle of grass, and a tiny mini-park raised up on stilts, complete with a street lamp and turf, hovers a few feet above the ground. In the centre of the main terrace is a large pile of broken glass that is supposed to mimic, a plaque informs us, the sundial on the front of the villa, shattering our concept of time in the process. Beyond it, a huge black basalt egg squats on the grass. The Japanese group files obediently past it, even their antenna-waving guide reduced to silence. Several of the men slip off and take videos of the view.

Billy wanders towards the top of the walls that border the Boboli. We're eye to eye with the garden's treetops up here, so close that we could lean over the waist-high balustrade and touch the new feathery leaves. Birds flit back and forth in the branches as Billy scents along the edges of the ramparts like a lazy hound. She nudges little piles of gravel with the toes of her All Stars and peers over into the gardens below. The sun has come out, and the urgency that propelled her up here seems to have slipped away. She bends to talk to a stray cat, and I dawdle.

There's a dreamy quality to this place despite the surreal piles of metal and glass dotted across the ragged lawns and gravel paths. A woozy sense of timelessness seems to come from the villa itself, which, in true Renaissance style, is a perfect cube of stucco. Deep porticos run the length of it, front and back, making it Janus-faced, and when I climb the shallow steps and stand in the central arch I feel as if I'm hovering above time itself.

Looking one way, I see the plain of red roofs, the Duomo and the mountains. In the other, there're the green waves of the olive groves and the striped façade of San Miniato. Below the walls, wild orchids are pinpricks of purple in the long grass, and far away, on the last hill, the sun hits a splash of pink stucco, which must be the villa I peered at through its gates, above the bumblebee houses. The fluorescent bars we saw last night have been turned off for the day, but neon words preaching the meaning of art, oddly enough in English, have been installed around the inside of the portico. Already some of the letters have shorted out. 'Art is the co text of our li es', they read. 'All tim passes.'

I look for Billy to point this out, but she's vanished. At first, I think she must have just disappeared behind one of the wretched sculptures, but after I watch for a few seconds, there's still no sign of her.

From where I'm standing, I can see virtually the whole of the ramparts, and suddenly I feel sick. Pierangelo said that the reopening of this site was controversial, not least because not all the walls are safe. The drop over them is a good thirty feet. Some of the city officials were afraid of getting sued.

I walk faster than I mean to down the steps, and almost trip. The cat Billy was patting scuttles across the gravel and disappears under a scraggly hedge of lavender.

'Bill?' I feel my palms start to sweat. 'Billy?' Some of the Japanese tourists turn to look at me, but by this time I'm trotting towards the walls that edge the Boboli.

'Billy!' I call again. By now I can hear my own personal nightmare, the Santa voice singing in my head.

'Billy!' I jump over a solidified chain curled like a snake, bang into a sign explaining who made it and why, and hear a burst of laughter. The tops of the trees in the Boboli shimmer and sway in front of me, and all I can think is that she must have climbed over the wall, or fallen and somehow survived.

'Billy?' I call again, and this time she answers.

The laughter's close, and when I spin round I see a shaft of steps sinking into the overgrown lawn, leading down to nowhere. Billy is standing at the bottom laughing up at me. 'Avon calling,' she says.

About ten minutes later, the guard throws us out. We weren't supposed to go down there. It turns out Billy moved a sign that said so, and he's mad. She curtsies to him when he calls us 'stupid Americans' and takes my arm going back down the tunnel under the ramparts.

'The Medici built it,' she explains. 'There's a door at the bottom so they could escape through the Boboli up into the fort if the going ever got ugly. I guess there's a tunnel too, somewhere. I found it in a thing on the Pitti. Anyways, you're the architect, I thought you'd like it.'

'I thought you'd fallen over the wall, I really did.' It's not like me to get so worked up, and I'm annoyed with her because of it.

Billy squeezes my arm. 'Don't be grumpy,' she says. 'I'm too smart for that sort of thing. And besides, I can fly.'

'Oh yeah?'

'Yeah. I have to. It's part of the job description.'

'What job is that?'

'Oh didn't you know?' Billy asks as we come out of the tunnel and into the sunlight. 'I'm your guardian angel.'

Chapter Thirteen

THE NEXT DAY is the beginning of the city's Easter festivities, and it starts out badly when the guardian angel wakes up in a very cranky mood. She doesn't tell me why, exactly, but she had dinner last night with Kirk and that, I suspect, has something to do with it. She comes with me to the shop when I go to buy our morning pastries, and when she drops her purse and spills her change all over the floor, she swears so violently that the signora stops talking and crosses herself and Marcello turns as red as his apron. I try to help her pick up the coins, but she bats my hand away. When I ask what's wrong, she only mutters that 'men always want too much.'

Back in the apartment, I notice that Marcello has given me six *croissants con marmalata* again, instead of the four I paid for, but even this doesn't cheer Billy up. She just 'humphs' and stomps off into her room. I figure she'll tell me what the real problem is when she feels like it, so I make coffee, empty the pastries onto a plate, and shove the dirty dishes and ashtray aside so I can spread the newspaper over the whole kitchen table.

'Who's that?' About a half-hour later, Billy comes in and peers over my shoulder at a picture of D'Erreti opening some kind of clinic out near the airport. 'Oh,' she says as she studies the photo, 'the hip-church cardinal. Is it true he dresses up in jeans and hangs out so he can parlay with the youth?'

'I don't know. Is it?'

'I guess,' she says. 'That's what I heard anyways. Celibate, my ass,' she adds. 'Just look at him, he's got it written all over his face. Who's the kewpie doll with him?'

I look at the picture closely for the first time, and sure enough the familiar face is hovering like one of those weird little disembodied angels behind D'Erreti's left shoulder.

'That,' I say, 'is the one and only Father Rinaldo.'

'That's him?' Billy leans in for a closer look.

'In the flesh.' I'm not surprised he's there, since Rinaldo's a big follower of D'Erreti's, but Billy's right, he does look kind of like a kewpie doll, I'd just never noticed it before. He's grinning as the cardinal cuts a ribbon stretched across the door.

Billy raises her eyebrows. 'That's the one who tried to get you to join God's Children and give up the Rose Petal?'

'The very same. I'm surprised you don't recognize him,' I add. 'He's the priest who came here looking for me.'

Billy peers at the picture and shrugs. 'I didn't have my glasses on,' she says. 'Anyway, all priests look the same to me. Like pigeons. Or chorus girls. Get 'em in their costumes, it's hard to tell the difference. Listen,' she adds, 'I'm sorry I was such a bitch earlier. I think maybe I just need some time to myself.' Billy looks at me and laughs. 'Not you, honey,' she says, ruffling my hair. 'Kirk. He's driving me crazy. He's so intense sometimes he makes me feel like running a hundred miles. Or doing my old act: the Disappearing Woman.'

'One of my favourites. You want to hide out here, I won't tell.'

'I just might do that,' she says. 'Or, since it's Easter, maybe I'll go away for three days and come back again.'

Billy grins at her little joke and pours herself the rest of the coffee. She grabs a croissant and a shower of crumbs falls across the newspaper.

'Have you seen Elvis?' she asks, a second later. I shake my head and she puts her cup down and begins to rummage through the kitchen drawers. 'I can't find him anywhere.'

She pulls out a corkscrew, a wine stopper and a paring knife, and dumps them on the counter. A minute later she bangs the drawer shut. 'Are you sure you haven't seen him?' she asks again, and I nod, but I'm not thinking about Elvis, I'm reading about the preparations for Easter. There are piazza parties—like the one we're going to in Santo Spirito—across the city tonight, and D'Erreti's booked like a rock star all week, holding court in the run-up to his big Easter performance when he sparks off a lot of fireworks outside the Duomo.

'If Kirk's kidnapped Elvis, I'll kill him,' Billy announces, and lights her cigarette from the stove, holding her hair up so she doesn't set it on fire.

Around noon, Pierangelo texts me to ask where I will be tonight, and I text back that we are going to the party in Piazza Santo Spirito. It's billed as a cross between a rave-up and a concert, and I have a sudden fit of inclusiveness. Why doesn't he join us? I ask. The fact that he's never met the others is getting sort of silly. He doesn't reply, which annoys me.

I love Piero, but he can be high-handed, and I know he basically considers Americans to be inferior beings, except for me, of course. My irritation with his silence builds through the afternoon, and finally I try him again, this time by voice, and leave a message. I tell him we'll be at the bar from seven o'clock onwards and he'll know me because I'll be the most beautiful woman there.

By this time, Billy is in the shower, and as I hang up I can hear the sound of running water, punctuated by the lyrics from *The Wizard of Oz*. A few seconds later, the door opens and she shouts, 'Bathroom's all yours!' As if I am at least halfway across the city.

Her mood appears to have rebounded, and she's spent the better part of the last few hours painting her nails and ironing her dress. Then she packed her hair in hot olive oil that she infused with rosemary on top of the stove. Half of it is still sitting in a sludge in the bottom of one of Signora Bardino's fancy little copper pans, and I stir it desultorily as she sticks her head round the door.

'The rosemary's great,' she says. 'You should use it. I don't know what it would do to your stripes, though. Might turn 'em green. By the way,' she asks, 'all that eye of newt and crap'—she is referring to the various potions and soaps from the Farmacia Santa Novella that Pierangelo orders for me—'does it actually work?'

'I guess,' I say. Pierangelo insists I use them, and although I like the smell of acacia too, I revolted once over the stuff for my scars, said it was pointless, which made him all ratty, so I gave in. I think he took it as a personal insult. He swears the recipes are ancient Florentine elixirs, and maybe they are. Although, as far as I can tell, most of it's made from distilled weeds. Enormously rare ones, if the price is any indication. 'I mean,' I add, 'the stuff costs enough so you feel as if it works.'

'Ah,' Billy says, 'illusion and marketing.' I've noticed that she's become increasingly prone to these Zen pronouncements, and I remember Kirk's love of sushi and wonder if it's his influence. 'It's a gorgeous night,' she adds rather more concretely. 'So the piazza's going to be packed. We don't want to be late.'

This is a not very veiled warning to me. One of the many odd things about Billy is that she's fanatically punctual. I, on the other hand, am what Mamaw used to call 'born five minutes behind'.

By the time we leave the apartment, we can hear music. The city lights are trapped under a thick scrim of cloud, and threads of sound, the ripple of a saxophone and the higher whine of a violin, corkscrew into the hazy yellowed darkness. In the street, a crowd is moving towards Santo Spirito. Billy locks the gate and drops her keys down the front of her red dress. She wriggles until they nest somewhere in her cleavage. The dress itself is a recent find, the result of one of her excursions to the markets up behind Santa Croce, and in its boned corset, nipped waist and flared full skirt, Billy looks like a crimson ballerina. She even has red satin shoes to match.

The hum of the crowd grows louder, swelling and gathering like surf. Beams of coloured light shoot into the sky, and suddenly there's a blast of sound and the band starts. All around us people murmur. Some clap, some even cheer. By the time we step into the piazza, it feels as though we're at a carnival.

A stage has been set up on the terrace in front of the church. The plain creamy façade is washed with red, and then blue and green and red again. In front of the giant doors, the band looks tiny. There are a lot of them, two sax players, a drummer, a violinist and several others. They look like brightly dressed puppets in a shadow play. Against Santo Spirito, even their huge amplifiers are dwarfed.

More fairy lights than usual lace through the trees, and people are everywhere. Most are dressed up. Skirts and dresses and embroidered blue jeans revolve around us. Some of the younger men are wearing jester's hats or striped crocheted caps, and a few people are in costumes or wearing masks. A witch runs by in a tall peaked hat, while at the bar that has been set up beside the fountain Galileo raises a glass of beer.

We push our way towards our bar and get almost next to them before we see Henry and Kirk and the Japanese girls waving to us. They have staked out a large round table in the corner of the enclosure, right beside a low plastic hedge that borders a wooden dance floor. A selection of carafes and bottles and plates of snacks surround a burning candle lantern.

'Isn't this great? Ayako came early and bagged a table!' Kirk announces as we sit down. Ayako beams in delight when he smiles at her.

If Billy ever really suspected Kirk of kidnapping Elvis, she seems to have forgotten about it. He pours her a glass of white wine, and she kisses him as if he's delivered up nectar of the gods instead of tepid Pinot Grigio. Whether this is for Ayako's benefit or his, I'm not sure. Henry leans over and drops a plaited rope of ribbons around my neck.

'Some guy was selling these for the homeless,' he says, and I notice that everybody is wearing one, even Kirk. 'It suits you.' Henry smiles at me and winks.

In the next hour the darkness, which had not been much more than twilight when we arrived, deepens. The lights in the trees glitter like electric snow. The band takes a break, and a new one comes on. They start to play Chubby Checker, and Henry grabs my hand.

'Come on, Mary,' he says. 'You may not believe this, but I won first place at my High School prom for the twist.'

Actually, I do believe it. There's something unexpectedly graceful about Henry. In the Boboli Gardens I saw him jump into the air to pick a leaf he wanted to admire, and the effect was surprising, like watching a Newfoundland or a St Bernard transformed as they suddenly find their element and bound through snow.

I, on the other hand, am a lousy dancer. And I am about to say so, to fink out and turn him down, when I hear the Japanese girls giggling. They don't think Henry is anywhere near as cool as Kirk, and now their cheeks are flushed with too much wine and with the idea that someone as big and ungainly as Henry should even think of dancing. My hand tightens around his, and I get to my feet. If I could give them the finger and climb out over the plastic hedge at the same time without falling down, I would.

'Let's Twist Again' bleats across the piazza, as Henry and I join a herd of gyrating, wiggling twisters. The best are middle-aged couples. So far, they've been standing reasonably sedately around the outside bar, or sitting at the restaurant tables picking at antipasto and smiling at the wildness of youth on display, but now they take to the floor with a vengeance. Beside us a woman in Ferragamo shoes and what looks a lot like a Chanel skirt, and her husband, who must be sixty-five if he's a day, put Henry and me to shame.

In my case, that's not saying much—I look like a scarecrow caught in high wind—but Henry's hot. His hips swivel. His knees dip. A blissful smile comes over his face, and his glasses slip cock-eyed on his nose. He catches me watching him and laughs.

When the song finally finishes and I glance back at the table, I see that Kirk's gone and Billy and Ayako are leaning across his empty chair, talking head to head. Blonde and dark, they seem suddenly as Naomi and Ruth. Bonded for life. Ayako's hands move as she speaks, and the other girls nod in agreement with whatever it is she's saying.

Henry says something that I only half catch and steps away into the line by the fountain bar to buy us a glass of wine, which is fine by me, because I don't really want to go back to the table. I don't know what Billy's up to but, just looking at her, I'm pretty sure it's something. I look around for a space to sit down on the edge of the fountain, and I've just found one, on the far side of two old ladies who are eating *gelato*, when the lights on the front of the church shift, and I see Pierangelo.

Dressed in jeans and sweater, he's threading his way through the crowd towards me. His eyes meet mine, then someone speaks to him and he stops and rests his hand on their shoulder. He smiles and nods, laughs, then mouths 'ciao,' and something inside my stomach twists. I feel as if I'm sixteen again and the boy I have a crush on is coming to ask me to dance.

The music is slow this time, and familiar. It's the Stones' 'Till the Next Goodbye.' Pierangelo stops in front of me and holds out his arms. 'Most beautiful woman on the piazza,' he says. 'The paper's gone to bed. And I'm all yours.'

This is the first time I've actually seen him since Graziella told me about his mother, and now that I've had time to get used to the idea I lean back in his arms, look into his face and imagine

I see, not the elegant man I know, but someone else: a little boy abandoned, a child growing up, struggling to be an adult and find his place in the world, loved by an aunt and uncle, but knowing that his own mother couldn't be bothered to raise him. How much hurt does that still cause, I wonder. How much sadness?

I reach up and run my fingers down the smooth line of his cheek and across the full-flush curve of his lips. 'I love you,' I whisper, and Pierangelo smiles at me with his lazy-cat eyes, pulls me close and kisses the top of my head. He smells of citrus and something else, the Colonna de Russe he buys at the *farmacia*. The cashmere of his sweater is a deep liquid blue, and soft.

'I love you too, *piccola*. More than anything.'

He says the words with his mouth close to my ear and I feel his body moving, his breath on my skin, and right now I don't think I'll ever care about anything else again.

The music shifts and quickens and Piero and I dance the next dance too. At some point, we spin around and I glimpse Henry through the crowd. Standing by the fountain, holding a glass, he looks like a big shaggy dog somebody has yelled at, and I feel bad. I should go to him, I think, say something. Really, I should explain. But then Henry's lost in a whirl of lights. Colours swing past us, and I get a dizzying glimpse of the table and see the white moon faces of Kirk and Billy and the Japanese girls staring, which makes me laugh. I'm half tempted to wave, as if I'm flying by on a ferris wheel or a merry-go-round, and they're stuck, grounded in their clutter of bottles and empty glasses.

Eventually the music stops and Pierangelo and I find a place to sit on the steps of the church. There are people above us and below us. I'm at eye level with heads and legs, knees and rear ends. Voices rise in a wave. There's some French, some English and something that sounds like Dutch, all of it a counterpoint to the rippling chatter of Italian.

'So,' he says, 'did you miss me?'

'No!' I laugh. 'What do you think?'

Pierangelo grins and shrugs. 'With you women, you never know.'

The lights play across his face, bathing it in red and then blue so his high cheekbones and the sharp angle of his nose stand out. Before, I might have taken this more as the joke it's intended to be, but now, knowing what Graziella told me, I don't.

'You do too,' I say. 'With me. That's why I came back.'

Piero ruffles my hair. '*Cara*. I was teasing you. And,' he adds, 'now the article is put to bed and I'm all yours.'

'Until next week.'

He shrugs. 'It's Easter, we're not so busy.'

'Are you happy with it?'

It's not meant to be a complicated question, but Pierangelo's face sobers. He shakes his head. 'Yes,' he says. 'Sure. No. I don't know. I told you, I admire D'Erreti more than I'd like. I guess.'

Pierangelo thinks for a minute, his eyes fixed on the throng of people below us, but not seeing them. I've seen him do this before, vanish while he is right in front of me, travel deep into his personal landscape where I can't follow. Finally he says, as much to himself as to me, 'The problem is, maybe I don't know how to talk about the church any more.'

He runs his thumb across the back of my hand. 'If you don't mention things,' he says, 'you soft-soap. If you hit too hard, it's nothing but an endless diatribe. For some of us, I think, writing about the church in this country is like writing about a parent who you love, but who's gone crazy. Turned senile and mean.' Pierangelo smiles, but the smile is sad. Looking at him, it occurs to me that he's exhausted, and I feel like a heel for even suggesting he come here.

I take his hand, about to suggest that we go home right now, when there's a commotion. The band starts, then stops and Pierangelo gets to his feet and I stand up too, but I can't see anything, so I climb a step behind him.

A column of white figures has appeared out of nowhere. Wearing long robes and something weird on their heads, tall pointed hats, they seem to have materialized in the middle of the piazza. Maybe sixty or more of them walk two by two, in a long white snake cleaving the crowd.

A few seconds ago the people below us had been putting their drinks down, happy, ready to dance again, but now a hush falls over the square.

I stand on my tiptoes, holding on to Pierangelo's shoulders as the column comes level with the fountain, and that's when I realize that the white figures are wearing hoods, not hats. The tall peaked cones rise from their shoulders and cover their heads, leaving nothing but slits for their eyes.

'Shit,' I whisper to Pierangelo. 'What are they? Klan?'

He shakes his head. 'Penitents,' he says. Then he adds, 'They do this in Spain, during Holy Week, march around the cities, especially Seville. But I've never seen it here before. In the last few years I've heard of it, in the south, but I've never seen it.'

The leader of the column is swinging a censer. Smoke trails out of it in a thin dribble. A Vespa engine coughs to life a few streets away. A dog barks. Colours wash over the white figures, and as they get closer to us I hear something like a swarm of bees, the low, dull, relentless hum of chanting.

They step up and over the dance floor like a column of army ants or sleepwalkers, and the crowd shifts uneasily. Then someone shouts, loud and harsh, and a bottle flies through the air. It explodes on the cobbles, wine splashing up and spattering the long white gowns, staining the material, and dribbling away to pool at the leading penitent's feet.

The censer hovers, losing its rhythm, and the chant falters. Figures in the back jam into others in front and the column stalls, bulges like a train wreck. I feel Pierangelo tense as the crowd shimmies. Blue lights wash the tips of the trees and the fountain, catching the strange coned shape of the leader's head as he swivels, the slits of his mask moving across the banks of faces that surround him. Someone yells. The shout hangs in the air. Then the leader looks down, slowly, lifts his foot and steps forward, his hem dragging in the puddle of wine and shattered glass.

For a second I think they are going to come up the steps, maybe even enter the church, but they don't. Instead, the penitents skirt the bottom of the terrace, throwing strange peaked shadows against the façade of Santo Spirito, and wind away down towards the river into the dark of the city, the smell of incense hanging in the air behind them.

The crowd surges defiantly back towards the fountain bar and the dance floor. The band strikes up again, almost frantic, and as we sink back onto the steps with the other people around us there's a palpable sense of relief, as though something awful has been narrowly avoided. We are still catching our breath when Billy materializes in front of us like a hologram.

'Now that the KKK's left,' she says, 'we're about to order food, and we'd be so pleased if you'd join us.' She beams, doing an excellent imitation of Beaver Cleaver's mother.

'Mary,' she adds, 'I don't believe you've introduced me to your friend.' Pierangelo stands up. They're almost the same height. 'Of course,' Billy grips his hand and looks into his eyes. 'You're the handsome man who brought the roses! And gave Mary this beautiful necklace.' Billy plucks the little nest of gold off my chest and swings it back and forth on its chain as if she's dowsing. 'I guess I just didn't recognize you, after dark.'

'I've aged in the last week,' Pierangelo says. 'Significantly.'

It might sound light-hearted, if you didn't know him, but there's an edge in his voice. He doesn't like her and I wonder why. Billy doesn't catch it. Instead, she laughs, and I gather they've been having a good time back at the table, because I swear I can smell alcohol rising off her, layered over the perfume I recognize as mine.

'We were thinking of going home,' I say suddenly.

'Well, you can't leave! You just can't.' Billy grabs Pierangelo's hand. 'I have money riding on this. A bet. The others think you don't even exist. They think Mary's been making you up!'

Pierangelo's presence has an immediate effect on the Japanese girls. As soon as he sits down at the table, they go mute. Like polite children, they answer questions when he asks them directly, but otherwise they don't say a word. When the food arrives they concentrate on their plates with the kind of dedication I normally associate only with child-proof aspirin bottles or the *New York Times* crossword puzzle.

For my part, I'm aware that I owe Henry an apology, but this is hardly the time or place, so instead I end up smiling at him inanely, trying to send some kind of telepathic signal that says I'm sorry for leaving him standing there. Henry is good at this game. He smiles back, and even winks. He makes conversation with Pierangelo, asking him about Florence. As usual, Henry is making an effort, being nice. Kirk, on the other hand, is not being nice.

He leans back in his chair and eyes Pierangelo as if they're two Alpha male baboons. The situation is not helped by Billy, who's behaving as though Pierangelo is the most fascinating man she's ever met in her whole, entire life. She passes him the bread. She leans forward when he speaks. She laughs in a high lilting giggle when he asks what we think of the signora and her academy. And when Kirk asks Pierangelo what he does, it's Billy who answers.

'He's a journalist,' she announces. 'A famous one. At least that's what Mary says.'

Billy gives me her 1950s beam again. She sounds like Doris Day on speed, and I wonder what the hell is the matter with her. After this morning's sulks she's all lit up, sparkly and excited, cooking with nervous energy. Or maybe just cooking. Henry's told me he's suspected more than once that Kirk has a cocaine problem—that maybe that's why he's taking this 'leave of absence'—and I wonder if he and Billy have been sneaking off and doing lines in the bar bathroom, or dropping Ecstasy tabs into their wine. I try to catch Henry's eye to run this idea past him via our new lines of telepathic communication, but he's not looking at me. Like everybody else at the table, he's watching Billy.

'So, you're doing this big thing on the cardinal,' she says to Pierangelo, making D'Erreti sound like a baseball team. He agrees that he is, and Billy witters about how fascinating it must be and asks what it's like in the Vatican. Kirk shifts in his chair and drinks more, and the Japanese girls eat, shovelling risotto into their mouths, breaking bread and tamping up the crumbs with their fingers.

'Well,' Billy says, after Pierangelo's said something about the Pope's summer residence at Castel Gandolfo, 'it must make a nice change, at least. I mean, after that awful stuff, those terrible murders you covered.'

There's a silence at the table, like a beat in music. The Japanese girls stop chewing and Kirk puts his glass down. But Billy's on a roll, and I have a horrible feeling I know where this is going to go next.

'I mean,' she goes on, 'that poor prostitute they found in the park, and the nun, and the nurse. That is so terrible. Mary and I disagree,' she adds brightly, 'about how much she should worry about those women.'

'Billy!' I start to rise out of my chair, not sure exactly what I plan to do—anything, I guess, to shut her up. But Pierangelo puts his hand on my knee, literally holding me down, and before I have a chance to say anything else Kirk and Henry both speak at once.

'What women?' they ask.

'There's nothing to worry about,' Pierangelo says. He smiles and takes my hand. 'Mary's right about that. And so are you, signorina. The cardinal's much more interesting.' But it's too late to change the subject. Like Pandora, Billy's cracked the lid on her box and released all sorts of mischief.

When I catch her eye and glare at her, she smiles, looking awfully pleased with herself. Her deep blue eyes hold mine, defiant as a kid sticking her tongue out, and all of a sudden I get it. She's been mad because I wouldn't pay attention to her worries over Ginevra Montelleone's vigil, and because I teased her and wouldn't listen to her yesterday at the fort. So now she's going to rat me out, and enlist the others to help bully me into 'taking things more seriously'. If I thought Pierangelo would let me up, I'd kill her.

'What murders?' Kirk is asking. There's a high, insistent edge in his voice. Like a shark—or a prosecutor—he smells blood, and he's not about to be deflected by talk of some guy in a red dress. 'What the hell are you talking about?' he asks.

Pierangelo almost never smokes, but now he produces a silver cigarette case and matching lighter I've never seen before, and lights up slowly. He blows smoke, and eyes Kirk the way a cat eyes a bird on a feeder. I glance around the table, at the shiny bowed heads of the Japanese girls, who are practically counting the grains of their rice, and at Henry and Billy, neither of whom is looking at me. I feel as if I'm in High School again, watching two guys square up in the parking lot, and I open my mouth to say this is all ridiculous but, before I can, Pierangelo shrugs.

'She's right,' he says. 'There have been women killed in the city, and my paper has written about it. It's hardly unusual.'

'Women? How many?' This is Henry.

Pierangelo looks at him. 'Four,' he says.

'Four!' Kirk reaches out and takes Billy's hand, the one with the heart ring on it. He winds his fingers through hers, holding on as if it's a gesture of solidarity in the face of immediate danger. 'There's been nothing about it in the press recently.' He turns to me. 'You know about this?'

I nod, fiddling with the stem of my glass.

'How long has it been going on?' Kirk is closing on me the way I imagine him closing on someone lying in court.

'A couple of years, I guess.' I don't sound as offhand as I'd like to.

'So, it was happening the last time you were here?'

Under the table, Pierangelo squeezes my knee. 'These things happen in big cities.' He taps his ash on the edge of his plate.

But Kirk's like a dog with a bone. 'I mean, what?' he asks. 'What are we talking about here? A serial killer? Is that what you're saying?'

He's raising his voice now, grandstanding. The people at the next table glance over their shoulders, but there's too much noise in the piazza for them to make out what we're saying.

'Should these women be afraid?' Kirk waves his free hand across the table theatrically, suggesting that Billy, the Japanese girls and I are all under his care. 'Is there some maniac running around?' he asks. 'I mean, if there is, we have a right to know. People have a right to protect themselves.' Kirk glares at Pierangelo as if he might wield the knife himself.

Piero doesn't say anything and in the face of his silence, Kirk goes quiet. He stares down at the table, one pale hand still holding Billy's, the other playing with his fork, rocking it back and forth on its tines as if he's about to flip it like a weapon. Then something moves across his face. He twitches, his pros-ecutor's instinct clicking in.

'That's what happened to the girl in the river, isn't it?' He looks up, the histrionics vanished from his face, leaving it cold and still as marble. 'She's one of them, isn't she?'

There's complete silence at the table. Henry pulls his beard, giving it a little jerk, and Billy stares with total concentration at the edge of her plate. She glances up at Pierangelo, her look distant and considering, as if she's curious to see how he'll get out of this one. Mikiko suddenly puts her fork down.

'She committed suicide.'

Mikiko's beautiful black eyes are wide, and she's staring at us as though we're all crazy, or she would certainly like us to be. 'Right?' she asks. 'That's what happened to her, right?'

There's a thin knife-edge of fear in her voice. She looks at Pierangelo, pleading for him to agree with her. 'Florence is a very safe city.' Mikiko nods, the dark cap of her hair shimmering in the lights. 'That girl jumped, from the bridge,' she says. 'Nobody killed her. It said in the newspapers.'

Piero stubs out his cigarette. 'As far as I know,' he says, 'she drowned.'

Mikiko favours him with a nervous smile, picks up her fork and dives back into her plate. Henry stops pulling his beard. Kirk reaches for his glass and looks slightly put out, as if he's been reminded again that you never break the cardinal rule and ask a question you don't know the answer to. And I just want to go home. Then Billy takes a bite of her food, looks up at Pierangelo and smiles.

'That's interesting,' she says. 'But let's just say for a second it isn't true. Just for the sake of argument. I mean serial killers, they don't usually stop, do they? Isn't that something to worry about? I mean, I heard that sometimes it's even like a game,' she adds, impaling another tube of pasta with her fork. 'That they leave clues and stuff, deliberately. For instance, the kind of knife that was used—'

'Knife?' Mikiko puts her glass down and stares at all of us. 'Someone killed her with a knife? But you just said—'

'Oh for God's sake!'

Henry picks up a carafe and splashes dark red wine into our glasses. Some of it spatters and spills on the white table-cloth, spreading like an ink blot under the breadcrumbs. 'Come on, you guys,' he says. 'It's a party tonight. Let's cut it out. OK? Some women were attacked, a long time ago, and a girl jumped off a bridge. We're not talking about the Monster of Florence here.'

I could kiss him.

Ayako pats Mikiko on the shoulder. 'See,' she says. 'No monsters in Florence.'

She hasn't understood Henry's reference to the city's most famous serial killer, and no one feels the need to enlighten her. Kirk's collapsed back into his chair, and even Billy's shut up.

'Well, it is pretty scary! Like a bad movie!' Mikiko laughs and lets Henry pour her more wine, and Tamayo even joins in.

'Miki is a really big coward,' she says.

This is almost the first thing Tamayo has said all evening, and the fact that she is speaking at all takes us by surprise. Normally, she's incredibly shy. Billy looks up from the pattern she's been tracing on the tablecloth with her fingernail, and Tamayo looks around as if she realizes her own shock value and finds it funny.

'Miki can't watch scary movies,' she announces, giggling. She picks up her glass and shakes her head in disbelief. 'She puts her head in my lap. Even pictures scare her, in museums. Fraidy Cat!' She laughs. 'You should have seen her in Mantua!'

'What did you guys do? Go see *Son of Dracula* with Signor Catarelli?' Kirk actually manages a smile, and when Mikiko laughs and makes a face at the idea we all laugh with her, the black mood around the table splintering into tiny bright pieces.

'Nooo. Yuck. But there was this picture by Mantegna,' Ayako says, the wine flushing her face and making her suddenly voluble. 'I was telling Billy, it was really gross. Hate was in it, and she was like a horrible old monkey, and she had these bags of seeds hanging from her shoulders.'

The band has started again. A wave of jive music washes across the piazza, and some people start to clap. Couples get up from tables around us, and clamber over the plastic hedge to the dance floor. One woman is drunk and half collapses on the spiky fake leaves. I see her open mouth, but I can't hear any sound. I feel as though my ears are blocked up and I'm in a plane that's climbing to a place where the pressure in my head will explode.

'Bags?' At first, I'm not sure I've said anything because Ayako doesn't seem to have heard me. Then I realize she's returned her attention to her food and doesn't want to talk with her mouth full.

Billy has taken her free hand out of Kirk's and reaches for her wine glass. The wine meets her lips, and she flicks at it with the tip of her tongue. Now I know what she was talking to the girls about earlier. It was their trip to Mantua. It was the picture they had seen, of Hate and her bags of seeds. That's what set Billy off.

Ayako finishes chewing and nods. 'Signor Catarelli explained it. Somebody is trying to chase Vices from the Garden of Eden. And Hate is like, you know, this monkey-woman. She's all shrivelled up, and she has only one breast and these four bags hang from her shoulders.'

Billy makes a point of not looking at me. 'Four?' she asks.

'Right,' Ayako says.

'And they're filled with the seeds of evil. Isn't that what you said?' Billy mentions this as if it's perfectly normal, as if what we're discussing here is nothing more than the effect of Classicism on the Renaissance.

'Yeah. And they're scarlet,' Mikiko adds. 'The colour of sin,' she laughs. 'You know, just like you, scarlet woman! You should go to Mantua.'

'You really should.' Tamayo nods in agreement. 'It's a beautiful town. And an amazing picture. Mantegna is really an interesting artist. You'd like it.'

'I bet,' Billy says. 'I just can't wait.'

Chapter Fourteen

PIERANGELO AND I decide to leave a few minutes later.

Kirk has led Billy off to dance, and the Japanese girls seem to have changed their mind about Henry's cool-ness, or lack of it, because they set on him like a trio of Munchkins, giggling excitedly as they drag him over the plastic hedge and out onto the floor where couples are clutching each other, stumbling slightly and swaying to the slow syrupy music.

As we stand up Piero runs his hand across his face and shakes his head, and I feel limp, like one of those animals—a possum or something—that plays dead when it's cornered. *Billy, one, me, nil*, I think. She might as well have taken the red bag they found pinned to Ginevra Montelleone's shoulder and thrown it in my face.

'What do you think it means?' I ask Piero as we begin to work our way through the crowded piazza.

He shakes his head again, and takes my hand as a couple almost crash into us and stagger away, giggling. 'I don't know.'

'But you think it means something? It has to.'

'Yeah. Probably.'

'Will you tell Pallioti?'

'*Certo.* Although,' he adds, 'they probably already have it. I think they have specialists who work on that kind of stuff, the homicidal version of the Stendhal syndrome.'

'But you will call him?' I stop, tugging on his hand like a stubborn child. 'You'll make sure? Even if he has it anyways?'

Piero turns to me. 'Of course I'll call him, *cara*,' he says. There's a hint of exasperation in his voice now. 'I promise,' he adds.

The whole piazza's taken on a slow, drunken feeling. A saxophone wails, and behind us the singer starts crooning in something that might, or might not, be Italian. Pierangelo's so tired that he sways slightly to the music, eyes half closed.

'Let's go home. Please,' he says. And I nod. Then I remember I haven't told anyone we're leaving. Pissed off as I am with Billy, I still feel that I should let her know. I'll tell Henry, and he can tell her. I edge my way back along the side of the piazza, Pierangelo following me. But when we step up by the fountain and get a clear view of our table, both of us stop.

The fight must have blown up as fast as a summer storm, because five minutes ago Kirk and Billy were dancing. But they certainly aren't now. Now they're standing beside the empty table, screaming at each other. Kirk is holding the back of a chair as Billy leans towards him, and although we're too far away to hear them, I know right away this is much worse than Fiesole.

Billy's arms are straight, her fists balled. She's virtually spitting with anger. I've never seen her like this before, neck rigid, back braced, and the effect is creepy. It's like seeing someone else in Billy's body. She pulls herself up straight, and in her red dress she's fearsome. And beautiful. And, I suspect, enjoying herself. A diva giving an epic performance.

Kirk, however, looks stricken, and I look around instinctively for Henry, thinking he'll know how to stop this. After all, it's his stock in trade. But when I spot him in the crowd, I see at once he's oblivious. Surrounded by a bevy of witches and half-masked men, Henry's grinning blissfully, his glasses askew as he dances with the Japanese girls like Pan with his nymphs.

More people in fancy dress have appeared. They must have seeped into the edges of the crowd while we were discussing Mantegna and serial killers. A Dante and a monk, each clutching a Botticelli angel, circle past us. On the church steps, I glimpse Romeo making out with Juliet, and someone in jeans and sneakers has gotten hold of one of the penitents' hoods and walks solemnly through the dancers swinging a beer bottle for a censer and blessing couples who cross in front of him. He stops and raises his hand, making a half-finished sign of the cross over Henry as Ayako and Mikiko and Tamayo orbit around him like woozy stars.

Back at the table, Kirk is white and immobile. He wraps his arms across his chest, and raises his chin, as if he expects Billy to slap him. They have quite an audience now. The people at the next table have given up trying to ignore them and stare openly. Others watch from where we are, laughing and whispering, cheering for one side or the other. Someone claps. Billy leans into Kirk, so close she could almost kiss him. Her lips move as her hands chop up and down, dancing to a choreography of their own, and then, abruptly, she pulls the heart ring off her finger, throws it at him, and turns away.

Kirk reaches for her, but she jumps over the trampled plastic hedge, leaving him standing beside the littered table, his hand hanging uselessly in the air, a cop with no traffic to direct. A second later, he bends down and gropes amid the old paper napkins and spilled wine for the ring. Finally he straightens up and sinks down in his chair.

I start to step forward, feeling that I should say or do something, but Pierangelo puts a hand on my shoulder. He shakes his head, and I guess he's right. Kirk would probably just be embarrassed. Then Piero inclines his head, and I see Billy too.

She's already dancing with someone else. The music has picked up, morphed from the slow sticky groping song to an erratic swinging jazz. She twirls and pirouettes across the dance floor, the skirt of her red dress fanned out around her like a parasol. People move back to make room for her, and the guy she's dancing with, who's wearing a *Carnivale* mask, gold one side and silver the other, spins her so fast her hair comes loose. A wild cascade of snarls and ringlets ripples down her back and falls away like the froth from a waterfall as he dips her low to the ground.

When the man swings Billy up, she puts her arms around his neck and catches my eye, and I'm sure I see her smile.

The next morning is Palm Sunday. It rains, and Pierangelo and I sleep late. I wake up once, early, and hear the hard beat, like a shower turned on up on the roof terrace. Grey light filters through the linen blind, and I drift off again. I don't know how long it is after that when I roll over without opening my eyes and reach out to feel Piero sleeping beside me. Or apparently not. Because he takes my outstretched hand and kisses my fingertips.

'Hey, sleepyhead,' he says, and I open my eyes to see him sitting on the edge of the bed, already dressed.

'How long have you been up?'

He shrugs and smiles. 'A while. It's almost ten.'

'You're kidding.' I sit up and run my hands through my hair. We were so beat when we came in last night that we virtually passed out, but even so I feel stiff, as if I've been in a wrestling match. The dancing. I'm getting too old for my scarecrow act. 'I must have slept ten hours. I think my muscles have atrophied.'

'Have a hot bath.' Piero stands up. 'I'll run it for you.'

The night comes back as I watch him walk towards the bathroom: the sickly shifting lights, the weird white penitents, Billy and Kirk fighting. The awful dinner.

'Did you?' I ask suddenly.

Pierangelo turns round and smiles at me, his hand on the bathroom door. 'Yes, *piccola*,' he says. 'I told you I would, and I did. First thing this morning.'

'And?'

Pierangelo laughs and goes into the bathroom. I hear water start in a gush. Ispettore Pallioti sends you his best wishes,' he calls.

By the time I get out of the bath, the table is set. There are pastries and fruit and coffee and a vase of roses in the centre. And the Sunday paper. Two copies. Pierangelo's article on D'Erreti is a six-page spread. 'Fifty Years Lived in the Shadow of God.' We read in silence, cups of coffee in hand.

The piece is at least partially in honour of the fact that this Saturday, the day before Easter, is Massimo D'Erreti's fiftieth birthday. Pierangelo runs through his career in the church, concentrating especially on his early missionary work in Africa, where D'Erreti was heavily influenced by some of the more right-wing African bishops. He was tagged as a star from early on, and by the time he did a stint in the States and returned to Italy in the early nineties, his mindset was pretty well gelled.

Like Savonarola five centuries before him, the cardinal has warned of a 'Black Cross' hanging not only over Florence, but over the whole of Western society. In a recent interview His Eminence stated that: 'The Liberal moral equivalence of the 1960s and 1970s has seduced us all onto a wrong path. In our own country, we have seen the scourge of the Red Brigades, the Anni Piombi, the Years of Lead. In Africa and across the world, we see the scourge of AIDS. We see the innocent unborn who die in the name of their mothers' "rights." As we have fallen away from God, we have become lost. Now the true job of the church is to be our captain in the storm, to guide us safely home to God.'

His investiture as the Bishop of Florence was, D'Erreti claims, an occasion for humility, a chance to serve the native city he so dearly loves, and I understand at once part of the reason Pierangelo identifies with him, albeit reluctantly. Not only are they the same age and both love Florence, something Piero considers virtually a moral duty, but Massimo D'Erreti is apparently a genuine populist, something I know Pierangelo admires. I wonder if, having lived through the same decades and come to virtually opposite—but equally strongly held—conclusions, they're flip sides of the same coin, one politically left, one politically right.

> Like the protagonist of Morris West's novel, *The Shoes of the Fisherman*, His Eminence has been known to slip away incognito in order to mingle with the citizens of the city. 'There is an old saying, "The Franciscans love the plains and the Dominicans love the cities." And I will only know my children if I can walk among them,' he says. 'After all, Our Lord walked into the marketplace as well as into the temples. And when I see the unfortunate, the drug addict, the prostitute, the beggar, what can I do but look into her face and see a woman who could be my mother? Indeed, who could be the mother of us all, for we share a universal Mother. All of us are the children of Mary. And whether we are aware of it or not, all of us live out our childhood in front of God.'

I look at the top of Pierangelo's head as he bends over some other article, his curls showing a faint tinge of grey, and understand his frustration, why he had such a hard time with this article. *Massimo D'Erreti, Man of the People*. The cardinal's been working on the performance all his life and it plays well, so it must be frustrating as hell to know what really lies underneath, and have to figure out how to reveal it. The original Savonarola at least was ugly.

The next page is given over almost entirely to pictures, which is what caused Piero such a headache earlier this week. Digging them out was hard enough, especially the early ones, and verifying them and providing accurate captions was a nightmare. I see D'Erreti as a young man, newly ordained and at seminary, and even before that, as an altar boy. Then there's one of a row of children sitting outside a building, motley and unhappy, a priest standing on either side of them. D'Erreti is the third from the left, a wimpy-looking little boy who looks cold in dark shorts and lace-up shoes. School, I think. Then I read the caption, and my heart flutters. 'Raised as a foundling by the church, the young Massimo found refuge in God and felt his calling early.'

I stare at the page in front of me. Now I understand the other part of Pierangelo's *sympatico*, even fascination, for the cardinal. It's the instinctive tug that makes him recognize one of his own, like me with pictures of the dead women, makes him see, perhaps, if circumstances had been just a little different—if there had been no loving aunt to take him in, no uncle to be his father instead of God—what he might have been. It's not just that Massimo D'Eretti and Pierangelo Sanguetti are both idealists with a special love for Florence; it's that they're both orphans.

I get up and wind my arms around Piero's shoulders, rest my cheek on the top of his head. He reaches up absently and takes my hands, his fingers lacing through mine.

It's after five p.m. when the telephone rings and Pierangelo comes back from answering it to ask me if I want to drive out and have dinner with some friends of his in Tavarnuzze. Nothing fancy, he says, but they have a villa to die for. I'll like the buildings. This is a tease, of course. He knows perfectly well I want to go. I know almost none of his friends, and I'm eager to meet them. But I won't go dressed like this, in my clothes from last night. My hair is clean, but I want my makeup. Earrings. Shoes and a dress. Piero shrugs. No problem, he says. We'll stop by on the way out of town so I can change.

It's still pouring when we get there. The wind has come up and splats of rain hit the side of the car so hard it feels like someone's throwing buckets of water at us. Piero pulls up opposite our building and I tell him to stay put and listen to his favourite CD of Puccini arias, I won't be more than fifteen minutes.

A gust hits me as I run across the road, almost turning my umbrella inside out. I'm still wrestling with it, trying to hang on to it with one hand and get my keys out of my pocket with the other, when a shadow appears under the entrance arch and thickens into the solid black shape of a priest who must have just finished saying Mass for Signora Raguzza. With his rain cape and old-fashioned hat and umbrella, he looks more like one of the nuns from the convent over by the Carmine. His gloved hand holds the gate for me as I run up the steps and brush by him.

Pools of rain have formed in the courtyard and the lemon trees look miserable. Sophie-Sophia's windows are shuttered; the family must have gone away for the holiday. The downstairs door to our vestibule is closed against the wind, and the stair-wells so dark that I hit the lights. The grille of the elevator looks like a cage, dark and unwelcoming, and I take the stairs two at a time instead.

Billy's not home. I sense it as soon as I get through the door, the apartment has the cold feeling of unoccupied space. But I call anyways, and then check the rooms, just to be sure. Pawing through my closet, I settle finally on a skirt and boots, and a deep blue-green blouse Pierangelo gave me. What it needs, I think as I twist around in front of the mirror, is a belt. Something big and funky. The sort of thing I don't have, but Billy does. She came home from the market with a fabulous heavy leather one covered with coins and turquoise bits just a few days ago. Just my luck, she'll be wearing it, but when I go into her room I find it right away, coiled in her top drawer. After putting the belt on, I have a fast paw through her jewellery box. Billy's an earring queen, and sure enough there's a pair that match. As I grab them, my fingers collide with a pretty blue wristwatch. Typical Billy, I think as I close the drawer, to prefer bugging everybody by asking what time it is every fifteen minutes. I check her lipsticks to see if there are any colours I like, but our skin tones are too different.

Then, as I'm fastening the earrings and admiring the result in her mirror, my phone starts cheeping. I glance at my watch as I run into the kitchen to fish it out of my jacket pocket. I've been gone exactly fourteen minutes. Men are amazing. *I C U,* the text says. I duck into the living room, look down into the street and wave at the car. Then I text back, *CU2,* drop the phone in my pocket and write Billy a note that I prop against the television. 'Staying at Piero's. Stole your belt and earrings, will return with rent of bottle of wine—M.'

The BMW's windows are so steamed up I can't even see inside, and I have to tap on the glass to get Piero to open the door, which is annoying because I'm getting wet. When I jump in and throw the umbrella in the back seat, he leans over and kisses me, then raises his finger mouthing, 'Wait.' The aria from *Madame Butterfly* fills the car, the notes a high, sweet counterpoint to the clatter of the rain. Pierangelo's eyes are closed, his face blissful as his hand moves slightly to the music.

'Tebaldi,' he says as the last notes linger in the air. 'Sublime.' He turns the engine over and we pull out into the wet street.

A few seconds later, we stop at the lights on Via Maggio. Ghost figures scurry in front of us, someone wrapped in a mackintosh and carrying a dog, two nuns clutching each other's arms and running, and a tall woman, scarf over her head, who I'm sure is Billy. I twist round as she heads up the sidewalk, rubbing a patch in the fog on my window, and waving. But she doesn't notice me, and a second later she's lost in the blur of the rain as we glide forward, windshield wipers thunking in rhythm, and turn up towards Porta Romana.

I don't see Billy the next day, or the day after that. Which is not surprising because I visit the apartment for a grand total of maybe ten minutes, just enough time to put her belt and earrings back in her room and grab a couple of changes of clothes for myself.

Pierangelo takes Monday and most of Tuesday off. We drive out to Vinci to see the Leonardo museum, wander among the wooden flying machines and admire the rebuilt model of the submarine, then the next afternoon, after Piero spends a couple of hours in the office in the morning, we go to Pisa. We have a long lunch, take pictures of each other leaning under the tower, buy a snow globe with the Campo dei Miracoli imprisoned inside, and linger beside the Arno admiring the beautiful little jewel box that is La Spina, the perfect tiny chapel built to house a thorn from Christ's crown. In the evening, we stop in Lucca, walk on the ramparts holding hands, and have dinner in Piazza San Martino where we watch the swallows dive and swoop against the backdrop of the cathedral.

Now the mini-holiday is over. It's early Wednesday morning and, knowing he has to be back in the office in a few hours, I watch Pierangelo sleeping. A thin haze of beard has grown on his cheeks and chin, and his eyes move under his lids as he dreams. His hand flutters on the duvet like a restless bird.

I pick up my shoes, ease the door open and slip into the living room. I've been awake for a while, and since it's six-thirty, and Piero's alarm will go off in a half-hour anyways, I figure I might as well leave him alone in his habitual pre-work chaos. I rummage in the kitchen drawer for a pen and a piece of paper, and write a note telling him to call me later. Then, as I'm about to prop it up by the coffee pot where he can't miss it, I notice the silver cigarette case he used at the party the other night and I can't help myself. I slide it across the counter and open it.

I'm no expert on silver, but even I can tell that this is nice. It's heavy in my hand, smooth and cool. The lid springs up with a satisfying click. There are two cigarettes, held down by a silver band, but they're not what interests me. What interests me is the inscription. It's nice too, done in heavy mannish Roman letters, very tasteful and surprising. I expected it to be from Monika, but it isn't. 'To Piero, with all my love for ever— Ottavia' it says, and I feel a nasty little wince in my stomach. Then I look at the date underneath and laugh at myself. *'21*

April 1980'. Whoever Ottavia was, she was long before my time. I snap the lid shut and put the cigarette case back where it was. Then I carry my shoes across the living room so I won't wake Piero, and let myself out.

The sky is the colour of unripe peaches. A tiny puff of cloud floats above the buildings and turns faint yellow as the sun hits it. I take a short cut through Piazzetta del Limbo, listening for the rustling sighs of the unbaptized babies, then reach the Lungarno, and hear the whirr of street cleaners. The little drone-like trucks move along the broad avenues ahead of me, and turn abruptly away from the river, buzzing up towards the cathedral.

In four days it will be Easter, Florence's biggest event of the year, celebrated with an odd mixture of the pagan and the Christian, as if—despite D'Erreti's best efforts—the city is still hedging its bets, appeasing whatever gods might be out there. While the cardinal celebrates Mass in the Duomo, a fancy-dress parade will wind its way through the city, its main feature a tall decorated cart pulled by garlanded white oxen and filled with fireworks. Surrounded by flame-throwers and trumpeters, the *scoppio del carro,* as it's called, will finally come to a halt directly outside the doors, and as the service ends, the cardinal will release a mechanical white dove from above the high altar, sending it racing down a guy wire to dive-bomb the cart outside and, hopefully, set off a magnificent display of fireworks. The dove is supposed to contain flints collected by Mary Magdalene from the foot of the true cross, and the general idea is that if the fireworks explode with enough vigour, Florence will be happy and prosperous. If they fizzle, it'll be a rough twelve months.

Billy is adamant that we should all follow the parade together, and have the traditional glass of Prosecco on Ponte Vecchio afterwards before Henry treats us to a feast in the apartment at Torquata Tasso. She's even written invitations in her favourite purple gel pen. Ours arrived in the mail yesterday, and while we've decided we'll join them for the parade and the fireworks, we're ducking out of the feast because Pierangelo's arranged a special treat. He's taking me to the Villa Michelangelo up in Fiesole for Easter lunch.

On the Ponte Vecchio, I stop to watch the river. A sculler glides by on the still, smoky water, and I wonder if he's the one who found Ginevra. He shoots out of the far side of the bridge, silent and straight as an arrow, glances up, sees me and smiles before he bends and pulls and bends and pulls again, rowing in perfect time with the metronome in his head.

The railings around the Cellini statue are festooned with padlocks painted with the initials and names of lovers who have vowed to stay true for ever. The shutters of the jewellers' shops are closed and locked down, making them look like rows of giant bread boxes. A few homeless people have been dossing out by the drinking fountain, their blankets neatly arranged, bulging plastic bags piled at their heads in makeshift pillows. Two of them are sitting up, getting ready to face the day, but one, still rolled in his sleeping bag, opens an eye clouded with dreams, and watches silently as I go by.

At the grocery, the signora's in a frenzy. The morning's pastries and papers have arrived, but Marcello hasn't, so she has to handle the line of customers herself. She's muttering crazily about irresponsible youth, telling every person she serves it would never have happened when she was a kid, as she drops croissants into brown paper bags and yells at the guy who's just arrived with the morning's strawberries. Secretly, I think she's enjoying herself, and when at last he arrives, Marcello seems to agree. He pulls up on the vegetable Vespa just as I'm leaving, and when the signora shouts, he winks at me. His eyes are shiny and he doesn't even blush when I wink back. Maybe he had a really good night at the wine bar last night. I catch the strawberry he plucks from a box and throws to me as I pass.

The apartment is completely silent. I slip my shoes off so I won't make a noise clacking around on the marble floors, and slide in my socks towards the kitchen. The door to Billy's room is ajar. I tiptoe over to close it so I won't wake her, and as I pull it to, I expect to see the shape of her body in the bed, clothes hung over the brass rail, shoes tipped on the floor. But the room isn't even dark. The big metal blind is up, and her pale yellow counterpane is tucked over her pillow. I look round the door and see her belt, still draped over the back of her chair where I left it on Monday morning.

Stepping inside, I see that her earrings are on top of her dresser too, right where I put them. They're surrounded by lipsticks, barrettes and an array of bottles of hair goop. Postcards of Billy's favourite paintings are stuck into the edge of the mirror. Bronzino's portraits of baby Marie de Medici and her mother, Eleanora di Toledo, stare back at me. It's strange, but of all of us, Billy is probably the best student. She is the one who actually takes notes, and reads books. A stack of them, Gombrich and Burkhardt on the Renaissance, and Malraux's *Voices of Silence*, are piled on her bedside table beside a framed, muzzy picture of a house sitting in the middle of an overgrown field that she told me once was her grandfather's farm, or rather what was left of it after he was ruined by the Depression and the Dust Bowl.

Suddenly I feel like a kid caught snooping and whirl round, sure I'll see Billy standing in the doorway. But there's no one there. Unnerved, I tiptoe out. Then, for good measure, I pull the door closed behind me.

In the kitchen, I dump my bag on the table, throw the French windows open and step out onto the balcony where a thin layer of grit sticks to the bottom of my socks. All of Sophie's windows are still shuttered, so the whole opposite wing of the house looks as if it has its eyes closed. Back inside, I put the coffee on and sing to myself, out of tune. Then, while the little silver pot begins to perk and bubble, I wander into the living room.

Milky sunlight spills through the tall window and the cushions are mussed up on the couch, a pair of Billy's pink socks balled beside them. There's a wine glass, one of Signora Bardino's good ones, on top of a pile of books on the side table, a brown film forming in its base that will crystallize and be hell to clean. And there are the postcards. Billy's been at it again, but this time she's pushed the coffee table back so she had the whole rug to work on. Which was necessary, I guess, because since I saw it last, her collection's grown.

I glance at the couch and the glass and I can almost see her, wine in one hand, butt in the other, surveying her creation. There's even a dent in the cushion where she sat. The coffee pot screams suddenly, like a train coming into the station, and I go to take it off the heat, pour myself a cup and come back. As I sink down onto the sofa, I notice the green tin ashtray wedged in beside the books. Sure enough there's one stubbed-out cigarette, its filter perfectly ringed in bright red lipstick.

This time, Billy's made a sort of spiral. The outer circle are scenes that feature Florence: Ghirlandaio's pictures from the life of Mary with the Loggia dei Lanzi in the background, di Bonaiuto's scenes from the Spanish Chapel, a marriage procession on its way to the Baptistery, the Santa Trinità from Stradano's fresco in Palazzo Vecchio. And of course, the burning of Savonarola.

As the pictures circle inwards, the city recedes and groups of people become more prominent. There's Piero della Francesca's eerie resurrection from Sansepolcro, the expulsion of Adam and Eve from the Brancacci Chapel, and a bunch of others: Christ mocked from San Marco, spat at and whipped by disembodied heads and hands, a Giotto crucifixion, a St Sebastian I can't place, a naked woman with a halo and long dark hair covering her body, and another holding a tray. After that, the postcards spiral inwards in a series of Madonnas. Botticelli, Simone Martini, Michelangelo, Raphael. And the photo of Billy as a Perugino.

Without meaning to, I give a slight start because right in the centre of the coil there's a postcard of a painting I've never seen, but recognize anyways. A young man raises his sword and drives creatures, fleeing, from a garden. They stumble and crawl and fly, and among them is a monkey with the face of an old woman. Her breast is wizened, arms scraggly, and she walks upright, four red bags dangling from her bony naked shoulders.

It's grotesque. Billy must have looked all over to find it, combed the postcard kiosks and museum shops. Who knows? Maybe she even went to Mantua to retrieve this trophy. Because that's clearly what it is—the centrepiece of her collection that she's left here, displayed on the living-room rug for me to see.

Forget performance art, this is make-your-point art. Rub-Mary's-nose-in-it art. I sit there for a second staring at the snake coil of images, then I get up and leave the room, slamming the door behind me.

It's all I can do not to go back into the living room and slew Billy's postcards across the floor. But I don't. She did this to get a reaction out of me, just like she tried to goad me in front of all the others on Saturday night, or left my make-up all messed up on my bureau, and I'm damned if I'll give her the satisfaction. I feel as if we're in a sort of silent battle of the wills, and I have to marshal my forces. Telling her anything was a mistake, I think. Really, really stupid. I should have followed my instincts and shut up. I take a long bath to calm down, and afterwards I apply myself to cleaning the kitchen with grim determination.

I scrub and polish and dust, even stand on the table and take a few wipes at the chandelier. Then I wash the outside table and chairs and sweep our little balcony, sending a shower of grit and what look like seeds cascading over the edge, down past, and very possibly through, Signora Raguzza's open window. I am considering washing the French windows when the phone rings.

I know it won't be Pierangelo because he always uses my cell phone, so it's probably for Billy. I stand in the hall for a second, my hand on the living-room door knob, wondering if I should just let it go through to the machine. Then I figure it might be Henry, or someone else looking for me, and answer it. As I reach for the receiver on Signora Bardino's little ormolu desk, I'm extra careful to step over the postcards, not disturb a single one.

'Bill?' the voice on the other end says when I pick up, and it takes me a second to realize it's Kirk.

'It's Mary,' I say. 'Sorry, she's not here.'

There's a longish pause. 'Well,' he says finally, 'do you know where she is?'

Despite the fact that Kirk can't see me, I shake my head. I guess I was assuming they'd made their fight up and she was over there.

'No idea. I came back a couple of hours ago, but she was already gone when I got here. I thought,' I add, 'she might be with you.'

Kirk gives a long and theatrical sigh. 'I don't think she's talking to me. At least, she hasn't replied to any of my messages. Goddam it,' he says. 'I told her to get a cell, I even offered to buy her one, but she won't let me. I'm sick of pleading with her through Bardino's machine!' I look down at the little black box, but the red number says 0. Billy must have wiped them off.

'Look, I'm sure she'll get over it,' I say. Although, to be honest, I'm not sure what 'it' is, and I'm not as optimistic as I sound. Billy can probably stay mad for quite a while—the wiped messages aren't a good sign—but the poor guy sounds so miserable that I feel I have to try to say something positive. 'Look, if you got her a cell, she probably wouldn't turn it on anyways,' I point out. 'You know what she's like. She won't even wear her watch. I'll get her to call you,' I add. 'As soon as she shows up. I promise. You know how she can be.'

'Yeah. Crazy.'

'She'll forget about it sooner or later. Probably sooner. Bet you.'

Kirk makes a humming sound as though he's not so sure. 'Well, I'll be here,' he says finally. 'And we're supposed to be at the bar tomorrow, for lunch. Signor Catarelli's joining us, at one. I left Billy a message. The poor guy's back from Genoa and La Bardina's dispatching him, as an Easter treat, to explain the inner meaning of the *Primavera*. Catarelli's Botticellis.'

He puts the phone down and I hop my way back out of the room, jumping over Billy's art installation, 'Very innovative, Bill,' I say out loud. 'But not convenient.'

Then I write a big note in her purple gel pen: 'For God's Sake Call Kirk, He's Going Crazy!!!' and stick it on her bedroom door where she can't possibly fail to see it.

In the afternoon I go to the covered market and do all the shopping for Easter weekend. That's our deal: I'll shop if Piero cooks. Then I spend the afternoon reading. When he comes home, we have a drink on the roof terrace while he tells me about a big series they're thinking of doing on Italian female writers, and then he starts dinner while I lie on the couch, listening to the news. My Italian is good enough that I can get most of it, but I still have to concentrate, so the first time he calls from the kitchen, I don't really hear what he's asking. The second time, he sticks his head round the door.

'Do you want to come to the football tomorrow night? There're tickets for a bunch of us from the office.'

I shake my head. 'You go, have a good time.'

It's nice of him to ask, but I'm not really a fan, and I know these tickets are precious. Besides, it's good for him to go out and do boy stuff without me. 'I'll stay at the apartment,' I yell. That way he won't have to worry about coming home smelling of beer. Not that I'd mind. But I ought to make things up with Billy. I'm not mad about the red bags any more, just curious as to what the hell she's been up to.

'You sure? You're welcome.'

'I'm sure. Have fun.'

I wave and he vanishes back into the kitchen. A few minutes later he appears again. 'The big yellow dish,' he says. 'I swear it was under the sink.'

There's something about the illegal sex trade and human trafficking on the news, and a map with complicated lines I'm trying to follow, so without even thinking I say: 'Graziella borrowed it.' Then I think, *Oh, shit*, and sit up.

Piero is standing in the kitchen doorway, his head cocked

like a dog that's just heard a strange noise. 'Graziella?' he asks. 'She came and took it?'

I nod, reach for the remote and turn off the TV.

'When? Did she leave a note? I didn't see it.'

'No.' I look at him for a second. There's no way out of this. 'It was about a week, ten days ago. I was here. I gave it to her.'

Maybe I can do this without actually breaking my promise to Graziella. If he doesn't ask, I won't tell him she was going to Monte Lupo. Or who with.

'You met her?'

I can't tell whether Pierangelo's annoyed with me or not, and I nod again, trying to read his face.

'I was here doing laundry. Actually, she frightened the life out of me. I didn't hear her come in. I thought I was by myself, and the next thing I knew, there was somebody in the kitchen.'

Pierangelo thinks about this for a second, then he laughs. 'Typical,' he says. 'In Zella's world the intercom was never invented. So,' he asks, 'what did you think?'

He doesn't seem to be annoyed with me for not mentioning it, which is a relief.

'Of Graziella? She's beautiful. Stunning. She looks like you, has your eyes exactly. It's almost creepy. And nice. She was very nice to me,' I add quickly in case he gets the wrong idea.

A wide fatherly smile breaks across Pierangelo's face, and I remember what Graziella said, that she was his child and Angelina was Monika's. Now, looking at her father, it's patently true. He's flushed with pride.

'Well, I'm glad you liked her,' he says. 'I've been meaning to introduce you, but with Zella at college...' He shrugs. 'The plate's a pain, though,' he adds. 'It's one of my favourites. Let's just hope she doesn't break it. Zella's got a good heart, but she's not the most careful person on earth.' He laughs as he turns back into the kitchen.

I sit on the couch for a second. It feels like a window of

opportunity is open here, and if I don't ask now, I might never have the chance again. I get up slowly and follow him into the kitchen.

'Piero?'

He turns round from whatever he's doing at the stove. With a spatula in one hand and an apron almost as big as Marcello's tied around him, he looks like one of those TV celebrity chefs.

'When Graziella was here—' I take a breath, feeling as though I have to say this all right now, really fast, or I might never say it at all. 'When she was here,' I start again, 'she said something about your mother.'

Something happens to Pierangelo's eyes. Their pale warm green dulls, as if he's retreated behind them, taken a step back inside his own head. 'What?' His voice even sounds flat.

Damn, I think, this was a mistake. But I can't stop now. I screw up my courage and spit it out. 'She said that you and Monika were fighting over Monte Lupo, that Monika wanted it, but that she shouldn't get it because it belonged to your mother. Your real mother. When I asked her what she meant, Graziella said that you never really knew her. That you were raised by your aunt and uncle. It wasn't Zella's fault,' I add quickly. 'I mean, she assumed I knew.'

Pierangelo stands there looking at me and I honestly have no idea what he's thinking. He puts the spatula down, slowly, turns the stove off so whatever it is he's got in the sauté pan won't burn, and walks to the refrigerator. He opens it and takes out some white wine. 'Want some?'

'Sure.'

Pierangelo pours us two glasses, slowly, as if now it's him weighing up what to say, what to tell me and not tell me. 'What else did Zella say?'

He hands me my glass and I shrug, choosing my words carefully. I've got poor Graziella in enough trouble already. 'Just that,' I say finally. As if 'that' wasn't enough.

Pierangelo looks as though he doesn't believe me, or knows

Graziella better. 'Nothing about Angelina?' He sips his wine. 'Or her mother?'

'Oh sure.' This is almost a relief, I was working myself up to lying to him about the boyfriend. 'She said Monika was angry with you. That she blamed you for everything, and that Angelina sided with her, but she'll probably come round. She also said Monika was crazy,' I add. 'Crazy as a bug, actually.' I leave out that she called her mother a bitch.

Pierangelo actually smiles. 'Well, she's right there.' He shakes his head. 'Monika's a very unhappy woman. Partly my fault. She's been very unhappy for a long time, and she blames me. According to her, I ruined her life.' He sips again, swishes the wine around in his mouth and swallows. Then he says, 'Angelina no longer loves me.'

'I'm sure that's not true.' Pierangelo has made the words matter-of-fact, but I can hear the hurt underneath. 'Really. She's just hurt. She's just trying to defend her mother. From what Graziella said, Monika makes it that way.'

Pierangelo shakes his head. 'You don't know Angelina,' he says, and turns back to the stove.

I watch his back for a second. Then I put my glass down and come up behind him, put my arms around his waist and lay my cheek against his back. I can feel the warmth of his skin through the fine material of his shirt. He pats my hand.

'She'll get over it,' I insist. But Pierangelo doesn't say anything.

Finally I kiss his back, let go of him and retrieve my glass.

'She will.' I take a sip of the cold wine and feel a pang of relief as he smiles at me over his shoulder, normal again. I thought his mother would be the sore point, I had no idea about Angelina. Probably, I think, this has more to do with the rivalry between the sisters, each of them staking out a parent, than with Piero himself. And it doesn't sound as though Monika helps.

'Why didn't you ever tell me?' I ask a minute later. 'About your mom?'

Pierangelo is layering something in a baking dish now, bending down to check the heat in the oven and slide it in, so I can't see his face.

'I guess,' he says as he shuts the oven door, 'because I don't think of her that way.' He straightens up and picks up his glass. 'As my mother, I mean. She wasn't.' He shrugs and grins. 'What do you want me to say? She gave me away. So I gave her away.'

'Did you ever know her?'

'No.' He shakes his head. 'I never met her. I was very little, a baby.'

He turns back to the counter and starts rinsing things, putting them in the dishwasher. 'I think she tried to contact us, a couple of times. I don't really know. And Graziella's right, she did leave me Monte Lupo. Not that there was anyone else. She didn't have any other children.' He shrugs. 'But it doesn't matter, *cara*. Really. My aunt was a wonderful mother.' Pierangelo turns round, wipes his hands on his apron and smiles at me. 'That's what she was,' he says. 'My mother. I didn't need another one. One Italian mama is enough for any boy.'

He comes across the room, puts his finger under my chin and kisses me. 'Anything else you want to know about me?' he asks.

'Yes.' I put my hands on his hips, feel the supple curve of his waist. Tug at the knot in the apron strings.

'What?' Pierangelo is already unbuttoning the top of my blouse. His fingers brush my collarbone. His free hand reaches down and pulls at the zip of my jeans.

'Who was Ottavia?'

'A mistake,' Pierangelo says, and lifts me onto the counter so I can wrap my legs around him.

Chapter Fifteen

THE NEXT DAY, my note is exactly where I left it. I stand in the hall looking at it for a second, then open Billy's bedroom door, half expecting to find her burrowed in her high brass bed. But her room's the same as yesterday, empty.

Either she hasn't been here, or she has and simply left the note where it was. The third possibility is that she came back last night, saw what I wrote, and went straight to Torquato Tasso, where she stayed because she has made up with Kirk. I pull my cell phone out and call to ask, but all I get is Henry's voice on their machine. Kirk's cell goes straight to message and Henry's doesn't answer.

The kitchen is still pristine from my cleaning fit. Definitely no evidence of Billy here. She invariably hits it like a tornado, and there's not so much as a coffee ground out of place. The bathroom is undisturbed too. Her toothbrush is still beside the basin. Finally, just as I'm beginning to feel like I'm stalking some elusive animal through the jungle, watching for pug marks and broken branches, I find evidence of her in the living room. Her spiral of postcards still takes up the whole floor, but the picture in the centre, the bullseye so to speak, has been replaced. This morning, instead of Hate and her four nasty bags, it's a snapshot of Billy and me.

I crouch down and pluck the photo out of the spiral so I can get a better look at it. We're sitting at a café outside some-where, and I'm laughing, turning away from the camera, my streaky hair flying across one cheek. Next to me, Billy sits with one elbow on the table, holding the inevitable cigarette, smiling straight into the camera. I don't remember seeing this particular photo before, but that's hardly unusual. She has about a million, addicted as she is to her disposable cameras. She claims she's working on some kind of project, and she's always getting poor unsuspecting passers-by to take pictures of us. Tourists she pounces on. Shopkeepers. Waiters. I smile to myself, stand up and pocket it, sure it's meant for me, a weird Billy-esque peace offering. An apology for rubbing my nose in her discovery about the red bags.

The living room stinks of cigarette smoke, and when I look, sure enough, there's another butt in the ashtray. The lipstick's lavender this time. She really is incorrigible. The room smells as though she didn't even open the windows. The smoke's probably in Signora Bardino's precious curtains and cushions by now, and although I suspect it's too late to save us from a horrendous dry-cleaning bill, it's worth a try. I pick up the ashtray and the dirty wine glass from the side table, and hop across the post-cards to unlatch the French windows.

Too late, I realize it's a gusty day, and the latch gives as I turn the handle, blowing the doors open. The curtains huff, papers lift off the desk, rising and falling like leaves, and before I can do anything about it the wind slurs Billy's postcards, pushing the Madonnas into the devils, blowing the judgement of Christ up against the pierced, bleeding body of St Sebastian, and sending the naked hairy lady scooting under the couch. Sorry, Bill, I think, as I get down on my hands and knees and sweep the postcards into a pile, but I'll make it up to you. I'll buy a bottle of Prosecco and we can drink it on the balcony tonight, sitting at my shiny clean table. The naked lady, who I fish out from among the dust bunnies, turns out to be St Agnes. I don't know what the story with her hair is, but I'm sure Billy will have a good time telling me, especially if she makes it up.

While everything is pushed aside, I vacuum the rug. Then I replace the coffee table, put Billy's socks in the dirty laundry hamper, and finally do the Italian equivalent of Windexing the windows. When I'm done, it still smells like smoke—well, smoke and furniture polish—but it looks a whole lot better. I could spray some air freshener around but, given the way most of that stuff smells, I'd really rather opt for the cigarette smoke.

It's just before noon, and I figure I'll run out to buy the Prosecco now, and get something for dinner. In the end I even stop at the signora's shop for flowers. She has tulips in today, red ones, and I get two bunches. Inside, she's chatting with two of her friends and working the till herself. When I pay, she shakes her head and grumbles.

'An hour,' she says. 'I say an hour, and he's gone an hour and a half. For two deliveries. In my day, my father would have smacked me up the head.' Her father would have had to be pretty big, I think. Even as a girl, I bet the signora was no shrinking petal. 'I should have hired an old-age pensioner; at least he wouldn't waste time, chatting with his friends all day when he's supposed to be working. That's where he is now, you'll see. Probably taking his girlfriend out to lunch on my time,' she adds.

'On a scooter covered in carrots?' One of the other women winks at me.

'Girls today,' the signora says darkly as she drops the euros into my palm, 'maybe they dress proper, speak nice, but they're not so picky.'

'Young man like that, I don't care what it is painted with, I'd ride his scooter.'

This provokes a ribald burst of laughter, and the three women shout *ciao* and wave as I go back out onto the street.

The wind is still bouncing around, sending an empty cigarette pack scuttling along the gutter and the awning over the wine shop ripples and dances. Places are shutting for lunch now, crates disappear from the sidewalk and doors lock. Between that and the fact that it's the holiday, this corner of town is dead. For the next few hours, if you're not in a trattoria or sitting in a bar on a piazza, it will be possible to believe that no one lives here at all. A man passes me, shrugging his jacket on and talking into his cell phone at the same time, a sudden breeze sending his hair straight up, as though someone's riffled it from behind.

Despite the gusts it's not cold—a sure sign that spring is really here, teetering on the edge before it falls over into real warmth, the long predictable days and velvety dark blue nights that lead up to summer. I shift the bag with the Prosecco and the flowers from hand to hand as I turn the corner into our street and see, walking half a block ahead of me, a tall thin man in a blue shirt. Trotting behind him is a little black and white dog.

The sight is slightly unreal, the empty street and the blowing paper making them look like a film clip or a dream, something I've almost been expecting, and I stand watching, half wondering if they'll disappear, melt in the sunlight or turn sideways and vanish, but they don't. Instead, the man and the dog cross to the other sidewalk and step up into the shadowed portico of a tiny old church that is virtually opposite our building.

At first I think they've gone inside, which surprises me, because every time I've walked past the doors have been padlocked. Then a long thin leg ending in a running shoe appears out of the shadows, and the dog circles and lies down at the top of the steps. They're only finding a place to sit.

My heart is thudding uncomfortably, but I tell myself not to be stupid. It's broad daylight in the middle of the city. If I ever want to find out who this person is, now is the time. I step off the sidewalk and cross towards the church, wind fingering my hair.

As I get closer, I see that the space is bigger than it looks. Cool and shadowed, it makes a narrow little room where he's sitting, his back against the side wall, one long leg bent, the other stretched out, disjointed, like a puppet whose strings have been cut. One of the scuffed running shoes has a new lace, an incongruous bright white against the worn shoe, tied in a floppy bow. I flatter myself that the dog recognizes me, since he sits up and gives me his snaggle-toothed grin, but probably he just smells dinner in my bag. Now I make out the edge of a folded blanket and an old duffel bag. They've been dossing here.

I stop for a second, knowing that if I glance behind me I will see our living-room window, and the window of Billy's bedroom, looking down on us.

'Hi.' Finally I reach out to pat the little mutt.

The man's face is in shadow, one arm is propped on his knee, and, even though I'm prepared for it this time, I feel a creepy shock of recognition as our eyes meet. The familiar amber colour almost glows. Next to him there are two dented metal dishes for the dog, one with water in it, the other with some food.

'I've seen you before. At Santo Spirito. And in the Loggia dei Lanzi. You're one of the white men.'

He watches me while I speak, his face immobile, and I wonder for a second if he hasn't heard me. If maybe he's deaf, or blasted out of his mind on something. But although he's thin, his skin looks healthy, and he doesn't have that addled look druggies usually do. His big hands, which have a rime of dirt under the short clipped nails, don't twitch or jump. I try again, smiling this time.

'My name is Mary.' Maybe he's not Italian, I think. Maybe he doesn't speak it. The dog wriggles under my hand, sniffing towards my bag. 'Look,' I say in English. 'I have some extra. Would you like it?'

I open a bag, pull out one of the rolls I just bought, and then a package of mortadella. I'm not really sure why I'm doing this, or why I'm not scared, but I'm not. I hold the food out and the dog wags his tail.

'Here,' I say. 'Please.'

The dog hums in anticipation, and his owner looks at me before he shakes his head. Then he points. I'm not sure what it is at first. Some cheese? The Prosecco? Is he just another drunk? Something in my chest deflates at the idea. And then I understand. It's not the pecorino or the wine he wants, it's flowers. The tulips. I lift one of the bunches out and hand it to him, and just for a second I imagine I see him smile.

While he slips the rubber band off, I give the dog a couple of pieces of mortadella anyways, and break the bread into his dish. Then his owner leans down and props the flowers in the dog's water bowl. He holds them upright, his big square hands cradling the pale green stems and long pointed leaves, then he lets go, and the tulips fall in a fan, a bright splash of colour against the dank grey wall of the shuttered church.

We stare at them gravely before he nods, apparently satisfied.

I should go now. I don't want to crowd his space, this tiny bit of the city that, however temporarily, he's made his own.

'Mary,' I try again, enunciating in case he can lip-read. I tap my chest. '*Mi chiamo Maria*. Goodbye,' I add, as I step down onto the sidewalk. 'Happy Easter. Maria. *Mi chiamo Maria*.'

'He can't answer you.'

The familiar voice is so close behind me that I swear I feel a puff on the back of my neck. Whirling round, I find myself face to face with Rinaldo.

'He's a mute.'

Father Rinaldo is standing on the sidewalk outside the church portico, the long black skirt of his soutane blowing around his ankles, making him look vaguely as if he's at the helm of a ship. The sun is hitting his round cheeks, blushing them bright pink and shiny.

'What are you doing here?' I step down into the road, gripping my bags, my fingers twisting the cheap plastic handles as though Rinaldo might snatch them from me.

'The ministry, my child.' He smiles, towering above me, and I think again that he's a bigger man than I remember. It's his doll face and his soft slug fingers that are deceiving. 'It's Easter week,' Rinaldo says.

He gestures vaguely across the street as he speaks, and beyond him I see a couple of young men and a girl. I'd say they were university students, but they're dressed wrong. The boys are in dark slacks and long-sleeved shirts, the girl in a straight grey skirt and flat ugly shoes. Even at this distance I can tell she's wearing panty hose, thick cheap ones that make her young pretty legs look as if they've been painted beige. They're carrying bags of some kind, and the girl is bending over, trying to give a sheet of paper to a wino who sometimes hangs out by the corner and doesn't seem to want what she's offering.

'As Our Lord would have us do, in this, the week of his Passion, we are reaching out to the less fortunate,' Rinaldo says. 'Just as you are, Maria.'

I begin to object, to say that that was not what I was doing at all. Then, instead, I turn away. I have nothing to say to Rinaldo. Crossing the street towards our building, I try as hard as I can not to run, and not to feel the caress of his eyes on my back.

Safely inside our courtyard, I drop my bags and sit down on the lip of one of the huge pots, my hands shaking. The sun washes across the paving stones and a lemon leaf skitters into the portico while outside on the street I hear footsteps and the low perk of voices as Rinaldo and his acolytes pass by, spreading God's work through the city.

The first thing I spot when I round the fountain a half-hour later is the black wing of Kirk's coat. He and Henry and the Japanese girls are already at our table at the bar, and as I pull out a chair he turns on me.

'Where's Billy?' Kirk asks. But before I can say I don't know, we're set on by Ellen and Tony, who are climbing over the low plastic hedge, each of them holding Signor Catarelli by an elbow, as if they have him prisoner.

Kirk glares at me, as though Billy's vanishing act is my idea, and the Japanese girls shift uncomfortably in their chairs.

Henry smiles half-heartedly and shakes hands with Signor Catarelli, while Ellen, completely impervious to the atmosphere at the table, hands out postcards of the *Primavera*.

'Here,' she says. 'I bought one of these for everybody.' She beams and sits down as I stare at the card in my hand.

The last time I went to the Uffizi, the Botticelli room was too crowded, so I stuck with Simone Martini's slant-eyed Virgins, but here in my hand the three half-naked Graces still cavort on their field of flowers. Mercury still holds the clouds back, and Venus still blesses the scene with the sort of absent benevolence that makes her look as if she's stoned. All while Primavera herself scatters flowers from the skirt of her hippy dress. In the corner Zephyr, looking bluer and meaner than ever, grabs Flora, making her spit flowers.

Maybe it's just today, but I don't think so. The truth is, I've always found this picture slightly nightmarish. It has the dream-like effect of beauty on the surface, while something dark and bad is going on underneath. Zephyr's cold and blue-grey, like something dead, and I can almost feel his chilly hands on poor, pudgy Flora's soft white stomach. She's terrified, and the rest of them are oblivious. She screams and screams, but nobody takes any notice.

'So,' Signor Catarelli is saying, 'the three Graces may also be manifestations of Venus herself. Three aspects of one goddess, three images of one whole.'

'Just like the Trinity!' Ellen chirps.

'Jesus Christ,' Kirk mutters under his breath.

'Exactly,' Signor Catarelli smiles.

Bent over their notes, Ellen and Tony miss this exchange, and the Japanese girls are too busy eating. But Henry suppresses a smile as Signor Catarelli goes on, bringing his explanation to a close.

'It is an obscure picture,' he says. 'Which some argue only adds to its greatness; the fact that what seems clear on first glance becomes less clear the longer we gaze upon it. So we must accept that the images mean more than one thing at any given time.'

Ellen bursts into vigorous applause as he stops speaking, causing a brief flash of panic to dart across the poor man's face. His lunch sits untouched in front of him, and I'm sure he's terrified that now Ellen's going to pepper him with questions, preventing him from ever picking up his fork. Henry rescues him, pouring him a glass of wine and urging him to eat.

'I wonder if he was having second thoughts when he painted it,' Henry says. 'Botticelli, I mean. Didn't he finally reject humanism, end up a huge fan of Savonarola's?'

'Card carrying,' Kirk says. 'Right?'

Signor Catarelli nods, stabbing eagerly at his ravioli. 'According to Vasari, he felt a deep need to re-examine his faith in the last twenty years of his life. So the work becomes both prophetic and apocalyptic, and yet he cannot leave behind him the immense richness of Ficino's Neoplatonism, or perhaps the memory of his great patron, Lorenzo. Which God do you betray? In that way,' Signor Catarelli says, reaching for his glass, 'he typifies Florence.' He takes a sip and smiles ruefully. 'Perhaps,' he says, 'he typifies Italy. The seduction of beauty, literature, art. Petrarch, Dante, Michelangelo, Botticelli himself. The surface of the ocean. But underneath, always, there's that other tide, the pull, pull, pull of the church on our hearts.'

We have become so used to hearing jokes from him that there is a momentary silence at the table. A round, ageing man in a beautifully cut threadbare tweed jacket, Signor Catarelli looks at us and smiles, but there is nothing in his face but sadness.

It's perhaps a half-hour later when Ellen and Tony escort him away, their chatter as bright and sharp as broken glass.

'Well,' Henry says, 'that was certainly jolly. I think I'll have a grappa with my coffee to recover. Possibly two. Anyone else?' He signals to the waitress, and Kirk nods. He's fiddling with some-thing in his pocket, and I can't help thinking it's Billy's ring. I can practically see the tiny hearts pushing against his fingers.

'I would like one.' Mikiko looks back at us, widening her eyes when we all stare at her. 'Well, why not?' she says. 'We don't just drink tea, you know.'

Unexpectedly, it's Kirk who reaches over and pats her hand. 'We never thought you did,' he says. He smiles, looking almost as sad as Signor Catarelli, and when the waitress comes to the table, he tells her to bring a round of grappa for everyone. Then they all look at me, and this time it's Ayako who asks the question.

'So?' she says. 'Where's Billy?'

I tell them I don't know. That I haven't seen her because I haven't been at the apartment much, but that I do know she's been there. I describe the postcards, and the wiped-off messages on the machine. The cigarettes and the lipstick.

'Well,' Mikiko says finally, 'maybe she went away. Just for the day, or something. She said she wanted to see Siena. Maybe she decided to spend the night.'

'She's a big girl, she'll show up when she's ready.' Henry shrugs.

Kirk doesn't say anything. A second later the tiny glasses of grappa arrive, and he throws his back in one gulp. 'She could at least call,' he says.

'She could,' Henry agrees. 'But then she wouldn't really be Billy.'

Back in the apartment, I turn on all the lights. The wind has stopped, and it's just warm enough to sit outside, so I wipe the table again and put the tulips in the centre. At dusk, I set the table for two, using Signora Bardino's pretty flowered plates and mismatching old-fashioned silver. It looks lovely, like a scene from one of those movies about Americans who come to Italy and make all their dreams come true. I even find a candle lamp and light the flame so it flickers in the glass. Then I sit down to wait.

There's the occasional click of steps from Signora Raguzza's apartment, a rustle of voices. Someone turns on the lights in the courtyard. The lemon trees throw shadows, filigree patterns against the walls of Sophie-Sophia's wing of the building. After a while I go back inside, take the salami, cheeses, prosciutto and olives I've bought and lay it all out on a serving plate. I put the crusty rolls in a little porcelain basket and lift two wine glasses down from the top shelf of the dresser. Then I stand at the rail, watching the darkness under the archway, waiting to hear the clang of the gate and see Billy's figure thicken out of the dark, the gold crown of her hair sparkling in the light.

At just past eight, there's a burst of voices. The security gate clangs, footsteps ring on the paving stones, and I wonder who she's brought with her. But when they emerge from under the archway, I see a middle-aged couple, well dressed and dragging two small children. The woman is carrying a covered dish, hanging on to it precariously as she hauls a little boy in best clothes, a mini dark blue blazer and long pants. The man has a bottle of champagne, and looks slightly as though he's contemplating thunking it over the head of the little girl who hangs on his free hand.

Signora Raguzza's family coming for dinner on Holy Thursday.

'Don't you want to see Nonna?' the man demands, as they disappear through the lower door. A second later I hear clattering on the stairs and a burst of voices.

At nine I pour myself a glass of red wine, pick at the salami and eat most of the olives. At ten I put the food away. At eleven-fifteen, Signora Raguzza's family leaves. The lights go off in the courtyard and I clear the table on the balcony, bring the tulips in, and tie the latch of the French windows in the kitchen with some cooking string I find in the back of a drawer.

Kirk's right, I think, she could at least call. Then I tell myself that she assumes I'm at Pierangelo's, and it's no big deal. The 'gift' has probably let her down, so she doesn't know I'm sitting here waiting for her. I imagine her in a bar in Lucca or Siena. Maybe she made it all the way to Ravenna to see the mosaics, and went on to Ferrara or even to Venice, where right now she's sipping spumante by the Grand Canal and seducing twenty-year-olds. I check the phone in the living room, listen to the empty buzz of the dial tone as if it could tell me something, then check my cell's turned on and prop it on the side table next to my head while I lie on the couch, reading.

I don't know what time it is when the book falls onto my chest, maybe midnight. I should go to bed, I think, but instead I pull Signora Bardino's satin throw off the back of the couch and read one more chapter. This time, when the book falls out of my hand, it lands on the floor.

I hear it vaguely, a thud, and reach up and turn off the lamp as I close my eyes. I'll go to bed, I think, when Billy comes home. After I've talked to her. Which will be any second, because I can hear her keys in the door.

'Bill!' I sit up with a start.

My heart's racing, banging all through my body, in my ears, my throat, my stomach. Fragments of dreams jangle around, and I realize I'm clutching the satin throw, pleating it into a rumpled ball. I sit there in the crackly stillness, knowing I shouldn't move, and wondering what woke me up.

Street light filters in through the tall windows, making the room black and white. I slide my eyes to the living-room door. I can see a wedge of the kitchen: the corner of the table, a block of floor, the white stripe of the linen blind on the French windows. Nothing moves. It feels too still, as if the apartment's holding its breath. Is someone in there? Or just down the hall? Around the corner, flattened against the wall beside the spindly ornamental chair? Is that what woke me up? The skin on my face feels hot, as if someone's held their hands on my cheeks while I slept.

A knot of panic lodges in my throat, and my hand reaches backwards, groping, fingers fastening on the wine glass I brought in from the balcony. Shoved hard, straight into someone's face, it would do some damage. I slip my bare feet out from under the throw and place them on the cold marble floor.

It seems to take for ever to stand up, to make my knees straighten and bear my own weight. The throw slithers to the floor with a hiss, and I freeze, waiting to see if the sound alerted whoever's here. But nothing moves. So finally I take the first step, the wine glass held at my chest, grasped by the stem, my elbow bent like a spring.

The second step is easier. The third brings me to the door. I can see into the kitchen now. It's empty. The French windows are still tied shut. Across from me, the bathroom door is ajar and my bedroom door is closed, just the way I left it. So is Billy's. Then something shifts, a movement in the air, less than a sigh, and my eyes focus on the end of the hall, and the tall front door. There's someone on the other side. I can feel them. I can feel their heart beating.

'Billy?' I whisper. But nothing moves.

I slide forward, past the half-moon table and the little chair. Past her bedroom door, until I'm not six inches from the polished mahogany panels. Until I can put my cheek against the dark glossy wood, my lips to the crack above the big brass locks.

'Billy?' Her name is no more than a breath.

'Billy, is that you?'

Then I realize there's something else, a smell, wafting under the door. Sliding through the cracks. Sweet and redolent and familiar, acacia hangs in the night air like half-heard music.

Chapter Sixteen

'DO YOU REALLY think it was her?' Pierangelo asks. 'Why would she do that?'

'I don't know. I have no idea.'

It is just past eight in the morning, and I have caught him on his way to work. A car honks in the background and I can hear the rush of traffic as he walks along the street.

'So you didn't actually see her?'

'Well, no.'

I'm beginning to wish I hadn't made this call. 'I didn't open the door,' I add. 'It was three in the morning.' As if that explains everything. Which, from the sound of his voice, Pierangelo thinks it does.

'Ah,' he says. Then he adds, 'Look, *cara*, something woke you up and you got spooked. It happens. As for Billy, the Three Little Maids from School are probably right. Most likely she took off for a few days.' Pierangelo has adopted Kirk's name for the Japanese girls. I told him about lunch yesterday and Mikiko's suggestion. *It's Easter,* I hear Billy saying, *maybe I'll go away for three days and come back again.*

'She could have missed her train coming home and decided to spend in the night in Siena,' Piero says, 'or Lucca or—'

'Mantua.' I told him about the postcards too.

'Yeah, OK, Mantua. Look,' he says, 'maybe she got sick of Dracula and his bat cape and sushi and ran off with the guy in the mask for a lost weekend. It's been known to happen.'

'So why doesn't she call?'

'Why should she? For all she knows you're staying here all week. It's not like you tell her what you're doing all the time,' he points out. 'She's not your mother.'

I seem to remember telling Billy the same thing relatively recently.

'Are you sure you're OK?' Pierangelo asks.

'Yes, I'm fine.' I laugh, but it sounds more like a cackle.

'Why don't you just come home?' Piero says. 'I have a meeting in about a minute, and I'm late. But I'm going to finish early. Even the paper packs up on Good Friday. We'll go somewhere.'

'So, call me when you're done,' I make my cackle voice brisk and businesslike. I'm going up to Settignano this morning,' I add. 'But I'll be back.'

'I should hope so.' Pierangelo laughs. 'OK, *cara*, I'll call you. I have to go.' Another horn blares and I imagine him darting across the street. '*Ciao, ciao*,' he shouts.

'Be careful! I love you,' I shout back, battling the sound of the cars, but the phone's already dead, and I realize too late I didn't even ask him how the football was.

I look at the phone in my hand, feeling like an utter fool. I don't know how long I stood in front of the apartment door last night, convinced there was someone on the other side. It could have been a minute or a half-hour. Eventually, I told myself that if I really thought Billy was standing out there playing some weird hide-and-seek game, I should open the door. Or go and call Pierangelo, who I knew would come over right away, even if it was three in the morning. The idea of doing that and having to explain myself sobered me up pretty fast, and finally I settled for sliding the half-moon hall table under the door knob, wedging it there so if someone tried to come in they'd virtually have to break it in half. I didn't share that part with Pierangelo. Or how I had looked in the closets and under the bed and in the shower. I pull the photo of us out of my back pocket, smooth it out, and look at her. 'Thanks a ton,' I say. But all Billy does is grin.

I hadn't actually planned to go to Settignano until I realized what a witless wreck I was sounding like, but now it seems quite a good idea. There's a garden up there I've been meaning to visit, and it's going to be a beautiful day. I might even stay for lunch. It's been a while since I did any drawing.

Suddenly energized, I collect my sketchbook and pencils, decide I don't want to take the time to go for pastries, and have one of the rolls from last night with my coffee instead. As I'm putting the bag away, I come face to face with the platter of cold cuts, more than I'll ever eat, so I make two thick sandwiches. Then I add a bottle of water and an orange and put it all in a plastic bag. As I lock the front door and go down the stairs, I remind myself to check next time I'm in the signora's shop and see if she carries dog biscuits. It's silly, but I feel as excited as I used to when I was a little kid and had a special present to bring home from school for Mamaw, a clay ashtray, or autumn leaves ironed between sheets of waxed paper. I close the security gate, drop my keys in my bag, and trot across the street to the little church, bearing my improvised picnic.

But when I get there, the portico is empty. I bite back a pang of disappointment. There are no dog dishes, no duffel bag. In fact, there's no sign that anyone's ever been here, nothing at all but three crimson splashes against the stone; tulip petals curled as tight as babies' fists.

The garden is beautiful, and I stay much longer than I'd planned.
I wander from 'room' to 'room', through separate mini-gardens
walled by high, square-clipped hedges. Water plays in fountains
and pools, and the view over Florence from the top terraces is
sublime. I start some sketches, and as my hand moves over the
page I feel as if I'm getting myself back, as if it's OK to care about
landscaping, and the shapes of walls and buildings again. By
the time I finally put my pencils away, it's almost two, and I'm
starved. I'd thrown the sandwiches out and Pierangelo hasn't
called, so I wander into the village where I buy a newspaper, find
a trattoria with an outside table and settle down.

I'm on coffee when the bill arrives and my phone cheeps. A
text starts, then goes blank: failed connection. I pay and it comes
through again. *In Bargello. Meet me.*

It's one of Piero's favourite museums, and if I hurry I'll just
be able to catch the bus.

Because of the holiday it's crowded, and I have to stand. We
swing round corners and lurch into the centre of town, and by
the time I get off I'm hot and a little crabby. My phone cheeps
while I'm standing in line for my ticket. *Where R U?* I guess he
needs to know exactly. *BRgeloticket,* I text back. *U?* But there's
no reply, so I switch it off and drop it into my bag. He'll find
me.

When I get to the window I find out that the museum is
closing at five this afternoon because it's Good Friday. As she
takes my money, the girl reminds me I have only an hour. As
I cross the courtyard, I look up and see dark sky. Clouds have
been gathering all afternoon, and now a sharp squall of rain
throws itself against the walls.

The first room is still crowded despite the late hour. I keep
a weather eye for Piero, but don't spot him, and am distracted
instead by the child Eros perched on his pillar. His baby wings
sprout from his back, not yet big enough to carry him into flight,

his pudgy legs and arms stretch as he reaches for the sky. I have some talent with pencils and paint, but I can't imagine what it would be like to be able to sculpt, to release faces and figures trapped in stone, ensnare souls in bronze. Most people come here for the Davids, Donatello's long-haired naked boy, and Verrocchio's Roman-skirted youth who stands with the monumental head of Goliath weeping at his feet. But I love some of the odder pieces, the sad-faced Marzocco lion, paw resting on his shield, Donatello's sweet St George, who looks as though he feels faintly sorry for the dragon, and the still marble busts of forgotten young men and women who died five centuries ago in Florence.

I wander into the chapel, look at the ghostly Giotto frescoes, and linger over the strange collections of jewels and daggers and coins trapped below the glass. Billy loved these cases. She said they were the best fleamarket display in the city.

By the time I come back into the main gallery there are fewer people. They've stopped selling tickets now, so those who trickle away are no longer replaced. If Pierangelo is here he's probably up on the third floor, with the displays of armour and weapons. The little boy in him still loves that stuff, lances and pikes, swords and shields. Secretly, I think he believes he's reincarnated, and that in some former life he was a *condottiero*, fighting for the glory of his city. The ragged Baptist, his eyes hungry and crazy-looking from a diet of locusts and honey, stares at me as I walk past him out onto the loggia.

The roof out here is painted with stars. Under them, Giambologna's birds rest on their marble pedestals. The owl leans forward, its eyes beady, something like a scowl on its face. The big hawk digs its talons into bronze earth and twists its neck, beak sharp and ready for prey. Beyond the stone pillars, the rain falls steadily now, muffling noise as a school group clatters down the steps, the teacher stopping to point at the crests of the *Podestàs*, the mayors of Florence who occupied this fortress before they moved to the Palazzo Vecchio. Their shields are mounted on the lower pillars, not feet from where a scaffold once stood beside the fountain. The fact that this was once a prison probably interests the kids a lot more than sculpture. Watching them, I wonder how many people died here and why, what crimes they confessed to, whether they had committed them or not. The children get herded away. Rain slicks the courtyard stones, but for centuries they ran with blood. Crimson, like the glint on the puddles.

I blink. And blink again. But I'm not imagining it. It's there, a shimmering wash of red on the mirror-like surface. It's only on the puddles, so it must be a reflection, from above. And sure enough, when I look up, there, standing in one of the leaded windows on the third floor, is Billy in her red dress.

Her outline is blurry behind the diamond-paned glass. She raises her arm and waves. Startled, I wave back. Then I call out, and realize she'll never hear me.

'Wait!' I gesture towards the stairway, and hurry down the loggia, making for the long flight of stone steps that leads to the upper floor. She watches me, a column of red, her face nothing but a pale smear behind the rain-streaked glass. Just before I get to the door, I wave again. And she waves back.

My phone doesn't have caller ID for numbers I haven't entered, and since Pierangelo has three phones—any one of which he can be using at any time—my phone sometimes knows him and sometimes doesn't. I just assumed it was him who texted this afternoon, but now I realize it must have been Billy. What she is doing here, and why she is wearing her red party dress, I have no idea, but I'm sure she'll tell me. I reach the top of the last flight and push the door, praying they haven't closed it yet for the night. But it swings under my hand, and I slip through before a guard can come along and stop me.

The glass cases up here hold porcelain, a mishmash collection of figurines, plates on little legs, and cups with etched scenes on them, the sort of stuff I imagine Signora Bardino's house to be full of. They wink under display lights as I trot by, making for the end door that leads to the armour gallery, where Billy had to be standing. Typical of her, I think, not to just call the apartment. Or, for that matter, my cell—using her voice instead of messages. Typical of her to spring surprises. I remember the set of steps at the Belvedere. If, as Henry pointed out, she did things normally, she wouldn't be Billy.

Just as I reach the end of the long cases, the lights go out. Sure enough, it's five p.m. on the dot. I push open the armour-gallery door, and step into twilight.

Life-sized knights ride model horses down the centre of the long room. Dressed for war, their mounts are covered in ornate silver. Embossed faded fabric hangs from their flanks. The knights' visors are down, their shields raised. Long pikes, lethal and tipped with steel, are mounted on the walls, hanging above display cases of swords and hand-to-hand combat knives. Suits of armour stand here and there, hollow, and looking like giants.

'Billy?' My voice reverberates, bounces off the thick stone walls and echoes back at me. 'Where are you?'

I walk up the gallery between the cases of weapons and the mounted cavalcade towards the window where she must have been standing, braced for her to jump out from behind a suit of armour. Expecting to hear her disembodied laugh.

'Billy?' I stop. There's the soft pat-pat of rain against glass, but nothing else. Could she have mistaken my hand signal? Gone downstairs to meet me?

'Billy, are you here?'

I walk a few more steps, to the window at the very end of the gallery, and when I look down I see the loggia across the court-yard below me, the archway where I was, empty. Could I have seen something else? A red flag or banner? I look around, but there's nothing like that, nothing red that could have been so close to the glass. And, besides, she waved. A flash of exasperation shoots through me. 'Damn it, Billy,' I say out loud, then the door closes. I hear the thud as it hits the frame, and the click of a latch.

'Billy, come on. Cut it out.' Anger ripples through the words now. She will probably call it 'a sense of humour failure' but, between this and last night, I've about had enough.

Watery shadows worm their way across the floor, and I think of all the times Billy has snuck up on me. Remember how quiet she can be when she wants. Without meaning to, I edge towards the end of the gallery, looking for a way out. Usually there are connecting doors. But not here. This is just another wall of armour, iron balls attached to chains and studded with spikes, helmets with no faces behind them.

'Billy! Stop it!' I shout. 'I'm scared!'

But there's no reply.

My throat goes, dry and my tongue sticks to the roof of my mouth. I realize my hands are trembling and I clutch the strap of my bag harder to stop them, remembering the alley near the Carmine when I thought she was following me. When I saw her. And it wasn't her.

I slip one hand down inside the soft suede of my bag, feeling for my phone. All I have to do is get my hand around it, punch '1' and Pierangelo will hear me. My fingers hit my wallet, my new purse, my pencil case, all the other junk I keep, scrabbling, because a stifled, hot feeling is rising up in me. The walls feel as if they're sliding inward. Then a shadow moves, and I panic.

I whip around the horse in front of me, throw myself towards the door, and scream just once before my feet fly out from under me. The floor is slippery, the phone shoots out of my hand, and I skid into something heavy and metallic, bringing it crashing down with me as I fall.

Pierangelo comes right away. When he arrives, I am sitting in the museum administrator's office throwing what Mamaw would call 'a hissy fit.' Specifically, I am insisting they call Pallioti. I've more or less threatened to sit here until they do.

'Birdseed!' I announce to Pierangelo when he comes in. He stares at me and I hold my hands out, show him how it still clings to the arms of my sweater and soles of my shoes. 'It was

all over the floor! And I saw her,' I add, my voice rising dangerously. 'I know I saw her.'

The administrator, a middle-aged man in a tweed jacket and
a tie with little lions on it, sits behind his desk looking worried. The
head of security looks worried too. I did no damage to the suit of
armour I pulled over, but, as far as my story goes, they're baffled.
They just think I'm crazy, because no one can remember a woman
fitting Billy's description either entering or leaving the Bargello
this afternoon, especially not one wearing a red party dress. And
they admit they have no idea where the birdseed came from.

I have been clutching a little pile of it in my palm, and
Pierangelo finally persuades me to dribble it into a paper cup,
but even then I won't surrender it to anyone but Pallioti. There's
a sick, twisting feeling in my stomach, something writhing, and I
need to see the *ispettore* the way, in my previous life, I sometimes
needed to see a priest. When he arrives twenty minutes later, I am
so relieved I actually start to cry.

Pallioti looks exactly the same as I remember him. I'm not
even sure he isn't wearing the same suit and tie, soft nondescript
grey and red silk. He pulls up a chair and watches me with his still,
grey eyes, then, after Pierangelo has handed me his handkerchief,
he says, 'I wish I could welcome you back to Florence in happier
circumstances, signora.'

I rub my hands across my eyes, trying to stop the tears that
are streaming down my face. Pierangelo kneads my shoulder.

'Thank you for coming,' he says to Pallioti, who inclines his
head, but doesn't take his eyes off me.

Pallioti watches me the same way he did when I was lying flat
on my back in the hospital two years ago, and for some reason I
find his gaze calming, like a cool hand on my forehead. Eventually
he says, 'I only know what Signor Sanguetti told me on the phone.
Why don't you tell me what happened yourself?'

And so I do. Haltingly at first, and then faster, as if the words
are a ball bouncing downstairs, I tell him about last night, and
today. And then I tell him everything I know about Billy, which
I realize isn't actually very much. And only what she's told me,

which may or may not be true. When I'm done, I hand him the paper cup.

'It was on the floor,' I say. 'In the armour gallery. I slipped on it. It wasn't there when I went in.'

Pallioti looks at the cup, his eyes impassive, then he glances at the museum administrator and the security guard. 'Perhaps,' he says, 'gentlemen, you'd be so good as to excuse us for a moment?'

At first, I think they're going to protest, especially the poor administrator, who's not only seen his Good Friday evening evaporate before his eyes, but now is being kicked out of his own office. In the end, however, all he does is shrug and mutter, '*Certo.*' He glances at me on his way out, clearly thinking I'm a mad woman and wondering why on earth I couldn't have gone to some other museum, the Opera del Duomo or the Accademia, if I wanted to smash into things and pitch fits. The door closes behind them, and Pallioti glances at the cup in his hand, then at me.

'Now,' he says, 'Signora Warren, why don't you tell me what it really is you're so worried about?'

I stare at him, his still, pale face, the thin-lipped straight line of his mouth. 'I told her,' I say. 'I told her everything, about the nun who was killed, and the nurse. And Ginevra Montelleone.' I try not to look at Pierangelo as I say this, and I know a red blush of shame is creeping up my neck and into my face. He told me, and then I told Billy. Like a little kid, I can't even be trusted with a secret. 'She knows about the red bags, and the birdseed.'

Pallioti doesn't move, doesn't register any reaction at all. I can't tell if he's angry or not, that I know all this in the first place, and that I've told someone else. 'I don't know what she's doing or why,' I add finally. 'But I'm scared.'

Pallioti glances at Pierangelo, his face opaque.

'Of what?' Pallioti's voice is quiet. He leans forward, his elbows on his knees, and looks at me. 'Can you tell me, Signora Warren, exactly what it is you're scared of?'

'I—' Something is still writhing and twisting in my

stomach, and I am afraid that if I even whisper it I will make it real, that it will jump to life like a spark exposed to wind.

'Signora?' Pallioti asks, his eyes not leaving my face.

'What if the person I saw wasn't Billy? What if someone else sent me the text, and waved to me from the window? Wanted me to go up there?'

'Who?'

I shake my head. 'I don't know.'

'And why would they do that?'

'I don't know!' My voice is almost hysterical, and I'm afraid I'm going to start to cry again.

Pallioti pats in his pocket with his free hand, comes out with a rumpled cigarette, looks around the office, and thinks better of it. His lizard eyes flick from the little pile of seeds in the paper cup to my face.

'I can understand why what happened to this girl, Ginevra Montelleone, must be deeply upsetting to you,' he says. 'To you especially. But from what you have told me, I see nothing that leads me to conclude that these incidents are truly related. I think it is far more likely,' he adds gently, 'that your friend is making some kind of practical joke.'

'Billy wouldn't do that!' The protest springs out of my mouth, but even before I finish speaking the words I wonder if they're true. She wouldn't, would she? Why?

'I will have the seeds checked, of course,' Pallioti is saying. 'To see if they are the same kind that was found on Signorina Montelleone's body. But from what I can tell,' he shakes the cup, 'this looks like sunflower and maize. Corn. The kind of thing sold in snacks. Do you have your phone with you?'

I nod, pull it out of my bag and hand it to him. It may be broken, I'm not sure.

'I didn't save the text. I thought it was from Piero.'

Pallioti glances at him. 'But you didn't send it?'

Pierangelo shakes his head.

'I'll have our people look at it,' Pallioti says. 'Sometimes, you never know, in the memory...' He shrugs and drops the little silver lozenge into his pocket, probably squishing the cigarette. 'She had your number, of course?'

'Yes. Probably.' I don't remember if I ever actually gave it to Billy. But I lent her my phone more than once, so I assume she knew it.

Pallioti nods. 'I'm sorry, signora,' he says. 'I know it is unpleasant to hear, but it sounds as if your room-mate is playing a trick on you, an especially disturbing one. You said you told her what you knew about the Montelleone girl, and also about what happened to the other women. Does she know also what happened to you, how your husband died? You told her that as well?'

'Yes. Sort of. Well,' I add, thinking of Billy standing in the rain at Fiesole, 'she discovered it. She ran a Google search on me, and then she looked up the newspaper articles.' Or went through my drawers, I think. But I leave that out.

'And when was the last time you actually saw—what is her name? Billy?'

'Saturday,' I say, 'in the piazza at Santo Spirito. At the street party. We left at around eleven o'clock and she was still there.' At least this is something I can answer, something concrete I can get right or wrong. And then I remember the rain, the wind-shield wipers, the nuns running across the street, and correct myself. 'No,' I say. 'It was Sunday. Sunday evening. We, well, I, saw her on the street. We were in the car, she didn't see me.' Pallioti nods.

'Where was this?'

'Just near our building. Santo Spirito. Via Sassinelli.'

'But, *cara*,' Pierangelo interjects, 'we got our invitation to her Easter party on, what, Tuesday? So she must have mailed them on Monday. And she's been to the apartment. You know that. Maybe as recently as yesterday.'

He's right. I take a breath, feeling as though I am slowly drifting back down to earth, as though Pierangelo and Pallioti between them are pulling me down so I can find solid ground underneath my feet.

'She was definitely there,' I tell Pallioti, 'either on Wednesday night after I left, or yesterday morning. Or maybe both. She changed the picture. In the collage in the living room. And she was there last night.'

'But you didn't see her? You didn't actually see anyone?'

I shake my head. 'No. I didn't actually see anyone. That's right.'

'Then how can you be sure she was there?'

'I smelled her.'

I have not mentioned this before, to either of them, and now both Pierangelo and Pallioti are staring at me.

'You smelled her?' Pallioti says. And I nod.

'My perfume,' I explain. 'Pierangelo buys me special soap and oil and perfume. From the Farmacia Santa Novella. And Billy used it. She uses my things. My perfume is acacia, and last night, when I was standing in the hall, I smelled it. It came from the other side of the door.'

There's a silence while both of them digest this, then Pierangelo asks, gently, 'Couldn't it have been you, *cara*? Your skin you were smelling? You use the perfume too.'

I nod again and reach for his hand on my shoulder. Suddenly I feel incredibly tired. 'Yes,' I say finally. 'It could have been me.'

'You didn't sleep much last night, did you?' Piero runs his hand across the crown of my head, smoothing my hair the way you smooth a child's. Pallioti gets to his feet, starts to reach for his cigarette again and stops again.

'I will tell you what I'm going to do,' he says. 'We'll have a look for Mrs Kalczeska. What is her first name? On her passport?'

'Anthea.' I hear Billy's voice, as loud as if she's in the room. 'She uses Billy, but her real name is Anthea. I don't know what's on her passport. I've never seen it. Signora Bardino might. She must have records. For the school.'

Pallioti nods. 'If she's staying in a hotel, she has to register. We'll run a check. Siena, Lucca, Ravenna, Venice, Rome. The obvious places.'

'And Mantua.'

Something that might be a smile flicks across his face. 'And Mantua,' he agrees. 'Actually,' he adds, 'it will cover the whole country. Even Sardinia. She's not missing, technically, but I think we'd like to talk to her.'

He pulls an envelope out of his inner pocket and pours the seeds from the paper cup into it as I stand up and Pierangelo puts his arm around me. 'And perhaps tomorrow,' he says, 'if you have a moment to drop one at my office, a picture would be helpful.'

'I have one here.'

This morning I transferred the photo of Billy and me from my back pocket to my wallet. Now, as I take it out and hand it to Pallioti, I get a brief glimpse of me with my hair in my face, the little table littered with glasses, and Billy, smiling.

Chapter Seventeen

THE NEXT MORNING when I get up, Piero is already in his study. He takes my hand, kisses my palm and presses it to his cheek while he scrolls pages down his monitor. When he finally looks at me and sees I'm dressed, he raises his eyebrows.

'I'm going to the apartment, to see if Billy's back, or has left a message.'

'Do you want me to come with you?'

I shake my head. 'I won't be gone long.'

Pierangelo opens his mouth and closes it again, deciding he knows better than to argue. Instead he squeezes my hand. 'I'll be here,' he says. 'Call if you need anything.'

If you need anything. The words go around and around in my head. What could I need? I have everything I ever wanted. Pierangelo. The run of one of the most alluring cities on earth. Next week lectures will start again on the most beautiful buildings, the most magnificent pictures. The weather is turning, summer's coming. I don't have to worry about money. So what could I possibly need? Except for this not to be happening. For Billy to come back. But Pierangelo can't give me that. I lied when

I told him I was fine. Last night I had horrible dreams. About Billy's laughter. And things that writhe. About Karel Indrizzio. And the skins of snakes. And drops of blood, crimson and curled as the petals of tulips.

I know, even before I turn my key in the lock, that Billy hasn't been here. There's no sign of her. No clogs left in the hall. No message on the machine. Already the air is gelling, turning solid without our bodies and voices to stir it. Absence builds up like dust.

'Shit, Billy,' I mutter, standing in the living room. 'Where are you?'

I don't want to go back to Pierangelo's. And I don't want to call Henry and Kirk and hear that Billy isn't there. I don't actually even want to be inside, boxed by walls. I switch my loafers for my running shoes, and for a perverse few minutes I actually consider going to the Boboli Gardens. It's the same impulse that makes you pick at a scab, eavesdrop on conversations you know you're not going to like, basically do things to make yourself feel worse than you already do.

In the end, however, I give it a miss and head towards the bumblebee houses instead. What Pallioti says makes sense, but I can't understand why Billy would do it. Why deliberately frighten me? We're friends. And yet, if that's not what she's doing, why doesn't she call? Why doesn't she come back and talk to me?

Restless as a caged cat, I prowl past the cars parked in the broad avenue that leads to the Art Institute. Half restored, it sits like a great wrecked battleship, 'Bravo Mussolini!' spray-painted across its boarded-up windows. People walk dogs and play frisbee, their shouts following me as I pick my way along the worn path to the gap in the railings and slip into the world beyond. Like Alice through the looking glass.

Grouped around their toy piazza, the little houses are as neat and still as ever. Their glossy doors shine in the sun. Their window boxes are pert with marigolds and pansies. Behind them, the soft grey tops of the olive groves sway in the breeze, while directly in front of me the derelict villa sits like a rotten tooth in the middle of a smile.

Its shutters blister in the sun. The two squat towers perch on the roof, looking as though they might break loose and tumble down. A brand-new chain twists through its door handles like a silver snake. I wander up the side and look down the narrow little alley that separates the villa's rear wall from the house closest to it. The kitchens should be back here, and the garden. Sure enough, when I peer down into the cool darkness, I see ivy climbing over the high wall, and what looks like a fruit tree, its branches long and spindly from lack of pruning, but still sporting blossom, puffballs of white in the overgrown shadows. There's a strong smell of urine. A cat jumps from the wall, saunters through the weeds, and I catch the glitter of broken glass.

Beyond the villa, the little neighbourhood's order is soothing, and I wander along until I come to a dead end at a low stone wall that marks the edge of the groves. San Miniato hovers on the horizon, and up the hill to my right I can see the pretty pink façade of the House of the Birds. Pale shapes of statues stick up from the terrace, probably gods and half-naked ladies, and it's easy to imagine Byron living there or later, the Brownings, sitting out of an afternoon, drinking tea, while the strains of a piano drift down the hill from the villa above, where Tchaikovsky is busy dying.

'Ha! The Madonna of the Steps!'

The old man has come up behind me so quietly that when I turn round I almost step on his tiny poodle.

'I know you,' he says, and gives me a toothless grin while the dog wags her stumpy tail.

It takes me a second, then I remember the first time I ran into him. Back then it had been chilly, the wind blowing off the mountains and slapping its way down the valley, but today it's beautiful, almost hot, which doesn't seem to have affected his outfit. He's wearing the same fawn-coloured raincoat and a navy-blue woolen beret, like an ancient member of the French Resistance.

'Perla,' he commands, tweaking the ancient poodle's leash, 'say hello to the Madonna of the Steps.' The dog continues to wag her tail and smile at me, blinking her watery eyes.

'Deaf as a post,' the old man shouts, as I lean down to rub the little poodle behind the ears. 'Deaf as a post! Just like me!'

Perla wriggles in pleasure while he shakes his head and taps his cane on the sidewalk. 'It's a crime!' he announces suddenly. 'To leave a building like that, closed. Abandoned. You like houses?' he asks. He fixes me with his bright black eyes, and I look down towards the tear-streaked villa, its towers sticking up above the bumblebee roofs, and imagine what it must once have been.

'Yes,' I say. 'Yes, I do.'

'So do I.' He shakes his head. 'And there's no excuse for it. Leave a beautiful house like that. And them with plenty of money. More than God himself.' He bangs his cane on the sidewalk again and lets out a bark of a laugh. 'God's bankers. And what do they do? Send a caretaker round once a week. A stupid youngster who doesn't even cut the grass, that's what. How can a house live like that?'

He leers at me, his toothless smile stretching over half his face, wrinkles accordioned almost to his ears. 'A house is like a woman,' he says. 'It has a soul. And it has to be kept warm. Not with fires. With love!'

Before I can think of a suitable answer to this, my friend yanks on Perla's leash, almost tipping the little dog over. '*Arrivederci.*' He turns to go as suddenly as he came, winking at me over his shoulder. 'Don't be gone so long this time, Madonna of the Steps.'

I walk all the way up to Viale Galileo, and down past the cat colony to the San Niccolo gate, then across the river and up through Santa Croce, and by the time I reach the Palazzo Vecchio, I am in a much better mood. Perla and my French Resistance friend have cheered me up, and I wonder if I've also discovered the secret to brown-field regeneration: *Love your house as you love your wife and both will blossom.* I imagine the poster. Then, as I cross Piazza della Repubblica and see the crowds sitting out at the cafés, I imagine Billy. In Siena, drinking wine in the late-afternoon sun on the Campo. Or by the seaside, eating grapes and telling lies to a new lover. Suddenly I'm certain she'll turn up tomorrow on the Ponte Vecchio, just like she said she would, and express great surprise that anyone might have been worried about her.

The flower seller has set up outside the big bookstore in the arcade and I stop and buy a bunch of daisies for Pierangelo, to apologize for being such a pain yesterday.

He isn't there when I get home, and I'm putting the flowers in a vase, smashing the stems with the handle of a knife, and making sure the water is not too cold for them, when he finally comes in doing what I can only call 'beaming'. I have seen him look pleased before, but never like this. His whole face is creased in a smile and before I can ask him what's made him so happy, he takes both my hands and kisses them.

'Ah-ha. Don't ask,' he says. 'Not one word! I'm taking you out to dinner to celebrate!'

'What? What is it?' His smile is infectious, and I find myself starting to laugh. 'Has Pallioti called? Have they found Billy working in a travelling circus?'

Piero dances me round in a little circle in the kitchen. 'This has nothing to do with Billy,' he says. 'It has to do with you and me. And don't be so nosy. I'll tell you when we get there.'

'Get where?'

He names one of the fanciest restaurants in the city, and I look down at my clothes in dismay. Jeans and running shoes.

'I can't go like this!' I have returned Billy's belt and earrings but, if I hurry, I have time to retrieve them, then I can wear what I wore on Sunday. I start reaching for my bag. 'What time is the table?'

'Nu-huh!' He shakes his head and grabs my bag. 'You're my prisoner!'

Before I can protest, Piero puts my bag back on the kitchen counter and leads me into the living room where he pushes me down on the couch. 'Stay there,' he says, 'and close your eyes.'

The box that he places in my lap is huge and tied with a bow. The gold letters spell the name of one of my favourite boutiques, for window shopping. The place is just off Tornabuoni and has price tags I can't even dream of affording.

'Open it!' Piero commands. He's as excited as a child.

The dress inside is a beautiful blue-green silk, long and sleeveless, and there's a little angora shrug jacket to go with it. Underneath are a pair of high-heeled sandals that match.

'Do you like it?'

'It's beautiful. It's perfect!'

The designer is a famous name from Milan. I've never had anything like this before, and I jump up and put my arms around him. 'Thank you, thank you. I love you,' I whisper in his ear, and Pierangelo laughs and lifts me off the floor.

Outside, the night is warm and the streets are alive. Swallows slice through the dark blue sky. Piero is leading me towards Santa Croce, and as we cross the Piazza della Signoria he puts his arm around my shoulders. At Rivoire, couples sit at outdoor tables, people-watching, and sipping cocktails. Neptune rises from his fountain, slick and silvery in the floodlights, and in the Loggia dei Lanzi, Perseus stands dangling the snake-infested head of Medusa. No white men are around tonight, and the steps, watched over by the lions, are left to the pigeons, who strut and coo.

When we arrive at the restaurant, it's crowded, I'm amazed Pierangelo was able to get a reservation at such short notice. The girl at the desk, who is fashion-model sleek, leads us towards the back of the magnificent room where several tables for two sit up on a dais. I try not to gawk, but it's hard. We're on the second floor of a palazzo, the ceilings must be twenty feet high, and the walls are frescoed. The fading, haughty faces of medieval knights and pages look down on us while lean hounds chase deer and horses plunge and whinny, their manes rippling on an ancient wind. The lights are low, hidden high up behind heavy beams, and the candles on the tables flicker like stars amidst the pretty dresses and expensive suits. Flowers are arranged in sconces on the walls. On my plate there's a pale pink rose.

We have ordered, the waiter has poured champagne, and when I look across the table at Pierangelo, I realize how patrician he really is. He's one of the city's aristocracy, and completely at home in a place like this. I, on the other hand, feel like a Cinderella who's been lucky enough to get asked to the ball, and I wonder if my dress is awkward, too obviously expensive for me, and if I'm wearing the jacket right.

Pierangelo must see something pass across my face because he raises his glass. 'You look beautiful, Mary,' he says. 'You are beautiful. In any room, anywhere. But especially here. Florence suits you.'

I know that in Piero's book, there is no higher compliment. He regards this city as almost human, loves it as much as he will ever love any woman. He told me once that Florentines actually believe that they never leave. Superstition says if you die here, you'll walk the city's streets for ever.

'To Florence, then.' I raise my own glass.

'To you, *cara*.' Pierangelo touches the rim of his flute to mine. 'To us,' he says.

He sips his champagne and his eyes flit around the room. In the candlelight they're even paler, glittering with the excitement that's been lighting him up since he came home this afternoon.

'Piero, for God's sake.' I put my glass down. 'I can't stand this. What is it?' I ask. 'What's happened?'

His eyes come back to me, and he actually laughs. 'Everything, Mary,' he says. 'Everything.' He reaches out and takes my hand. 'Monika's given up.'

'What?'

The truth is, I don't know much about what's gone on between Pierangelo and Monika, except for the fact that they've been fighting over assets, as Graziella said.

'Everything.' Pierangelo says again. 'Her lawyer called me today. She's finally quit. She's given up all claim to Monte Lupo.'

Monte Lupo, his mother's house. I can see how much it means. Lines I didn't even realize he had have vanished from his face, and he actually looks younger. For the first time, I understand the phrase 'years falling away'.

'That's wonderful. You must be so relieved.' I pick up my glass again and raise it. 'I'm so happy for you. Really.'

'Happy for us, Mary,' Pierangelo says. 'For us.' He reaches into his jacket pocket. The box he places on my plate is small, and black, and velvet. The room goes still, voices around us suddenly muted.

'Open it.'

The ring is a ruby, circled by diamonds. Pierangelo reaches for it, takes my left hand and slips it onto my finger. 'Marry me, Mary,' he says. 'Please.'

I have dreamed of this moment for so long and now it's here I don't know what to say. All I can do is nod. I don't even dare look at him, because I'm afraid that, if I do, he'll vanish.

'Yes,' I manage finally. 'Yes.' And Pierangelo takes my hand, and holds the ring up to the candlelight and kisses it.

'We will have a beautiful life,' he says. But before I can even agree, something happens. People stop eating and murmur and, as if on some secret cue, everyone looks towards the entrance as Massimo D'Erreti steps into the room.

The cardinal is attended by a small entourage, and I find

I am searching among them for Rinaldo's face, and feeling almost giddy with relief when I don't see it. The girl at the front desk practically curtsies. A tall man who must be the owner approaches His Eminence, and D'Erreti offers his hand. For a second I wonder if the man is going to kiss his ring, but he stops just short of that, greeting him effusively instead, then guiding him towards the rear of the room.

D'Erreti is wearing not crimson, but a severe black suit. With his silver hair and dog collar he looks like a raven gliding among peacocks. He stops at almost every table, shakes hands with the men, who rise to their feet, and, on more than one occasion, kisses the hands of their wives, who don't. Then he turns towards us.

Pierangelo rises while he is still several yards away, but even after D'Erreti steps up onto the raised platform, the two men are not at eye level. The cardinal is shorter than his pictures suggest, compact and built like a bull. Up close he has the stocky, solid stature of a peasant. His hair is the colour of steel, cut as close as a U.S. marine's, and the fine black material of his jacket strains across the barrel of his chest. As he grasps Pierangelo's hand, clutching his upper arm, his face breaks into an open, easy grin.

I don't know why it surprises me—after all they have spent a great deal of time together—but the affection between the two of them seems genuine. As different as they are, for a second, they could almost be brothers. D'Erreti says something, then Pierangelo turns to me.

'Eminence,' he says, 'may I present *la mia fidanzata*, Signora Maria Thorcroft.'

All my life I have been taught to stand or kneel in the presence of priests, and that is my inclination now, to fall on my knees in front of this man. It's embarrassing, as if I'm possessed by a doppelgänger I can't banish. I offer my hand. D'Erreti takes it in both of his. His fingers are strong and hard, his skin, callused like a labourer's, and the ring he wears in place of a wedding band, the thin strip of gold that binds him to God, glows in the candlelight. When he smiles, his teeth are white, and blunt and even.

'My dear,' he says, in perfect English, 'I had no idea Pierangelo would be lucky enough to have such a beautiful wife.'

The words are gracious but, despite myself, I recoil. Everything about the man, from the pressure of his hand to his smile, is overtly sexual. His eyes meet mine, and they're as black as marbles. Bottomless.

'God be with you, Maria,' the cardinal murmurs, and before I can move away he leans forward and gives me the mark of blessing, the pad of his thumb rubbing the sign of the cross into my forehead.

That night, Pierangelo and I make love like never before, as if, rather than the rest of our lives, we have only these few hours to be together. The sky is turning silver when we finally fall asleep, and it seems like just seconds before the phone is ringing.

'*Pronto.*' Pierangelo answers. His voice is thick and unfocused. Then it changes. '*Si,*' he says. '*Si. Quando?*' And although I have my head buried under the pillow, trying not to wake up, I know he's frowning.

When I finally look, surfacing as groggily as a turtle coming out of water, he's already throwing the covers back. I catch the clock. It's just seven a.m. We've had a whopping two hours' sleep.

'*Si, si.*' Pierangelo says. '*Non. Sono andato.*' I'm going. '*Si. Subito. In men the non si dica.*' Immediately. In less than no time.

He puts the phone down. He's already reaching for his clothes. 'The paper,' he says without looking at me. 'Something's happening, at the Belvedere.'

He dives into the bathroom and I hear running water.

The taps turn off, then he shoots through the bedroom into the living room, pulling a sweater over his head as he goes.

'Stay here,' he calls. 'I'll be back as soon as I can.' And there's something in his voice, something wrong and sharp, that makes me get up and follow him through the door.

Pierangelo's rummaging for his car keys.

'Why are you going? You're an editor. There are plenty of reporters.'

The creature that has been sleeping in my stomach rises up and jams itself into my throat. 'I'm coming with you,' I hear myself say, and Pierangelo stops.

'It's Billy, isn't it?' I ask. And the fact that he doesn't answer is enough.

Chapter Eighteen

T HE BLUE TAIL of a police car is visible as we come over the hill. It's parked at a strange angle, skewed across the entrance to the Belvedere where, in another life, the Japanese tour group lined up to buy tickets. There are other cars here too, and behind us, somewhere far away in the city below, I can hear the high alternating wail of an ambulance.

Pierangelo slams to a halt and jumps out of the BMW, groping for his press card and approaching the young *carabiniere* officer who is walking towards us, his face pale, his hands gesturing frantically. '*Chiuso, chiuso!*' he says. '*Affare polizia.*'

I follow Piero, raising my hands. '*Mi amica—*' My voice falters, but my feet are still moving even as the words stop in my throat. Pierangelo grabs my arm as I almost run into the cop.

'*Chiuso!*' he shouts. Fear flickers across his face, as if he thinks I'm crazy, or at least deaf, and his free hand twitches too near the ultra-shiny holster clipped to his belt. Pierangelo steps between us, talking softly, his hand on the younger man's shoulder.

The *carabiniere* officer is still shaking his head as Pierangelo speaks to him, and I begin to back away. I make myself move slowly, almost nonchalantly, towards the city gate that leads into Costa San Georgio. The wail of the ambulance becomes deafening, and I glance back in time to see the white van cresting the hill, the single word *Misericordia*, Pity, emblazoned on its front. Then, as soon as I am through the archway and out of sight, I run. I hurtle down the hill, making for the lane that leads to the hole in the fence the junkies use.

It's just like I remember from the morning Billy and I discovered it, the torn wire, the trampled path. I duck through and skid down the steep grass bank that ends at the base of the ramparts, then I sprint along the fort walls, back towards the ticket kiosk and the mouth of the tunnel. Inside, my feet slap the steps, and I almost trip and fall, blinded in the dark. Then I burst out and stop, panting, my breath coming in great heaves as if I can't suck in enough air.

The Medici villa looms up on my left, pale and white, the stupid neon letters still flickering under its portico. The morning fog hasn't burnt off yet, and the big junk-pile sculpture looks as if it's floating. In front of me, the street lights on the weird little platform park stick up like fence posts in a prairie snow.

Billy's up here. I know. I can sense her, smell her, the way I smelled her the other night. *I'm your guardian angel*, she says, her voice echoing out of the tunnel behind me.

Her secret doorway, I think. That's where she'll be. She'll be in the same place she was hiding before. It's simple. All I have to do is find her. I sniff the air. There's something acrid and not right, but I can't place it. My mind isn't working very well, maybe because I'm tired. There are white empty spaces, blanks where there should be other things. *Carabinieri*. Cars. A phone call. An ambulance. The Santa Claus song runs through my head, too sharp and high for this hour of the morning.

I reach up absently and wipe my cheeks because my eyes are streaming. Hide and seek, that's all she's doing, I tell myself. Playing hide and seek. And I'm 'it.' I have to find her. Then everything will be OK.

I can hear voices now, coming from beyond the villa. Pieces of words fly up like spit from waves, and I walk towards them, carefully. I don't want to slip and cut myself on the broken-time mirror or slam into the basalt egg. I make it up the steps and through the villa's central arch, then I stop.

Beyond the ramparts the olive groves roll away in a silver sea, the Casa degli Uccelli a sugar-pink square in their midst. The Torre de Gallo breaks the skyline. San Miniato looks down from its hill. It's a perfect Renaissance landscape, but in the foreground, in the centre of the ragged lawn that tops the ramparts of the Belvedere, there is a new and grotesque work of art.

I can't stop looking at it. I am vaguely aware of people, Pallioti and some others I don't know. They're looking too. Pierangelo, panting from having chased me, comes up the steps behind me.

'Mary.'

He touches my shoulder, but I shrug him away. Then I call her name.

It's a garbled murmur at first, nothing more than a combination of sounds. Then it's a word. And finally a scream. A long, thin wail as I run towards her, my feet skidding on the grass, my hands stretching out as if even now I can reach her in time, somehow pull her back.

Pierangelo grabs me, as does another policeman. They hold my arms while I shriek at Pallioti; the thing that has been twisting and writhing in my stomach finally bursting free, exploding up through my throat and out of my mouth. '*Credimi adesso?*' I scream. '*Credimi adesso?*' Now do you believe me?

Billy is lying on what looks like a smouldering bonfire. Half-burnt branches, sticks and leaves are piled underneath her. The smell of gasoline hangs in the air, and the skirt of her flowered pinafore is in tatters, half burnt, half ripped. Her painted sneakers are still on her feet.

I concentrate on them because I don't want to look at the rest of her. I don't want to see that her throat has been cut in a slash so deep her head is almost severed. That it hangs backwards and sideways at a horrible angle, and that even that is not the worst thing. The worst thing is her hair. It's been shorn. Tufted and scarred, Billy's scalp is naked.

Robbed of her golden halo, she looks like a filthy plucked bird. Her hands hang down at her sides, frail and useless, her heart ring nothing but a spot of green and pink amidst the grime. And on her shoulder there is an obscene bulge. A fat, red silk bag pinned to the rags of her dress.

Afterwards, time slides. It slips like oily string. And every time I try to pin down a thought or a word, it slithers away. Everything divides, shimmers and rolls off, like the globules of mercury we used to play with in High School science class, back before they figured out it wormed its way into your brain and killed you.

One of the mercury blobs is Billy's arm. In it I see her wrist, her hand and her painted nails. In another I see her mottled filthy legs. In another, the tatters of her pinafore dress. And a silver sky that turns the colour of apricots. And dirty smoke in the morning air. And after that, fireworks; the hiss and crack of rockets that shoot into the Easter sky and blossom, bright blue, green and red, shedding their petals in a shower of sparks over the Duomo.

I understand that this is due to the drugs, this mixed-up sense of smell and sight and sound, and that it's to be expected. Lack of clarity, after all, is the point. Sometimes, Piero says, it's better not to feel or think for a while, so as soon as we got back to the apartment a friend of his who is a doctor came right over with the pills. I have three bottles, each a different colour. Brown for sleep. Pink for calm. White for amnesia.

While the rest of Florence has Easter lunch, the police go to our apartment on Via Sassinelli. They dust for prints and find nothing, and come to Pierangelo's to talk to me. I tell them how Billy bought her clothes and shoes in the market, and how she painted her nails, and went to the party in the Piazza Santo Spirito looking like a ballerina. I tell them about the Bargello and the text message on my phone and the birdseed. I repeat every detail over and over again, until the globs of mercury get all mixed up in my head and finally Pierangelo asks the police to leave.

That night it rains. Heavy splashes hit the long windows and wash down the skylights above the sunken bath. Lying beside Piero in the dark, waiting for the pills to work, I think we're in a ship at sea that's hit a storm. I can almost feel us pitch and roll. The pills aren't working. I get up and take another from the brown bottle, and when I wake up it's almost noon on Monday and the rain has stopped. Piero is in his study. He turns when I come to the door, his hands poised over the keyboard of his computer, and all I have to do is look at his face to know what he's writing.

'I'm sorry,' he says. 'But someone has to, and it's better if it's me.' He's right, of course, it is. And besides, in the beginning, back with Eleanora Darnelli where all this started, it was his story.

He watches me for a second, his eyes clouded with a concern that I both want and don't want. Want because I would like to climb into his lap and hide like a child, and don't want because it makes me uneasy, as if I might be crazy or dying. I glance around the room, fishing for a topic.

'These are nice.' I point to a series of photos of the twins as little girls. I must've seen them before, but I don't remember. 'Did you take them?'

He shakes his head, as relieved by this effort at normality as I am. 'Monika. She was the shutterbug in the family. Actually,' he adds, 'that's how we met. On a shoot.'

I take the frame down. It's a collage, kind of, one of those big frames with square and oval holes in the matting. Holding it, I feel as if I'm staring through the windows of a building into other people's lives.

The twins ride ponies, dress in school uniforms, wear party hats. In one picture they climb on a younger Pierangelo, who is laughing and fending them off. In another a pretty blonde woman crouches down with her arms around them. She wears a swirly Pucci dress and she looks a lot like Catherine Deneuve, or she would except for the fact that her left eyelid is half closed and the left corner of her mouth dragged downwards in a grimace by a scar that runs from her eyebrow to her chin. Can this be Monika? Surely I would have known, if she was disfigured?

'Is this Monika?' I hold the frame out and he looks, shakes his head and laughs.

'No. I don't have any pictures of her.' Pierangelo takes the big frame from me and peers at where I point. 'That's Angelina's godmother, an old friend of Monika's.'

'What's her name?' He looks at me for a second before he places the frame back on the shelf, and I already know the answer. I can feel it. 'That's Ottavia, isn't it?' The cigarette case and lighter. Pierangelo stares at the picture for a second and finally nods.

'Yes.'

'What happened to her?'

'An accident.' He shrugs. 'She was lucky to keep the eye. It was a long time ago.'

I let it drop. Today I'm really not much interested in Pierangelo's old girlfriends. Instead, I find myself thinking about Billy. Looking at the twins and wondering what she looked like when she was a kid.

'Get the picture from Pallioti,' I tell Pierangelo. 'For the paper. Don't use her university pass or anything like that. They look like mugshots. She'd hate it.' He nods, and takes my hand, holds it against his cheek, and doesn't need to ask who I'm talking about.

A couple of hours later, Pallioti sends a car to bring me to the Questura, the police headquarters. They need to talk to me, he says, if I'm ready.

Easter Monday is a big holiday. People throng the sidewalks and the streets. They walk arm in arm, eating ice cream and showing off their new spring clothes. In the Piazza della Repubblica the carousel spins and the painted horses rear and charge. Four women sit in a pink boat shaped like a shell, their mouths open, twisted by laughter I can't hear behind the sealed windows of the car. Boys in leather jackets stroll in front of us, looking like Mercutio and Romeo out to pick a fight with Tybalt. The driver puts his siren on and flashes his lights, and we nudge our way through bodies that bend like corn in the summer wind to let us pass.

Today Pallioti is different. I'm not sure what I expect from him, but when he sits down opposite me in the interview room, there's no special familiarity. If, forty-eight hours ago in the Bargello, he felt like my father confessor, now he feels like a stranger. Or a policeman. His lizard eyes are empty. Clear as glass, all they give back is a reflection of what looks in, and suddenly, more than anything else, even more than seeing Billy's body, this frightens me. I feel the way a vampire must feel when it looks in the mirror and sees nothing. Sitting here in this interview room opposite Ispettore Pallioti, it's almost possible to convince myself that I don't exist.

The woman who sits beside him, however, is different. Plump as a ripe fruit, with pampered middle-aged skin and the kind of dark red hair that has nothing to do with nature, she regards me with open curiosity. Her name is Francesca Giusti, and she's the investigating magistrate who is handling Ginevra Montelleone's case, and Billy's. She smiles at me as Pallioti opens the file that lies on the table between us.

'Signora Warren,' Pallioti says, 'as we established on Friday, you entered Italy on Alitalia flight 557, from New York to Milan, on the first of March this year, using a passport in your unmarried name. Since then you have been enrolled as a student at the

Florence Academy for Adult Education, and have been living in an apartment in the Palazzo Sassinelli owned by Signor and Signora Bardino, which you shared with Signora Kalczeska.'

This isn't a question, but I nod anyways. Dottoressa Giusti and Pallioti regard me silently for a moment. Then Pallioti says, 'I have to tell you, signora, I'm disappointed. On Friday, you asked for my help. I would have thought you might at least have also told me the truth.'

'What?'

I'm not sure I've heard him right, but before I can say anything else Pallioti jams a cigarette between his lips, gets up, opens the door of the room and vanishes. A second later he's back.

'You should know,' he says, as the door swings shut behind him, 'that yesterday we removed this from a bureau in the bedroom of the apartment you shared with Signora Kalczeska.' He holds the manila envelope in both hands, carefully, as if it might contain anthrax powder, or a bomb. 'So,' he says, 'perhaps you would like to explain?'

Even with my brain fogged up by the pills, I realize what the problem is. He's in a snit because I didn't tell him about the envelope. Probably he was made to look like an ass when it was found in my drawer and he didn't know anything about it. Or he thinks I was holding out on him deliberately, that somehow I haven't been straight with him because I didn't share my fetish for the dead. Or both. Compared to everything else, it seems so minor I almost laugh.

'It's nothing. Just some things I kept.' Pallioti fixes me with his lizard look, unimpressed.

'Look, I'm sorry,' I add. 'It was personal. I honestly forgot,' I say, lamely. I start to add that on Friday I didn't even think about it. It didn't seem relevant. But now, in light of what's happened, it's such a stupid remark, I don't even bother. The fact that it's the truth hardly matters.

Pallioti sits down, and there's a minute of silence while all three of us look at the envelope.

'Really,' I say again. 'I'm sorry. I should have told you. It didn't seem important to me at the time.' I feel as if I'm confessing to keeping sex toys. Although the reality may be worse. Sex toys are common. Pictures of murdered women I imagined I communed with aren't. A flush of shame creeps up my neck.

Pallioti pulls an empty coffee cup across the table, taps his cigarette ash into it and says, 'Should have told us what, exactly, signora? That you and Signora Kalczeska had decided to open a detective agency, perhaps?'

'No!' I have the sudden sense that, without my realizing it, everything has slipped out of control. And I have a horrible idea of how this must look from their side of the table. 'That isn't true,' I say. 'Honestly. I would never do anything like that.'

'You went to the candlelight vigil for Ginevra Montelleone.'

'That's true, but I told you, only because I wanted to pay my respects.' There's a whiny, defensive edge to my voice that even I find distasteful. 'Billy knew some friends of hers, of Ginevra's, from the university. We go to lectures there.' I'm trying to make this better, but I'm not sure I'm succeeding. 'But that stuff,' I wave at the envelope, wishing it would miraculously disappear, 'the rest of it, I kept the articles, the pictures, for myself. That's all. I never showed it to her. Billy didn't even see it.'

'Are you sure?' Francesca Giusti leans across the table towards me. 'You've said she used your things, your make-up, your perfume. How can you be sure she didn't go through your drawers? See all this, and decide to do some "investigating" on her own?'

'I—' The words stutter and die in my throat. I can't be sure. And we all know it.

Smoke wreathes around Pallioti's head. If it bothers Francesca Giusti, she doesn't let on. Instead, she watches me, her expression both attentive and deliberately non-judgemental, like a shrink's. I resist the impulse to squirm in my chair.

'You must realize, Signora Warren,' Pallioti says, 'that as

much as we may understand, and even sympathize with your interest, the police are not sympathetic to those who meddle with the law.'

'I told you, I've never done anything, I was—' The more I say, the worse this seems, but I don't know what else to do, other than try to explain. 'Curious,' I say finally. 'I was curious.' I swallow, trying to make it sound less obscene than it does. 'I wanted to know what had happened to the other women. To the women Karel Indrizzio attacked before me. I wanted to know, exactly, how they were killed.'

'Why?' Francesca Giusti asks it so quietly that at first I'm not even sure I've heard her. Her fingernails are clipped short, and painted deep red, the thumbs faintly spade-shaped, and I concentrate on her hands, which are completely still as she holds a gold pen above a leather pad she hasn't opened.

'Because—' I am seeing Eleanora's Darnelli's throat. Benedetta's folded hands. The tiny feathered body of the gold-finch resting on Caterina Fusarno's stomach.

'Because?' Francesca Giusti asks.

I raise my eyes and look at her.

'Because I should have been one of them.'

She looks at me, Pallioti's smoke drifting between us. Then she lowers her gaze, traces the edge of her pad with the pen tip and nods. 'Certo,' she says.

Pallioti waits a second before he gets to his feet, taps the envelope with his index finger. 'Where did you get this material?' he asks.

'The library.' I say it too quickly. 'Mainly,' I add. 'Some from the internet.'

'Not the crime-scene photographs.'

He stares at me and I stare back at him. It doesn't take Einstein to figure out that my source must be Pierangelo, but I'm damned if I'm going to say so, and cost whoever his contacts are in the morgue and the police their jobs. This whole thing is awful enough. Billy is dead, probably because of me. That's clearly what Pallioti thinks, anyways; that I urged her to play girl detectives. That we went looking for trouble and found it.

It isn't true, of course. But it does look as though Billy was right on one count; that whoever this creep is, he's aware of me. That must be how he fastened on her. He looked at me, and saw Billy.

The realization seeps into my head like an ink stain. She tried to warn me, she told me I didn't take him seriously enough. But in the end it wasn't me who was in danger.

Pallioti grinds his cigarette into the coffee cup, pulls out his chair and sits. He leans forward and rests his elbows on the table.

'Let me tell you what I think,' he says. 'I think you developed a little extra-curricular interest, that somehow you thought your own experience might give you some special insight into whoever killed Ginevra Montelleone.'

'That is not true.'

'I sincerely hope not. Because if it is, it was a very, very foolish idea. And a dangerous one.'

Pallioti leans back in his chair and looks at me. Then he says, 'I would have thought you, of all people, might have understood that. First a husband, then a room mate. You're becoming a dangerous woman to know, Signora Warren.'

The words hit like a slap.

I am struggling not to burst into tears, pressing my nails into my palm to make it hurt, to make little stigmata marks the way I used to when I was young and about to get a shot at the doctor's office, reminding myself that no matter what, Jesus' pain was always worse than mine.

'Thorcroft,' I say finally. 'I don't use the name Warren any more.'

Pallioti picks up his pen. 'Then tell me,' he says, 'Signora Thorcroft, if you can, about the last time you saw Signora Kalczeska.'

'It was in the street, as we drove by, on the night of Palm Sunday.'

'But not to speak to? You didn't speak to her then?'

'No. I waved, but she didn't see us.'

'And she was wearing?'

I close my eyes, hear the slap-slap of the wipers, see the nuns run across the road, the tall, blurry shape through the window.

'I think a raincoat. It's long, and pink. Maybe her tweed coat. I'm not sure.'

'And the last time you spoke to her?'

'The last time I spoke to her was at the party in the piazza the night before.'

'What happened?'

'We were all there. We had a table.' My head is beginning to throb. 'They asked me about all this yesterday. Over and over. I've already told you.'

Francesca Giusti leans forward. 'Then tell me,' she says.

I guess this is how they play good cop, bad cop here. I swallow, hating myself for having to dig in my bag for a Kleenex.

'We had dinner, all of us together. We talked about the murders. And the Japanese girls told us about the Mantegna painting and the red bags. I've already told you everything I can remember. The last time I saw her that night,' my voice sounds thin, and ripply, 'she was dancing with someone. I don't know who. I didn't recognize him. He was wearing a mask. A lot of people were. His was half gold and half silver. Like something from *Carnevale*.' I take a deep breath, trying to fend off the hollowness that's blossoming in my chest.

'And what time was this?' Francesca Giusti asks.

'About eleven. Maybe eleven-thirty.'

The picture of Billy's body hangs in front of me like a canvas. Did he kill her up there at the Belvedere? Under the half-burnt pile of sticks and leaves is there blood on the ground? Is that why he set the fire? How much would a fire like that even destroy? And speaking of destroy, why didn't I do that? Why didn't I take the articles and photos and burn them? All of this, just like Ty's death, all of this is my fault. The past is repeating itself, bleeding through into the present.

'The man Signora Kalczeska was dancing with,' Pallioti asks, 'would you know him again?'

I shake my head. 'He was medium height, wearing dark pants, or maybe black jeans, I think. I can't remember. And maybe sneakers. Have you talked to Kirk?' I ask. 'Her boyfriend here?' A picture of him rises in my mind, standing beside the table, his empty hand raised, staring after Billy. 'They fought that night,' I say slowly. There's something wrong with the picture in my head, but I can't put my finger on what it is. Everything is getting all mixed up again. 'I don't know what happened afterwards,' I say finally. 'We left. But he was watching her. I'm sure he would remember the person she was dancing with.'

'We have spoken to Signor Taylor.' Pallioti waves his hand in the air, either fanning smoke or dismissing Kirk, I'm not sure which. 'Now,' he asks, 'back to Signora Kalczeska. She came home that night?'

'I don't know.' I feel a prickle of exasperation. 'How would I know? I told you. I wasn't there. You should ask the old lady downstairs, she might have heard something.'

'I assure you, we have.' Pallioti looks at me with what I am sure is supposed to be a withering gaze, but all it does is irritate me, make me feel like a cornered animal that's being poked with a stick.

'You know,' I say suddenly, 'it was Billy who was interested in these killings. She brought them up at dinner that night, not me. She did find out about what happened to me, yes. But I didn't tell her. Not at first. Not until she found out, anyways. I don't tell people,' I add. 'I didn't come back here because of it, and I don't talk about it. And I didn't show her what was in that envelope. I'm sorry if she found it. If that's true, I'm sorry I didn't burn it myself. But I didn't show it to her. I wouldn't have done that. I couldn't have done that to them.'

'Them?'

I didn't realize what I'd said.

'The other women,' I mutter. 'I couldn't show her their pictures. It would have been wrong.'

Pallioti and Francesca Giusti exchange a glance, then she asks, 'Signora Warren—I'm sorry, Signora Thorcroft—why did you come back to Florence?'

'Because my boyfriend—no, my fiancé,' I hold up my ring, 'my *fidanzato* is here.'

'Signor Sanguetti?'

I nod.

'None of this is his fault,' I say. The wobbly tone goes out of my voice. Defending Pierangelo is something I can do. 'None of it,' I repeat. 'He didn't even know about the stuff I kept. I wanted to know about what happened to Eleanora Darnelli and Benedetta Lucchese because no one ever told me. I guess I thought I'd find out at the trial. But when Karel Indrizzio was killed there wasn't a trial. And I didn't feel then that I could ask.'

'So you decided to find out for yourself?'

'Yes.'

I'm grateful that she doesn't actually make me say I took the material from Pierangelo. Or lie about whether or not I told him afterwards. She glances at Pallioti again, but he appears suddenly fascinated with his pen.

'How much did Signora Kalczeska actually know?' Francesca Giusti asks. 'About the other women?'

'Everything. Everything I knew. I told her.'

'Why?'

'Why?'

She nods. 'You said you didn't like to talk about it.'

'I don't. But Billy found out, I told you. And after that, well. We talked about a lot of things.'

'But you never showed her the pictures?'

'No.'

'And the'—she hesitates, choosing her words carefully— 'the little gifts, left on their bodies. You told her about those?'

I nod. 'Yes.'

'Interesting,' Dottoressa Giusti says. 'You realize of course, or perhaps you don't, that that information was never released to the press.' She smiles almost ruefully. 'We do that sometimes. To conserve the integrity of the investigation. You'll find, I think, that there is nothing about them in the newspaper articles.'

She smiles at me again, not having to make the point that she's trapped me. The only way I could know about them is if someone told me. Someone with an inside source, like Pierangelo.

'But,' she changes tack suddenly, 'Signora Kalczeska knew what happened to you? You told her all about it? You talked about everything.'

'Yes.' It wasn't actually what I said, but I'm so relieved she's moved away from Pierangelo that I don't correct her. 'So, you were friends?' she asks.

I'm not sure where she's going with this, or why, but the word 'friend' sounds alien to me, almost laughable, as if such a pedestrian term could not possibly encompass Billy.

'I guess,' I say, eventually. 'She was, well, yes. For lack of a better word, she was my friend.'

'What would be a better word? Than "friend"?'

'What?'

I feel Pallioti shift in his chair.

'A better word than "friend." Lover?'

I stare at her.

'Were you lovers?'

'No. That's ridiculous!'

'Is it?'

Francesca Giusti focuses on my face, and suddenly I feel Billy's fingers, as she plucked open the buttons of my blouse, stood in my bedroom and traced the road map of my scars, her hair still glistening with damp from the rain at Fiesole.

Something dangerous is happening here. Somehow this woman, whom I have never met before, has put her finger on the one thing, touched the exact moment, when Billy reached out and stepped over all the boundaries I'd built around myself.

I look straight at her. 'We were not lovers.'

Dottoressa Giusti considers me, as if it were not so much the truth she was after, as how I would respond. What exactly I would say. A moment later she says, 'You're a private person, aren't you, signora?'

'Aren't we all?'

'Of course,' she smiles. 'But you have secrets. Hidden pictures. Things that, perhaps, you'd rather forget in order to build your new life here. You say Signora Kalczeska found out herself about what happened to you. Confronted you with it. It's not something you like to talk about, understandably. Not, perhaps, something you want revealed.' She pauses. 'That intrusiveness, signora, someone you barely knew probing into your life like that, it must have been difficult. We understand,' she adds, 'that Signora Kalczeska could be pushy, had a temper. That she could be...volatile. That can't have been easy.'

'Listen.' I lean forward, looking into the hard bright light in Francesca Giusti's eyes. 'There's something you need to understand. I would never have done anything, anything at all, intentionally, to hurt Billy. You may not believe that, but it's true.'

What's unintentional, though—who I am and what happened to me and what it means; who might come looking for me and find Billy instead—all that hangs in the air between us. Francesca Giusti leans back in her chair, watching me.

'You know,' she says finally, 'we have found no record of a text message on your phone.'

I look straight back at her. 'I'm not surprised. I told the *ispettore*, I erased it.'

She doesn't answer. Instead, she smiles.

'Tell me, Signora Thorcroft, is there anything else you think we should know? Anything strange or out of place that you can remember? It doesn't matter how trivial it seemed at the time. It might help us now.'

'A priest.' Francesca Giusti blinks and Pallioti glances up. 'Billy said a priest came to the apartment. About—I don't know, maybe two or three weeks ago. Looking for me. She said he asked for a Mary Warren. At the time, I thought it might have been a mistake. The old lady downstairs is an invalid, and her priest comes to her. I thought—' I shake my head, trying to remember exactly what Billy said.

'You thought what?'

'I thought she might have been mixed up. That it might have been a coincidence. But I don't now. She didn't know my married name at the time. This was before I told her anything.' Pallioti is watching me, the pen still in his fingers. 'After I was attacked, you talked to a Father Rinaldo who'd been with us that day.' Pallioti nods. The motion of his head so tiny it's almost imperceptible. 'I think it was him.' I say. 'I think he came looking for me, and met Billy. He was at the vigil for Ginevra Montelleone,' I add. 'I saw him. Her family, or at least her mother, used to worship at San Miniato. And I've seen him near our apartment. On the street.'

Francesca Giusti has been making notes in her leather notebook and now she glances up. 'Is there anything else, signora?'

The white man. The El Greco saint with the pirate dog. I open my mouth and close it again. What can I tell them? That I keep seeing a mute homeless man who has my husband's eyes? That I gave him a bunch of tulips? I shake my head. 'No. Nothing.'

Dottoressa Giusti stands up, extending her hand to me as though we've just met at a cocktail party. Her grip is firm and cool. Obviously this interview, at least as far as she's concerned, is over.

'Thank you for coming in this afternoon, signora,' she says. 'We appreciate your cooperation. I understand that this must be a very difficult time for you. All the same, please accept our congratulations on your upcoming marriage.' She lets go of my hand. 'We've finished with your apartment,' she adds, as if it's an afterthought. 'You're free to move back there any time you choose. And,' she says, smiling again, 'I'm sure I don't need to remind you that anything said in this room is entirely confidential? It's very important, given the nature of our investigation. We'd appreciate it, if you don't leave the city, for now.'

Francesca Giusti gathers up her leather pad and her fancy gold pen. As she reaches the door, she turns and looks back at me.

'Obviously you know quite a bit about all this, signora.' She nods at the manila envelope still lying in the centre of the table. 'Not least, I'm sure, that Karel Indrizzio indulged in the rather common practice of keeping souvenirs. Signorina Darnelli's shoe, the Lucchese girl's watch. Caterina Fusarno's handbag was missing, and Ginevra Montelleone's clothes.'

She looks at me for a second, as if appraising what she's going to say next, and whether or not I can be trusted.

'We think that whoever is copying him,' she says finally, 'may be doing the same thing. I'm sorry that you saw Signora Kalczeska's body. But given that you did, and that you knew her well, may I ask you, do you have any idea? Any thoughts at all, about what he might have taken from her? A piece of jewellery, perhaps? Something you noticed? A necklace? A watch?'

'She didn't wear a watch.' I shake my head. 'That's not what he took.'

Now they are both looking at me, Pallioti holding another unlit cigarette, Francesca Giusti with her hand on the door knob.

'What he took,' I say, 'was her hair. He took her fucking hair!'

By the time I get down to the lobby a few minutes later, my hands are shaking and I have to stop and lean against the cold marble wall. I wonder if I should put my head between my knees, if maybe that would miraculously stop all this from happening.

Today's a holiday, but at the Questura people are coming and going. Nutcakes and psychopaths probably don't take a day off for Easter. In fact, they probably consider it prime time. Young men, obviously cops, race by in pairs, which seems to be how they travel. Maybe, I think, they're like geese, and mate for life. Then I see Pallioti. He's coming down the wide steps of the main staircase, slowly, his face sheepish. Or possibly I'm imagining that.

'Shall I call a car for you, Signora Thorcroft?' He looks around the lobby of the Questura, vaguely, as though his mind is really somewhere else, and for the first time it occurs to me that he's probably tired. That this case, and maybe his whole job—dealing with the kind of people who cut women up with knives and leave them 'little presents'—is hell. 'The driver was supposed to wait,' he says, 'but these guys—'

Pallioti shrugs, and pulls the cigarette package out of his pocket. I can see now that they're Nazionale, the same brand that Billy smoked. This time when he offers me one, I take it.

The silver lighter flicks, and the smoke is warm and familiar. For a second, the act of standing here smoking together almost makes us friends, and I wonder what he's giving up to be here this Easter Monday. A special lunch? Time with his children? His wife? Or does he live in a solitary apartment somewhere?

'Can I ask you something?'

He raises his eyebrows, presumably in acquiescence.

'The case against Indrizzio,' I say, 'not for me, but for Eleanora Darnelli and Benedetta Lucchese, how strong was it?'

Pallioti considers the end of his cigarette for a moment, then he shrugs, as if telling me cannot possibly do any more harm than has already been done.

'He was charged with your husband's murder and with attacking you, as you know. The similarities with the other two were strong,' he glances at me, 'as I presume you also know. Circumstantially, both were possible. He had no alibi, and was seen in the area the night Benedetta Lucchese was killed. We were still working on a connection to Eleanora Darnelli when he died. And then the killings stopped.'

'Until this January.'

Pallioti inclines his head in a little bow. We smoke for a while in silence.

Then I say suddenly, 'I should have asked you about Karel Indrizzio. I'm sorry. I know that now. I should have come to you.' The words are coming out faster than I intend them to. 'But you understand, don't you?' I ask. 'You understand at least why I wanted to know?'

It's suddenly important to me that he say yes, that this man who sat in the hospital, who travelled with me through the days when I veered close enough to the dead women to touch them, should understand. I look into his face and the grey eyes look back at me. This time, though, something moves deep inside them, like a fish stirring under a frozen river.

I'm sure he's going to say something. I can feel the words forming in the air between us. Then he changes his mind.

'You could have asked me, signora, of course. But I'm not sure what I could have told you.' He shrugs, and adds, 'The past and the future, it's all around us, but so difficult to know. We live in the picture,' Pallioti says, 'but we rarely see it.'

He takes a long pull on his cigarette and stubs it out into the sand ashtray beside us. Now,' he smiles. 'Shall I find you a car?'

I stare at him. Then I drop my own cigarette into the sand. 'No, thanks,' I say. 'I think I'll walk.'

By now, it's late afternoon, and I begin, automatically, to walk towards Pierangelo's, then I turn away. I'm not ready for company yet. I took one of the pink tranquillizers before I left the apartment, but it must be wearing off because I feel anything but calm. I don't think I could sit still if I tried. It's a relief, of sorts, not to be numb, to escape the dulled haze I've been more existing than living in for the last day and a half. But now, instead, my insides are simmering and popping. What I feel, I realize as I turn into the narrow warren of streets behind Piazza della Signoria, is angry.

Oddly enough I'm not mad at Francesca Giusti, who was just doing her job—and well, I'll admit, I wouldn't want to face her in court—but at Pallioti. I'm angry with him for not trusting me with whatever it was he had been about to say just now, for darting back under the ice and fobbing me off with some clichéd sidewalk profundity. I thought better of him. I thought, I realize with something of a shock, that he was my friend.

'They think I did it.'

'What?' Pierangelo is chopping, the knife coming down in sharp rhythmic smacks on the cutting board.

'They think I did it. Or at least that woman does, Francesca Giusti.'

'That's ridiculous.'

'Not from where they're sitting.' I pour myself a glass of wine and look at him. 'Think about it. I know everything, every single little detail. I was hiding gory pictures in my bedroom. I commune with dead women, and, according to them, Billy and I were lovers. She took me where I didn't want to go, so I killed her, and made it look like this creep did it. Makes perfect sense to me.'

'*Cara.*' Piero abandons the vegetables he's been mutilating and puts his arms around me, rests his cheek on the top of my head. 'I have some leave coming up,' he says. 'I'll take it. We'll go to Monte Lupo, as soon as this is over.'

'What makes you think it's going to be "over"?'

'Of course it will be.' He runs his fingers down my face. 'They'll find who did this. Pallioti isn't a fool.'

'What if it wasn't Indrizzio?' Piero frowns. 'I'm not kidding,' I say. 'What if it wasn't? I asked Pallioti today, and he said the cases against him for both Benedetta and Eleanora Darnelli were totally circumstantial. They never even charged him for them. He was in the area when Benedetta was killed, but so what? I mean, he lived there. In the gardens, or wherever. They never even put him in the vicinity when Eleanora Darnelli was killed, or at least they hadn't when he died.'

Piero has picked up his knife again and I can't see his face. 'The killings stopped,' I say. 'So they just dropped it. But what if whoever really did it was out there the whole time? And now he's back.'

'The case against Indrizzio for you and Ty was strong. DNA, and blood typing,' Pierangelo points out. 'He had Ty's wallet and your wallet. *Cara*, he described you.'

'But he never confessed, did he? And they didn't find my blue handbag with Indrizzio. He said he thought I was dead when he found us. So he took the wallets. Piero,' I insist, 'what if he was telling the truth?'

Pierangelo turns round and looks at me. 'He wasn't. So, he dumped your bag somewhere. So what? I'll accept that there's a question in the case of the other two. But you and Ty, no. Most of the time, when it quacks like a duck, it is a duck. *Cara*, the man who attacked you and killed Tyler is dead. He isn't out there.'

'And this guy?' I reach for my glass, but my hand is shaking again. 'They think maybe Billy decided to "investigate." I don't buy that, do you?'

'I didn't know her. So I don't know.'

'I don't think so,' I say. 'She wanted me to be more careful. That's why she brought all that stuff up at dinner at Santo Spirito. She was trying to shame me, bulldoze me, I don't know, into being more careful. She said if he was copying Indrizzio, he'd know about me. She said I didn't take it seriously enough and she'd have to be my guardian angel.'

I burst into noisy, bawling tears. Pierangelo stops with the food and holds me. He takes me into the living room and sits me on the couch, rocks me back and forth while I howl. And when I'm quieter he strokes my hair.

'Maybe you should leave,' he says. 'If you want to go back

to the States for a while, until this is cleared up, I'm sure Pallioti will understand.'

'No, he won't. Don't be dumb. And besides, what about you? I can't leave you. I just got you.' I look at my ring, at the beautiful cherry-coloured ruby and the winking diamonds.

'Matches your hair,' Pierangelo says, tugging my pink stripe. 'That's why I chose it.'

'What if I dye it green?'

'Well,' he says, 'then I suppose I'll have to buy you an emerald.'

Chapter Nineteen

I THOUGHT THE apartment would be different. That, despite what Francesca Giusti told me, the door would be sealed, and I wouldn't be able to get in. Or that it would be covered in fingerprint dust, the way places are in the movies, with drawers left open and furniture turned upside down. But it isn't any of those things. All it is, is empty.

The article on Billy's murder is coming out today and Pierangelo left early. He offered to come with me to collect some more of my things, but I told him I wanted to be alone. Now I wish I hadn't, and that he was standing here beside me, stirring the silence that's built up like silt.

The French windows in the kitchen are still tied shut. The first traces of the police are smudges of dark powder around the door handles in the living room, and the fact that the papers on the desk have been squared into too neat a pile. The shutters are up, the curtains open, and below on the street the city is coming to life again, stirring like a bloated animal after the Easter festivities. A gaggle of tourists heads for Santo Spirito, skirting the bollards and tape that have been set up by an open manhole in the middle of the road where a grey electricity van is parked, one set of wheels on the sidewalk. As I watch a moped comes by, threading in and out, then speeding off towards the piazza. The sound fades, and I pull the curtains. The sun needs to be kept off Signora Bardino's pretty little desk.

After the living room, I patrol the bathroom, put some of my things in a bag, then I stand in the hallway outside Billy's door. A shout rings up from the street, followed by laughter, and beyond the silence of the apartment I can hear music, high and tinny, coming from a radio. The announcer breaks in, the news bulletin from Rome. When I finally turn the knob, I realize I expected it to be locked, as if I should be barred from entering, punished for what I have done. But the door swings inward, whispering.

Sun streams through the window, highlighting streaks of dust on the floor and the bureau. Strands of Billy's hair are caught in her brush and glow golden white, spiralling and almost translucent. I force myself to open the wardrobe and look at her clothes, uncertain of what I expect to find. All the hangers point in the same direction, which is an odd little hint of order, since the dresses and skirts and pants are mixed up. A cardigan has fallen to the floor and I pick it up, untangling the arm from one of the pointy-toed crimson pumps she wore to the party in the piazza. I hold the shoe for a second, studying a stain on the toe, and then I return it to its mate, and, for some reason, get down on my knees and begin to pair off all the shoes, lining them up two by two—loafers, boots and heels. A few are left over. There's a single ankle boot, an old green sandal and a black patent-leather lace-up. They look lonely by themselves, so I put them all together at the end of the row, their toes touching in a three-way Eskimo kiss, and hear Billy laugh. My hands stop, and I turn round, still crouched on the floor of the closet. She's here. I can feel her. I think that if I closed my eyes I could touch her.

I stand up slowly, as if sudden motion might scare her away, and slip my arms into the sleeves of the cardigan. The cuffs fall down over my hands, but I button it anyways. The faint odour of cigarette smoke and the sweet flowery scent of her shampoo cling to the soft blue wool. When I stare into her mirror, I half expect to see her standing behind me, telling me my hair is dirty and that there are circles under my eyes. Which is true. I don't even remember which pills I took this morning.

The top of Billy's dresser is too orderly. The police have put the bottles of hair stuff in straight lines. Her bracelets are a pile of enamelled glass and silver, and the framed picture of the house has been placed beside the mirror. When I open her jewellery box I hear a few tinkling notes, as though it once played a whole song but no longer has the energy to remember the music. Inside, there are a couple of cheap necklaces, a chain with a ladybird charm on it and a pin in the shape of a butterfly. From behind my shoulder, Billy whispers I should take it, so I do. I pin the butterfly to the shoulder of her cardigan.

In her top drawer I find a dog-eared envelope of photographs, some of people I don't recognize, probably her family—her mother, a woman who might be her aunt Irene, and one of a boy who looks young enough be her son, but was, I suspect, her husband. The others are of us. Kirk and Henry and me sitting at the bar. The Japanese girls posing with Signor Catarelli in what looks like the gardens of one of the Medici villas. There's even one of Signora Bardino standing in front of one of her trattorias, one hand clutching her Ferragamo bag while the other holds the shoulder of a young man in a white chef's jacket.

I shouldn't, I know, but I take it, and her ratty old coin purse that's stuffed, not with coins, but with entrance tickets from everywhere we've ever been. She always said she was going to make a scrapbook. Or a collage. Maybe I'll do it for her. I dig through the rest of the drawers, looking for her collection of postcards, but I can't find them.

How did it happen? I stare at her things as if somehow they could tell me. Did someone call her? Did the guy in the mask take her number and ask her out for a drink, or to a party? Or was it different? Maybe she was just walking home from a movie or dinner, fitting her key into the security gate when he came up behind her and tapped her on the shoulder. Grabbed her and pulled her into the dark. But if that's the case, she would have been wearing a coat or jacket. It hasn't been warm enough to be without one at night.

I dart back into the hall and check, but yes, her tweed tent and her long pink raincoat are both here. So it didn't happen at night. Or when it was cold. She must have met him in broad daylight. Which means it was unlikely that there was a fight or struggle. Billy's a big girl, and tough. Surely that would have attracted attention. No. She must have gone with him willingly. Which means it's likely that he was someone she knew. And probably someone I know too.

It's past noon now, and I was going to go to the store for something to eat, a panini or a pastry, but suddenly I feel funny unlocking the door. I keep it open with my foot while I stand for a second on the landing, listening to the faint sound of Signora Raguzza's radio. The Sassinellis are back, I noticed their windows open when I came in, so there are plenty of people around. Even so, as I let the door click shut and start down the stairs, I shove my hand in my pocket and stick my keys through my fingers the way they taught us in self-defence class.

Outside it's turned sunny, and as I cross the courtyard I meet Signora Raguzza's priest. He's young, and he bows his head when he sees me, ducking like a rabbit, as if even the glimpse of a woman might be contaminating. His long skirt swishes as we pass, and his hands are folded into his black belled sleeves. He could be holding anything, I think. A knife. A gun. He's as bad as me with my spiked fingers buried in my pocket.

'Greetings, Father,' I mutter in Italian.

'God be with you,' he mutters back. And it seems both our voices are filled with shame.

The store is crowded. School has finished and a bunch of kids, all in messy uniforms and carting book bags, are buying candy. The signora is busy serving them, parcelling out little white paper bags to each one, so Marcello serves me. When I ask for the closest thing they have to cookies, he rolls the ladder over to the stacked shelves and climbs up to reach for them, his sweatshirt riding up, the pallid hollow of his back marked by a white ridge of scar tissue that snakes under the blue material. I feel my own scars prickle in sympathy, and when he comes down suddenly, hopping to the floor, I make an extra effort to smile. Marcello winks and drops a couple of Baci into the bag.

'You have an admirer.'

I don't hear the voice until I am stepping out of the shop, and when I look round, I see Sophie standing behind me. Paolo is beside her, his knapsack hanging sideways off his shoulder while he inspects the contents of the candy bag the signora has just handed him.

'Not really.' I glance back at Marcello, who is watching me out of the corner of his eye as he serves the next person in line. I hope he's not going to get in trouble. Probably the signora makes him pay for the extra treats he gives me. Somehow I don't think she misses much.

'Ah, young love,' Sophie says as we start down the street and I give her one of the hazelnut chocolate candies. There's a little strip of waxed paper, like in a fortune cookie, under the blue and silver foil, and Sophie extracts hers and reads aloud. "Knowledge can be learned and forgotten, but Venus' art is truly eternal". What about you?' she asks.

"Love comes with many faces, but it is always with you."'

'Sure, and I'm going to meet a tall, dark stranger.' Sophie laughs and pops the round chocolate candy into her mouth. Her cheeks bulge like a chipmunk's while she chews.

'Listen,' she says a few seconds later, 'I'm really sorry.' She's crinkling the Baci paper in her hand, rolling it into a little silver ball. 'About your friend. It's terrible. I'm really, really sorry.'

My step falters as I look at her.

'You haven't seen it?' She stops and her face colours. 'It's on the front page of the paper. They don't give her name, but I recognized her picture.' The later edition of the paper comes out in the afternoon, around now, and Sophie pulls a copy out of her bag and shows me the front page. 'I'm sorry,' she says. 'I thought you knew.'

I did. Of course, I did. But, nonetheless, I'm a little surprised at how much it startles me.

They've edited me out of the picture I gave Pallioti, so all that's left is Billy, smiling into the camera. 'American Art Historian Murdered' the headline says. Billy'd be thrilled they're calling her an art historian. I'll have to remember to thank Pierangelo. Sophie folds the paper again and puts it away.

'Are you OK?' she asks.

Paolo is pulling a black liquorice string out of its wrapper, threading one end of it into his mouth and sucking on it as if it's a straw.

'I don't know,' I say.

She touches my shoulder, just once, her pink manicured nails brushing the fabric of my shirt. 'If I can do anything—' The sentence peters out in awkwardness, and we start to walk again. 'You know,' she adds, 'I only live across the way.'

'Thank you.' She doesn't push any harder, doesn't get into some big fake grief act because she knows somebody who knows somebody who was murdered, and I'm grateful for it.

We come to the corner, stop to cross the road, and skirt the electricity van that's still parked there. One of the bollards has fallen over in the street, dragging its yellow tape with it. No one seems to be around to right it.

'Typical,' Sophie says. 'The Italian two-hour lunch break. Big Paolo's already furious because his driver couldn't get past them this morning. He had to go through the back and wait by the cellar door.' She laughs. 'As if the indignity of walking past a wine rack and driving down an alley makes him less of a man. I told him he should dump the Mercedes and get a Smart car, then he wouldn't have the problem, but he didn't think it was funny. They'll be there for weeks and weeks,' she adds, nodding at the van. 'You'll see.'

She pulls her keys out of her pocket, ushers Paolo up the steps and opens the gate. I follow her into the courtyard, and just before we part she turns to me, her soft, round face clouded with concern.

'Seriously, Mary,' she says. 'If there's anything at all I can do...' Sophie leans forward and gives me a quick, hard hug, then she turns towards her wing of the building, Paolo trailing after her, liquorice hanging out of his mouth.

The lights are off on our stairs, and I don't bother to switch them on. It's shadowy, and I count the steps as I go up. Twelve, then the landing, then twelve more to Signora Raguzza's door, and twelve more after that to our landing. My hand trails on the banister and I watch my feet as I climb, so it's not until I am halfway to the top that I look up and see the figure standing outside our door.

He's dressed in black, in what looks like a cape or a cassock. I stop dead, and must make some kind of noise, a gasp, or a mew, because he turns round, and I realize it's Kirk. 'Hey,' he says. 'I was just going to leave you a note.'

When he gives me a hug, his shoulders are stiff and unyielding. He smells of mint, and underneath it something slightly sour, as if he hasn't washed or brushed his teeth for a while, just thrown on aftershave and used mouthwash instead.

'So, does the coffee at the police station suck, or what?'

It's meant to be a joke, but Kirk's voice is cracked, and neither of us laugh. A second later he says, 'Henry's in the bar. He said he'd pay if I came over here and convinced you to give us an espresso. We tried your cell,' he adds, 'a few times yesterday. We didn't have what's-his-name's number.'

'Pierangelo. My cell's broken.' I don't tell Kirk I'm using one of Piero's spare ones, and I don't offer the number.

A flood of light hits us as I push the apartment door open, and I see that Kirk's already fair skin is sickly white, and the rims of his eyes are as pink as a hamster's. Despite the warmth of the day, he's shrugged deep in his overcoat. I remember what Henry said about cocaine, and wonder exactly how much chemical help he's had in the last few days.

'Kirk, are you OK?'

'Not really,' he says as he steps past me into our hallway. 'Are you?'

'No. I don't know.'

The door swings shut behind us, and it occurs to me that I haven't even asked him how he got in here. I didn't know Billy had given him a key. I open my mouth to say something, then stop. Kirk is standing in the hallway staring through the open door of her room.

'Fuck,' he says. 'Oh fuck.'

He looks like a hound scenting, as if he can smell her here. As if the memory of her might gain flesh and bone and actually appear, if he just stands still enough.

'Kirk?'

I say his name as softly as I can, reach towards him, half intending, somehow, to comfort him. But I don't get the chance, because what happens next happens too fast.

'You bitch!' Kirk yells. 'You fucking bitch!'

He swings round and hits me in the jaw. 'What are you?' he screams, as I stagger backwards. 'What are you? Some kind of fucking death angel?'

I drop the cookies, arms flailing, and collide with the little hall chair. One of the legs cracks and snaps as I fall, and I reach for it, for anything I can use to defend myself. The hall lamp. That's heavier, a better weapon. I grab the cord, start to pull it off the table, blood pounding in my ears, and look up, to see where he's coming from, how he's going to hit me next. But Kirk has apparently forgotten all about me. Standing in the hallway, staring into Billy's room, his hands hang at his sides. Long ugly streaks of tears run down his cheeks. His nose has started to run.

'I loved her,' he says. 'I really, really loved her.'

I don't know how long we stay like that for, me sitting on the floor grasping the chair leg in one hand and the electric cord in the other, and Kirk staring into Billy's room as if I'm not even here, weeping. It seems like for ever, but it's probably only a minute. Finally I lever myself to a crouch and crab around the wreckage of the chair, hoping he won't notice I'm moving. Then I sidle into the kitchen.

My head is hammering and my mouth is like sandpaper.

There's a knife. A sharp one. I bought it. Or I could open the windows and scream for Sophie, scream anything, to anyone. I remember waking up on the couch. Because I heard a noise. The door. He has a key. He was going to come in.

I glance backwards at Kirk, standing in Billy's doorway, and my hand reaches for the French windows, fingers scrabbling for the tight little knot in the kitchen string. 'Come on, come on, come on!' I whisper, certain that any second I'll hear him come up behind me. Then someone bangs on the front door.

It's a hollow thud-thud-thud, and my hands freeze. I can't make them work right.

'Mary,' Henry calls. 'Hey, Kirk, Mary, are you there?'

I sprint down the hall, my hands stretched for the big brass lock as though I'm reaching for the finishing tape in a race. When I open the door, Henry envelops me in a bear hug.

'Shit,' he says. 'I have been so worried about you. Your buzzer's broken, by the way. Some Albanian lady let me in.' He steps back and holds me at arm's length, looks at my face, his shrink's eyes sharp behind his round John-Boy Walton glasses. 'Mary?' Henry asks. 'What's going on?'

The blood in my head is slowing down, and I can hear my heart beating. I catch my breath, so relieved to see him that I actually laugh. The noise comes out of my mouth high and crackling. It sounds like electricity in a cartoon, a jagged yellow line. Henry looks past me, into the apartment.

'Kirk?' he mouths.

'In there,' I gesture with my head. 'In Billy's room.'

Her door is closed now, and Henry follows me inside. Cookies are scattered across the floor, and when I pick up the broken chair and prop it against the wall, Henry steps around it without saying anything.

'I'll get him out of here,' he mutters, as we come into the kitchen. 'Just give him a couple of minutes with her stuff and I'll get him out of here.'

My eyes tear up and blur as I nod, fill the kettle for something to do, and turn on the halogen.

'Mary?'

I don't turn round. I'd rather Henry didn't see that I'm shaking.

'How much do you know?' I ask. I don't know what Kirk has found out about me, but obviously it's something. Billy must have told him.

'Just what's in the paper, really.' There's apology in Henry's voice, and I glance at him over my shoulder.

'Haven't you seen it?' he asks.

I shake my head, standing on tiptoe to open the top cabinet and reach for the mugs we bought because we were so scared of using Signora Bardino's eggshell cups. 'No, not really,' I say, as I get them down. 'I saw the headlines. I guess she'd be happy they called her an art historian.' Henry makes a strange sort of noise and I turn round and look at him. 'What?'

He shrugs, as if he's embarrassed.

'I didn't mean that,' he says. 'I meant the part about you.'

'About me?' My hand stops in mid-motion, holding the cheap blue mug.

'Yeah. I thought you'd have seen it.'

'No.'

'Well, it just says it's a big coincidence that you were Billy's room-mate because you were attacked, before, two years ago, but survived. Just.'

I can't believe what I'm hearing. I had no idea there was anything about what happened to me in the paper, and part of me thinks it's a mistake, that it has to be. Pierangelo would never do this. Would he?

'In the Boboli Gardens,' Henry's saying. 'Right?' The kettle begins to whistle and I turn it off. A second later, Henry says, 'I wish you'd felt like you could have told me, Mary. I thought we were friends. Or at least I thought you knew I'm not the enemy.'

'I do know that.' I reach for the coffee, my hands moving

by themselves, my mind clicking over. What has Pierangelo written? Why didn't he tell me?

'Well, at least that's something.' Henry gives an uncomfortable little laugh.

I spoon coffee and pour water into the French press, and we watch in silence as it swirls and foams. Brown flecks ride to the top of the bubbles.

'Mary, I could help. Really. It's what I do, for Christ's sake.' I can sense the frustration in Henry's voice, but I can't give in to him. I'm afraid that if I do, I might dissolve altogether, melt onto the floor like the Wicked Witch of the West and never be able to get up again.

'I know, I just—' I have the sense that I'm going deaf, that I can't hear other people properly, or hear myself speaking, and I don't finish the sentence.

'Listen'—Henry glances at the door and drops his voice—'Kirk is going nuts. He'd asked her to go back to New York with him. To live with him. Did you know that? Did she tell you?'

I almost drop the coffee pot. I'd had no idea.

'That's what they were fighting about,' Henry whispers, 'on Saturday night. She wouldn't say yes. Or no.'

Typical, I think. Billy playing both sides of the deck. Keeping her options open. Refusing to be pinned down. A bright glob of mercury splitting and rolling away. I look at the doorway and see her standing there the afternoon before the party. What did she say? *He's driving me crazy.*

'Look,' Henry goes on. 'I tried to talk him out of it, but you should know that he went to the police. I know it's garbage, but he's convinced you had something to do with this.'

I put the kettle back on the stove, and turn off the switch, watching the little red circle flare and die, remembering the questions Francesca Giusti asked me, and the sheepish look in Pallioti's eyes.

'He was convinced she was seeing someone else,' Henry adds, and I almost laugh out loud.

'And he thinks it was me?' I ask. Then I remember the way

Kirk was looking at me in Fiesole, and something else clicks in my head. I've just remembered what I couldn't think of yesterday. Billy's ring. It sparkled in the grime on her dead hand. After she pulled it off her finger and hurled it at Kirk in the piazza.

'Henry,' I ask suddenly, my voice sinking to a whisper, 'how many times has Kirk been here before, to Florence? Do you know?'

Henry shakes his head. He starts to open his mouth, but before he can say anything we hear Kirk's footsteps in the hallway. He appears in the door holding one of Billy's shirts and a couple of her art books.

'I'm taking these,' he says. It isn't a question. His face is naked, stripped down to its thin, fine bones, his lips set in such a hard line that they've almost disappeared. When he rakes his hand through his hair I can see it's lank and greasy. Kirk puts the things on a chair and accepts the coffee I put on the table, but he doesn't apologize for hitting me.

'How much did Billy know?' he asks suddenly. 'Exactly, I mean. About you? About what happened here before?'

There's no trace of tears in his voice now. It's hard and clipped and I look him right in the eye, and remember that, for all the twisted, bottled-up jealousy and grief inside him, Kirk's a prosecutor, and probably a good one.

'Everything,' I say. 'She knew everything. I told her. A while ago.'

'She didn't say anything to me.'

I shrug. 'She knew it was something I didn't like to talk about. I guess she respected my privacy.'

Kirk digests this for a second, stirs four teaspoons of sugar into his coffee and looks up at me.

'Your privacy,' he says. 'Well. Isn't that nice? So why are you here, Mary, if you care so much about "privacy"? Why come back here? Is it lover boy, or closure? Isn't that why you really came back? To face your demons? Maybe even track them down?' His voice is nasty with sarcasm.

'Is that what you got Billy into?' he asks. 'Some kind of little detective game so you could finally face your attacker? A little truth and reconciliation, maybe? Or, who knows, vengeance? What were you going to do, cut his balls off?'

'Don't be ridiculous.'

'What's ridiculous about Billy being dead? Is that your idea of a joke?'

Henry shifts uneasily, and when I don't answer Kirk takes a sip of his coffee and says, 'So come on. Let us in on it. The paper wasn't all that clear. What, exactly, did happen two years ago?'

I pick up my own mug and stare at him.

'I was attacked. In the Boboli Gardens, on a Sunday afternoon.'

'But the guy didn't kill you.' Kirk looks up at me and actually smiles. 'Why not?' he asks.

'I guess,' I say, 'because he killed my husband instead.'

They leave a few minutes later, Henry following Kirk down the stairs, turning around and making phone gestures at me. I watch them sink into the shadows, listen until their footsteps cross the marble foyer and reach the courtyard below. Then I dart back inside, close the apartment door and lock it. My heart is fluttering, jumping around, and instead of the hallway and half-moon table and broken chair, what I see is Billy: her tufted head hanging sideways, her red-tipped hand, cut and grubby, the heart ring winking in the ashes.

Pallioti keeps me waiting. I left the apartment and almost ran straight here, and now I can barely stay still. My legs and arms twitch, and when he does finally appear, I take the cigarette he offers almost greedily and suck on it long and hard.

'I've remembered,' I say. 'That night in the piazza, Saturday, when Billy and Kirk had the fight.'

Pallioti looks at me out of the corner of his eye. I told him I didn't need to go up to his office, so we're standing in a narrow little interior courtyard, next to a modern fountain, an obelisk of granite that piddles into a shallow green pool.

'The thing is,' I continue, 'when I was talking to you and Dottoressa Giusti, I knew there was something wrong, but I couldn't remember what.' I close my eyes, squeeze them tight shut, and see Billy standing beside the low plastic hedge outside the bar, leaning forward, spitting words I can't hear over the music. Then I see her yank something off her hand. She hurls it to the ground and spins away, her red dress swirling in the coloured lights.

'She threw it at him.' I open my eyes and look at Pallioti. 'She was wearing this ring he gave her, two heart-shaped stones intertwined, and she pulled it off her finger and threw it at him.'

Pallioti looks at me, his face impassive.

'She was wearing it when she died!' I almost shout. 'It was on her hand when you found her at the Belvedere. I saw it.'

'So, she retrieved it after the fight.' Pallioti almost smiles. 'She wouldn't be the first woman,' he says, 'who thought better of throwing away a piece of jewellery.'

I shake my head. 'No. Kirk picked it up. I saw him. He put it in his pocket. And he has a key to our building. He turned up there today. He was waiting for me. Or maybe he was just about to let himself in.'

Pallioti narrows his eyes. He's looking at my jaw, at the red swelling that is already beginning to stand out, but he doesn't say anything. He just nods his head for me to go on, like old times.

'Kirk's been here before. I don't know when, or for how long. But he has. And I know he's been to Mantua. He said so, one day when we went to the gardens. At least ask him,' I beg. 'Please. At least find out the dates when he was here.'

Pallioti considers the cigarette in his hand, flips it into the green gutter of the fountain and nods. 'I will, signora,' he says. 'Thank you. Now, will you do something for me?'

I look at him. 'Of course. What?'

'Be careful.' Pallioti says this without so much as a tremor passing over his face. It's so deadpan, it's almost funny.

'I am careful, Ispettore Pallioti. Believe me.'

Something about this almost makes him smile. He reaches into his jacket pocket and takes out one of his cards. 'I'm sorry I can't let you have your phone back,' he says. 'But if you need anything, signora, or think of anything else, please don't hesitate. Call me.'

I tuck the card into my wallet. I know he's just doing his job, but it does make me feel better. And I thank him.

Pallioti ushers me back into the entrance hall, asks me if I want a car to take me home, and almost smiles again when I say no. Then he shakes my hand and starts to walk away. After a few steps, he stops and looks back at me.

'*Carpaccio*,' he says suddenly.

I look at him, confused.

'Raw beef.' Ispettore Pallioti shrugs. 'Some people think it's an old wives' tale,' he says. 'But, really, it is the best thing. At least that's what my mama always told me, when I'd been in a fight.'

After I leave the Questura, I pick up a paper, sit at a café in Piazza della Repubblica, and read the whole thing. Then I read it again, the music of the merry-go-round rising and falling in the background.

'You could have at least warned me!'

The newspaper skids to a halt at Pierangelo's feet where I have thrown it, Billy's face smiling up at us.

'I guess I should be thankful you didn't put my picture in it! And my birthday and my fucking phone number!' I shout.

Then I slam the study door. I am so angry, I barely know what to do with myself.

In the kitchen, I try to pour myself a glass of wine, but I can't even stand still for that. My jaw has begun to throb, and when I catch a glimpse of myself in the shiny distorted surface of the bread box, I see a big red blotch. Tears prick at the back of my eyes. Suddenly I miss Billy so much it's like a physical pain.

The piece about me was on an inside page, in a side bar, a neatly placed little black box that denoted 'special interest'. The headline was: 'Apartment-mates Share More Than a Kitchen.' As an article, it was straightforward enough, gave my name, noted that Billy and I were room-mates, and outlined the attack in the Boboli two years ago. All without mentioning that Ty had been killed. Or that he'd even been there. In fact, the article didn't mention Ty at all. He might never have existed, never mind been murdered, and I'm as angry about that as anything.

When Pierangelo comes into the room and puts his arms around my shoulders, I try to shrug him off, but he's too tall and too strong for me. He rests his chin on top of my head, holding me from behind so I can't see his face.

'I'm sorry,' he says. 'But they were going to put in the story about you anyways, and it was better if I did it. I was going to tell you this morning. I should have. I'm sorry.' I make a half-hearted attempt to squirm away, but he holds on. 'I said as little as I could,' he adds. 'But you had to know this was going to happen. It's too big a coincidence. We had to cover it.'

'You left Ty out. Altogether. You didn't even mention him.'

I'm aware that the grievance of this is vinegar poured on my own guilt, and I think Pierangelo is too. 'Isn't it better that way?' he asks as he touches the sore place on my jaw.

'I tripped over a chair,' I say.

'The chair belong to anybody I know?'

I shake my head. Stupidity or playground ethics, I don't know, but, either way, my instinct tells me that mixing it up between Kirk and Pierangelo will only make a bad situation worse.

'You need a treat,' Pierangelo says. 'Go wash your face and I'll take you for a Martini at the Excelsior.'

'Piero, what about Kirk?'

'Batman?' Pierangelo looks at me over the rim of his glass. 'What about him?'

'Do you think he could have done it? Do you think he could have killed Billy?'

The spindly palm trees in their pots bow in an invisible puff of air, and on the other side of the Excelsior bar, the pianist breaks into 'Night and Day.' No one could possibly hear us in the corner where we are nestled on a gold brocade sofa, but Piero lowers his voice anyways. 'Could have, or did?' he asks. His pale green eyes glint in the low light.

I shrug. 'Does it matter?'

'Sure,' Piero says. 'Almost anyone can kill anyone, given the right circumstances.' He contemplates the gold signet ring he wears for a second, then he asks, 'Did he? I don't know. Unless you think he's a serial killer.'

'You're sure the same person who killed the others killed her, aren't you?'

Pierangelo considers me then nods. 'Yes,' he says. 'I am.'

'And that's what the police think?'

'From everything I hear.'

'So, no matter what the story is with Karel Indrizzio, the same person who killed Caterina Fusarno and Ginevra Montelleone killed Billy?'

'In my opinion, yes.'

'Why?' I can feel something slipping into place in my head, pieces of a puzzle that I only need to tilt the right way for them to make sense. 'I mean, I agree with you,' I add. 'So I don't mean "Why do you think that?" What I mean is, out of all of the women in Florence, why pick those three? What connects them?'

Pierangelo is watching me as I go on, groping towards something I can't quite grasp, fuelled by the cold silky gin and vermouth.

'If Billy was killed because of me, because she knew me, which I think is probably true, then that's not the right question, is it? It's not what connects them to Billy, it's what connects them to me.'

Pierangelo watches me for a second before he says, 'You know, *cara*, Pallioti is really a very good cop. He's very highly thought of.' He reaches out and smooths a strand of my hair. 'Come on,' he says. 'Let's let the police do their work, and we'll do ours.'

'Ours?'

'*Certo*. We have a wedding to plan.' Piero reaches into his jacket pocket, pulls out his date book and drops it on the table. 'I'm going to the men's room,' he says, standing up. 'When I come back, we'll pick a date.'

I watch his back as he walks away, weaving between the tables, then I reach out and take the little leather book. I riffle through its gold-edged pages, but I can't see the dates. Finally I drop it and sink back on the sofa, taking in the room around me. The piano is playing something I don't recognize. The tune winds itself through the sounds of people's voices. Above me, chandeliers wink. A champagne cork pops. A woman walks past, her high heels clicking on the marble, and squeals in greeting, hands outstretched when she sees her friends. This place is a cocoon, its beauty makes it safe, and yet, during the war, a man was shot in this bar, perhaps not feet from where I'm sitting. It was in the winter of 1944. He stood up and shouted that Mussolini was a bastard, and someone took out a gun and shot him.

Sitting here now, I can imagine the silence that followed. The piano notes hanging in the air, the stunned terror as the dead man's blood seeped in rivulets across the floor. And then the music starting again, a little sharper, a little faster, and, quickly, the resumption of conversation, high and brittle; the voices of people with eyes averted, people who are trying not to look, trying to pretend that what has just happened has not happened at all. Or, worse, that it's perfectly normal.

Chapter Twenty

PIERANGELO HAS AN editorial meeting, and in the morning he's in more of a hurry than usual. As he rushes out of the door, still tying his tie, he suggests I stay home for the day, maybe watch a movie or read a book. Get some rest. I promise I will.

The lie rolls off my tongue too easily. I watch from the living-room windows as he comes out of the building and walks down the street. Standing up here, I'm like Rapunzel in her tower. When he looks back, waving before he turns the corner, I lift my hand, although I doubt he can see me.

I've left things out—committed sins of omission—but I've never actually lied to Pierangelo before, and it makes the inside of my chest feel heavy. Perhaps, I think, I'll tell him, eventually. Make right what I have done wrong. But not now. Because if I told him now what I'm about to do, he'd stop me.

Annika is sitting alone. Again. I have the feeling that she always sits alone these days, that it's almost part of an act, like the horrible clashing clothes she wears. Today it's a pink turtleneck and a purple-and-green-spotted sweater. Her jeans have patches in the shapes of daisies on them, presumably in deliberate contrast to the heavily inked eyeliner and dark gothish lipstick.

I have been lying in wait for her for the better part of an hour, lurking around the coffee bar where, according to Billy, Ginevra Montelleone held court. Now, I give her five minutes to buy herself a cappuccino and settle in before I make my approach. When I do, she looks at me with a mild amount of interest, then digs in her bag for a cigarette. I pull out a chair, half expecting her to tell me to fuck off.

'I don't know if you remember me, we met at—'

'I remember you.' Annika doesn't stop ferreting in her knapsack as she says this, but I think I see a flicker of a smile cross her face, like lightning in the afternoon.

'May I?' I nod at the chair and she waves a hand, either in dismissal or vague invitation. Today, her bitten fingernails are painted bright blue.

She pushes the rumpled pack across the table towards me. I don't really want one, but I'm trying to make her like me, or at least talk to me, so I take a slightly bent Marlboro and the box of matches that Annika drops on the table. The flame flares in front of my face with a whiff of sulphur.

'How are you?'

She shrugs, her thin shoulders jumping and settling again as if the bones aren't connected by much flesh. I wouldn't be surprised to hear them rattle. 'You know,' she says. 'Busy. I have exams coming.' She lights her own cigarette and pulls on it.

'She was your friend, wasn't she?' she asks suddenly. 'The one who was killed up at the fort. I recognized her picture. You left together,' Annika adds, as if I am likely to dispute this. 'From the thing for Ginevra. I saw you.'

'Yeah. She was my friend.'

'And it happened to you too. Some creep got at you with a knife. The paper said so.'

I nod.

'I'm sorry,' she says. 'That's too bad.'

For the next few seconds, we watch each other through our respective clouds of cigarette smoke, playing chicken, waiting to see who will make the next move. This is a game I'm really good at so, finally, it's Annika. She works on the cigarette some more, then stubs it out in the ashtray and runs her blue-tipped fingers through her short white hair, pulling it from the roots.

'So,' she says, 'now you come and see me. And I wonder why. To tell me, maybe, that you think Ginevra didn't jump off a bridge after all?'

'What do you think?'

'I think that's the only reason you'd have for wanting to talk to me again.'

She stares at me with her odd opalescent eyes. I can see a pale blue vein throbbing at her temple, looking as if it might burst through the thin papery parchment of her skin.

'So what are you going to tell me?' she asks. 'That you think some creep is running around killing women and Ginny was one of them? She didn't know your friend, if that's where you're going.'

I reach into my bag and pull out the envelope I took from Billy's drawer yesterday morning.

'Did she know this guy?' I drop the picture of Kirk and Henry and me on the table, and for a second I think she isn't even going to look at it. Then she reaches out with the tips of her fingers, turns it towards her.

'Which one?'

A horrible cold feeling grips me when she says this, and for a nightmarish second I imagine she's going to point to Henry. But she shakes her head.

'Not really,' she says, and my heart stops.

'Not really?'

'They came in here. Him, the red-haired guy, and your friend. I think maybe once or twice before Ginny died. And maybe a couple of times afterwards.' She shrugs. 'I mean, you guys go to lectures at the university, right? So it's hardly unusual.

This is where everybody comes. I've never seen him before.' She puts her finger squarely on Henry's face and slides the photo back to me.

Did Ginevra know them? I mean, did she speak to them?' I don't know how Annika can possibly know this, but I ask it anyways. She looks at me as if I'm a little crazy, which probably isn't too far off the mark.

'I don't know,' she says. 'But I doubt it.'

'Why?'

Annika gives a little cough of laughter. 'They're not Ginny's type,' she says, pulling another cigarette out of the pack and lighting it. 'Americans. There's this place called Iraq, remember?'

'We didn't all think it was a great idea either.'

Annika rolls her eyes and shrugs again. 'So what? You think that guy killed them? Why does it matter,' she demands suddenly, 'how it happened? The point is, Ginny's dead. So is your friend. It doesn't matter how it happened.'

I open my mouth, about to point out that it does, kind of a lot, actually. That other people are dead too, and more could be, but then I close it again. Annika is glaring at me, and although I know that her anger is really pain, rage at having her friend plucked out of the world like this, she still looks as though she half suspects that I might have wielded the knife myself. I slip the picture back into the envelope and drop it in my bag, trying to tamp down a little surge of disappointment. The fact that Billy and Kirk came in here for an espresso after a lecture one afternoon isn't exactly damning evidence.

'If she knew him,' I ask, 'would you know about it? I mean, could she have known him without you knowing?'

'Of course she could, I was her friend, not her jailer. But I told you, I doubt it. Ginny wasn't really into men.'

I open my mouth and close it again, digesting this. 'She was gay?' I ask finally.

Annika laughs, the short little coughing sound again. It makes it seem as though she has TB, and I wonder if maybe that explains the pale-skin-and-bones look. 'She just wasn't into men,' she says. 'Definitely not right now, anyways. She thought they were basically assholes.'

'Why?'

I expect her to laugh again, tell me this is obvious, but she doesn't. Instead, Annika studies the slowly burning tip of her cigarette, watching a column of ash form and drop onto the table. She flicks it away with her blue fingers, watches it disintegrate as it falls to the floor like snow.

'The last time we met, you told me that on the night she died, Ginevra was depressed. Is that why?' I ask. 'Because of some guy?'

At first I think she's not going to answer. The café is almost empty, and she looks away from me, staring at the newspaper racks that hang beside the big wooden doors. *Corriere della Sera* and yesterday's *La Stampa* flutter slightly in the draught as a couple come in and go to the bar. Eventually, Annika looks at me.

'You might say that,' she says. Then she adds, 'It was because of the baby. I guess I shouldn't say anything. But I can't see that it matters, now that she's dead.'

'Baby?'

I try to keep the surprise out of my voice. After all I didn't even know the girl, but surely, I think, Piero's contact in the coroner's office wouldn't have missed this. Was Ginevra going to have a baby?'

'Not any more.'

I am not sure if she means because Ginevra's dead or because she had an abortion but, before I can ask, she shrugs her bird-like shoulders again and tugs the cuffs of her sweater down over her hands as if she's cold.

'She got rid of it. A couple of months ago.' Annika shakes her head. 'It's not as if she was even sure who the father was, you know. But afterwards, it wasn't as easy as she thought maybe it would be.'

I stub my cigarette out and think about this for a minute,

about being twenty-one and coming face to face with the chasm between ideals and deeds.

'She was Catholic, you know,' Annika is saying. She smiles suddenly, and makes a strange sound, like something ripping inside her. 'I mean, everybody here is,' she says, 'aren't they? So, so what? It's not like Ginny went to church any more or anything, except at Easter and Christmas, you know, to make her mother happy. But I think it got to her, afterwards. The brainwashing's hard to undo when you're being told you're damned. You think you don't care, and you know you shouldn't. I don't see why the church bothers with damnation,' she adds. 'Isn't knowing yourself bad enough? Ginny loved her country,' Annika announces. 'She wanted it to be better. For everybody. She was like that.'

There's so much jumbled up in this that it takes me a minute to sort it out. I knew Ginevra was idealistic, of course, she was an activist. And I knew she was Catholic. I remember the picture in the wine bar, and Rinaldo. Something contracts in my stomach. Something familiar that Annika just said. Damned. Who told Ginevra she was damned?

'Annika, do you know if she went to church, maybe to confession, after the abortion?'

'Yeah. I think she hoped it would make her feel better. The habit was hard to break. You know?'

I do know.

'Do you know who her priest was?'

She shakes her head. 'I have no idea,' she says. 'Priests all look the same to me. She went to Mary Magdalene though, over by the synagogue. I know that. Because she liked the name. Mary Magdalene was her favourite saint. At least she wasn't a goody-goody.'

I know the church, Maria Maddalena dei Pazzi, but as far as I know Rinaldo has no connection with it. Which doesn't mean he doesn't. Or that Ginevra didn't go back to her family's church, to San Miniato, without Annika knowing about it. Or that she didn't run into him somewhere else. I think of the clean-cut boys and the scrubbed girl handing out leaflets on the street.

'Did she ever talk about a certain part of the church?' I ask. 'I mean, did she ever, for instance, mention a group called Opus Dei?'

'The right-wing cuckoo pots?' Annika shakes her head again, stubs the cigarette out and immediately lights another one. She seems to like to play with them as much as smoke them. 'No,' she says. 'I mean, we all know who they are. They think they're all secretive, but they stick out a mile. Like FBI agents in American movies. You know, they all have short hair and smile too much. They don't let women go in bars, right?'

For a second I'm not sure if she's talking about the FBI or the Opus, and I can't help smiling, thinking this is probably not the single thing Father Rinaldo would want them to be known for.

'That sounds about right,' I agree. 'Did Ginevra ever talk about them, or campaign about them, or anything?'

'You mean, was it one of her things?' Annika shakes her head. 'She was worked up about the clinics, yeah. And about Palestine and what's going on in Africa. But stuff in the church, no. I mean, she wanted to be a lawyer, like for people's rights.' She pushes her sleeves back and glances at her watch. 'Shit!'

Annika jumps to her feet, almost pushing the pile of books on the table in front of her onto the floor. 'I have a lecture I can't miss.' She shakes her head rapidly, and starts stuffing her books into her bag. 'I only meant to come in for a coffee.'

'I'm sorry.' I feel responsible for this, which I think is what she intends, and I stand up too, as if it will somehow help speed her on her way.

'Was there anything else?' She is shrugging into her jacket, which looks like something Billy would have owned, short and suede, and definitely second-hand.

'No. But thanks for talking to me. I'm sorry if I kept you.'

Annika shrugs, her peaky face closed and angry again. 'What the fuck does it matter?' she says again. 'What does any of it matter? You know? You can be twenty-one and end up dead on a river bank.' And with that she's gone, pushing through the big wooden doors, her canvas knapsack clutched to her chest, empty coffee cup and smouldering cigarette left on the table behind her.

Back in Pierangelo's apartment, I check all the rooms. I know he shouldn't be here now, but I want to be sure. There's a flickering feeling running through me, like electricity jumping between wires. This has been happening. Either I'm groggy, slow and stuffed up, or jumping and twitching. In the bathroom, I stand looking at the pill bottles lined up on my side of the basin. Then, before I can stop myself, I grab them and empty them into the toilet. I don't want to be calm and I don't want to forget. What I want is to think straight. I push the button, and feel a moment of sheer panic as the little dots whirl away like confetti at a wedding.

A few seconds later, the panic is replaced by a surge of excitement. My mind is hopping and snapping again, reaching for something that feels so close I can almost touch it. In Piero's study it takes me five minutes to find what I'm looking for—an article on Caterina Fusarno from a women's magazine, detailing how sad her story was because she was a single mother and ex-addict who was getting her life back together, kicking her habit with the help of a methadone clinic called Vita Nuova out in the north of the city.

Despite my best efforts, I end up getting on the wrong bus. Then I get lost, so it's late when I finally find Vita Nuova.

From the outside the clinic looks as if it's seen better days. It's the ground floor of a concrete-block building with wired-in, plate-glass windows, and somebody's painted the front bright yellow, presumably as a sign of optimism. Or maybe because it was Dante's favourite colour. Who knows? Outside there's a bench that's chained to bolts in the sidewalk. When I try the door, it's locked.

I'm more annoyed by this than I would expect myself to be, and I stand there for a second, frustrated, but telling myself I can come back tomorrow. Then I notice the security camera, and remember what I've read about drug-treatment places, how they keep the doors locked because of the stuff they have inside. I start to knock and notice the bell, camouflaged because somebody painted it yellow too. I don't hear the ring when I push, but the black eye of the little camera is watching me, so I look right into it and try not to be threatening. I even smile. It must work, because a second later the buzzer sounds, and I push the door open.

The clinic's front room is painted yellow too, bright yellow that collides with an icky brown rug that has worn patches. Plastic modular chairs are lined up below bulletin boards covered with notices and posters, and there's a round table with stacks of leaflets on drug addiction, AIDS and STDs. The reception desk is behind a thick panel of glass, like one of those things you see in the Mafia trials. It's brightly lit and empty, just like the room, and I'm wondering what to do, knock or holler or just wait, when a young woman in jeans and a white lab coat appears from somewhere in the back of the building. I imagine Billy would pinch me if she were here, because the woman's name tag reads, 'Beatrice Modesto.'

Beatrice has a suitably sweet-looking face, of the kind, gentle-nurse variety. When she sees me, she puts down the files she is carrying and smiles, which presents me with a dilemma because I have no idea what I'm going to say. The jumpy feeling comes back and my palms feel sweaty. I can't just ask about Caterina out of the blue, so I fall back on the only thing I know. I smile broadly and say I'm a journalist. That I'm doing a piece for an American women's magazine on drug-abuse treatments and single families and wonder if she can spare me some time? The babble comes out of my mouth so fluently I amaze myself. My nose must be growing longer by the minute, like Pinocchio's, and I'm sure Billy's grin hangs like the Cheshire Cat's above my shoulder. Beatrice apparently doesn't notice either, because she buzzes me into the back office and offers me coffee.

For the next fifteen minutes, I dredge up everything I've ever heard, from Ty, or on TV or anywhere, about methadone. We discuss the number of patients the clinic treats, the rate of recidivism, and the whole question of the treatment itself, or rather, thank God, Beatrice does. I listen and nod a lot and take notes in what is actually my address book.

The clinic, it turns out, is funded by the city, which also gives them money for outreach. Four doctors rotate through it on a regular basis, and others come in from the major hospitals as volunteers. The youngest kids, the teenagers, are the hardest to reach, Beatrice says. The older ones, who know exactly how much your life can get screwed up, mostly come and get help on their own. In fact, the place has a waiting list. When I have the wit to ask if they operate a 'three strikes you're out' policy for those who fall off the straight and narrow, Beatrice smiles and shakes her head.

'That is a very American idea,' she says. 'Here, we just keep trying. Some of the people who come here are already lost, and they always will be. We know that. Others only look lost, and make it. The problem is, unless you're God, how do you know the difference?' She shrugs. 'It's amazing how many times some people can get knocked down and get back up again. You can never tell. The ones who have children especially. People will try hard to keep their kids.'

'Like Caterina Fusarno?'

I try to say it matter-of-factly, but my heart goes still. This is the moment when she's either going to clam up or talk to me. A cloud passes over her face, and I reach into my bag, produce the article and hand it to her.

'That's how I heard about you. It sounds like a really sad story.'

Beatrice picks up the article and shakes her head. Suddenly she looks tired, and I wonder for the first time how old she is. Probably not even thirty. Her fine features crumple into a frown and she pushes her long brown hair off her forehead as if she's hot.

'She was going to be OK, you know? She even had a line on a real job, at the day-care place where her son went. They'd agreed to take her as a secretary, part-time, if she kept up the good work here. Then this happens.' She hands the article back and shakes her head. 'The police were such pigs about this,' she says.

'How?'

'Oh they were here about fifty million times. Wanted all her medical files, probably to prove she was nothing but a junkie. And they wanted other patient files too. Of course we weren't about to give them to them. We even had the fucking cardinal.'

'D'Erreti?' I ask, surprised.

She nods. 'God himself. He's trying to cut our funding because we counsel on contraception and abortion instead of preaching abstinence. Then he used Caterina to try to make the case that if we didn't give methadone to hookers they wouldn't get murdered. I'm not sure how that works,' she adds. 'Frankly, I just think men are animals. Every last goddam one of them. Probably we should do castration here too, like they do for dogs.' And to think, when I first saw her, I thought Beatrice looked kind and gentle.

'Did you ever run into a priest, a sidekick of D'Erreti's called Father Rinaldo?' Beatrice looks up at the ceiling, thinking for a second, then she shakes her head.

'No,' she says. 'I don't think so. I don't remember that name at all. Why?'

'He's Opus Dei. I thought it might be the kind of thing—'

'—they really get into?' She actually laughs as she finishes the sentence for me. 'Well, you're right there. But no,' she says, shaking her head again. 'We haven't actually had any trouble with them, but others have though, especially if they touch abortion.'

'Same thing in the States,' I agree. 'I guess,' I add as casually as I can manage, 'that the university's felt some heat about that.'

'Yeah.' Beatrice frowns. 'It's a damn shame,' she says, 'about that poor girl who threw the eggs at His Cardinal-ness.'

'Did you know her?'

'No.' She grins. 'But I'd have liked to shake her hand.'

She glances at the clock, and I realize my time here is up.

'Caterina wasn't into that kind of stuff, I guess? Protesting and all?' I ask it as I stand up, hoping that somehow she'll miraculously hand me a connection between the two women. But she shakes her head once more.

'I don't think so. At least not that I know of. She was probably too busy with Carlo. But you could ask her mother. Carlo lives with Rosa now,' she adds. 'Which is good because he stayed at the same care place and everything. It's no fun losing your mom when you're five. That's him right there, in the front.'

Beatrice points towards a picture on the wall. The group of people in it wear baseball caps and T-shirts and hold up paint brushes. Some of them have spatters of yellow on their faces. All of them are grinning. In front is an older woman holding a little boy. They're standing outside the clinic, with the bright yellow wall and the reinforced metal door behind them.

I peer at it, something niggling at the corner of my brain. One of the faces seems almost familiar, but with the baseball caps it's hard to tell. Those things make everybody look familiar, little white half-moon faces with yellow bills where their eyes should be.

'Church volunteer group,' Beatrice says. Not all of them are bad. Even I have to admit that. This one does work at the hospital too. Repairing things, painting, stuff like that. You know,' she adds quickly, 'if you go now, you can probably catch Rosa waiting for Carlo. He gets out at five, and it's just round the corner.'

'Would she talk to me?'

'She talks to anyone,' Beatrice says, leading me towards the door to the front room. 'Especially about this. She's very angry with the police, that they never really did anything, after making such a big fuss. It's disgusting.' Beatrice buzzes us back into the yellow front room. 'It was as though all they really wanted to know was did Caterina do drugs and have AIDS.'

Beatrice waves as she lets me out. 'Send us a copy of what you write,' she calls as I head off down the street. 'And mention our name, it's good for the money!'

Unlike Vita Nuova, the day-care centre is not hard to find. It fronts a small triangular park. The building is concrete block too, but this time the windows are open and someone has painted a mural of giant sunflowers on the outside wall. A red lion and a blue-striped zebra peer through the stalks. A pink giraffe pokes its head above the flower faces. Probably the church group again. There's the sound of children babbling from inside the building, and a bunch of women, and a few young men, sit on the round benches that circle the park's trees. The women chat among themselves, the guys read their newspapers. The big clock above the front door of the centre says ten minutes to five.

At first, I can't see anyone who even remotely looks as if she might be Caterina Fusarno's mother, and I'm about to give up and make the long trek back to the bus stop, resigned to coming back tomorrow, when a group of people walking their dogs move, and I spot an older lady sitting a little off by herself, knitting. She's wearing the kind of nylon flowered smock that house cleaners wear, and a big raffia shopping bag that's seen better days sits at her feet. Her fingers move over the navy-blue wool so fast it's almost possible to see the arm of the little sweater take shape as I walk towards her. This time, I think, I'll try just telling the truth.

When I get up close, I stretch out my hand and tell Rosa Fusarno my name. Then I ask if she's Caterina's mother. She studies me for a second before she puts the needles in her lap and asks what I want. Her voice is deep and determined, and she doesn't flinch. She's had practice, I think. She's been through this with the police, and the press, and God knows who all else.

'I'm a journalist,' I say. 'From America. And I'm a friend of the woman they just found murdered up at the Belvedere. I wondered if you'd have a minute to talk to me?'

'A journalist from America?' Rosa Fusarno laughs, which is not what I expected. 'What good is America to Martina?' she asks. 'Unless maybe it embarrasses the bastards.' She has a point, and I'm trying to figure out how to answer it when she pats the seat beside her, and moves over so I can sit down.

She knits for a few seconds, then, without looking up, she asks, 'How old was she? Your friend?'

'Thirty-five,' I reply, and realize with a shock that Billy's birthday is coming up. She wanted to go to Venice. Stay on the Lido. Ride in a gondola.

'You think the same person did it?' Rosa's needles click like summer crickets.

'I think maybe. That's what I'm trying to find out—if anything, or anyone, connected them. My friend and Caterina. Somehow he had to know them both.'

'Maybe. Maybe not.' Rosa doesn't look up from her tiny sweater. 'Maybe he was just mad at his wife and felt like killing,' she says. 'Evil son of a bitch. It's not women, you know,' she adds, 'who go around cutting people up with knives.'

'No. Not usually.'

Rosa glances at me out of the corner of her eye.

'You sleep at night?' she asks. 'They give you pills?'

'Yeah, they did. But I threw them out.'

'Pills for this. Pills for that. As if they can cure everything. My Martina, she was thirty-two.'

'I talked to Beatrice at the clinic. Your daughter sounds like she was a remarkable woman.'

Caterina's mother shrugs. There's the hint of a smile on her face, but it vanishes as quickly as it came. 'America,' she says again. 'So, are you going to tell them in America that no one's done a goddam thing here to find the man who killed my child? Maybe in America,' she adds, 'they won't care that she was a whore.'

The word isn't said with anger, or even bitterness. Rosa just states it as a fact. This was what her daughter did for a living.

'They looked at her room,' Rosa goes on. 'They took some

things away. Some of her pictures. And said they'd bring them back, but they never did. She had a job, you know,' she adds, 'here at the day care.' Her words peter out. She stares off at the building, as if she might see her daughter, along with the zebra and the lion, hiding in the bright green sunflower stalks.

'She was going to start the week after it happened.' Rosa's fingers slow and stop, the clicking winding down to silence. 'She was so proud of herself. She took a course on the computer and everything. At least she knew she got the job before she died.'

Rosa puts her knitting in her lap and her head swings round. Suddenly she reminds me of a snapping turtle I saw in the woods behind my grandparents' farm in Pennsylvania when I was little. It was huge, so big it looked as if I could ride on it. Its neck was crêpey and old, its beak nose pointed, but its eyes were bright and black and shiny, just like the ones that stare at me now.

'She didn't work that park,' Rosa says. 'Never.' Her hand comes down on the wood of the bench, flat and hard. 'She wasn't stupid, and she wasn't a streetwalker. She took bookings. She didn't need the extra. I told the police that too. You hear what I'm saying?'

'What about her man?'

Rosa makes a sour face. 'She didn't have no man,' she says. 'Didn't need one. She had a client list. Like I said, she was high class. She didn't work the streets.'

'And that night, New Year's Eve—'

Rosa cuts me off, waving her hand. 'She didn't share details with me. I was her mother. I watch Carlo.' I feel myself colour. Rosa reaches out and pats my knee. 'We were going to Mass,' she says. 'New Year's Day at the cathedral. My girl loved God. She used to say he was her best friend. I told the policeman that,' she adds, 'not that he cared, the cold-eyed son of a bitch.'

I see my white-tiled hospital room, and the quick image of a lizard sitting on a rock.

'Pallioti?'

'Yeah,' Rosa nods. 'That was the name. Of all of them, he

was the only one who didn't ask me about sex. From the looks
of him,' she adds, 'he probably doesn't know what it is. Men like
that, they hatch from eggs.'

'Did she have a priest? A regular confessor?'

'*Certo*,' Rosa nods, her eyes distant. 'Father Donati. He went
to the seminary with my cousin. Afterwards, you know, he went
right to the police and told them everything he could think of,
said the confessional wasn't so sacred after she was dead. He told
me too, but it didn't help. He always absolved her,' she adds. 'He
made sure she got to heaven, where she belongs.'

Hearing this, I'm pretty sure my next question is pointless,
but I ask about Rinaldo anyways, and Opus Dei. Rosa shakes
her head. She's never heard of Rinaldo, and Opus, she says, well,
from what she's heard, they only like fancy people. Finally I pull
out the picture of Kirk, but I draw a blank there too. Rosa's never
seen him before, but, like she said, the police took her daughter's
papers, her calendar. Told her they'd traced all of her clients, not
that Rosa believes it. She hands the picture back.

'You think he did it?'

I look at the three of us, me and Henry and Kirk, sitting in
the bar and shake my head. 'I did, I think. Now, I really don't
know.'

Somehow I can't imagine Kirk cruising hookers on New
Year's Eve. It just doesn't feel right.

Rosa tucks her knitting into her bag, and stands up. One
arm of the small blue sweater hangs over the edge.

'There are evil people in this world,' she announces, 'and
most of them are men.' She reaches out and pats the top of my
head. 'We, none of us, can do anything about it, *piccola*,' she
says. Then she adds, 'I just don't want Carlo to be one of them.'

Rosa Fusarno's hard calloused palm rests for a moment on
my head. Then she picks up her bag and begins to walk away,
shuffling slightly in her flat shoes. Other women are standing
up now too. The men fold their newspapers. She is maybe ten
yards away, her square, squat, flowered back to me, when she
turns round.

'In America,' Rosa calls, 'at least use her name right. She changed it to Caterina, but I baptized her Martina. You call her that, you call her Martina Fusarno.'

A sense of dejection stays with me all the way home, and finally I get off the bus early and decide to walk. I was so sure I was right, so certain that the link between Billy and Caterina and Ginevra was me, that I had all but convinced myself that it had to be Kirk, or maybe even Rinaldo, or Opus Dei, something—anything, anyone—I could identify, if only I looked in the right place and asked the right questions. So much for that. Maybe Rosa's right, and this is all random. We believe in cause, in chains of logic, or even God, because it gives us some sense of control. But maybe we live at the mercy of the butterfly's wing, after all. Chaos theory. A tiny breath of air shifts halfway across the world and, bingo, your life is changed for ever.

A dog barks, the high excited yip of a terrier, and I turn a corner and realize I'm closer to Santa Maria Novella than I thought. A group of students comes along the sidewalk and splits, flowing around me, their laughter ringing like a peal of bells. I turn another corner, then the next, until, without really being aware of it, I'm facing the building where Ty and I lived.

The front door opens, and a young woman comes out pushing a baby carriage. Watching her, I can almost smell the faint whiff of mould and vegetables that always filled that stair-well, almost see the peeling paper and the mustard-coloured paint on the banister. The girl is wearing jeans and sandals, and from across the street she smiles at me, half hesitantly, as if she thinks she should recognize me. Then she tucks the baby in and starts off in the opposite direction. I watch her go, her figure getting dimmer and smaller, and for just a second I allow myself to wonder how close that came to being me.

❄ ❄ ❄

Piero's waiting for me when I get back, and I know right away that something bad has happened. His face looks as though a shadow has fallen across it.

'What? What is it?'

He shakes his head, as if he is trying to clear it. Then he tells me he saw a copy of Billy's autopsy report today.

'She wasn't killed at the fort. She was placed there after. Well after.' He doesn't want to look at me. He opens the refrigerator and is fooling with something inside. 'They're pretty sure she'd been dead for about forty-eight hours when they found her,' he says.

My mind can't seem to process this, that she died on Thursday, not Easter Sunday.

'So I couldn't have seen her in the Bargello?' I ask stupidly.

'No.' Pierangelo shuts the fridge. 'Probably not. She was almost certainly dead by then.'

Of course. She was so filthy with dirt and ash from the fire, it was hard to see, but I remember the mottled skin of her legs.

I drop my bag, sink down onto one of the kitchen stools.

'Why would anyone do that?' I ask finally. 'Kill her, then keep her body before burning it.'

Pierangelo shakes his head. 'He wanted her to be found on Easter morning? Resurrected? I don't know. Maybe he couldn't get in until Saturday night. Maybe he had to get ready. Who knows? You tell me.'

But I can't. All I can think is that Billy was taken somewhere, to some terrible place, and killed.

'They looked, didn't they? After Benedetta? For where—' But I can't say the words.

'Of course.' Pierangelo walks across the kitchen, picks up a bowl and puts it down again. 'Everywhere,' he says. 'They got excited, for a while, about one of the sheds, in the groves. The growers park their trucks and stuff in them, and one of them looked as if the floor might have been turned, but it was nothing. A petrol spill. Then there was an abandoned warehouse, out by the airport. A couple of the boyfriend's construction sites. But they turned out to be illegal butchering. A fight. Nothing.'

'Do you think whoever it is took Ginevra and Billy to the same place?'

'Yes. Probably. I don't know. Assuming he has a car, it could be anywhere.'

Pierangelo's voice drops, as if this really doesn't interest him, but he's still pacing around the kitchen, restless as a cat. He's more worked up than I am, as if we've reversed places, and I know I have to be missing something here. A cold feeling comes over me.

'What else did the autopsy say?'

He stops and looks at me, and I know. I can see the pictures of Benedetta Lucchese's and Ginevra Montelleone's bodies. 'How bad?' The question sounds like a rock falling into the room

'*Cara*—' Pierangelo sounds as though he might try to say something soothing, and I wave it away. Nobody soothed Billy.

'How bad?'

'Bad.' He takes a breath. 'Under her clothes,' he tells me, 'all over her body, they found burns.'

Chapter Twenty-one

I READ SOMEWHERE once that someone did a study on exactly how many babies are conceived the night after funerals. The result was 'a lot,' and the theory was that the urge to start a new life makes up for the loss of an old one. But I'm not sure I agree. I tend to think those conceptions may in fact be the by-product of a more visceral, more furious act of defiance, a giving of the finger, so to speak, to mortality. A screeching back: *I'm alive and I'm going to stay living*! I think about this the next morning as I walk over the Ponte alle Grazie and turn towards San Niccolo.

Pallioti has deprived me of the faces in my envelope, but neither he nor anyone else can stop me from paying private calls to the dead. Behind me, on the opposite bank, is the spot where they found Ginevra. Ahead is the wine bar where she was last seen. Up the hill is the place where Benedetta vanished and, not far from that, the spot in the olive groves where she was found two days later. Almost directly above it are the walls of the ramparts where Billy's killer built her funeral pyre.

And somewhere, somewhere in this city, is the 'in between,'

the void those women were sucked into. The place where he takes them to burn, and cut, and strip the skin from their bodies.

The sun is coming out, burning off a thin scrim of clouds as I climb the steep hill beside the city walls. I meet ladies walking together, and joggers who huff and pant. Ahead, a father in a business suit gets out of a car, grabbing a briefcase in one hand and his little girl in the other. He stops to fix the ribbon on her long braid before they walk together up towards the school on Via San Leonardo, her tiny polished shoes taking two steps for every one of his.

At the top of the street I am momentarily surprised by the sight of a tour bus pulling up outside the entrance to the Belvedere. A group of people tumbles out, smiling and laughing. I didn't realize the fort was open to the public again, and then I think: *Why not?* It's Thursday. Four days since Billy was found. Plenty of time for the police to finish with the site, and for the city to clean it up. To remove all trace of her. Because for these nice people life goes on. For them, it never stopped. They trickle past me, chattering and adjusting the straps of their cameras and videos, and as I turn onto Via San Leonardo I find myself hoping they like the strange floating park and the broken-time mirror, and that the big old junk sculpture doesn't ruin their view of Florence.

No sinister black motorcycle whips past me this time. The morning is so still I can hear birdsong. Ten days ago the wisteria buds were puckered, but now they've opened and the long purple flowers reach across the tops of walls like languid hands, fingering the warm grey stones. Two elderly men come out of a gate, each with a small brown dog on a leash. Passing me in silence, they raise their hats in unison. I walk on a few yards until I'm standing outside the gates of the Lucchese house.

This is the last place Benedetta was seen alive, and I imagine her sister standing in the doorway, watching as she walked down this drive and passed into the dark. I wonder if she waved. Or called something? Perhaps if I listen, I'll hear the echo of her voice.

The gates are rusty. The *'Attenti Al Cane'* sign is tied on with wire, and I reach out to touch it, tracing the outline of the dog's nose with the tip of my finger. Then I hear singing and, almost as if I've conjured her, a woman appears. She's tall, thin and wearing blue jeans, and she comes around the side of the house pushing a wheelbarrow filled with brush. Her voice is slightly off pitch in the still morning air.

She could be the gardener. But even as I think it, I dismiss the idea. The drive is thinly gravelled and weedy. A tiny Fiat is the only car parked on the other side of the gates, and the bench set underneath a chestnut tree has a broken leg propped up by bricks. This house can't afford staff. She puts the wheelbarrow down and pulls her gardening gloves off, then she senses me and turns. As our eyes meet, I think that, although I've only seen pictures of her when she was dead, Benedetta Lucchese must have looked a lot like her sister.

I know this is the moment when I can walk away, when I can be just one more passing tourist trying to glimpse beyond villa walls. But instead I stand there with my hand resting on the sign, the rusted wire poking into my thumb. A real German shepherd, much prettier than the one on the picture, rustles out of the undergrowth, and the woman speaks to it, rubs the top of its head, which comes almost to her hip. Then she walks up the drive, the dog padding beside her.

Her fine features and wide-set eyes are creepily familiar. But where Benedetta was dark, this woman is fair. She has long caramel-coloured hair tied back in a braid.

'*Buongiorno.* Can I help?' Her voice is soft, the words rounded and smooth, cool as stones dropping through water.

'Signora Isabella Lucchese?'

'*Si.*' She cocks her head, her blue eyes watching mine. 'Do I know you?' she asks.

'My name is Mary Warren.'

She stares for a second, then her eyes widen. She won't recognize the newspaper pictures from two years ago, not now that I've changed my hair, but she'll remember my name. How could she forget? The man who murdered my husband killed her sister.

'The Honeymoon Killing?' She summons up the tabloid name, and I nod.

'Karel Indrizzio.'

'*Si.*' Her voice falls to not much more than a whisper. 'Karel Indrizzio.'

The air around us feels as if it has gone still, as if time has stopped. The dog senses it and whines. His golden eyes flicker to her face. Without looking at him Isabella drops her hand to his head.

'If you don't believe me,' I say, 'I have…I have some ID.' I'm scrabbling in my bag now, suddenly terrified that she'll tell me to go away. I fish out the old press card that I still keep in my wallet and my driver's licence, and proffer them through the rails of the gate. Isabella takes the cards, still watching me, glances at the pictures and names and passes them back.

'I need to talk to you,' I say. 'I'd like to talk to you, please.'

I can feel her wavering, wondering if perhaps she wouldn't be wiser to send me on my way, not make the mistake of opening the gates and letting me and whatever I might bring with me into her life. All at once, I feel as if I smell, as if there's a rotten sick-sweet odour rising off me that will never be disguised by fancy clothes or new haircuts or any amount of acacia oil. This was a terrible mistake. There is nothing this woman can do to help me, or Billy, and I have no right to intrude on her life. I'm not even sure what I want to say. Pierangelo was right. I should let Pallioti do his job.

'I'm sorry,' I say quickly. 'I'm sorry. I shouldn't have come, I—' I start to back away, to turn and walk as fast as I can, maybe even run down towards Viale Galileo, but Isabella Lucchese stops me.

'Why?' she asks. I hesitate and look at her. 'Why do you want to talk to me?'

The sun is warming the cobbles and the flowers that tip over the walls, scented hydrangea, a scraggle of red roses.

'I have a friend. I had a friend,' I correct myself. 'She was murdered. Last week. A week ago today. And before he killed her—whoever he is—he took her somewhere and tortured her.'

'*Santo Dio.*' Isabella crosses herself quickly.

'He burnt her.' By now tears are streaming down my cheeks, as if saying it out loud finally makes it real. 'All over her body, he burnt her. And then he killed her, and dressed her up. This time he put her on a fire. There was another girl he drowned.' Isabella is staring at me. 'It's happening again,' I say. 'It's happening all over again, just like it did before.'

I am only half aware of her opening the gate. She steps out into the road and takes me by the arm, the dog watching, bemused, as she leads me inside.

'Come on,' she says. 'Come out of the road. You can't stand here like this.' She even digs in her pocket and hands me a handkerchief.

Behind us the gate clanks shut and our feet crunch on the gravel. The smell of lavender rises up as we skirt the wheelbarrow, and Isabella guides me around a hedge at the side of the house.

'Come on,' she says as though she's talking to a reluctant animal or a child. 'Sit down. I was going to have a cup of coffee.'

She parks me on a bench at the back of the villa beside a low wall that gives onto a wild tangle of garden below. Behind us, grape and honeysuckle climb the columns of a pergola. The pale stucco of the villa glows faintly in the sun. The upstairs windows are shuttered, their eyes closed, but the lower ones are open, and vines wind themselves through broken slats and cling to rusted latches.

Isabella drops her gloves and vanishes into the house. The dog regards me solemnly for a moment, listening as I hiccup and sniff, wiping my eyes with his mistress's handkerchief, then he follows her halfway and plants himself outside the door, making sure I won't get in. Through the kitchen window, I hear a tap go on and off, a coffee grinder; and as I stop crying, and sit still, I can hear the sound of bees.

'I keep them,' Isabella says from behind me. She is holding a tray with a coffee pot and two cups on it. She puts it down on the seat. 'Do you know anything about bees?' she asks. We are speaking Italian, and at first I think I haven't understood her. She sees the look on my face, smiles, hands me a cup, and switches to English. 'I started keeping bees as therapy,' she says. 'After Benedetta was killed. Bees are very soothing.'

She sits on the low wall opposite me, stirring her coffee. 'Once,' she says, 'they swarmed. They do that sometimes, if they get scared. Run away from their hive. They went inside and I found them on the curtains. When that happens, you have to capture the queen. You just hold her in your hands and the rest of them will follow you anywhere.'

Behind her, beyond the tangle of the garden, the olive groves roll away. Below us, I pick out the roofs of the little bumblebee houses nestled by the walls of the Boboli.

The coffee is bitter and very strong. 'Thank you.' I finish it and put the cup down, not sure whether I'm talking about the coffee or the handkerchief or her kindness. It doesn't seem to matter. 'This is a very beautiful place.'

'Yes.' Isabella glances up at the house and smiles. 'They say Byron stayed here,' she says. 'But they say that about most of the villas in these hills. My mother's family built it in 1630. We've been here ever since. Almost all of us were born here, upstairs in the centre room. It's considered auspicious.' She waves towards the shuttered windows. 'But now there's just me. Well, just me and Fonzi.'

At the mention of his name the big dog gets up and comes and stands beside her. He nudges her arm with his nose and she rubs his ears. 'It's too big for us, isn't it?' she asks him. 'Just for us and the bees? But we can't bear to leave it. Sometimes,' Isabella says, 'in the evening, you hear a nightingale.'

She puts her cup down. 'Now,' she says. 'Why don't you tell me about what happened to your friend?'

I put my own cup back on the tray, consider the faded gilt rim and the tiny spoon. 'Her name was Billy Kalczeska. She was my room-mate. Well, I shared an apartment with her. I came back here to do a course, on art history.'

It feels important that I don't get this wrong, as if a lot is riding on it, and at first the words come slowly. Then they start to gather speed and flow of their own accord, and I tell her about Billy, and about Ginevra Montelleone, and what I discovered about Caterina Fusarno. When I finish, her face is pale. She gets up and stands looking out across the view, her back to me.

When she turns round, she says, 'But Karel Indrizzio is dead. He died in that accident when they were taking him to Milan. You know that?'

I nod. Isabella stares at me, her face disbelieving. I think if I hadn't told her Pallioti was handling this, she might be deciding by now that I'm making it all up and throw me out.

'So, what you're telling me,' she says slowly, 'is that there's someone else. Someone who's copying him. Or?' She sits down hard on the wall. 'Or that Indrizzio didn't do it. That's what you're really suggesting, isn't it?'

'I don't know,' I reply. 'Honestly. I really don't. I don't understand either. But I thought if I could find out why these women, of all the women in Florence, why these? Or if I could find out where he takes them, then maybe—' My voice just stops.

'I'm afraid,' I say. Isabella looks at me. 'I'm afraid of his four red bags.'

'Because he's used only two?' I nod. She picks at a piece of moss. 'Or because you think one of them is for you?' she asks.

'Both. I don't know. But I do know he's going to use them,' I add. 'For somebody.'

We sit there with nothing but the hum of the bees and the rustling of birds, an occasional twitter, around us. When Fonzi gets up, sniffs the air and lopes off down the steps into the tangled undergrowth, both of us watch him. Then Isabella throws the moss she's been picking over the wall. She takes a deep breath and runs her hands across the long, lean features of her face, and for half a second I expect her to do a clown trick, take her hands away and look like someone else. Now you see me. Now you don't. When she does finally look at me, I imagine that she has been here, with her dog and her bees, in this crumbling garden, for ever.

'It's not that I don't believe you,' she says. 'I never liked the case against Indrizzio. I mean, I wanted to believe it. I was even looking forward to the trial, because I wanted to be convinced, you know?' She shakes her head at this idea. 'But then he died. And there were no more killings. So I thought, oh well, that was it. I didn't know about the prostitute.'

'Caterina. No one did, really. And Ginevra Montelleone was reported as a suicide. They can't do that with Billy's murder, obviously, but I think they don't want to have a panic. Terrify people. It's the beginning of the tourist season.'

She looks at me out of the corner of her eye. 'Or to have to admit they were wrong all along. What about you?' she asks suddenly. 'Why don't you just get on a plane and leave?'

'I can't. I'm going to live here. I'm getting married. There's nothing in America I want to go back to.' It sounds facile, but it's true, and the realization comes as something of a shock, as if I've been on a boat, and so busy sailing out to sea that I've only just noticed I can't see land any more.

'Besides,' I add, taking a breath, 'I don't think it would do any good. For me maybe, but for no one else. I don't think it would stop him. He could have killed me if he'd wanted to, in the Bargello. Look.' I lean forward, as if I can will her to come with me, convince her that this time there's something, anything, that can be done about this. 'I believe Indrizzio is dead, and if he did kill your sister and Eleanora Darnelli, whoever this is knows a lot about him. What he did, how he killed. They must have known each other. And if Indrizzio didn't do it, if he didn't kill them, then—well I just keep thinking, if I can find out why he chooses the women he chooses, what the connection is —' I look at her. 'I know he chose my friend, Billy, because of me. So I need to figure out about the others. There has to be a link.'

'And you think it's you?'

'I can't think of anything else. If it's random, if he just kills, there's no way to find him, except luck.'

Isabella stands up and pushes back the rolled cuffs of her faded yellow shirt exposing strong arms, sinewy and tanned from wrestling with the wilderness of her garden. 'I don't know what to tell you,' she says. 'You can ask me anything you want about Bene, but the police have it all, pretty much. I'll give them that, they were thorough.'

'Was she fit? Could he have forced her into a car that night?'

Isabella shrugs. 'She was as fit as anyone. She rode a bike to work. But yes, I guess someone could have grabbed her. I've thought about it, of course. That's what they thought Indrizzio did. They found out that he actually belonged to one of those car clubs.' She laughs at the look on my face. 'I know,' she says, 'he was homeless. But this is Italy. Not having a place to sleep doesn't stop you from having a driver's licence. Apparently, he even worked sometimes. On construction, that sort of stuff. At least that's what the police told me.'

I think about this for a second. With the black economy, people do all sorts of things, live whole lives below the radar of the state.

'Whoever did this, or is doing it,' I say, 'I think they might be Catholic. Because of the stuff left on the bodies, the "presents." It's all vaguely liturgical. Eleanora's white ribbon: purity. The candle: transubstantiation. Caterina Fusarno was left with a goldfinch. They stand for Christ's passion, at least in painting, and the red bags belong to Hate in the garden of Eden. Do you think she could have known him from church somewhere?'

'Sure,' Isabella says. 'She could have known him from anywhere. He could be a parent of one of the kids she took care of at the hospital. Who knows?'

Kids. I see Rosa Fusarno's face. Sunflowers. Giraffes. 'She didn't work in a day-care centre did she? Out by the airport? Maybe a charity place?'

Isabella shakes her head. 'She was full-time at the hospital. She barely had time for a life.' So much for that idea.

'But she went to Mass, right? Before she came here?' I try another tack.

'Uh-huh. She'd had a fight with André, her fiancé, that night. That's when Bene was most likely to go to Mass.'

'At night?'

Isabella smiles. 'No, when she felt guilty. But she went at night, because of her work schedules. You fit God in when you can. I don't believe he minds,' she says. 'There are others who disagree.'

'Where did she go? That night, before she came here.'

'To Mass?' Isabella shrugs. 'San Miniato.'

I stare at her, my stomach feeling as if it's going down on a fast elevator. 'San Miniato?'

Isabella nods. 'Sure. Our family went there, when we were children. It was our family church.'

'Just like Ginevra Montelleone.' I say it as much to myself as to her. 'Tell me,' I ask quickly, 'do you know a priest there? A Father Rinaldo? He's very right-wing. I think he's even Opus Dei.'

'Opus Dei?' Now Isabella stares at me.

I nod, feeling my pulse begin to race. 'This group,' I say, 'they're—'

She waves her hand in the air, brushing my explanation away. 'I know who they are.' Isabella closes her eyes. '"Let us drink to the last drop the chalice of pain in this poor present life...Deny yourself. It's so beautiful to be a victim,"' she recites. Then she opens her eyes and looks at me. 'You know who wrote that?' she asks, and I shake my head. This time when she smiles, the smile is bitter.

'Josemaria Escrivá, Opus Dei's founding saint—literally —in his book, *The Way.* It's their bible. Their manual for day-to-day living. Bene's fiancé, André, has spent most of his adult life fighting them,' she adds. 'In fact, that's how they met.'

Pictures shoot through my head. Rinaldo's beautiful prayer group whispering and fluttering around me as I stand in the sacristy at San Miniato, Rinaldo himself, towering over me as I proffer tulips, the scrubbed boys and blank-faced girl standing in the empty street behind him; Beatrice Modesto shaking her head. *We haven't actually had any trouble with them, but others have, though, especially if they touch abortion.* Pieces of the puzzle click and shuffle.

'Benedetta was involved with Opus Dei,' I mutter. But Isabella shakes her head.

'No,' she says. 'I was.'

This takes me totally by surprise, and I open my mouth to protest, to actually argue with her, then close it again, quickly. Isabella is looking down into the garden, studying the whirring flight of her bees. 'I can't wear bathing suits,' she says.

I feel faintly sick. Too much sun. Or the idea of barbed wire digging into flesh.

'The cilice?'

She nods. 'I have holes.' Her eyes are still on the bees. 'Like stigmata. They said it was a special privilege, and I was so happy when I received permission to wear it.'

When she looks at me there are tears on her cheeks. 'It's like a chain of barbed wire. You wear it around the top of your thigh for two hours a day. More, if you're very privileged. And you use the "discipline" too. I suppose you know what that is?'

I nod. It's a rope whip, something like a cat-o'-nine-tails. In the Middle Ages the penitents used to beat their back and buttocks with it until they drew blood, flaying their flesh to grow closer to Christ on the Cross. The church took a dim view of it, even then, and eventually mainstream Catholicism banned it. But not Opus.

'That's not the worst thing about them,' Isabella is saying. She wipes her eyes with the back of her hands. 'The sleeping on boards and kissing the floor, all that nonsense. That's what the papers like, but it's not the worst. The real damage isn't what they do to your flesh, it's what they do to your heart. To your love of God. They take it.' Her voice turns hard.

'They kidnap Christ,' she says. 'Treat him as if he's their own personal property, and instead of him, you get them. You're supposed to surrender everything to them, and in return they tell you how to love God. And how not to love God. Then they tell you how he loves you. But, mostly, how he doesn't love you. And in return for that, they want everything. Everything. You give up your life.' She pauses. '"To live we must die,"' Isabella says. '"We must deny ourselves everything; the sacrifice must be the Holocaust."'

She smiles, her teeth showing, as if she might bite. 'That's what they teach about the Love of Christ.' She picks up her empty cup and puts it down, and when she starts speaking again I can hear the rage in her voice.

'They don't want just your faith and your mind, they want your money too,' she says. 'If you live in one of their houses they make you hand your salary over to them and give you an allowance in return. It's all part of the "Childhood Before God" idea. But that's not all. What they really want is for you to make your will over to them. They wanted this house.'

Isabella looks up, at the closed windows of the upper room where her family has been born, and probably died, at the buttercoloured stucco, at the pediment above the door engraved with a fading coat of arms, and shakes her head. 'I would have given it to them,' she says. 'That's the sick thing. God, I would have. I gave up my marriage for them. They told me I was giving it to Jesus, and I would have given them this house, too. That's what happened to André,' she adds.

'You were married?' I thought he was Benedetta's fiancé, and now I'm confused.

'Not to André.' Isabella smiles. 'No, to someone else, who I left for Opus. André's mother got involved with them, though. After his father died. They lived here, in Florence, and she signed everything over to them. But worse than that, they took her from him, and his sister too. When you live in one of their houses they discourage contact with family. They tell you who you can and can't write letters to, the whole thing. What you can read, what you can watch on TV. That's how Bene met André,' she adds. 'She went to him about me. He runs a group that helps families of Opus members. Or he did. After she was killed, he decided to stay in Morocco. Even when they got Indrizzio, he didn't want to come back here. There was nothing for him after Bene died.'

I'm feeling cold. The chill spreads from somewhere deep down in my insides. 'Do you think her death had anything to do with Opus?'

Isabella either doesn't hear me, or ignores the question.

'You love something—God—so you want to be close to it,' she says. 'You think it will save you. I thought Opus would save me, but instead all they did was take something beautiful and make it ugly. They say your heart is a traitor, that you should lock it away, and that your body and soul are enemies who can't escape each other. I don't know,' she says, suddenly answering my question. 'I've thought about it. I don't know if they regard a human life that can't be converted as especially sacred. I mean, when I left, they told me I would be without God's grace. Actually,' she adds, 'they told me I was damned.'

'Yes. An Opus priest told me that once too.'

'This Father Rinaldo?'

I nod.

'Did you believe him?' she asks.

'No,' I say slowly. 'In the end, I don't think I did. I guess I didn't believe God would really do that. Or that I'd want to know him anyways, if he did.'

Isabella smiles. 'I don't know this Rinaldo,' she says. 'And I doubt Bene did. Maybe. But she wouldn't have gone near him if she knew he was Opus. She wasn't their biggest fan. To put it mildly. I did suggest it,' she says, 'to the police. Of course I did. It was obvious. But I don't think they found any connection between Indrizzio and Opus. They've threatened André in the past,' she adds. 'Opus, I mean. But they leave me alone. I think they consider damnation enough. Which doesn't mean, of course, that we don't want them out of here.'

'Out of Florence?'

Isabella laughs as if this is genuinely funny. 'That wouldn't be possible, I don't think. People say Florence belonged to the Medici, but the Medici are dead and Savonarola's still going strong, so to speak. No. I mean out of this area. We've started a neighbourhood group, but there's not much we can do about them. It's not illegal to buy property. They own a couple of houses around here, and they're after a big ruined villa down near the Art Institute, you know the one I mean?'

I think of the mascara-streaked stucco, the squat crumbling towers, and the old man with his deaf poodle and his cane. 'Yes,' I say, 'actually, I do.'

'They got the oldest son to leave it to them. But the other brother and his sisters are contesting it. And the neighbours don't want them. They usually don't, when they find out about them. They burn books, you know,' Isabella says. 'Have little Bonfires of the Vanities in the back garden. '"The eyes. Through them many iniquities enter the soul. If you guard your sight, you have assured the guard of your heart."' That's from *The Way* too. We had to learn them. All Escrivá's little pearls of wisdom. And the sick thing was, we loved it. We thought they were incredibly profound.'

Sadness drifts across Isabella's face. 'I don't understand now,' she says, 'how I could have believed it all.'

'Listen,' I tell her. 'Father Rinaldo? He tried to snag me for Opus two years ago. And in other circumstances I might have bitten. They weren't that wrong. Their timing with me was just off, that's all. Another time, another place, I could easily have done what you did.'

I want to give her this, partly as thanks for what she's told me, and partly to say that whatever well of loneliness and neediness they spotted in her exists in us all. She nods, but she doesn't say anything.

A few seconds later the dog rustles up out of the bushes and trots up the steps. He throws himself down at Isabella's feet with a sigh and thumps his tail on the gravel.

'I usually take him out for a walk,' she says. 'He gets bored here. He likes to go and do the shopping.'

This is my cue to leave, to step out through the gates and let Isabella close herself back into the world of her villa where maybe time, or enchantment, or bees, will heal her. I stand up and thank her, for her coffee and her time and what she's shared with me, but she shakes her head. 'I'm going to drive you home.'

'I can't possibly let you.'

She looks at me and laughs. 'After what you've told me,' she says, 'you can't possibly not!'

Isabella insists that she has to feed Fonzi first, and I follow her into the kitchen. It's a cavernous room. Dented copper pots and knives hang above a gas range that looks as if it dates from 1900. She vanishes into a pantry and comes back with a slab of meat on a board while the dog paces behind her and then sits, eyes fixed on her hands as she chooses a knife. She runs her thumb down it, and reaches for a whetstone. The sound of the blade running across its edge is like nails on a blackboard, and I have to look away. I could never stand this noise. In school, when I was little, it used make me feel as if I had to pee. Now I distract myself by studying a dresser full of books and pictures.

'That's Bene,' Isabella says suddenly. She has stopped sharpening the knife, and stands watching me by the sink. The photo I have picked up was once brightly coloured, but now the green of the child's dress has turned dull and a little murky. The red ball she holds is mottled.

'I think she was seven then.'

From where she stands, Isabella cannot possibly see the picture I'm holding. She must know by the space on the dresser. She must have memorized every one, and I imagine her, sitting at the long empty table in the evenings, the dog at her feet, the lights pooling on the stone floor while she eats, cutlery clicking, in the company of ghosts.

When I look on the back of the snapshot, someone's written, 'A. Giugno 1975' in spidery handwriting. 'A?' I ask.

Isabella nods. 'Agatha. She hated it. Benedetta was her

middle name.' She turns back to the board, flips the hunk of meat over and begins to chop, the blade swishing down hard and fast as she hits the wood. A piece of gristle plops onto the floor, and is snuffled up by the dog. I put the photo back, careful to make sure I have it in exactly the right place.

When we leave, Isabella drives fast. After I close the gate and get back in the tiny Fiat, I barely have time to buckle my seat belt before she flies down the road. Fonzi lies across the back seat, apparently unbothered. The gears grind, and she swings into Viale Galileo so abruptly the car almost skids. We shoot down the hill and the big dog sits up, his breath filling the car with a meaty smell. I'd like to open the window, but when I reach for the button I find it's broken.

I've told Isabella where Pierangelo's is, but by the time we accelerate across the river, I kick myself for not asking her just to drop me at Signora Bardino's apartment, not because I want to go there, but because it's an awful lot closer. The tiny car and the dog are making me feel slightly sick. I tell myself not to be stupid, that we'll be there in just a second, but even so, I want to get out.

We stop at the lights after the bridge, then Isabella steps on the accelerator and jerks forward, taking a wrong turn. As I start to protest, she looks at me and smiles.

'Don't worry,' she says, 'this is a short cut.'

I have rarely driven in the city, and she's a native, but it seems to me, as we plunge into the maze of alleys and one-way streets that run from the river towards the station, that we're going in the wrong direction. Isabella turns, and turns again, and I realize I'm lost. Behind me Fonzi shifts, the fug of his breath hot on my neck.

Somewhere to our right are the fancy shops and bijoux restaurants of Via Tornabuoni—Prada, Gucci, the works—but Florence can change fast, parallel cities live alongside each other, and this area's seedy. The streets are like canyons, tall, dark and dirty. We pass a hotel with a flashing neon sign and Isabella honks at something small and dark that scuttles in the road. 'Rat,' she says.

My shirt is sticking against the back of the plastic seat, and I blot my palms on my jeans. My scars itch, and the dog's breath smells. I'm actually afraid I might be sick. Under my bag, I inch my fingers towards the seat-belt buckle. I don't care. When this car stops, I'm going to open the door. If I have to, I'll jump.

Isabella shifts, and we burst out of an alley and are at Santa Maria Novella. She swears at a pedestrian. The buckle clicks under my fingers. Then she slams to a halt in front of a crosswalk and I scrabble for the door handle.

'It sticks.'

I feel my skin turning red and hot. Our eyes meet and Isabella smiles. 'What, Mary?' she asks. 'Did you really think I was kidnapping you?'

Isabella looks at me for a second as cars pull up and stop on either side of us. 'It's all right,' she says finally. 'It's what happens. You end up afraid of everyone. And everything.'

She gives a little smile. 'You'll get used to it,' she says.

Chapter Twenty-two

SIGNORA BARDINO IS PLANNING what she calls a 'Remembrance' for Billy. I find out about this the next morning when Henry calls and asks if I want to meet for lunch at the bar. When I tell him I can't, he sounds genuinely sorry. He says he needs my help to stop the Remembrance 'getting out of hand', as though it's a riot, or an unruly child. 'Things are dicey,' he explains. 'Ellen's threatening to recite Elizabeth Barrett Browning.'

'Oh dear.'

'Billy would hate it,' says Henry. I have to agree. 'How Do I Love Thee? Let Me Count the Ways' was really not her kind of thing.

We talk a little more about nothing in particular, skirting around the mention of Kirk's name, until finally I can't stand it any more. Isabella's probably right, indiscriminate fear is like an infection, and possibly I overreacted, but I can't forgive him for hitting me. Eventually I just blurt it out.

'Kirk hit me,' I say abruptly. 'At the apartment, before you came the other day. That's how the chair got broken. He has a pretty bad temper, you know. He scared the crap out of me.'

There's a silence on the other end of the phone, then Henry says, 'I know. He told me.' I can almost see him pushing his glasses up his nose, preparing himself for whatever he's going to say next. I wait and finger the sore place on my jaw.

'You know he's full of shit, don't you?' Henry says finally. 'About this being your fault? He's only saying that because he's angry with himself. He thinks somehow he didn't take care of her. That he could have stopped this from happening. So he blames you. He has to blame somebody. Or maybe everybody. Mostly Billy.'

'Billy?' She didn't even love him. And she certainly didn't belong to him. She wasn't his to keep, like a pet or a toy.

'Sure,' Henry is saying. 'For being dead. Rational beings that we are, we hate the people we love when they leave us. Even if it's not their fault.' I don't say anything, but I think that if he tells me love and hate are really the same thing, I may scream.

'Kirk thinks if he hadn't fought with her that night, this wouldn't have happened,' Henry adds.

'Well, maybe he's right.'

My patience is fraying. Back in the real world, I'm tempted to say, Billy is dead, and it isn't her fault, and, guess what? Our actions do have consequences.

Henry doesn't reply right away. He wants it all to be simple, to fit into nice black and white squares like a crossword. Kirk's anger is just guilt. I have nothing to answer for. The only person responsible for Billy's death is the one who wielded the knife. Everything can be neatly explained, and we are all absolved. Amen.

Finally he says. 'That's not all, is it? It's not just the fact that he hit you that bugs you?'

Bugs me? What bugs me, I feel like shouting, is that women are being snatched. And tied up. And really hot things, cigarette butts, pieces of metal, are being put on their naked flesh before they're killed. That's what 'bugs me.' But I can't. I'm not even supposed to know about Billy's autopsy, about what really happened to her. And besides, there's no real point in picking a fight with Henry. He's just trying to help. Anyways, he's right, there is something else. And I probably shouldn't talk about it either, but I'm going to.

'When Billy was found,' I say, 'she had her ring on, the one Kirk gave her, with the two hearts. But when they had that fight, in the piazza, she took it off and threw it at him. I saw her. And I saw him pick it up afterwards. He put it in his pocket.'

Henry sighs, as if he knew this was going to come up, and even finds it vaguely tiresome. 'Kirk also told me that he gave the ring back to her,' he says. 'He says he wrote a note and stuck them both in an envelope and dropped it off in the apartment, last Monday, after she didn't answer the phone.'

I did go to the apartment last Monday, before we went to Vinci, back when the world was still normal, but I didn't see an envelope, or a note. If they were in Billy's things the police could have taken them away, of course. They probably did. But Pallioti didn't mention it.

'Do you believe him?'

It's a mean question—after all, Henry and Kirk are friends—but I have to ask it, and to my surprise, instead of defending Kirk outright, Henry weighs it up.

'I guess,' he says finally, after a few seconds. 'Yes. Probably. Kirk's competitive. You know, "I'm going to give you this whether you want it or not." And he didn't want to be rejected. Just like the rest of the world. That's pretty normal, don't you think?'

Now it's my turn to say, 'I guess.' But what I'm really wondering is what else Kirk tried to give her that she didn't want to accept.

Henry's obviously eager to change the subject by now, and the conversation drivels on for a few more minutes. He tells me that the Japanese girls have decided to leave the course early. They'll stay for Billy's service and then they're going to the Amalfi coast because it's safer than Florence. Henry pointed out that that's only true if you don't drive, but he didn't think they got it.

After we hang up, the conversation leaves a bad taste in my mouth, and I can't decide whether it's because I'm annoyed with Henry for finding neat little reasons why nothing is anybody's fault, which I guess is his job, or because I lied to Pierangelo again this morning. It was easy, just like lying to Henry about not being able to come to lunch. I did that to save his feelings, of course. I could have gone to lunch, but there's something I want to do more and I tell myself I'm doing the same thing with Pierangelo. Saving his feelings. Yesterday I told him I went to a lecture, on Classicism. And reassured myself it was for his own good. Saving him worry. Just like when I said we'd have to wait until this afternoon to meet at Signora Bardino's apartment to collect my suitcases because I am meeting Tony and Ellen at San Marco this morning. Which is completely ridiculous. An out-and-out lie. What I am actually doing this morning is going to see Gabriel Fabbiacelli.

Eleanora Darnelli's lover is doing a restoration job at a monastery up in San Felice. I know this because his mama told me. Pierangelo has the phone number in his notes, and when I called early this morning I said I was a 'friend from America.' Mamas always fall for that one. They like their little boys to have friends, and on the whole they approve of American girls, I'm not sure why. Maybe it's a sort of benevolent hangover from Grace Kelly. They think we're all clean and blonde.

San Felice is in the hills to the south of the city, and by the time I finally get there I'm afraid Gabriel will have taken a break, gone out for coffee or quit for an early lunch. The place appears to be deserted. As I come through the open gates and cross the courtyard I catch a glimpse of the chapel. Inside what looks as though it may possibly be a Giotto crucifix hangs above the altar, and I stop to admire it, unable to resist stepping into the nave, making my way past the shadowed flowers and pamphlets about missions in Africa, and standing for a moment in front of the lithe, golden-haired Christ. His wounds ooze, his halo shines. Above him in her nest, a pelican feeds her young, while beside him, his mother folds her hands and weeps. A car goes by. I hear the revving engine of a scooter or motorcycle, a slice of voices behind me as the door opens and closes. There is the familiar rustle of someone slipping into a pew, and I don't have to glance back to see them crossing themselves, or know that they're muttering the familiar words, 'Father, forgive me for I have sinned.' When I go back down the aisle, the shape is nothing but a hunched shadow in the corner, one more human soul begging for redemption.

Outside, the sun is momentarily blinding. It's so warm I don't even need my jacket. I follow my nose into the shadows of the cloister and, sure enough, I find Gabriel right where his mama said he'd be, high up on a scaffold among the angels he's named for.

Dark and lithe, with wild Italian curls and honey-coloured skin, he has a familiar quality. Pierangelo might have looked like this when he was younger. Gabriel Fabbiacelli is wearing paint-spattered khaki trousers and a blue denim shirt with the sleeves rolled up, and I wonder if this is how Eleanora first saw him, crouched like an overgrown faun, high up on his platform with a brush in his hand. When he finally senses me and turns to look, his eyes are almond-shaped, long-lashed and almost as blue as Billy's.

'You're late, American lady,' he says in Italian, and I must look surprised because he laughs and adds, 'My mama.' Gabriel pats his pocket. 'These days,' he says, 'even archangels have cell phones.'

He puts his brush down, wipes his hands on a cloth and climbs down the scaffolding to offer me his hand. 'I'm sorry I don't speak your language, Signora—'

'Thorcroft. I wish I spoke yours better.'

His grip is firm and warm, and as he lets go I decide that the best thing I can do is tell him the truth. 'I'm not an old friend you've forgotten,' I say.

'That's too bad.' A smile crosses his face, the reflection of it catching his eyes.

'To be honest, I want to talk to you about Eleanora Darnelli.'

The words are hesitant, even though I try not to let them sound that way, but if what I've said surprises Gabriel, or distresses him, he doesn't show it. He doesn't even stop smiling. Instead, he just inclines his head, gracefully, almost a little bow.

'Nothing makes me happier,' he says, 'than to talk about Eleanora. Shall we walk?' He takes my elbow gently, guiding me up the cloister. 'Are you a journalist?' he asks.

'No. No, not really.'

He looks at me sideways, but doesn't say anything. The silence stretches out, measured in the beats of our footsteps as we move slowly past the arches, light and dark playing on the faded paintings on the walls beside us. Gabriel doesn't rush me, and finally I say, 'Two years ago, I was attacked by the same man who killed Eleanora.'

'Indrizzio?'

I nod. 'My husband tried to save me, and he was killed. I think instead of me. I don't know, maybe you read about it. Anyways, I was lucky.'

He glances at me. 'Or it wasn't your time.'

I smile. Put it however you want: Chaos or grand design. 'God has something else in mind for you,' Gabriel says.

'Maybe.' This is the kind of thing Mamaw would have said, and if nothing else, the familiarity is comforting.

'Anyways,' I go on, leaving the divine aside, 'the reason I've come is that a woman I knew was killed last week.' I'm getting good at this now. It's almost like a routine.

'I'm sorry.'

'Thank you.'

I stop and look at him. Serenity is a word that's frequently misused but, in Gabriel Fabbiacelli's case, it's appropriate. It's not just his beauty, which is undeniable, there's something else about him, a stillness. He looks back at me without questioning, just waiting to hear what it is that I have to say.

'She isn't the first,' I add. 'There've been two others, one in January, and one about three weeks ago. I think they're connected to Indrizzio. That's why I've come. I think someone's copying him. It's almost as if they're trying to finish what he started.'

Gabriel nods, as though my turning up and telling him this out of the blue isn't completely crazy. Then he takes my elbow and we begin to walk again. Our feet pace the worn stones, treading in the footsteps of generations of men who walked here, heads bent and hands folded. My loafers click and flap, but Gabriel's wearing espadrilles, the old-fashioned, rope-soled kind, so his footsteps make no sound at all.

'Are you very frightened?' he asks finally, and I realize no one else, not even Pierangelo, has actually asked me this before. They've assumed it. But they haven't asked.

'I don't know.' The answer surprises me. 'Maybe I'm just too tired to be frightened,' I add. 'I can't sleep. I feel as if there are things I should know, and I don't. Or'—I struggle for how to put this—'as if there are things I do know, but can't see. It's like someone touching you in a dark room. Sometimes I think it's Indrizzio. Then I think it's someone else. I came to see you because I thought—'

The words die on me. Probably it's fatigue, but I don't know if I'm sure now, how to end this sentence. Because I thought if I could ask the right question then, bingo, I'd suddenly know who killed Billy. It seems ridiculous, but Gabriel Fabbiacelli doesn't seem to mind. Perhaps that's what drew Eleanora to him, that he didn't mind, wasn't fazed or weirded out because she was a nun.

He throws me his sideways glance, and says, 'To me it doesn't matter, signora, who killed Eleanora.' And the strange thing is, I know what he means. Annika said the same thing. In the end, the brute fact is the absence, not how it came about.

'Whoever's doing this,' Gabriel adds, 'must be in a great deal of pain. I think killing must be like a fungus that creeps across a canvas and eats what's there. Destroys something beautiful in the soul.' He smiles, suddenly. 'Eleanora was a great soul,' he says. 'Pure, you know? Some people are just put on earth like that. My mama says they haven't been born before, that they're brand new. But sometimes I think they've been born so many times before that all the creases have been smoothed out. Or maybe they've always been like that. Some people are just better.'

'Yes, they are.' And it's a shame we can't always love them for it, I think. Eleanora Darnelli was lucky. Luckier than my husband was.

We walk on for a second, then I ask, 'Could you tell me what she was like? I mean, as a person?'

I start to give him my spiel about what connects us all, or doesn't, and then I stop. I remember sitting on the cold floor of my room at Signora Bardino's, my door locked, studying the dead women's faces. Why lie? I wanted to know who they were. To meet the other members of the club.

'I feel as if I know her.' I must be exhausted, but it's a relief to actually say the words, and somehow I don't think Gabriel will think this is crazy. 'After Indrizzio attacked me,' I add, 'when he almost killed me, I used to think I knew her. It was as though she'd touched me. Her hand, I mean. Sometimes I used to dream we were sisters.'

The words hang in the air between us, mix with the chattering of the sparrows and the sweet drifting scent of the first roses that cluster in the sparse beds, fighting for space with bushes of scraggly lavender.

'Eleanora loved God,' Gabriel says finally. 'And me. I consider that a great blessing in my life,' he adds. 'That she loved me.'

He stops, and when he looks at me I see that his eyes are crystalline with tears. They don't fall, and he wipes them away with the back of his hand. It's an unusual gesture for a man, with nothing furtive or overly dramatic in it.

'She was the youngest of a big family, all boys,' he goes on. 'Her family didn't have much. That's why they sent her up here to school. I think she would have liked a sister.' I have no idea if that's true, but it's a kind thing to say, and I appreciate it. 'She was funny,' Gabriel says. 'She had—how do you say it?—a sense of humour like a fairy?'

'Impish.' I use the English word.

He smiles at me. 'Yes, that, exactly. That's why children loved her. She could laugh like them, you know? Play tricks. Probably her brothers taught her that. I think boys are better at it. Anyways, she wanted to be a teacher. Sometimes, I feel worse for the children who never knew her, you know? It was the convent school that interested her, and the orphanage they run.'

'Because she'd been there?'

'Sure. She wanted to pay something back.'

'So it was a good experience that she had at the convent?'

'People always sound surprised about that.' Gabriel stops, watching the sparrows. 'I don't know why,' he says. 'It's not so hard to believe. Nuns aren't ogres, they're just women who love God. And parents are not always wonderful for their children. Even mothers. A lot of kids are given away by parents who don't care anything for them. Or ignored. Or beaten. Hit. Even killed. More kids are killed by their parents than by strangers, did you know that? Everyone assumes that children should be with their mothers, but love comes from all kinds of people. Mothers don't have a monopoly on it. Sometimes they hurt more. It's only the things you love that can really destroy you. Not mine,' he adds.

Gabriel laughs, his face and voice changing as fast as wind moving over water. 'My mama, she's an angel.' He kisses his fingertips and blows the kiss into the air. 'You see,' he says. 'I'm a good Italian boy.'

Standing here beside him, I can't imagine the effect this man must have had on a twenty-one-year-old Eleanora Darnelli; Sister Darnelli, who not only was a nun, but had lived virtually her entire life among nuns. Or actually, maybe I can.

He glances at my face and laughs again, as if he can see my thoughts, and I'm disconcerted to find myself blushing. After that, we walk for a few seconds in silence.

'The day she told me she loved me, I knew I was the luckiest man on earth,' Gabriel says. 'I asked her to marry me then. That afternoon. On my knees.'

'And she said yes?'

'Yes. Yes,' he nods. 'But I knew it was hard for her. I knew what it would cost her. That's why I took the job in Ferrara. I wanted her to be sure. The last time she spoke to me, she was happy.'

'And that was in January?'

He nods again. 'The day before she died.'

'Do you know if she ever had anything at all to do with San Miniato?'

Gabriel shakes his head, 'No. I don't think so. She was up in Fiesole. And when she came to see me,' he shrugs, 'we borrowed a friend's apartment near Fortezza di Basso.' There's no lasciviousness or embarrassment in this because she was a nun. Just the acknowledgement: we were in love, we had to have somewhere to go.

'What about a priest called Rinaldo? Did you ever hear her mention him? Or a group called Opus Dei?'

Gabriel shakes his head again. 'Who are they?'

I start to tell him, then I stop. 'No one,' I say. 'It doesn't matter. Tell me more about Eleanora. She was happy in the convent, but...?'

'She wanted a bigger life.'

'And you.'

Gabriel shrugs. 'Sure, yes. And me. And she wanted to go to university. Not just for teaching, but for herself. For her heart. She loved poetry—Petrarch, Dante and the English. The "Romantics."' He rolls the word in English across his tongue. 'They were her favourites. That's why she took the name she took, you know,' he adds, 'when she became a novice. Sister Maria Agnes. The Maria, well, that's nun name number one, but the Agnes, that was for that poem by the Englishman. The one who died, coughing in Rome.'

'Keats.'

'That's right. Keats.' He winks. 'Next to God, when she was seventeen she loved Signor Keats.' Next to God and before she met you, I think.

Of course, I loved him too, from the time I was in High School, right after I wanted to be Jane Eyre and marry Mr Rochester. Soft, quiet, perfect Keats, who was so often drowned out by the bombast of Byron and the frantic beautiful madness of Shelley. One more thing Eleanora Darnelli and I have in common.

'She wanted to know other things too,' Gabriel is saying. 'About art, especially. That's the first thing Eleanora ever asked me, how I got my ideas. She wanted to know if they came to me in dreams.' He laughs at the memory.

'And do they?' I ask.

'Not often.'

Gabriel stops in front of a fresco set into the north wall of the cloister. 'This is mine,' he says. 'We're replacing some pieces. A lot was destroyed here during the war. Bombed, mostly by the Allies. That's one of the things the German Commissar here was most afraid of, that the British and the Americans would do what they did at Pisa and Padua and Cassino. So they arranged for the paintings to be taken away, hidden. But the frescoes—so much was lost. Now bits are being restored.'

Gabriel laughs and shakes his head. 'The Americans bomb us, then they come and lecture us on how to fix it,' he says. 'In time, maybe none of us will be able to tell the difference. After all, all of it's made by the hands of men.'

In the fresco that faces us, a group of angels crowds around Jesus. They hover over his shoulder, beating their great wings; they flock about him, reaching out to touch his hands, and hem and the bare skin of his sandalled feet. There must be fifteen or twenty of them, and their faces are exquisite, mobile and full of expression. But that's not what makes me gasp. It's one face, in the back of the group. Even here, he's taller than the others. The familiar golden eyes almost seem to move in the shadow of the cloister. He holds a lily in his long lean fingers, and, for just a second, I see not the white flower, but a crimson tulip.

'That man.' I point. 'In the back. What's his name?'

Gabriel looks at me, curious. 'I don't know,' he says. 'Do you?'

'No. No, I don't.' I stare at the fresco, at the face so familiar that I expect it to move. Then I ask, 'You've seen him too? You must have.'

'I'm sure.' Gabriel shrugs. 'I've seen them all. I collect faces, and eventually I paint them.' He points at a chubby laughing angel. 'That's the woman in our *salumeria*. And,' he says, 'that's Eleanora.'

He points again, and suddenly I see her, not dead as I've always seen her before, but alive and laughing, and looking out at me. Gabriel is watching me, studying my face. He nods towards my El Greco saint.

'Who is he?' he asks again.

I shake my head. 'I don't know. I see him, though. I gave him some flowers once because he—' I stop, embarrassed. 'It doesn't matter.'

Gabriel touches my arm. 'Just say it. It won't hurt.'

I look at him for a second, then I take a breath. 'He, that man, in your painting, I see him, in the street. I mean, I have seen him, more than once. I think he works as one of the white men. I don't know who he is, but the strange thing is, he has my husband's eyes, my husband who was killed. They're not similar. I mean, when he looks at me, they're exactly the same.'

'Then he's still with you.'

'I don't believe in that kind of thing,' I say quickly. 'And besides, we weren't—' My voice trickles off. 'We weren't very happy together.'

Gabriel laughs. 'What makes you think that makes any difference? That you didn't love him?'

I start to protest, to say that's not what I said. But of course, it is.

'For that matter, why do you think that what you believe

makes any difference?' Gabriel asks. 'Our belief in it doesn't make love real, it exists on its own. Whether or not we want it to. We think we have a choice. We like to think we have choices about lots of things. But we don't.'

We start to walk again. 'Isn't that really what Christ meant?' Gabriel shoves his hands in his pockets. 'That we're loved, whether we like it or not?'

'I don't know.' I shake my head. 'Maybe.' I'm tempted to tell him that I don't think I'm very well qualified any more to have any idea what God means. The truth is, I probably never was.

'I see Eleanora, all the time,' he says suddenly. 'I mean, really see her. In the street or in a shop. Or sitting on a train. Truly. Sometimes I think there's a whole other Florence. A city of the dead that no one ever leaves. And sometimes a curtain is pulled back and we get a glimpse of it.' Gabriel shrugs. 'Perhaps they're lonely,' he says, 'and they need to look at us. Or perhaps we're the ones who are lonely, and we need to look at them. Maybe that's why we paint them over and over again.'

He laughs at the look on my face. 'Haven't you noticed?' he asks. The professors and art historians analyse it and write about it and call it "The Florentine School," but really all it is is what we see. Every painting in Florence, centuries of them, they're nothing but our ghosts. Ghosts, and the faces of angels.'

Chapter Twenty-three

THE BUS RATTLES and swings down the hills towards Porta Romana. I hold on, staring out of the windows at the big villas and green-leafed trees, my own face looking back at me, watery and indistinct. When we come into the city, the doors open and close, and more faces flick by, coming out of shops, standing in lines, one after the other, as if they're pages of a book being riffled by the wind.

Angels, Gabriel Fabbiacelli said, and ghosts, as though there was no difference. I think of him seeing Eleanora and me seeing Ty. I didn't ask Isabella Lucchese if she sees her sister, if she glimpses Benedetta on the street. But maybe she does. And maybe Rosa Fusarno and Ginevra Montelleone's mother will someday see their daughters alive in the faces of other women's children.

The doors hiss and snap and I realize I've missed my stop. I get off at the next one and walk back through Santo Spirito. In a couple of hours Pierangelo will come to fetch me. It's time to pack my bags and leave.

As I let myself in and come through the archway, I glance up at our French windows and almost believe I see a figure, a shadow behind the white-linen panels. If Gabriel's right, it's not a trick of the light, but Billy, looking down at me. I don't know what will happen to her things. I suppose someone will come for them. And for her. Her mother's apparently terrified of flying and refuses to get on a plane, so maybe her aunt Irene, or her cousin Floyd, who bet her when she was eight that she wouldn't eat a fly, will come instead. She did eat the fly, incidentally, and made Floyd pay her, despite the fact that she threw up. Personally, I think she'd rather we talked about that at the Remembrance than Elizabeth Barrett Browning.

Sun darts between clouds as I come out of the portico and hear the noise. It unwinds in the warm spring air, and, unsure of what it is, I stop, listening. It's a low whine that spools down into the courtyard, and although I have never actually heard 'keening' before I know instinctively that that's what this is; an incoherent call of distress, grief and pain, all mixed up. Looking up, I also know what I am going to see. Two storeys above, Sophie's windows are open.

I start to walk on, to bow my head and plough past, telling myself that whatever it is, it's none of my business. But then I stop. This sound is not made by Little Paolo having a tantrum. This is a noise so anguished only an adult could make it. Sophie. I remember the look on her face the first time I met her, the loneliness that was so obvious and familiar it might have been my own. The door to their apartment is only a few feet away, in the corner opposite ours, but I've never been through it. I have no idea what's on the other side.

Their vestibule is much smarter than ours. There are no scuff marks on the marble stairs or scratches on the elegant curve of the banister. There's no elevator either, and when I look at the ground-floor door, which on our side would lead to the storage rooms under Signora Raguzza's, I see that it's propped open, revealing a dark passage. The wine cellars and back entrance that Sophie mentioned. Suddenly it dawns on me that they own this whole side of the building. Billy was right, Big Paolo's cashmere does indicate serious real estate.

I climb the stairs as quietly as I can, as if I'm trespassing, which is how it feels. The first flight is shiny, polished marble. Above, they rise in carpeted flights to what are probably bedrooms. On the first landing huge double doors stand open. The noise is louder now, coming from inside, but when I step in I don't see anyone. The room is vast, spanning the width of the building, four windows on one side looking out on the courtyard, four on the other staring across the side alley. Signora Bardino's whole apartment could fit in here. Groups of brocade chairs and two uncomfortable-looking silk sofas are arranged around tapestry rugs. Bowls of flowers sit on low tables, and there are portraits, one of Paolo in a sailor suit looking creepily like the Romanov children in those pictures they took just before they shot them, and one of an idealized Sophie in a pink ballgown. At the other end is a grand piano and a formal dining table with eight chairs, and beyond that an open doorway to the kitchen, where Sophie is sitting beside an open window with her head in her arms, making that awful noise.

'Sophie?'

I whisper, partly because I don't want to alarm her, and partly because I feel like I shouldn't be here at all, and at first I think she hasn't heard me. Then she looks up.

Her face is pasty. There's a red blotch on each of her cheeks, making her look like a clown or a Raggedy Ann doll, and her colourless blonde hair is matted to her forehead.

'I hate him,' Sophie announces, looking at me as though it's perfectly normal for me to be standing here. 'I just fucking hate him!' Then she puts her head down in her arms and starts crying again.

I don't know what to do. I'm not good at this sort of thing, and I wish Billy was here. Or Pierangelo, or Henry. Or Mamaw. Or Ty. Or virtually anyone but me. Finally I pat Sophie's shoulder as if she were a horse in a petting zoo, and make the sort of noise Mamaw used to make when I was sick or having a tantrum, a kind of low, out-of-tune hum.

Sophie's skin feels hot under her linen shirt and she doesn't stop crying, even when I crouch down and put my arms around her shoulders. The damp clamminess of her cheek meets mine, and her soft, sweaty hands reach out and hold on to me. We stay like this until my knees hurt. Until my body is as hot as hers, and the side of my face and neck is damp with her tears. Then, little by little, Sophie's shoulders stop shuddering and the awful mewing sound withers to nothing but wheezy breaths of air.

'I'm sorry,' Sophie says finally. 'Oh God, I'm so sorry.' She pushes herself away from me, and rubs her eyes, which are red-rimmed and swollen. Her lipstick is smeared too. 'I must look a fright.'

In this second she sounds terribly English, and the laugh she gives is fake and half-hearted, like a bad imitation of Mrs Miniver. She pushes her hair out of her eyes and looks at me. 'I'm pregnant again,' she says, 'and, to make it worse, that bastard I'm married to says if I don't have it, he'll take my son away.'

'What?'

There's a letter lying on the table beside a vase of irises. Sophie nods towards it.

'I told him I didn't want another baby, not with him. He's been bonking his secretary for years,' she adds, as if it's an afterthought. 'Not that I even care about that. I know he doesn't love me, so what does it matter? He can fuck the silly cow stupid for all I care. I told him that. I told him I didn't care, but I wasn't going to stay with him and have another baby since he doesn't give a damn about me. And he says if I don't, he'll have me declared unfit or crazy or something, and stop me seeing Paolo.'

I stand up, feeling a little woozy. And I thought my marriage had problems.

'All I want to do,' Sophie is saying as though it's obvious to the whole world, 'is take Paolo and go back to England. I don't want to stay with him!'

'Can he do that? Can he take your son away from you like that?'

'According to his *avvocato*, yes.' She pronounces the Italian for lawyer so it sounds like 'avocado', and flicks the letter contemptuously with her fingers, sending it sailing to the floor. 'Apparently he can do any bloody thing he pleases. And I pay for it!'

I bend down and pick the letter up. The paper is heavy, and engraved with the heading of a law firm in the city.

'That's why he really doesn't want me to go,' Sophie adds. 'He doesn't give a toss about me, or Paolo. Never has done. He just doesn't want to lose the money. And he'd quite like another carbon copy of himself, he has a right to that, he says. To His Baby. That's what he calls it, by the way: His Baby. As if I don't even exist. I hate him,' she says again. 'I just fucking hate him.'

Her pretty round face is transformed with a bitterness that seems so uncharacteristic it's almost more disturbing than her crying.

'And do you know what my priest said?' Her voice rises with outrage and I feel my stomach sinking. I start to say I probably do, but Sophie's there first.

'When I told him about the affair, about the bonking and the secretary, he told me my fucking marriage was fucking sacred, no matter what my fucking husband does, and that I should find room in my heart for forgiveness. No matter what. Have you noticed how it's always women who have to summon up forgiveness? I pointed that out, and all he said was that if I left my marriage I ran the risk of being "removed from God's grace." Removed from God's grace are the words he actually used. As if I were a chair or a sofa. Can you believe it?'

I nod. I could tell her that virtually the same thing was said to me, and is probably said to thousands of other women on a daily basis, but Sophie doesn't want me to talk, she just wants me to hear. I put the letter on the table, trying not to read the two neatly typed paragraphs and the flourished signature.

'I'm a Catholic,' she adds. 'I mean, I already was, I didn't become one when I married Paolo. So it's not as if I haven't thought about this. I have. I'm not entirely stupid.'

'Have you told your priest yet? That you're pregnant?'

'God, no!' she says, and bursts into tears again. 'I know what he'll say, so I can't!'

Sophie wipes at her eyes with her sleeve and I look around the beautiful room and try to think what Mamaw would say or do. There's a shiny copper kettle sitting at the back of the huge six-burner stove, and when I go to lift it up, it feels full.

'I don't believe God really feels that way,' I say. 'That's just the interpretation of men. God's better than that. He has to be.'

I'm not sure if I'm saying this to try to comfort her or me, but in either case Sophie doesn't reply. Just at the moment I doubt she's up for hearing a defence of God. As far as she's concerned, right now he's probably just another rotten man. She watches as I turn on the gas. 'Second drawer on the left,' she says, before I can ask.

The teabags are Earl Grey, and I wonder if she has them sent from home. I don't even like tea, but making it seems like a good idea, especially since she's English. From what I can remember of *Masterpiece Theater*, they use tea for occasions like this.

While I'm reaching for two of the mugs that hang on hooks under the cabinets, Sophie gets up and goes into the other room. A second later she comes back with a bottle of whisky in her hand.

'Only reason to drink tea, really.' She seems to be recovering, and she pours a stiff two fingers into each of the mugs.

'Personally, I think tea's filthy stuff,' she announces. 'But my mother keeps sending me the fucking bags in hampers from fucking Fortnum's, as if there's no proper food in Italy.' Sophie injects 'fucking' into her sentences like a schoolgirl who's just discovered it's a very bad word.

She looks at me and laughs. The sound has a high, slightly hysterical edge to it, and I wonder if this is the first time she's opened the whisky bottle today.

'That was the idea, you see,' she says, 'when Mummy sent me to art college. That the combination of being Catholic and my bank account would net me a fancy Italian and spare her the awfulness of having to wheedle me a receptionist's job at Christie's. I mean, look at me. I could hardly be expected to compete in London, could I? Everyone there is thin.'

She flumps down in one of the kitchen chairs and fiddles with a stem of iris. 'Of course, Mummy'd have liked a defunct title thrown in,' she says. 'You know, a contessa or marquesa, or something. That was a bit of a disappointment. But Paolo was the best I could do. Not that Sassinelli isn't a good name. Very Florentine. Very noble. A bunch of them died with the Pazzis. He was just too handsome.' She rubs her hands across her eyes. 'That was my mistake,' Sophie announces. 'I should have gone for someone short, and fat, like me. Then at least I wouldn't be such a joke.'

'You're not a joke.' I'm appalled at this. 'And you have Paolo. And,' I point out, 'your husband's affair isn't your fault.'

'Oh yes it is.' She looks up at me, her face suddenly older. 'It always is,' she says. 'At least partly.'

As she speaks, I remember what Billy said the night we saw them on the bridge, and turn away so she won't see my face.

'I have a friend in Geneva.' Sophie chews on one of her pink nails. 'I could just take Paolo and go,' she says. 'Leave the son of a bitch without his son or his baby.' There's a trembly defiance in Sophie's voice. She looks up at me. 'He couldn't stop me,' she insists. 'The children are mine too. He couldn't stop me taking them.' But she doesn't believe this for a minute, and neither do I. Big Paolo could stop her. And he would.

I start to point this out, trying to put it tactfully. 'Sophie,' I say, 'I really think—' But I get no further, because there's a crash in the other room.

Sophie lets out a little shriek and I almost knock one of the mugs onto the floor. In one motion, we turn towards the door, both of us certain that Big Paolo will be standing there, glowering, and threatening to—what? Kill us? Have us locked up?

But the doorway's empty. I actually heave a sigh of relief, and Sophie starts to laugh.

'My God,' she says. 'Look at us.' Finally she gets up and ventures out among the brocade sofas and cut flowers. When she returns a second later, she's carrying a grocery bag and laughing again.

'Culprit!' Sophie announces, holding up a can of tuna. 'It rolled down the stairs. I've started using Dinya for extra little jobs, and when she heard you she must have bolted. The poor thing's incredibly shy and she doesn't speak English.' Sophie dumps the bag and can on the table. 'Actually, she doesn't really speak Italian either,' she adds. 'Raguzza Minor says that's why she gets along so well with his mother, can't understand a word the old bat says.'

I think of the radio, the priest, and what Dinya's silent life must be like, closeted below our apartment with Signora Raguzza. Maybe life was much the same for Karel Indrizzio. I don't know how much English he spoke, or Italian either.

'How much of the economy do you think is made up of that?'

'Illegals?' Sophie shrugs. 'A lot. Most of it probably, in service anyways. Everyone complains about the Albanians and the Roma, but no one else wants to do those jobs.'

I pour boiling water into the mugs and the teabags float to the surface like little bloated animals. The concoction I've brewed up is roughly the colour of sewer water, but it seems to cheer Sophie up. 'Foul!' she exclaims when she tastes hers.

The tea is revolting, but in a bracing way, sort of like those awful herb liqueurs. Sophie regards me over the rim of her mug, her face suddenly impish. 'I knew you were Catholic,' she says. 'I could tell, the first time I saw you.'

'How?'

She shrugs. 'The way you walk.'

This is ridiculous and we both laugh, but I know what she means. It's tribal recognition, something like the way zebras identify each other from the pattern of their stripes. She grins at me, and I see the seventeen-year-old Sophie—round-faced and soft, a little shy, but gutsy. All of a sudden I hate Big Paolo too. He should have picked on someone who was fair game, some lean, sharp-boned creature who cares about silk sofas and wouldn't have fallen in love with him.

'At our convent,' Sophie says, 'everyone was frightfully interested in the martyrs, and had anorexia.'

'We made macramé pot-holders.'

She giggles, reaches for the bottle and pours a little more into both of our mugs. 'I think things are nicer in America,' she says.

We sip our tea, which is mainly whisky now, for a few more seconds. Then Sophie puts her mug down. 'Did I scare you?'

I consider this. The light's falling onto the irises, making them look as if they're made of velvet. A couple of dust motes swirl through the air. Below us I hear footsteps and the sound of the security gate clanging closed. 'A little.'

'I'm sorry.' She studies her immaculate pink-polished fingernails. They're cut short and rounded, like a child's. 'My mother says I cry like a broken Hoover. I think people who don't cry much don't really know how to do it properly.' She glances up at me. 'It's not the affair, you know,' she says. 'I've known about that for ages. He takes her away sometimes, on "business trips." I don't mind. I haven't minded for a long time, not until I knew I was going to have this baby.' She shakes her head and reaches for her mug. 'I actually used to think I'd make a life for us in England. Me and Little Paolo. I had it all worked out in my head. Don't know why,' Sophie adds. 'I hate England.'

She studies the flowers on the mug, then says, 'It was the letter that did it. The fact he went and discussed it all with some man in an office and then had them write to me like that.' She looks up. 'I think that really proves he hates me,' she says.

'Take Paolo anyways,' I say suddenly. 'Just take him and go.'

Sophie smiles as if this is a nice idea, but impossible. 'I'll be all right,' she says, more for herself than for me. She sounds tired. Deflated. As if the tea, or maybe the whisky, has drowned the little flame of defiance that flared up in her.

'Sophie, look, if I can do anything—'

'No.' Sophie shakes her head. 'No, honestly. I'll be fine.' She takes a sip of her tea. 'It was the shock, that's all. Of the letter. I'm sorry I frightened you.' She laughs but the look in her eyes isn't funny. 'I'm better now,' she says. 'Really. I'll get used to it.'

I get up to leave maybe ten minutes later. Sophie says she has to meet Paolo at school, and while she runs upstairs to change out of her crumpled crying clothes I wash the mugs in the white porcelain sink. Then I wait for her in the big room, looking at the portraits and the bowls of flowers, and imagining Sophie spending the next eighteen years here, waiting for her children to grow up so she can leave, and getting used to it.

Back in Signora Bardino's apartment, I lay clothes out on the bed. Pierangelo will be here any minute. I survey my collection of high-necked blouses and turtlenecks, my jeans, the skirt and jacket I bought to win Piero back when I was convinced Graziella was a secret girlfriend. My life to date, piled up in a few square feet. I have some stuff in Philly, but nothing I really care about, and it seems odd to be packing the past into a duffel bag and a suitcase. If there is anything of Billy's I want to remember her by, I think, I should take it now. I won't have another chance.

I know she wouldn't mind, but in the end there isn't much. Her clothes are all too big for me, and so are her shoes. I try a few on anyways, but they won't work. The black-patent lace-up almost fits, and it might be nice with pants, but I can't find the other one, even under the bed, so I abandon it, and take a few of her books instead, the ones Kirk left—her Burkhardt, her dog-eared copies of Gombrich and *The Dictionary of the Italian Renaissance*—more for sentimentality than anything else. I'm tempted by the blue wristwatch she never wore, but it has an engraving on the back, 'B. 4/7/92', so it was probably a gift her family would like back. I do snag the belt and earrings I borrowed. No one will miss those.

The buzzer is still broken, so Pierangelo calls when he arrives. He offers to park and come up and help me, but I tell him not to bother. All I have to do is put my bags in the elevator, close the door and say goodbye.

Outside by the lemon pots I turn and look back, but this time there's not even a shadow behind the linen panels of the French windows. I can't hear the echo of Billy's laughter, or smell her cigarette smoke. She's gone.

The next day is Saturday, and Pierangelo and I sleep late, go out for a long lunch, and generally laze about. The football is on in the evening, and when I eventually finish unpacking and come into the living room, I find Pierangelo on the couch, bouncing up and down, punching wildly and swearing every time the ball leaves the ground. He doesn't look especially stylish or elegant, but he does look completely happy, and I wonder how much of a bitch Monika must have been to outlaw something so harmless that gives him so much pleasure. Don't be stingy on the little things, I think, as I watch him. That's one of my resolutions for this marriage. Little things make up life. I kiss the top of his curly head as I pass by on my way to the kitchen.

Our Chinese food has been delivered and the boxes are ranged across the counter. The air smells distinctly of egg roll, something else Monika probably wouldn't approve of. I poke through the offerings to see what tempts me, settle on pork fried rice and some kind of chicken, and have just spooned it onto a plate when the phone rings. It's Henry, wanting to know if I have a picture of Billy. Signora Bardino wants to use one for the Remembrance. Frankly, the idea gives me the creeps, but after he promises there'll be no votive candles, I say I'll see what I can do. When I ask why Kirk can't help, Henry hems and haws, then says that actually Kirk got in a fight with La Signora about the Remembrance, and has gone off to Venice in a snit. It's not all bad, though, he has convinced Ellen not to read Elizabeth Barrett Browning.

'Oh, Henry, I was joking. Browning's not that bad.'

'Yes, she is,' Henry says. 'And Ellen's worse. But now you have to come up with something else for her to read instead.'

'"I Sing the Body Electric"?'

'Please,' Henry says, 'we're talking Signora Bardino here. And while you're at it, she feels it should have an Italian connection.'

'Easy. Keats.'

'Better than Shelley?'

'Much better than Shelley.' Although I think Billy herself would probably have preferred Byron. They would have gotten along like a house on fire. She would have just loved the pet bear.

Henry is asking me which poem, and I suggest 'Ode to a Nightingale,' or maybe one of the sonnets, let me think about it. We can discuss it tomorrow. He's happy with this, but after he hangs up I stand by the phone, staring at my plate. The football blares from the other room and Piero shouts, '*Che cosa, diavolo, fai!*' What are you doing, you idiot! And rushes in for another beer and rushes out again.

I love 'Ode to a Nightingale.' Who wouldn't? But my favourite Keats has always been the first one I ever learned. In High School I had to memorize a poem and I chose part of 'The Eve of St Agnes.' Mamaw suggested it, and she helped me learn it, covering the page with her hand and prompting me. We liked the part about the owl who 'for all his feathers was a-cold,' and the hare who 'limp'd trembling through the frozen grass.' Mamaw said the holy man praying over his frozen rosary reminded her of Pennsylvanian winters and of freezing at midnight Mass when she was a girl, before they had real heaters. It was cold in the poem because St Agnes' Eve is in January, which is odd, because Eleanora took the name Agnes because of Keats, and that's when she was killed.

I feel as if someone's slapped me.

Putting my plate down, very slowly, I adjust the fork. Then, as gently as I can, I open the drawer where Pierangelo keeps the phone books and appliance pamphlets. I lift each one aside, as if I'm handling something fragile, and pick out Monika's old Catholic calendar. As I stare at the pages, a picture forms in my mind. Colour bleeds in from the edges, filling it out. Making it real. I shake my head to clear it, but the picture's still there. Walking down the hall to Pierangelo's office, I try to ignore the sound of my heart banging against my ribcage.

I open the filing cabinet carefully. And when I get my hands on the file I hold my breath as if I'm dismantling a bomb.

Finally, I grab a pen and piece of paper, check and recheck, and finally realize the answer has been sitting right in front of me all this time. I just didn't know how to see it.

When I switch off the TV, Pierangelo starts to protest, then he sees my face.

'*Cara?*' he asks.

'I know,' I say. I hold the calendar up, and I'm surprised that my hand doesn't shake. That my voice is so steady. 'I know what connects us,' I tell Pierangelo. 'I know what he's doing.'

Chapter Twenty-four

FRANCESCA GIUSTI'S HOUSE is a modern villa on the outskirts of the city. I don't know why this surprises me. Maybe I imagined her living in the Questura, or in some palatial Bardino-like residence. But this is a new cream-coloured stucco cube with a bright red-tiled roof, and in this nice suburban neighbourhood, even early on Sunday morning, people are already out mowing lawns and walking dogs.

Pierangelo tells me he grew up in a place like this but that when he was a kid everyone would be in church on Sunday morning, including his aunt and uncle, who probably didn't even believe in God. And, oddly enough, Dottoressa Giusti set up this meeting here, and not at the Questura, for just that reason. Her husband needs to take his mother to Mass, and she promised to stay home with the children. By midnight last night when Pallioti fixed all this, it was too late to make other arrangements.

Now a violent drum roll comes out towards where we are sitting in the garden, on a patio by the pool house, and Francesca Giusti winces. 'My son,' she mutters, 'he wants to be a rock star.'

Pallioti, who is wearing the suit I'm beginning to think he was born in, sits beside me, and across from us is a short man who he has introduced as Dottore Babinellio, a forensic psychiatrist. The drum roll dies, and starts again, and everyone looks at me.

The setting is so unreal that I feel as if I'm about to make a presentation in school. When I square up Monika's calendar on the table, I notice there are grubby fingermarks on the front.

Finally, I look at the four expectant faces and meet Pallioti's eye. 'I didn't understand at first,' I tell him. 'But it was right in front of me. It's actually very simple, once you understand, because this guy, whoever he is, isn't just killing women.'

'Not just killing them?' Babinellio raises his eyebrows, as though I might be his subject myself. 'If he's not "just killing" them, signora,' he asks, 'then what is he doing?'

'He's martyring them.'

This is what I saw on Monika's calendar last night, the connection that has been sitting right under my nose. Pallioti was right. We live in the picture, but we can't see it.

There is complete silence at the table. Even the drumming has stopped. I turn the calendar around so they can see.

'Look,' I explain. 'Each of these women had a different name, another name, one they didn't use, so it isn't obvious at first.' They look at me as though I'm crazy, or at least confused, but I'm beyond caring. I tick them off on my fingers.

'Eleanora Darnelli was Sister Agnes. Agnes was martyred on the twenty-first of January, the day Eleanora was killed. Benedetta Lucchese's first name was Agatha, Agatha Benedetta, but she hated it, so she just used Benedetta. Agatha was martyred on the fifth of February. Billy Kalczeskai's real name was Anthea. Billy was just a nickname, but it stuck. Anthea, the eighteenth of April. Caterina Fusarno was christened Martina. The first of January. And Ginevra Montelleone's middle name was Theodosia.'

'And Theodosia, I suppose you will tell us, was martyred on, the second of April.' Pallioti runs his hand over his eyes. 'Right.'

I've underlined the dates in red, and I hand the calendar to Dottoressa Giusti. She takes it almost gingerly, and as she flips the pages she starts shaking her head almost exactly the same way I did last night. When she's done, she hands it to Babinellio. He looks at it for a few seconds, hands it to Pallioti and nods.

'There's more.' This time it's Pierangelo who speaks. 'After Mary explained to me,' he says, 'we looked on the web. You can find indexes of martyrs that tell you how each one was killed. Listen to this.'

He spreads the pages we printed off out on the stone table and begins to read.

'"Agnes was cast into flames but the flames were extinguished by her prayer. She was left untouched, so she was slain with the sword, thus consecrating, by her martyrdom, her claim to chastity."' He looks around the table. 'White for chastity, purity. The white ribbon Eleanora had tied around her wrist.' Francesca Giusti nods and he goes on.

'"Agatha endured buffets, mutilation, imprisonment and torture." Benedetta Lucchese was badly beaten before she was killed. "Martina was subjected to various kinds of torture, and finally obtained the crown of martyrdom by the sword." The Fusarno girl was also badly beaten up before her throat was cut.'

Pierangelo pauses. Then he reads: '"The flesh was torn off Theodosia's breasts and sides to the bone. At last she was hurled into the sea." We know that Ginevra Montelleone's lungs were full of water, but no one could ever understand why. Well, it's because she was flayed alive, just like Theodosia. Then she was drowned.'

He looks back at the pages on the table. '"The Bishop of Illyria,"' he reads, '"endured a red-hot iron, a gridiron, a pan filled with boiling oil, pitch and resin cast to his loins, and endured no harm by them. Finally his throat was cut. His mother, Anthea, underwent the same death."'

In the silence that follows, Francesca Giusti stands up and walks away from us to the middle of the lawn. We can hear the drums again through the open windows of the house, the same riff being played over and over, not particularly well. A telephone rings. Beyond the fence cars go by, and I am aware of two fat bumblebees in a planter of lavender, humming and buzzing as they work their way over the newly opened flowers.

When Dottoressa Giusti turns back to us she runs her manicured hands through her thick dark hair and gives her head a little shake, as if she's trying to rid herself of a bad dream. 'All right,' she says. 'All right, let's just say this is true. What do we do?'

In the pause that follows, Babinellio actually smiles. 'It's fascinating.'

He leans forward, his chubby hands on the table, tapping his finger on the edge of the calendar to some secret rhythm of his own as he turns the pages.

Pallioti lights a cigarette, looks in vain for an ashtray, and finally settles for tapping his ashes into the lavender pot. 'This is all very well,' he says. 'But how do we find him?'

Pierangelo shifts in his chair. 'He has to have known Indrizzio. There's no other explanation.'

'There is.' Babinellio nods, his round head wagging up and down like one of those things in the back of cars. We all look at him. 'Maybe it is Indrizzio.'

'Oh for Christ's sake!' Pallioti grinds his cigarette out and immediately lights another one.

'Well,' Babinellio asks. 'Are we really certain he's dead? It wouldn't be the first time the police screwed up totally. The accident was bad, right? Bodies burnt?'

'Yes,' Pallioti nods, 'the petrol tank caught fire and the van exploded. The driver and one of the guards got out, but they couldn't rescue the others.'

'And you ran DNA?'

'Yes, we DNA-tested. Of course we did.'

'DNA isn't infallible.' This is Francesca Giusti. 'Mistakes can be made,' she says. 'Sometimes it isn't even very good.'

'And,' Babinellio adds, 'this is a very strong profile. The

continuity between these killings was undeniable to start with, even if the exact method was not the same. Of course, now that is explained. The death fits the martyr. But the rest, the staging, the souvenirs. They all point of the same perpetrator. And with the dates the signora has discovered, now it all fits.' He stops speaking and looks around the table.

'Except for Signora Warren.' Pallioti has slipped into using my old name again. He stares off across the lawn, then he looks back at me. 'There's no date for you, is there? Presuming, of course, that he intended to kill you on—what was it? The twenty-fifth of May?'

'No.' I've recognized this, of course. 'All I can think is that there may be some martyr not recorded, maybe not accepted, someone he knows about and we don't.'

'Or the date is significant to him for another reason altogether,' Babinellio suggests. 'An anniversary perhaps? A birthday, or the death day. Of his mother. Sister. A lover. Who knows?'

'"Who knows" does not help me,' Pallioti barks.

'The only thing I could find,' I say quickly, 'is that I was attacked on the name day for Saint Mary Magdalene di Pazzi. It's also the church Ginevra Montelleone went to, when she went. Maybe there's a connection there, and that had to be good enough for him.'

'Well, not everyone is perfect all the time,' Pallioti says. He smiles tightly, but the frustration in his voice is palpable.

'How much of a practising Catholic was Indrizzio?' Babinellio asks.

Pallioti shrugs. 'Nothing special. As far as we know, he went to church occasionally. Most of the homeless do,' he adds. 'Especially if it's raining and there's food.'

'Well.' Francesca Giusti picks up her gold pen and puts it down again. 'As I see it, gentlemen,' she says, 'we have three choices. Either Karel Indrizzio got out of that accident, by luck or because he wasn't in the van in the first place, and he's come back. Or he's dead, and we have a copycat. Or,' she says finally, 'he's dead and he never did it in the first place. In which case we've had a serial killer loose in this city for more than two years.'

No one seems to want to address the last possibility, and eventually Pallioti stands up.

'You know, no matter who it is,' he says, 'the point is to stop him.' He picks up the calendar, his voice getting increasingly agitated. 'And there is nothing,' he says, 'nothing in this—is there?—that helps us predict why he chooses these women, specifically. Or when he'll do it again.'

He walks across the terrace, then comes back and sits down. 'I mean, good God,' his voice rises in exasperation, 'there are martyrdoms for most names on every damn day of the year on these calendars. So, how does he choose which ones?' He glares at Babinellio, as if the doctor should be able to answer this. 'Out of all the women in Florence,' Pallioti asks, 'how does he choose, huh?'

'Maybe he doesn't.'

They all look at me, as if they're a little surprised to find I'm still here, even Pierangelo. 'Maybe he chooses the women first,' I say, 'then waits for the right day.'

Pallioti considers this for a moment, and when he speaks again his voice is a little softer.

'That still doesn't help us, signora. Unless we know why he chooses these women, specifically, we can't anticipate him. And if we can't anticipate him, we can't stop him. And if we can't stop him, we are at his mercy. All we can do is wait and react. Which means, unless he makes a mistake or we get very lucky, more women are going to die. You don't think he'll stop, do you?' he asks Babinellio suddenly. 'I mean, there was a hiatus of—what? Eighteen months?'

'That doesn't matter,' says Babinellio. He shrugs. 'If it's the same person, there are a hundred things that could explain it. He could have been out of the city, even out of the country. Workers move easily, thanks to Brussels. For all we know he could have been anywhere in the EU. The world, for that matter. But whether he's a copier or not,' he adds, 'no matter who killed the first two women and attacked the signora, we do know two things. One: the same person who killed the Fusarno woman also killed the Montelleone girl and Signora Kalczeska. Two: he's in Florence now. And no,' Babinellio turns to Pallioti, 'I see no reason to believe he'll stop.'

Babinellio leans back in his chair, his fingers laced across his stomach. 'On the contrary,' he says, 'in cases like this, the hunger feeds itself. You'll notice the intervals are getting closer. The staging becoming more dramatic.'

'He's getting bolder.'

'Possibly,' Babinellio says. 'Or more terrified. He feels possessed by this need. He can't stop himself, so he may be begging us to stop him.'

'A cry for help,' Pallioti's voice is acidic. 'That's very touching. And I would love to stop him, but how do you suggest I do it? I can't very well warn every woman in Florence.'

'Why not?' I ask.

Pallioti ignores this and picks up the calendar. 'I'm not sure what we do with this.' He turns to Babinellio. 'I'm not even sure what it tells us about him that we don't already know. That he has access to a car or a van, he has access to somewhere to keep the victims he kidnaps, he knows how to buy a carving knife in a shop.' Pallioti shrugs. 'With rental agencies and car clubs, apartments, garages and storage units, that could describe virtually anyone in this city. Male or female, for that matter. We don't even know he's a man, since he doesn't rape.'

'Well,' Babinellio says, 'the vast majority of sexually ritualistic crimes are, like it or not, committed by white males. Especially when the victims are white, which these were. And make no mistake about it,' he adds, 'although he doesn't rape them, these killings are sexual. And ritualistic. And they're not random. So, chances are good that he's a white male, and we know he's organized, a planner. He may be reassured by structured situations, plans. They'll be part of the ritual for him. For instance, he'll pick out the presents for his victims, probably far in advance. The gifts are chosen very carefully. They're loving.'

Babinellio leans forward and rests his elbows on the table. 'You have to understand,' he says, 'that the hunting, the planning, it's like a courtship for him. Foreplay, for the rest of us: the building up to the act of penetration, the orgasm, which is the killing itself. That doesn't mean, incidentally,' he adds, 'that he sleeps with women. He could even be gay. But more likely he's dysfunctional. And ritual is important to him. Very. In all probability, he's a Catholic.'

At this, Pierangelo actually laughs and Pallioti smiles, as if it's a very bad joke.

'Everyone in this city is Catholic,' Pallioti points out. 'Except for the Jews and about five Muslims. Does it mean he's a priest? A monk? A fanatic? A penitent? Where do I look?'

Babinellio regards him for a moment. Then he leans over, takes Pallioti's package of Nazionale and lights one for himself. 'He's certainly a fanatic,' he says slowly. 'But a priest or a monk? Maybe. Not necessarily. He may no longer even be a practising Catholic. But he was at some point. That's what's important. And when he was, it meant a lot to him. It's possible,' he adds, 'maybe even probable, that he feels that he's doing the women a favour. After all, martyrdom is glory.'

Babinellio leans back in his chair, the tip of his cigarette glowing red as he draws the smoke down into his lungs. 'He loves them,' he says. 'He hates them. He's trying to save them. In that, he's much like the rest of us. But for him, the sadism, the ritual, it's part of his hatred. And his love. It's his "signature."' He raises his hands and makes little quotation marks around the word. 'He's acting out the same brutality again and again. In all probability he's fucking the same woman again and again. It's his need to degrade her. To punish her. Constantly, until he's satisfied.' Babinellio shrugs and holds up his small round hands. 'Which,' he adds, 'may be never.'

There's a silence around the table while each of us contemplates this idea. From the house I can hear someone calling the children. It's a man's voice. The drumming stops. And starts again.

'He's interested in you,' Babinellio says suddenly, turning to me. 'He's killed two people close to you. It's possible that he's showing off for you. Trying to impress you.' Pierangelo reaches for my hand.

'So I know him?' I ask.

Babinellio shrugs. 'Not necessarily.' He smiles. 'But in his mind, anyways, he certainly knows you. That doesn't mean the situation is reciprocal. You may never even have met him.'

I have a cold, shrinking feeling inside as if my stomach is withering. Pallioti shakes his head.

'That doesn't get us anywhere,' he says. 'It still means it could be anyone. Some nut who saw Signora Warren on the street, or in a piazza, or in a bar. He could even have read about her in the paper when she was attacked. There was a lot of coverage. It doesn't narrow the field enough.' He smiles at me. I think he's trying to be reassuring, but it isn't working.

'We can't attack it that way,' he says. 'What we have to do is anticipate him. And to do that we still need to know what connects these women. Something will. Something always does.'

Pallioti reaches into his briefcase, pulls out a folder and deals a set of eight-by-ten pictures across the table.

'Eleanora Darnelli. Benedetta Lucchese. Caterina Fusarno. Ginevra Montelleone. Anthea "Billy" Kalczeska.' He slaps their photos down like a dealer in a casino. 'Signora Warren's right,' he says, 'the dates, the desire to martyr, is significant in what it tells us about him. But in terms of catching him, why he picks his victims is even more significant. We've checked schools, professions, neighbourhoods, hair colours. Even horoscopes. So, any ideas, anyone?'

These aren't crime-scene pictures, and we reach for them, all of us except Pallioti, secretly fascinated, I think, eager to look behind the curtain and catch a glimpse of who these women were in the days before they were made special by a serial killer. I realize that I've never seen a picture of Benedetta alive as an adult, or of Caterina Fusarno alive at all, and it occurs to me that these are like photos of the famous and the infamous as kids, the ones you study in magazines, looking for a hint, a clue, that they had any idea of what they would one day become

Francesca Giusti is looking at the portrait of Ginevra Montelleone, the same one that was in the bar. Pain flashes across her face. Ginevra looks so like her, they could be mother and daughter. I reach for a photo of Eleanora and find that Gabriel Fabbiacelli is as good as I thought he was: she looks exactly like his painting of her in the fresco. Except in this picture, she's wearing her nun's habit, not angel's robes.

Eleanora stands on what looks like a playground, smiling into the camera, one child hanging on her hand, another peeking around the edge of her skirt. The brown serge of her nun's habit looks hot in what is obviously summer sun, and she's hitched it up in the work apron she wears so it hangs at mid-length. I wonder how stifling it must be to pass the whole summer in black stockings and black lace-up shoes. Shoes so highly polished they shine. Like patent leather.

Without thinking, I snatch the photograph of Benedetta.

Pallioti is talking, saying something to Francesca Giusti about the number of men he can make available. His words blur and mix with the buzzing of the bees in the lavender pot and the tattoo of the drum set. The photograph in my hand is in colour. Benedetta sits on a park bench in her nurse's uniform, one arm draped along the back, the pretty blue watch she's wearing setting off the tan on her arm.

'He's been in the apartment.'

The talking at the table stops.

'He's been in the apartment!' I stand up, the chair behind me almost tipping over.

Pallioti gets to his feet. 'Signora?'

Pierangelo stands up too. He reaches out, but I duck away. I don't want anyone to touch me.

'He's been in the apartment,' I say again, louder this time. 'That shoe, the one he took from Eleanora Darnelli, it's in the bottom of Billy's closet. And she found black nail polish in the bathroom. She thought it was mine. But it was Caterina's.

Caterina Fusarno was wearing it when she died, it must have been in her bag. And Benedetta Lucchese's watch. It has a B and a date, 1992, I think, engraved on the back, doesn't it?'

I don't even have to see Pallioti nod.

'It's on Billy's bureau. In her jewellery box. I thought she didn't wear it because she was being difficult, but she probably didn't even know it was there.'

I sit down, suddenly, groping for the chair. 'He's been coming in the whole time.'

Pieces of the puzzle are falling around me like hailstones, clattering out of the sky and locking into place. The picture grows and grows, seeping like a stain across the weeks we spent in the apartment.

'My keys were missing. I lose keys. He must have got hold of them, somehow, and had them copied. Then he came in and out. He did it all the time.' I close my eyes and see my room, my lipsticks and eye shadow all messed up. I thought it was Billy. But it wasn't. He sprayed my perfume. He took my toothbrush.

'That's how he got my cell number.' I feel sick. 'He left things and he took things. I think he made designs on the floor, with postcards. It wasn't Billy outside on the landing, last Thursday. It was him.'

I feel the door panel against my cheek. Hear my own whisper in the dark.

'I smelled him. He used my perfume. He was right on the other side of the door.'

My skin starts to crawl. Rats' whiskers tickling my scars. I see my room, Signora Bardino's pretty pink counterpane, and the indent, the unmistakable shape of a head on the pillow.

'Oh God,' I wail, 'he was on my bed! He lay on my bed!' And the drumming stops abruptly.

In the next few minutes, Pallioti makes a series of phone calls while Francesca Giusti takes me into the house to use the bathroom and wash my face. She runs ice-cold water and hands me a pink fluffy towel. When she walks back with me across the lawn, she puts her arm around my shoulders. By the time we sit down again, Pallioti is pacing back and forth. The rats are still tickling me, but as he speaks I feel calmer.

'When was the last time you think he was there?'

'Yesterday.'

All of them stare at me.

'I saw him,' I say slowly. I'm way too embarrassed to confess I thought it was Billy's ghost, but I tell them about the shadow in the kitchen. 'He left while I was at Sophie's. Signora Sassinelli,' I explain. 'He must have.' I stop, remembering how close I came to not going up to Sophie's at all. 'He took Billy on Wednesday or Thursday.' I run my hand across my eyes, trying to stop the days sliding together. 'And he's come back since,' I add. 'That night, he didn't think I'd be there; I called Billy's name when I woke up, and stopped him coming in. But he came back yesterday. There were cigarettes,' I say slowly, remembering the red and lavender bands. 'He uses my lipstick.'

'Mary should leave,' Pierangelo says suddenly. 'She should leave Florence today.'

There is silence at the table. Babinellio, Francesca Giusti and Pallioti exchange glances.

'Of course,' Francesca Giusti says, 'Signora Thorcroft is entirely free to do as she wishes, and her safety is our primary concern.'

'Good.' Pierangelo stands up.

Babinellio looks at me. 'I think it would be a great shame if you left.'

His small black eyes are almost glittering with excitement. 'You see,' he says, 'it appears I was right. Not only is he interested in you, signora. He wants, even needs, to be close to you.'

'What Babinellio is saying,' Pallioti interjects, 'is that you're the only certain way we have of catching him.'

The argument goes on for the better part of an hour, and finally it's me who settles it. Francesca Giusti and Pierangelo both suggest using a policewoman who looks like me, someone in a wig who will come and go from the apartment while the police stake it out. But one look at Babinellio's face is enough to tell me that he thinks this idea is pointless. And so do I. Because whoever it is who's doing this, whoever's plucking women out of Florence to offer them his peculiar brand of salvation, will know. I can sense it. I don't know who he is. I can't pick his face out in a crowd, as familiar as it may be. But he's caressed my clothes. And used my toothbrush. He's rested his head on my pillow. He's my secret friend. And he won't be deceived.

I consider this as I stand outside the door to Signora Bardino's apartment with Pallioti, two other policemen I don't know, and a forensics team. It's just past five a.m. on Monday, and I feel as if I've been away for years.

The Sassinellis and Signora Raguzza and Dinya, her companion—in other words everyone who lives in the building—have been eliminated as suspects, so it was decided yesterday that we would come here this morning, immediately after dawn. Coming at night would have meant using lights, which would be unusual because I haven't been staying here, and appearing during the day would have attracted attention, which Pallioti is desperate to avoid. The only chance for springing this trap is for everything to appear completely normal.

So that's what I've been instructed to do; be normal. All the time. Twenty-four seven. The apartment will be watched continuously, and in the meantime I'm supposed to go to lectures, and go to Pierangelo's and go out to eat, and go shopping. A panic button has been installed in Piero's apartment, and another one will be put here. My cell phone is still being monitored, and the phones at Pierangelo's and here are tapped. I won't know who the police are who are shadowing me, in case I do something to give them away, but I have been assured that somewhere, close by, they'll be watching, looking for someone, anyone, who is looking at me. I don't need to worry, Pallioti says. I'll be fine. Because from now on, I'll never be alone.

'Ready?' He turns the key in the lock, and I nod. All I have to do is walk in, go through the apartment and notice everything: anything I think he might have touched or taken or left behind.

In the dull light, the rooms look dead. The bed counterpanes are smooth, there's no indent on the pillows. I wear gloves to open my own closet and stare at the empty hangers. In Billy's room, dust is collecting again on the top of her bureau. In the kitchen, I go through the cupboards, the bottles of oil, the spices and sugar to see if he's left a little gift there. When I look at the eggshell cups and ugly mugs I wonder which one he drank out of. If he opened packets and stuck his fingers in our food. What did he lick? What did he spit in? Who knows?

After I have finished, the forensic crew seem to take for ever. It's crucial that the chain of evidence be preserved, so everything has to be photographed and rephotographed, annotated and bagged. There are three of them, and before they go inside, they zip themselves into white paper spacesuits. Pallioti and I only have to wear gloves and little paper bags over our shoes, and we stand in the hall, which seems to be a neutral area, while they brush and swab everything in sight.

Yesterday, Pallioti asked me over and over again when I first noticed things: the nail polish, the shoe, the watch. Papers out of place. Food missing. And I told him everything I could remember. But now, actually standing here, I am no longer certain of anything. The past has been all shaken up; what I thought was our life in this apartment, the days Billy and I spent coming and going that seemed so ordinary, have been put into a kaleidoscope, whirled and rearranged, and nothing I look at is what I thought it was.

I want to ask Pallioti if this is what happens to him, if this is what police investigations do. If, when you know the 'real facts'—who had murderous intent, who plotted and hated, cut and killed—does the picture change? Does what is beautiful become ugly? I'd like to ask him that, and ask him how he ever manages, then, to know what he is seeing, to believe in anything. But I don't dare. Because he's getting agitated. The forensics are taking too long. The bells are ringing for early Mass, and the day is starting.

Finally they finish with the kitchen, the living room, Billy's room and the bathroom. They just have my room and the hall to do, and two of them will leave while the third finishes up. We move into the kitchen while a man and a woman strip off their paper suits and fold them away. They put their stuff into a backpack and a toolbox. The woman loosens her hair and suddenly she looks like a student. She goes first. The guy waits and goes ten minutes later. When I watch him sauntering across the courtyard, wearing a blue coverall and carrying a toolbox, he's nothing but a plumber.

I stand on the balcony—after all, someone had to let the plumber in for this early appointment—while Pallioti hovers in the kitchen. I hear him shift uneasily when a howl is unleashed from the apartment opposite. Little Paolo is unhappy with his breakfast again. The howl rises and crescendoes, and I'm about to reassure Pallioti that this is entirely normal, when the tiny figure explodes from the Sassinellis' lower door, runs into the courtyard and disappears under the portico. He's still in his pyjamas, and I expect Sophie to appear any moment, chasing him.

When she doesn't, Paolo skulks back into the court-yard. He looks both ways, to see if he's being pursued, then wanders, barefoot and tousled, over towards one of the giant lemon pots and sidles behind it so he's out of sight of his own door. From where I'm standing I can see him clearly, playing with something he has clutched in his fist. Behind me I hear Pallioti talking to the remaining forensics guy, then I see a flash, which appears to startle Paolo almost as much as me. A second later he giggles and opens his hands as though he's got a secret.

Matches. I did this when I was a kid, and set the sleeve of my sweater on fire. I don't know if the fancy pyjamas Sophie buys are flame retardant or not, but since there's no sign of his mother, I don't think I want to wait and see.

'I'll be back in a minute.'

I push past Pallioti, pulling the gloves off as I go down the hall. On the stairs, I almost slip and fall. Great. I'll break my neck, and Paolo can play Buddhist monk and immolate himself. Along with Mr Martyr running around town, that should start the week off well. I pause to rip off the stupid booties and stuff them in my pocket.

The voice from Rome is reading the morning news in Signora Raguzza's apartment, and by the time I get out into the courtyard Big Paolo is already coming out of their door. He's carrying his tie and he's obviously just shoved his shoes on. His hair is still wet. Little Paolo sees him and screams, 'Mommy, Mommy, Mommy! I want my mommy!' And dives behind the lemon pot again.

We converge on the little boy at about the same time and, to my surprise, Big Paolo actually looks relieved to see me, as if he's under the mistaken impression that because I'm a woman, I might be good with children.

'*Dispiace, Signora, dispiace!*' he says, and smiles at Little Paolo. 'Come on, *piccolo*.' He stretches his hand down to his son. 'You have to get dressed for school.'

At this, Little Paolo melts down onto the flagstones, turning suddenly boneless, the way small children can. When his father reaches for him again he squeals and wiggles away, clutching his hands to his chest as though he's holding the last possession in the world.

Big Paolo looks at me and rolls his eyes. 'My wife is away,' he explains. 'Paolo is very used to having her do everything for him.'

'Away?' So Sophie made up her mind, after all. But she didn't take Little Paolo. Which seems completely weird.

The little boy's concentrating on whatever it is he's got gripped in his fist, employing the old kid trick of pretending we're not here so we'll go away, and I sink down on my haunches to be at eye level with him.

'Hey, Paolo,' I say. 'Remember me? I'm a friend of Mommy's.' I speak to him in English, the way Sophie does, and he looks at me, slyly, out of the corner of his eye.

'You have pink hair.'

'That's right. I do. When did Mommy go away?' I ask. He can burn himself to pieces for all I care, I just want to know the answer to this question.

'Come along, Paolo.' His father reaches for him again, but I hold my hand up like a traffic cop and, amazingly, he stops.

'When did Mommy go away, Paolo?' I ask again.

'Yesterday,' he says in English, and smirks at his father.

'When yesterday?' I turn and look at Big Paolo. 'Where did she go?' I ask. It's obnoxious, but there must be something in my voice because he actually answers me.

'She went to Mass and left directly afterwards.' He sounds exasperated. 'My wife does things like this sometimes. She's staying with a friend.'

Geneva, I think. Then I look back at Little Paolo. He's twisted his hands around behind his back and is looking from one to the other of us, probably fascinated that I even dare speak to his father. Would Sophie have left him like this? Without saying anything? Maybe. Maybe saying something to him would just make him hysterical. Then he'd give her away. She must be planning to come back for him. That must be it.

'I'm sorry.' I stand up and smile sheepishly. I'm sure Sophie has a plan and I don't want to mess it up for her. 'I thought I could help,' I say finally. '*Dispiace*. I'm so sorry to interfere. Paolo seemed unhappy.'

'Without his mother,' Big Paolo snaps, 'Paolo is always unhappy.'

His temper is clearly fraying. He reaches down and grabs Little Paolo, who shrieks again and curls himself into a ball. As he's lifted off his feet, he bats at his father, his fists flailing angrily.

'Stop it!'

His father's shouting only makes Little Paolo shriek and kick harder, and although I know I'm overtired, just at this moment I think that if Sophie has taken off and left them both I really wouldn't blame her.

Little Paolo is boiling himself into a tantrum, and Big Paolo shakes his head and lifts him higher. As he starts to walk away, his son lets out another shriek of rage.

'MOMMY!' he screams, trying to slap his father's face. His little fist flies open, and Billy's pink lighter falls at our feet, Elvis's hips wiggling on the pale grey stone.

Chapter Twenty-five

'TELL ME AGAIN.'

Pallioti walks back and forth across the Sassinellis' living room, one hand pressed against the small of his back and the other against his forehead, as if he's literally trying to hold himself together.

Little Paolo, who seems to sense that something terrible is happening, has finally shut up and nestles in his father's lap. Big Paolo, holding him, sits on one of the uncomfortable sofas, his face a sickly, chalky white. The Elvis lighter is in an evidence bag, already on its way to the crime lab, and as we sit here, white-space-suited people are assembling in the vestibule of the Sassinellis' apartment.

'She went to an early Mass, yesterday morning.' Big Paolo's voice has no sign of bullying aggression in it now. Quite the opposite, he sounds terrified.

'At San Miniato?' Pallioti asks.

Big Paolo nods. He's already told us this once. 'Yes, at San Miniato.'

'Did she take the car or walk?'

'She walked. My driver has Sunday off. We usually go to Mass together on Sunday, at ten, as a family. We walk,' he says miserably, 'because Sophia says the exercise is good for us, but yesterday she said she wanted to go alone. Early.'

'That was unusual?'

Paolo strokes the crown of his son's head. 'We weren't getting along very well,' he mutters. Then he looks up. 'Ispettore Pallioti, my wife is expecting a baby. She hadn't been—Well,' he stammers, 'she could be irrational at times.'

Pallioti stops and looks at him. I have already told him about the conversation I had with Sophie on Friday. 'Go on,' he says.

'There isn't much more to tell. I saw her before she left. We... we had words.' He uses the nice old-fashioned term for 'fight.' 'I told her to go and talk to our priest,' he adds.

'Who is?'

'Father Corsini.'

'Not Father Rinaldo?' Pallioti has asked him this before.

'No. I told you. I don't know him.'

Pallioti glances at me and then back at Paolo. 'Go on,' he says again, his voice impatient now. 'You told her to go and talk to her priest. She left at what time?'

'About half past six. There's an early Mass at seven. She wanted to be back in time. She likes to be here,' he says, 'when Paolo wakes up. She says she wants to be the first thing he sees every morning.'

To my amazement, tears begin to pour down the big man's face. He's either a really good faker or he's suddenly forgotten his secretary. He reaches up to wipe them away, then gropes in his pocket for a handkerchief. 'I didn't see her when she came back,' he says. 'I was angry with her. I got my son up and took him out for breakfast. As a treat. Just the two of us together. We went to the Excelsior. The roof terrace is open. You can ask them,' he adds. 'They know me. When we came back, she wasn't here.'

'Did you check, to see if any of her things were missing? A suitcase? Clothes?'

He shakes his head. 'I thought she'd gone to stay at a friend's. You know how it is,' he adds miserably, 'with wives.' Pallioti just stares at him. Maybe he does and maybe he doesn't.

'We were supposed to be at my parents' for lunch yesterday,' he goes on finally. 'She doesn't get on with my sister.' I swear he starts to say, *You know how it is with families*, but thinks better of it. 'I thought she was just being awkward. So I took Paolo and went without her. I was certain she'd be home by the time we got back.'

'But she wasn't?'

'No.'

'And you found the lighter when?'

'When we got back; at about six o'clock. It was on the kitchen table. Paolo found it. In a pile of seeds.'

My stomach flips. This hadn't been mentioned before. Until now, it was just possible to believe that Sophie had fled to Geneva or Rome, or wherever, and that Little Paolo had had Billy's lighter all along. I don't think Pallioti thought it likely, hence the space-suits, but now it's not even possible. I open my mouth and close it again, remembering the Bargello. And the grit I swept from our balcony the day before that almost went through Signora Raguzza's window. If I'd looked more closely, would I have noticed that it was birdseed?

Sophie's husband looks from me to Pallioti, who has stopped pacing and stands, staring at him.

'A pile of seeds?' he asks. Pallioti deliberately doesn't look at me. 'Where are these seeds now?' he asks slowly.

Paolo isn't stupid, and though he may not know what this means he knows from the looks on our faces that it's not good news. He closes his eyes. 'I swept them up and threw them out,' he says. 'They went in the rubbish last night.'

'You still have it?'

He nods. 'In the kitchen. We've started using Dinya, Signora Raguzza's companion as a cleaner, but she doesn't come on Sunday.'

Pallioti calls, and the woman from forensics who looked like a student when she left our apartment an hour ago sticks her head round the door. Now she's back in her white get-up.

'The kitchen,' Pallioti says to her. 'Pay special attention to the rubbish. There's birdseed in it.'

'*Certo.*'

Another of the cops from this morning shoulders past her, comes into the room and hands Pallioti a calendar. I don't have to ask what kind it is. He flips through the pages quickly, then his face freezes.

'Ispettore Pallioti, please,' Paolo says. 'Tell me. Anything I can do to help you find my wife.'

'Pray,' Pallioti snaps. He gestures to me and turns towards the door. 'Pray, signor,' he says.

Forensic people and cops come streaming in, and I almost have to run to catch up with Pallioti, who is already at the bottom of the stairs. Without saying anything, he hands me the calendar. Today is 28 April. On 30 April the virgin and holy martyr Sophie was beheaded.

'You have to arrest Rinaldo! You have to!' Little Paolo had an epic temper tantrum earlier, and it looks as if I am having one now.

'I told you, he came here. He was looking for me, but he met Billy. He was in the Boboli when I was attacked, and he has a connection to Sophie!'

'Get in the car, signora.' Pallioti is holding the door.

'But—'

'Now!' Pallioti snaps. 'I don't have time for this!'

I crawl into the back seat, feeling like a child. Pallioti gets in beside me and taps on the screen that separates us from the driver. The city streams by. Beyond the tinted glass, everything looks as though it's in a movie. We pass the grocery store, where the signora stands on the front step, her hands on her hips, looking up and down the street while Marcello unloads some sort of crate from a delivery van. At the head of the Ponte Vecchio, tourists are already flocking. The chic policewoman, the one with the long blonde hair who is always there, waves us out onto Lungarno Torrigiani, and as we fly along the river, we pass people walking dogs, and bicycling, and taking pictures of the bridge.

'Opus Dei,' I say, without looking at Pallioti. 'Rinaldo's involved with them, I told you. Isabella Lucchese was too. She says they own a bunch of villas. You should talk to her. Please. She says they're trying to get hold of that big derelict villa down by the Art Institute. It's not far from where Benedetta was found. Or Billy. How did he get her in?' I ask suddenly. 'How did he get Billy up to the fort, after he killed her?'

Oddly enough, I have never asked this before, and I don't think Pallioti is going to answer me now. He's completely distracted, and sick of me. We drive over the Ponte alle Grazie, and he sighs.

'He has a car,' he says. 'One of the villas on Costa San Giorgio reported hearing a car in the early hours of Easter morning. Shortly after two a.m.' He runs his hands across his eyes. 'They didn't bother calling the police. It was the holidays and there are often kids up there.' He shakes his head, then he makes a sound like a snarl, half laugh, half snort. 'They thought it was normal. And why shouldn't they? The owner told me he didn't want to bother the *carabinieri*. They thought the police had more important things to do.'

I think of the hole, of Billy's body being dragged through the ripped chicken wire. Did he have her in a bag? Did he roll her down the bank? Is that what he'll do to Sophie? I start to cry. It's a beautiful spring day, but the kaleidoscope's turned and all I can see are ugly, shattered pieces of light.

Pallioti may be sick of me, but he does call Pierangelo's apartment at about four o'clock in the afternoon to tell us that Rinaldo is 'cooperating' with the investigation, and that the family who own it have agreed to give the police access to the derelict villa by the Art Institute. Piero talks with him for a few minutes, and when he gets off he says they've made the decision to go public with Sophie's disappearance. A reward is being offered. Pallioti will be on the news tonight.

We tune in to watch him. They don't say anything about the other women—Piero says they don't want to start a wholesale panic in the city—so all they talk about is the abduction of a young mother. Pictures of Sophie fill the screen. In one she is holding Paolo and laughing. Just like Caterina Fusarno must have held Carlo. I can't watch this. Finally I have to get up and go into the bedroom. Pierangelo comes in later and sits beside me. He strokes my hair and tells me that Big Paolo was on too, appealing directly to whoever was holding his wife to release her. He looked awful, Pierangelo says. I tell him everything about my conversations with Sophie, and he adds that it's strange how often people don't realize who they really love until they lose them.

After that, I can't sit still. While Piero cooks dinner, which he knows perfectly well I won't eat, I wander around the apartment, going back and forth and back again through the rooms, until I know I must be driving him crazy. I take the file from his study and bring it into the living room, but Pierangelo takes it away from me.

'They're good, *cara*,' he says. 'The police will find her. Really, they will.'

I don't know if he believes it, but at least he's making an effort. I take the glass of wine he gives me, not really tasting it as I thumb through Monika's calendar. Some martyrs get more details than others, but nothing says Sophie the virgin and martyr was tortured. Just that she was beheaded. It's a strange thing to take comfort in.

Finally I fall asleep on the couch, drifting down into shallow dreams that toss and rock. Sophie's in a dark place and I want to bring her tea, but I can't find a teabag. I look and look, getting more and more frantic. Then the bell rings and Sophie laughs. 'Time's up!' she says, 'Mary! Mary!' And I wake with a start to see Pierangelo standing above me holding the phone.

'Pallioti just called.' He sits down on the edge of the couch. 'They have a lead.'

'From the news?' I sit up and Pierangelo nods.

'They're sending over a picture they want you to look at, of the Sassinellis' driver. His ex-girlfriend saw the broadcast and called in. Apparently he had a prior conviction, in Rome. For stalking.'

I remember the basement door propped open because of the electricity van parked in front of the apartment. But he'd have a key anyways. And of course, Sophie would get in a car with him.

'They need to know if you recognize him,' Pierangelo is saying, 'if you ever saw him hanging around, or if Billy knew him.'

I nod and get up. My head feels fuggy. I need to splash cold water on my face. Maybe it wasn't me, I think suddenly. Maybe I wasn't the connection after all. Maybe it was Sophie all along, and he noticed Billy because of her.

When a policeman arrives fifteen minutes later, I stare at the eight-by-ten he shows me of a thickset man with bulldog jowls and a shadow of beard.

'This is a mugshot. He probably looks a little better now. Cleaned up. His name is Fabio Locci,' the cop tells me. But I shake my head. I even go and get the envelope of Billy's pictures and spread them out on the dining-room table to see if Fabio Locci might appear in any of them. But he's not there. I've never seen him before.

'OK,' the policeman says finally. 'Well,' he shrugs. 'Thank you, anyways.'

'But you can just bring him in, and at least Sophie will be safe.' The cop hesitates by the door. 'You have him, right? You know where he is?'

He shakes his head. 'No, signora,' he says. 'I'm afraid not. We have the car, of course. But Signor Locci has disappeared.'

'Locci's from the Abruzzi,' Pierangelo tells me the next morning when he brings coffee up to the roof terrace. 'Did his time in the army, and a stint in the *carabinieri*. Three years ago, his ex-wife brought charges against him for stalking. He did six months and community service, and left Rome. He's been working for Paolo Sassinelli for two years.'

For a change, Pallioti actually wants Pierangelo to run a piece on this. They can't risk giving away what they know by mentioning the timing or the martyrs, so the paper's been on the phone almost all night, working on stories about Sophie and Locci, figuring out what they can say and what they can't. The police are scouring the city, even as we speak, but the public are still their best eyes and ears. A story's coming out this morning, 29 April, and anything Pierangelo's going to run for this evening has to be ready by noon.

'Oh, and I thought you'd want to know,' he adds, glancing at me, 'you were right. We did some digging around, and Batman has a nasty past.'

'Kirk?' I put my cup down and look at him. I don't remember ever actually suggesting this, but maybe the bruise on my jaw was enough. Or maybe he spoke to Pallioti. I told them Kirk had gone to Venice.

'Our guy in New York did some ferreting,' Piero says. 'Your friend's left a bad smell behind in a couple of offices. Nothing that's stuck yet, but allegations of sexual harassment, that kind of stuff. There was an incident at some conference. The word "rape" was never actually used, and the woman, a junior associate, got a pretty nice vacation package.' He shrugs. 'You know how it goes.'

I guess I do. I think of Kirk's fist flying towards me, and of Billy, telling me he was 'too intense'. Of the phone calls. The temper. The cocaine. Of her asking me about the stuff I got from the *farmacia*. Did he hit her? Or worse? Would she have told me if he did? Pierangelo is watching the expression on my face.

'He's apparently a very good prosecutor, *cara*. Puts a lot of bad guys behind bars.'

Oh yes, the 'greater good' argument. Pierangelo pours more coffee into my cup and says, 'Paolo Sassinelli is a big donor to Opus Dei.'

'You're kidding?' I exclaim. Then I think, *why should this surprise me?* They're Catholic and they're rich. Or rather, they're Catholic, and she's rich. I bet she doesn't even know about it.

'How did you find out?' Opus is notoriously secretive about its financial dealings.

Pierangelo raises his eyebrows. 'Ve have our methods, Seegnora.' It's a silly effort to make me smile, but I try.

'Go.' I say suddenly.

'What?'

'Go. Go to the paper.' I have been so selfish. This is a potentially huge story breaking, and Pierangelo has been sitting here holding my hand.

He shrugs. 'They're fine. It's time I started handing over more to the sub-editors anyways.'

'Oh crap! This is important, Pierangelo. He could kill her any time after midnight. Go on, get outta here. Go! Go talk to the cardinal. If Opus is mixed up in this, he can find out. The Vatican's meant to have the best intelligence system in the world.'

He looks at me, and I can see how desperate he is to be there, running this story in person, not from the end of a telephone. I've been so mired in my own self-pity I didn't even notice.

'Go,' I say. 'Please. It's where you belong. Please, Piero,' I add. 'I want you to. Honestly. What goes in the paper could make a difference.' It could make *the* difference, and we both know it. The evening editions are the most widely read papers in the city.

'Well—' He's seriously wavering, and I stand up and push him towards the door.

'I'll be fine,' I say. We both look at the bright-red panic button mounted on the garden wall. There's another in the living room. 'Believe me.' I even manage a smile. 'There is no date any time soon with my name on it, and the one thing I am not, is alone.'

A few seconds later I watch from the window as his big BMW shoots out of the garage and into the street, and realize I'm actually jealous. At least he can make a contribution. All I can do is wait.

The whole morning passes. I have a bath, but when I go to get dressed I don't want to put on any of my clothes. Every time I pick something up, I think of Fabio Locci, of his big fat sweaty hands stroking the fabric, holding it up to the bulldog jowls of his face. Finally, I just wear my robe. Sophie is all over the one o'clock news bulletin, and this time her mother's here too. A huge woman in an expensive-looking suit, she grasps Little Paolo by the arm as if he's a squeegee toy and talks about her daughter. She pronounces Sophie's name with a slight lisp. It sounds like 'Tho-fay.'

I switch the set off. I can't bear the news any more and I'm not even hungry. Eventually I go to get Billy's old books and curl up on the sofa. But sitting isn't possible either. I feel like a caged cat. I get up and riffle the pages, making the photos she used as bookmarks fall onto the floor like leaves. None of them is particularly interesting. Billy was not discriminating about what she shot and these are of our street. The sky is leaden. The wine shop man rolls down his awning, and the vegetable signora glowers, hands on her hips, her gorgeous legs protruding from her barrel-shaped mini-skirt. Standing beside her, Marcello looks like those people you see on death row in the newspaper, half smiling and desperate, his red apron binding him like a sarong. In the next picture Billy is holding a tomato in each hand, and in another she leans against the Vespa, her arms around a man and woman I don't recognize. Or do I? The picture quality is really bad. I squint and feel a pang of recognition. The guy's hair is cut too short. His shirt is too white, and the girl's jacket falls open to reveal a dowdy grey skirt and legs that look as if they've been painted beige. Rinaldo's friends. What do you know?

I flip the picture over, looking for a date mark, but before I can find it, the phone rings. It's Pallioti. They've got some mugshots he wants me to look at and they're very busy. Can he send a car to bring me to the Questura? I don't even have time to tell him about the pictures in my hand before he hangs up.

When I leave the apartment with my escort, it's ten minutes past two in the afternoon. In nine hours and fifty minutes, it will be 30 April.

The second floor, where I am taken, looks like a riot scene. A confusing number of people shout into phones and run in and out. Pallioti sees me for just a second. He nods when I show him Billy's old pictures and hands them to someone who he says will 'take them away for comparison'. Pallioti still has the same suit on. It has ash down the front of it and his face is pasty. He looks awful, but the adrenalin flying around the place is palpable.

They've found other pictures of Locci they want me to look at. Then, Pallioti asks, would I mind going through their other crime books? Locci might have help, there might be a face I've seen. On my way down a glass-walled corridor, I glimpse Rosa Fusarno. She is sitting with a policewoman at a computer terminal, staring at photographs on a screen. The man who's with me, probably one of my 'shadows', follows my glance and nods. He tells me they've brought everyone in. Somewhere in the building Isabella Lucchese and Ginevra Montelleone's family are also staring at screens. Gabriel Fabbiacelli's been here too, and even Eleanora's Mother Superior. And they've questioned everyone who's had access to the Sassinelli building in the last two years. Sooner or later, someone's going to recognize a face. Someone may, but it isn't me. Finally, sometime after six, a cop I don't know says they'll have a car take me home. I have looked at the faces of so many men that my head is swimming. I can't believe there are that many people in Florence I don't know.

Pallioti has gone off to be on the news again, and when we walk back through the second floor, the riot scene has changed. Now people talk in quieter voices. They hunch over phones, tap pens on the edge of desks and don't meet each other's eyes. A big blow-up of the picture of Sophie and Little Paolo looks down on the room.

'Thanks for these, we made copies,' the cop says when he hands me Billy's photos. We are standing in the lobby and I can see lights coming on outside.

'Do you think you'll find her?' I know I shouldn't, but I can't help asking.

'Sure, yes. Of course we'll find her,' he says. But he doesn't look anywhere near as confident as he sounds. He's relieved when, a second later, he gets a phone call and excuses himself, telling me my driver will be here in a minute, if I just wait.

So I do. I wait and wait. Cops fly by, still looking like pairs of mated geese, but no one comes for me, and finally I think this is ridiculous. The *passegiata*'s in full swing. My 'shadow' is probably hanging around somewhere, and the only person that anybody, certainly Fabio Locci, is thinking about is Sophie. It sure as hell isn't me. In fact, I think, as I push through the revolving door onto the street, I feel safer than I have in days.

Instinctively I start to walk towards Pierangelo's. Then I stop. He's working on tomorrow's edition and won't be back until late, if at all, and I can't face the empty apartment. I'll go crazy. If there's really nothing I can do, I'd rather do it with someone who understands what this feels like. There's a cab in the rank outside the Savoy Hotel, and I get in and give the driver Isabella Lucchese's address.

It's only after I pay and the taxi pulls away that I realize her drive is empty. It seems deeply unfair, as if she should have known I was coming, and I almost rattle the gate in frustration. Then, just as I am about to walk away, Fonzi bounds out of the shadows like a mythical wolf. He stops and looks at me and I think he's going to start to bark, but instead he glances backwards and, sure enough, Isabella emerges from the tangle of the garden.

Seeing her again, I remember what an idiot I was in the car when she drove me home, but she doesn't seem to care. When she lets me in, she even smiles.

'I thought you might come,' she says. 'It's hard to be alone, isn't it?'

I nod. 'You were at the Questura.'

'You too?' She pushes the gates closed, and as I follow her down the drive, I ask, 'Where's your car? I thought you weren't here.'

'In the garage. I'm getting the brakes fixed.' Any other time I might think that was funny.

The villa rises above us, the twilight making it look even bigger than it is. Its shuttered windows are blank squares, and when we come around the edge of the house the light spilling from the kitchen looks yellow and garish. Vines throw tangled shadows onto the gravel and something rustles in the heavy bank of overgrowth. Isabella goes inside without looking back, and I follow her.

'You want wine?' she asks. The bottle is already open. She holds it up and pours me a glass I don't really want.

'Listen, I've found something. You know about Sophie?' Of course she knows about Sophie, she was at the Questura. Isabella looks at me as though I'm stupid, but I pull Billy's pictures out anyways. 'This is my friend, the one who was killed. I didn't know she had any connection to Opus at all, then I found this.' I put the snapshot of Billy leaning against the Vespa on the table. 'Do you recognize either of them?'

Isabella takes the photo and holds it under the light, examining the clean-cut boy and the pale, doughy girl. She takes so long that I'm sure she's going to say yes, give me a name and a criminal record, but she shakes her head and hands it back to me. 'Are you sure?'

She nods. 'I've never seen either of them.'

I actually whimper with frustration.

'Take it down to the Questura in the morning,' Isabella says. 'Maybe they can match it.'

'In the morning? It will be a little fucking late in the morning.' In the morning we'll find Sophie laid out in some terrible place, clutching her ghastly little present. I can't believe Isabella said such a thing. And then I remember. She doesn't know. The police haven't told anyone about the martyrs, and the time. She stares at me as I reach for the glass. Then I tell her.

When I'm finished, Isabella sinks down onto one of the old cane-seated chairs. Then she glances at the big clock above the table, and I look too. It's almost eight p.m., and I know she's thinking about Opus, I can tell by the look on her face.

'It has to be them,' she says. 'It just has to be.' She bangs the table with her palm making our glasses jump. 'I've always thought, always, that they killed Benedetta. Even during Indrizzio, I had this thing in the back of my mind. I've always thought they killed her,' she says again, 'and I've always thought they did it not too far from here. How else could they have taken her, moved her?'

I don't know, but I'm remembering something else she said. *Bonfires of the Vanities in the back garden.* Things other than books burn in fires. Clothes, for instance. Evidence. I see a map of Florence in my head, with coloured pins on it like the ones I sometimes imagine Piero stakes me out with when he asks *Where R U?*, but these pins are for the dead women.

'Three of them,' I say, thinking out loud, 'Benedetta, Ginevra and Billy, have been laid out, or whatever you want to call it, pretty close to here. And Benedetta and Ginevra were last seen close by too. Ginevra at that wine bar in San Niccolo.' It's not more than a five-minute walk away. 'Eleanora and Caterina both disappeared further away. But they weren't tortured,' I go on. 'Caterina was beaten up, but not burnt or cut or anything. They were killed where they were found, essentially. "Put to the sword." But the others were tortured. He has to do it somewhere.'

'Will Sophie be tortured?' Isabella's eyes don't leave my face.

'It doesn't actually say so in any of the martyrdoms I've found, but I don't know. All we do know is that he's taken her, because he told us.' I think of Elvis and the little pile of birdseed, and try to concentrate.

'He has to take them somewhere where he can get to them, but secluded enough so if something happens, if they scream or struggle or something, no one will hear. I think there's an Opus connection too. It's like somebody's taking *The Way* literally.' I remember what Babinellio said. 'Martyrdom is salvation, right?' I ask her. 'An honour, even? Like the cilice. The mortification of the flesh. This guy may think—I mean, he's crazy, clearly—but he probably thinks he's glorifying them. "It's so beautiful to be a victim."' I quote that pearl of wisdom back to Isabella, and she nods.

'They've searched the villa down by the Art Institute,' I add, 'but you told me there were others.'

'They're all used. They're Opus Dei houses,' she says. 'People live in them, quite a lot of people. It wouldn't be possible, unless you're suggesting—?'

'—a group effort, some organized rite?' I shake my head. I don't buy that. The more I think about it, the more I'm convinced that this is one person who's taken an already dangerous message and warped it out of all recognition. Run it through the zealot's prism in his head and come to the appalling logical conclusion: mortification for God is good, torture for God is better. Death best of all.

I feel suddenly exhausted. But Isabella gets up, standing in the middle of the kitchen, a pool of light at her feet.

'There are two houses,' she says. 'And a third place they use for teaching. Then there are the properties they have their eye on. We've been concentrating on those, because once they move in it's harder to get them out.' She thinks for a second. The clock has become like a third person in the room. Neither of us look at it. Its soft tick-tick-tick drops through the air.

'I'm sure,' Isabella's saying, 'at least I think—' She hurries out of the room before she can finish the sentence, and I hear papers and books being shuffled in the hall. A few seconds later, when she comes back, she has glasses on and a letter in her hand.

'We track this,' she says. 'We have a pressure group, and the idea is to try to stop them before they get in, because, afterwards, it's almost impossible. And I thought I remembered correctly: there is a property they're after. It's been empty for years. The family tried to give it to the city, but that didn't work out, and Opus has been trying to buy it for ages. The issue went dead about a year ago, when it looked as though an American college was going to buy it. I haven't heard much about it since, but I think it's still empty.'

'Where?' It's all I can do not to rip the paper she's holding out of her hand.

'I'll get a map.' Then she grabs my arm. 'Even better, I'll show you!'

Isabella is dragging me into the hallway towards the stairs. It's dark, and her grip is like a claw. As my energy's ebbed, hers seems to have grown, as if there's a finite amount between us. She's every bit as strong as she looks, and she virtually hauls me up the stairs.

'In here, in here,' she's saying. 'It's still light enough to see.'

Isabella throws open the door to the centre bedroom, and I can see the bulky shape of a high *matrimoniale* bed, dressers, and the ghostly reflection of us in the mirrored front of an enormous wardrobe. Something looms up behind me in the glass, and as Isabella pushes the shutters open I whirl round to see an altar in the corner, complete with a prayer rail and a crucified Christ. She pulls me to the open window.

Below us, beyond the dark mass of the garden, the olive groves spread in a silvery carpet across the hills. Tiny specks, bats or swallows, dart through the navy blue of the sky and in the last glow of the day the old villas are creamy squares backed by spires of cypresses. In a few of them, lights have come on, pinpricks of yellow making the evening darker than it is.

'There.' Isabella points. 'That one. Just there.'

I follow her finger, but somehow I already know where she's pointing. I remember the old man standing beside me, how I thought he was talking about the Art Institute villa when he talked about the house that had to be loved like a woman, and how I was surprised that he called it beautiful, because it isn't.

But the villa he was actually talking about, the one I was looking at at the time, is. In the fading light, as Isabella points, I can still make out the statues on the terrace, the cypresses that line the drive.

'Over there,' she says. 'It's called—'

'La Casa degli Uccelli.'

She nods. 'The House of the Birds.'

Chapter Twenty-six

ISABELLA LOOKS AT me, her figure fading in the darkening room. 'You really think she's there?' she asks.

'I don't know.'

I am staring at the pale pink stucco and the beautiful line of the roof, and at the tiny blank squares of the windows, as if I could will myself to see through them, know what lies inside. But I can't. There's only one way to do that.

As I think it, I'm already turning away, starting back towards the stairs.

'The fastest way is through the groves,' Isabella's voice floats through the dark behind me. 'There's a gate at the bottom of the garden. It's quicker, especially without a car.'

She runs down the stairs, pushing past me, and rummages in a drawer in the hallway. Then she bolts out onto the terrace and down the overgrown garden steps, leaving me no choice but to follow. There's a bulky rustle in the hedge as Fonzi flies past, and I can smell flowers. The cool leaves of rhododendrons brush my cheeks.

The gate is high and old, and Isabella has to put her shoulder against it to half lift, half push it open after she gets the key in the lock. Before us, the groves are sylvan after the dark wilderness of the garden. Fonzi shoots out through the trees and vanishes.

'This way.' Isabella waves.

'No.' I pull Piero's spare cell out of my pocket, hitting the 'on' button, but it won't get a signal down here. 'Take this.' I shove it at her. 'Go back to the house and call the police.'

Isabella swipes the phone out of my hand, sending it flying. 'Don't be stupid, Maria,' she says, anger lighting her voice. 'He killed my sister.'

She darts into the trees, and by the time I find the little silver phone Isabella's nothing but a shadow. The long grass hides dips and rubble, and it's all I can do to keep her in sight. Finally I catch up, and about five minutes later she stops and points.

'There.'

I have lost all sense of direction, but now, rising above us, I can see the wall of the terrace and the strange still figures of broken statues. 'I came here once, as a kid,' Isabella murmurs. 'Bene and I prowled around. But I've never been inside. I can't remember, but there's usually a gate, like ours.'

She cuts to the right, staying in the cover of the olives, slipping through the trees like a ghost. Weeds grow out of the retaining wall, their roots jamming into the cracks. One section has bulged and fallen down, causing a landslide of earth and brick. We skirt it, but when we finally find the gate it's high and spiked, and locked. The steps beyond lead up into darkness. Isabella points and I see the glint of a brand-new padlock on the rusted chain that winds through the railings.

'We won't get over this,' she whispers. 'We'll have to go around and try the front.'

Until this second, I hadn't thought about how we'd actually get into the villa, but I know enough to know that the fronts of these places are usually exposed, with fortress-like doors, and barred or shuttered windows. Assuming we have to break in, we're going to have a better chance from the back.

'Come on.' I turn round and head back to the bulging, broken place.

The scree of earth and rubble is old. Grass has taken root in it, and it's not very difficult to claw our way up. I go first. I can hear Isabella breathing behind me. She swears as my foot slips, sending pebbles and earth down over her. Then I slip again, falling down the scree like a mountain climber, hands outstretched, clutching at nothing. Isabella grabs me and hauls me up again, and when we finally get to the top and scramble through the gap in the wall, the House of the Birds looks much bigger.

The last light is almost gone now, and instead of glowing, its pink walls hold the dark. There's a little moonlight, and I can see that the garden is overgrown, wild, but not totally unrecognizable. Wisteria's run rampant across a half-ruined portico on our left, and lumps of shrubbery crouch against the bottom of the walls. There are a few broken benches, and what looks like an old wheelbarrow lies on its side in front of a glassy circle that must once have been a fish pond. A gravel path leads in a straight line towards the back of the house, and we follow it, sticking to the edge so our shoes won't crunch on what's left of the putty-coloured stone.

Halfway to the house, I see the burn mark, a round imprint of charred earth, like a devil's footprint. When I crouch down beside it and brush its edge, little feathers of white and scabs of coloured paper shift in the dirt. Somebody's been doing God's work here, saving souls from the temptation of the printed word. I scrabble around some more, and my fingers meet a shred of fabric. I drop it fast, and tell myself it may mean nothing. Behind me I hear Isabella shift. As I stand up, our eyes meet in the dark.

She steps past me, making for the side corner of the house. From behind a screen of bushes we can see the wide gravel apron that stretches across the front. It's empty. There's no sign of a car or outbuildings where one might be hidden. Another padlock and chain glimmers in the handles of the front door. I feel in my pocket for my phone and swear.

'What?' Isabella's face is pale in the thin moonlight.

'The phone. I must have lost it when I slipped.' I turn to go back but she grabs my arm.

'Sophie!' she hisses in the dark. 'He's not here now. But if she is here, he'll come. We don't have time.'

She's right. Either this house is empty, and there's no need for the police, or Sophie's inside and every second counts. Isabella grabs my hand and turns towards the back of the villa, treading silently across the overgrown lawn.

The terrace at the back of the house is paved, and we step on dark lumps of weed and moss in an attempt to be quiet, neither of us mentioning the possibility that if Sophie is here, she may not be alone. Maybe he walked or used a bicycle we didn't spot. Maybe he's going back for the car later, after he's done his job. We reach a pair of crumbling stone lions that stand on either side of a set of tall wooden shutters.

They creak obligingly as I pry my fingers into the slats and pull. Isabella gets her hands in above mine, and one good yank does it. The inner latch gives, revealing an old French window. I stand back to let Isabella put her shoulder to it, and a little shower of termite-eaten wood falls at her feet. When she pushes again, a glass panel cracks, and I pull my sleeve over my hand, knock the edges out with my elbow and reach through to slide back the bolt.

The first thing that hits us is the smell of cats. It rolls out of the dark in a stinking wave and I put my hands over my nose and mouth as I step inside. The room must run almost the whole length of the building, and, beyond the cats, there are other smells too. Mould, and something feral. I have no idea what bats smell like, but I have a feeling this might be it. Isabella comes in behind me, and I hear her gasp. When I look, she's clapped her hands over her face too. We should have brought a flashlight. Stupid, I think, unbelievably stupid. I take fast shallow breaths, telling myself it won't kill me.

'Should we shout?' Isabella leans close, her voice barely more than a breath, and I shake my head.

'If he's in here, he might kill her. It only takes one stab.' He'd be a few hours ahead of schedule, but somehow I don't think he'd care. 'Let's look first. If he isn't here and she is, we can get her out.'

Beyond the thin haze of light from the open door, it's pitch-black, and it takes me a moment to figure out there's no furniture. As my eyes adjust, I see something glimmering on the far wall, and catch a motion which almost makes me scream. Then I realize it's a long mirror, set into the panelling. Once, it must have been pretty, reflecting the French windows and the garden. Now it throws nothing back but the darkness, a liquid black that makes the room look as if it recedes for ever. Two chandeliers hang in pale bags from the ceiling like cocoons. Beyond our breathing, there's no sound. Not even a rustle. If he's here, he's being really quiet. And if Sophie's here, she's either trussed, or unconscious. Or dead.

'We need a light, even a little one.' Isabella pulls my shirt. 'Kitchen.' She points. There's a door to our left, and I follow her, moving gingerly, trying not to catch our reflections drifting in the darkness of the mirror.

The tall doors give on to a corridor, and even following Isabella, I have to put a hand on the wall to feel my way along. My fingers meet damp plaster, crumbly and soft as bread-crumbs. She's right about the kitchen. And as an added bonus, one of the windows isn't boarded or shuttered. After the hall, it seems almost light. I make out two white porcelain sinks and what looks to be a marble-topped table. Isabella is pulling the drawers open, but there's nothing in them. Then she whispers, 'Eureka.'

On the shelf above one of the sinks, she's spotted a box of candles. At the same time I see a newish box of matches on the draining board. As I reach for them, I try not to think what this means.

The immediate effect of the candlelight is to make the corners of the room darker. Shadows bounce up towards the ceiling. The kitchen is a dead end, except for a pantry. Isabella looks in, shakes her head, and we go back along the little corridor.

In the big room our flames flick and gutter, moving like fireflies in the mirror. A closer inspection reveals that there's nothing in here at all, and when we try a door in the panelling, it's locked. I put my face to it and whisper Sophie's name, but all I get is a mouthful of dust.

'Look,' Isabella whispers. 'Let's make sure he's not here, then we'll yell. If we have to, we'll kick doors in.' She squeezes my arm. '*Courage, mon brave.* If this son of a bitch has her here, we'll find her.'

Isabella has grown stronger as I've faltered, and as she leads the way out of the room I realize that she must have thought there would never be anything she could do for Benedetta. Now she has a chance to do this. She leads the way towards an arch at the end of the huge empty room, and we come into the front hall.

In the faint light from a fan above the doors we can see that the stairs run straight up the centre of the villa. On the far side there's an archway identical to the one we've just come through, and we find another long room. In here there are ordinary windows, all boarded up. Beyond is another passage leading back to store rooms. Wood is stacked in one, but the other is empty. The cold flagstone floors weep underneath our feet. This time, it's me who leads the way back. Now, the only place Sophie can be is upstairs.

Both of us are more accustomed to the dark and move more easily. In the store room, Isabella picked a heavy short stick out of the woodpile, and I did the same. Wax has begun to drip on my hands, but I ignore it.

The stairs curve upwards into shadows, and I wonder how you would drag a struggling woman up them. Maybe she'd be drugged, or hit on the head. Or maybe he hasn't dragged anyone, and we're in the wrong place altogether. Maybe there's nothing up here but feral cats, and Sophie is somewhere else, her life ticking away while I'm being afraid of the dark.

Suddenly I don't want to go on. I put my foot on the first step of the stairs and stop. When I look back at Isabella, I see the mirror of my own face. Her eyes are huge in the candlelight, and I know she's felt it too; the sense that something ghastly is above us. We stand there together, remembering our dead and terrified of what we might find, until finally Isabella nods, and I put my hand on the banister, and begin to climb.

The front hall is vaulted to the roof, and what have to be bedrooms open off a three-sided gallery. The cat smell isn't so bad up here. Something rustles and a flutter of wings brushes past us in the dark. Isabella swears under her breath. The first door we open is over the front of the house. The room appears to be empty, another long rectangular space. When we go in, the candles catch glints of gold from the moulding. We see what looks like a cupboard, but is in fact just an alcove full of dirty, empty shelves.

Back on the gallery, we listen, then Isabella steps forward and opens the next door. It's another bedroom, its windows shuttered and black. Her candle catches a wash of colour on the wall, mauve or pale blue. In the centre of the room there's the unmistakable shape of a bed. Behind her, I stop in the doorway. Suddenly my heart is beating in irregular little skips. Sweat is breaking out across my chest. This is it. I can sense it. I can sense him. Just as surely as if we've come face to face.

'Isabella!' I whisper. But she's already stepped into the room. Her candle throws a halo of light.

The bed is huge, an old-fashioned monstrosity. Sitting in the centre of the empty room, it looks like a stage set for an erotic performance. Isabella lowers her candle and I see two pieces of cord hanging from each of the bedposts. Knotted, they're plenty long enough to tie someone down with, to go around a wrist or an ankle. Without really meaning to, I walk up close. I stand beside Isabella, and when I move my candle I see the cords are dark, stiff and crusted.

There are stains on the bed too. I thought there was a coverlet, or a blanket, but now I realize it's the mattress. It's covered in something dark, as if paint has been thrown at it.

Isabella is just standing here, staring. She looks as if she can't move. I step aside, winging my little light around the room, and see a door in the far wall. Sophie. My mind's darting around now, going faster and faster like something about to explode. It's not midnight yet, I think crazily. So he can't have killed her. She has to be alive.

My sneakers slap on the floor. I'm not even trying to be quiet any more, but the sound surprises me, and when I look down I see the boards are pale, almost as though they've been scrubbed. Just for a second I allow myself to think I'm wrong, and that because there's no blood under my feet, maybe no one died here after all. Maybe this is just some kinky place to tie people down and use the 'discipline.' Then I open the little door.

The candlelight catches the shine of old-fashioned porcelain. A basin, a bathtub. Shadows and flame bounce out of the mirror. The room feels alive, as if the walls are throbbing, and it takes me a second to understand what I'm seeing.

Brown smears run across the white tiles like finger-paint. When I look down, I see footprints and skid marks. The bathtub is streaked and the little basin spattered, as if someone threw a can of rust-coloured paint at them. But that's not what makes the bile rise in my throat so I have to clamp my hand over my mouth.

What does that is Billy's hair. Long springy strands of it stick to the sides of the basin, and lie in trampled, matted wads in the bathtub and on the floor.

Tears are streaming down my face and my nose is running. I drop the piece of wood, back up, and bang into Isabella.

'Don't look!' I scream. 'Don't look, don't look, don't look!'

But it's too late, she's already seen. Her mouth opens and closes, then she turns, and runs.

We fly onto the gallery, screaming Sophie's name now. Over and over and over. Isabella throws her shoulder against doors, flings them open, one after another, cracking and splintering rotten wood, but it's me who finds her.

At the very end of the gallery, there's a linen closet. It's not much bigger than the chair that Sophie is tied to. She has a sack over her head and I snatch at it with my free hand, screaming for Isabella. When she takes both the candles, we see a bowl, a spoon and strips of sheet like the ones he's bound and gagged her with, and a plastic bucket she's been forced to use as a toilet.

I undo the gag first, and Sophie chokes. She leans forward, gasping and coughing, and I put my arms around her, feeling her matted blonde hair and the heat of her skin. The closet is unbelievably hot and it stinks.

'I wet myself,' she says when she finally looks at me. One of her eyes is swollen closed.

She is still wearing her church dress, but it's soiled and ripped, and when I get her hands undone I see that one of them is horribly swollen. 'I hit him,' Sophie says. Her voice is raspy as if her tongue is swollen. 'He shut my hand in the car door.'

'Locci?' I'm working on the knots around her legs. They're not as easy as they should be and the sheet is damp with urine.

'I don't know.' Sophie shakes her head and winces at the motion. 'I never saw him. He put a bag over my head, from behind. And when he fed me, he wore a mask. He wore a mask and he didn't say anything!'

The words come out in a howl, and Sophie starts to try to kick and claw at the knots, panicked, like an animal that's realized it's about to be slaughtered. She hits me in the side of the head, and would tip the chair over, except the space is too tight. Finally Isabella drops the candles, stands on them to put them out and grabs her by the shoulders. She pushes Sophie backwards, holding her against the wall, murmuring in Italian, while I feel my way through the last knots.

When we try to stand her up, Sophie almost falls down. She howls in pain. She has no shoes and he's done something to her feet. Cut them. Burnt them. We might get her down the stairs, but then what would we do? Drag her down the long drive? Across the olive groves? He'll be coming soon and he'll find us.

I turn to Isabella. 'Maybe one of us should go for help? Go and find the phone?'

'Don't leave!' Sophie wails. 'Please don't leave! He'll come.'

Isabella looks at me in the dark, both of us terrified. 'We have to get her out of here,' she says. 'We can only do it if we stay together.' She's right. He would almost certainly overpower one of us and Sophie. The three of us have a chance. I grab Sophie's arm and sling it over my shoulder, and Isabella does the same. Between us, we lift her off the chair and out of the fetid, stinking closet.

'Come on,' Isabella says. 'We can carry her like this.'

We each get an arm around Sophie's waist, and she holds on to Isabella's shoulder with her good hand. Without the candles it's dark, but we can see well enough to make our way along the gallery.

'OK,' I hear myself saying, 'that's great, that's fine.' It's mindless, words to reassure myself as much as Sophie.

We work our way to the head of the stairs, then we have to stop, trying to figure out how to get Sophie down without hurting her more. We decide Isabella will go first since she's tallest, Sophie will follow a step or two above, her arms over Isabella's shoulders using her as support, and I will come last, holding Sophie from behind. When we get ourselves in place, Sophie even giggles. Then a glow of lights washes the fan window above the front door.

It's dim but growing brighter, and for a wonderful second I think it's the police, that they have somehow found out where we are, that my shadow followed us, and called help. I even whisper, '*Polizia*.' But Sophie shakes her head.

'It's not blue.' Her voice is very small. 'A police car or an ambulance would be red or blue,' she says and I freeze. Isabella looks back at me.

'It's him,' Sophie mews. 'It's him.' The lights are getting brighter. Now we can hear tyres crunching on the gravel.

Sophie starts to scream, but Isabella shoves her hand over her mouth. 'Quick,' she hisses, 'quick, quick!' And we stagger backwards.

Isabella throws open the door of the first empty room. 'We have to hide,' she says. 'We have to hide!' But there's nowhere here to hide except the alcove, and even there there's barely room for the three of us.

'We wait,' Isabella whispers. 'We'll hear him go by. Then we run. We can get downstairs. To his car.'

We all nod, but I think: *With Sophie?* I can't see Isabella's face in the dark, but I know she's thinking the same thing I am. Whoever he is, he'll be strong and fast. He's abducted four young, healthy women. And we'll have only a few seconds between the time he goes along the gallery and the time he realizes Sophie's not in the closet. I can't even remember if we shut the door. If he sees it open, he'll know. And he'll come looking for us. Right away. Both of us grip Sophie's arms, and she whimpers. Below, the car stops and we hear a door slam. Footsteps crunch on the gravel and then, all at once, the night is ripped with an explosion of sound.

There is the furious barking of a dog, yelling, running, and more barking. Fonzi. I had completely forgotten about him. He must have followed us up from the groves. A gun cracks, and there is the screeching sound of acceleration, then another shot.

Isabella lets go of Sophie's arm and screams. She doesn't care any more who hears her or what they do about it. Instead, she leans against the grimy wall and howls, for her sister and her dog and everything that has been taken from her.

Isabella is still crying when, a few seconds later, the house is washed in lights, and filled with the sound of running footsteps and men yelling, '*Polizia!*'

In the confusion, slamming of doors and shouting, I am more afraid now than I have been all night. Clinging to Sophie, I feel as if I'm drowning, as if a dam has broken inside me, and all the awfulness of what has happened in the last few weeks is rising up in one terrible black wave of fear. When Pallioti finally takes my arm and tries to speak to me, I can't even hear what he's saying.

Medics take Sophie away on a stretcher. They wrap Isabella in shiny paper-foil blankets, and even though she is told over and over again that Fonzi is fine, that he screwed up a police stakeout, but nobody shot him and he's downstairs waiting for her, she can't stop crying. She apologizes, repeating herself as if she can't stop saying the words, and finally the police guide her down the stairs, wrapped in a cocoon of blankets.

I sit on the stairs where someone has put me, wrapped in a foil blanket, although it isn't cold. Below me, half of the Florence police force seems to be streaming in and out of the front door of the villa. There's an air of euphoria. Policemen slap hands and pat each other on the back. Until they follow the forensics spacesuit people upstairs. Then they come down rather more subdued.

Eventually I hear that, though he got away, they have a clear sighting and, despite the dog, they got a shot at the car. It's only a matter of time now before they bring him in. He was medium height, medium build, dressed in black. The sports bag he'd taken out of the boot, and subsequently dropped when Fonzi attacked him, is being examined by the scene-of-crime people. A few minutes later a murmur goes around: it contained cord. A knife. And a red silk bag.

From my perch I pick out the cop who fired the shots. He was outside when the car drove in, and would have nabbed this guy, except that he couldn't bring himself to shoot the German shepherd when it got in the way. He's tall and thin, with nubbly bones at the back of his neck, and when he finally turns round and climbs the stairs towards me I feel as if I've known him a long time. He fixes me with his strange golden eyes. 'I should thank you,' he says, 'for the tulips.'

'I brought you lunch too. But you'd gone.'

He nods, and we watch each other for a second. Then I ask, 'Where's your dog? Or isn't he your dog?'

He laughs. His face creases up and suddenly he doesn't look as thin as he did in the portico of an abandoned church. Now he looks like a greyhound. Lean and mean. Like he could be a policeman, if he wore the right uniform. 'Oh he's mine all right,' he says. 'I left him at home with my wife tonight, though. Sometimes we argue over who gets to take him to work.'

'Is she a cop too?'

'No,' he laughs. 'She's a travel agent.'

'I thought you were an angel.'

"It's a common mistake.' He holds out his big El Greco hand. 'Lorenzo Beretti, Signora Thorcroft. I'm pleased to meet you, officially.' His grip is warm and strong.

'How did you know I was here?' I ask. 'Tonight?' Then it dawns on me. He's my shadow. He always has been. I look over his shoulder for Pallioti, but I can't see him.

'You told me,' Beretti's saying. 'I tailed you as far as Signora Lucchese's. I was waiting to pick you up as you came out, then we got a signal from the cell you were carrying. You left it on long enough so we could triangulate it.' Of course. I turned it on when I tried to hand it to Isabella, and never turned it off. 'When we saw that the signal came from here, and not Signora Lucchese's, we put two and two together.'

'I'm glad you came up with four.'

Beretti shrugs. 'I got here first, that's all. The rest of the cavalry took a little longer.'

'But you'd been following me before. For weeks.'

He inclines his head. 'I prefer to think of it as being—what did you say? Angel? You've had a few guardian angels, actually. We usually work in teams.'

I think about this for a second. 'The electricity van?'

He laughs, and I don't need more of an answer. Then he says, 'I'm sorry if I frightened you. You weren't supposed to notice me quite as much as you did. My fault.'

'No.' I shake my head. 'No, you couldn't know. You—' I shrug, wondering how I can possibly explain. Finally I just settle for: 'You look a lot like someone I used to know.'

'Well,' Lorenzo Beretti says, 'I hope he was nice. The someone you used to know.'

'Yeah. He was.' Lorenzo smiles at me and turns away.

Pallioti's standing in the gallery. I don't know how long he's been there, but he snaps his cell phone closed. Without being aware of it, I stand up. Something's going on. There's a palpable buzz in the hall below.

'Signora.' Pallioti takes my arm. 'I'm sorry,' he says, 'but I'm going to have to ask you to come with me.'

He hustles me down the stairway, through the crowd, and out into the night. Vans, police cars, unmarked cars and another ambulance are pulled up on the gravel in front of the villa. People turn, looking at us as we hurry by, but when I ask Pallioti again what's going on all he will do is shake his head and say, 'I am afraid we have a situation.'

Pierangelo, I think. I stop, feeling like Niobe, turned to stone. But Pallioti takes my arm again. He's putting me into the back seat of a car.

'Please,' he says. 'I'll explain on the way. We have to hurry.'

He gets in the other side, and his driver spins us round and down the drive. The carnival-like lights that wash the House of the Birds recede, and soon all I can see is Pallioti's profile against the window as Viale Galileo flies past. We dive through Porta Romana, the driver switches the siren on, making people part, cars move over, and Pallioti turns to me.

'We were following him,' he says. 'Our most important goal was Signora Sassinelli's life, so we hoped he'd lead us to her. You got there about the same time. Beretti was going to let him get inside and trap him, separate him from his car. But the dog startled him.' Pallioti's face goes still. He looks out of the window past me, as if he's seeing something on the street. 'Beretti got off a couple of shots. We found the car.'

'Is he dead?' My head feels hollow, like an echo chamber. The words ring back and forth, but Pallioti doesn't seem to hear them.

'He must have known the game was over,' Pallioti says softly. 'Maybe Babinellio was right, and he wants it to be finished. Anyways, we have him.'

'You have him?'

Pallioti nods. 'But he wants to talk to you.'

I stare at him, my tongue as thick and dry as cotton wool.

'You don't have to do anything you don't want to, signora,' Pallioti says. 'But I promised the cardinal I would try.'

'The cardinal?'

Pallioti nods. 'The cardinal has been following this case closely,' he says. 'He's been very distressed by it.'

The car swings sideways, jumps over a kerb, and as I look out of the window, I realize we've turned up past the Uffizi, and are nosing our way into the Piazza della Signoria. Ahead of us, the Palazzo Vecchio is bathed in floodlights. Neptune and David are bright, icy white. Banners fly off the battlements, but no one is sitting at the cafés or buying ice cream. The carriages are gone. There are police cars, and a crowd mills around looking up towards the high-arched windows on the upper floors of the palazzo. We stop, and Pallioti gets out and opens the door for me.

'Please,' he says. 'He's waiting for you.'

He escorts me past barriers that have been thrown up around the building, and through the courtyard tourists usually come out of, past frescoes and under the little arches where the fountain plays. A *carabiniere* officer pulls aside a red velvet rope, and Pallioti leads me up the stairs, going faster and faster until finally I take two at a time to keep up with him. Even if I wanted to think, I don't know if I could. My brain's closed down, and I see myself from far away, running after Pallioti like a wind-up toy, following him through room after room of the Palazzo Vecchio, as if we're working our way to the centre of a maze.

Pallioti leads me through the Queen's apartments, past the entrance to the loggia, through the chapel. People are standing in clumps, whispering. Finally doors swing open, and we come into the anteroom of the Sala dei Gigli.

A knot of men in dark suits stands by the door. One of them is Cardinal D'Erreti.

He's forsaken his crimson, and is wearing just a suit and dog collar, like he was the last time I saw him, at the restaurant in Santa Croce. This time, though, he doesn't bless me. Instead, he takes both my hands in his.

'Signora,' he says, 'thank you. I know how difficult this is for you, but you must remember that every human life, every soul, is God's, and precious. You are the only person he has asked for.'

The cardinal looks at Pallioti, and the doors to the room of the lilies swing open.

The windows are big, and arched, and very high off the floor, the sills themselves shoulder height, as if it's a room made for giants. Iron grilles run halfway up the glass, so getting up there can't have been easy. The building's open late for civic work. He must have got in and run up here before anyone realized what he was doing, then grabbed the chair he's kicked away, and climbed up to where he's perched now—balancing on the railing, and holding on to the moulding to keep himself from falling two storeys to the piazza below.

Behind him, lit up like a postcard, I can see the dome of the cathedral, and it occurs to me that's probably why he chose this window. I wonder how long he's had it in mind for. He must have bought a ticket like the rest of the world, walked through here with tourists, stood and pretended to admire the Gozzoli frescoes, while really he judged the height, noticed the guards, the chairs, figured how fast he would have to be to grab one before he could be stopped. Babinellio said he was an excellent planner. But this must be at least a change of schedule. Surely he planned to clean up Eden completely, use all four of the red bags before this.

He's pale. There are bright patches on his cheeks, and his lips look red too, as if he's wearing lipstick, maybe one of mine. A breeze blows in from the river and I catch the distinct, familiar perfume of acacia.

'Please—' I don't even know who I'm talking to, or what I'm asking for. Apart from not to be here. Not to have this happening.

The cardinal squeezes my shoulder. 'Every life is sacred, Maria,' he whispers. And I want to say: *He didn't think that.* He didn't think that when he killed my husband, and Eleanora. When he plucked Isabella's sister out of the dark and dressed her up like a doll, or flayed the skin off Ginevra Montelleone and took Carlo Fusarno's mother away from him for ever. Did he think life was sacred then? Did he ever care? But I know the answer. No. No, he didn't. He didn't give a damn about their lives. He was way too busy saving their souls.

Marcello sways like a branch hit by a breeze, and everyone in the room gasps.

His eyes are fixed on me, and I can't stop staring at him either, although I'd like to. He's barefoot, his toes curling at the edge of the rail, his naked feet pale, the skin stretched taut as if it might split. I see him in his ridiculous red apron, winking, throwing me Baci, kisses with a fortune locked inside. Then I close my eyes and see Sophie.

I turn to the cardinal. 'I don't think I can.'

'Yes.' Massimo D'Erreti nods. 'You can.' His dark eyes look into mine. 'No one,' he says. 'No one is beyond God's love, Mary.'

I turn round and step towards Marcello, not sure what I'm supposed to do.

'Come closer,' he whispers. So I take another step, then another, until I have broken out of the semicircle of men standing around the window and entered a space that contains only him, and me.

'Closer.'

I reach the stone wall. Marcello's feet are in front of me. The railing is just wide enough to stand on, and I can see the tendons in his ankles straining.

'The chair.'

I right it, drag it over and climb up on the seat. Now I can feel night air on my face, and see the rooftops, the campanile, the top of the Baptisery, and the Duomo, Santa Maria del Fiori, lit up against the sky. Someone shifts uneasily behind us, and without looking back I know it's Pallioti. Marcello reaches down for my hand and I reach up until our fingers meet.

His eyes are wide, the whites, bright white, and under the perfume a strange smell is rising off him. Fear. Babinellio was right. He's terrified. Probably he always has been.

'Maria,' he whispers. I can barely hear him. I stand on my toes, his fingers cupping mine. 'I had to give them to God.'

'I know.' I tighten my hand around his.

'Flesh shall pay for the sins of the flesh. To live we must die,' Marcello whispers. Then he says: 'They were lost, and I brought them back. But not you, Maria.' Marcello bends towards me, his eyes on my face. 'I never hurt you.'

'Marcello, please.'

'*Serviam!*'

He shouts. His fingers leave mine and he throws his arms open.

For a split-second, Marcello balances, framed in the window, the Duomo lit up behind him. Then he's gone.

My hand is still outstretched, and I am still standing on the chair when I feel myself begin to shake. It's the cardinal who lifts me down like a doll.

Minutes later, when we drive out, my face pressed to the glass, I see Marcello for the last time. His bare feet are white in the lights, and kneeling beside him, cradling his head in his lap, his hand raised to deliver the last rites, is Father Rinaldo.

Chapter Twenty-seven

IT'S TWO DAYS later when Pallioti calls and asks if I would like to come to the Questura. They've found out some things about Marcello, if I'm interested, and he'd like to talk to me. I am interested. And I'd like to talk to him too. In fact, if he hadn't called me, I was going to call him.

This time, Pallioti sees me in his office. I have slept for almost eighteen hours of the last forty-eight, and am feeling distinctly more chipper than on my previous visits to this building. The first thing I say when I sit down is, 'You had me followed. All this time.'

'Not followed, watched.' Pallioti slides into the chair behind his desk.

'Is there a difference?'

'Oh indeed, signora.' He smiles. 'If I had had you followed, I assure you, you wouldn't have known about it. I just had an officer who happened to be in the area keep an eye on you.'

'An angel?'

He shrugs. 'If you like.'

'From the time I arrived?'

Pallioti nods, resting his elbows on his desk and regarding me over the top of his steepled fingers.

'Why?' I find this outrageous. He seems to find it amusing. 'Don't tell me you didn't have a reason! I can't believe the Italian police don't have anything better to do than follow American adult ed students around.'

Pallioti regards me for a moment, then he says, 'Signora, the last time you were in our city, you were attacked and your husband was murdered. So, when you came back, let me just say I was concerned.'

'What did you think I was going to do? Run around wreaking vengeance? Karel Indrizzio was dead, for God's sake.'

He stares at me without saying anything. It feels like old times. He doesn't even blink. 'I don't understand why you'd—' I stop before I finish the sentence, the realization dawning on me. 'You weren't sure Indrizzio did it,' I say. 'You were never sure.'

Pallioti reaches for a cigarette, lights it and offers me one. I shake my head.

'In your case,' he says, 'the evidence was strong. DNA confirmed the blood samples on his hands and clothing matched yours and your husband's. He was seen in the immediate area, and he was found with your possessions. In the others, I thought the balance of probability was good, but not decisive. Until Caterina Fusarno was killed.' Smoke wreathes above his head in a nicotine halo.

I think about this for a second, about the doubt that must have seeped in like damp, peeling back what he thought he knew.

'And then there was Ginevra,' I say. 'And the similarities were too great. The way the body was arranged. The bag. So it was either a copy, or Indrizzio didn't kill the first two women.'

Pallioti nods. I feel somehow betrayed by this. I had always assumed his belief that Karel Indrizzio committed the first two murders was total. He never expressed any doubt. But, I remind myself, he wouldn't, to me, would he? Just because he sat by my hospital bed, it doesn't mean our relationship was equal. The idea comes as something of a shock. Then I wonder if that's fair. The police aren't in the equality business any more than priests are, they just like you to believe that while they're trying to get you to tell them things.

I have thought this over, and I know I first saw Lorenzo Beretti on the day we went to the Boboli. The first official day of summer, when the clocks went forward. Billy with her basket. The Japanese girls in Mantua. Ginevra Montelleone was definitely dead by then.

'And if it was a copycat?' I ask finally.

He shrugs and pulls an ashtray towards him. It's big and glass. The light from the window beside us bounces through its prisms. 'A copycat could have been as dangerous for you. Your case was in the papers. He might have wanted to really copy Indrizzio, finish what the master left incomplete.'

I think of Billy arguing with me about going to Ginevra's vigil, making the very point Pallioti has just made. Except that already it was too late. Already, Marcello had appeared out of the dark to see me safely home.

'I think I'll have that cigarette after all,' I say, and Pallioti smiles and pushes the pack and lighter across the desk towards me.

As the heavy silver lighter flares, I look at Pallioti. Were you really just protecting me? I wonder. Or did you think that if you watched me, you might see someone else watching me too?

In which case, my coming back would have been a gift. What's the saying? The best way to catch a wolf is to stake a goat? They probably couldn't believe how lucky they got. Anger rises up in me, then dips again. Why should I blame them? In their place, wouldn't I have done the same thing? And it did work, in the end. Sort of. I know now that they had Marcello on a 'watch list', that they were suspicious of him, but didn't want to risk bringing him in, in case he led them to Sophie.

We smoke in silence for a moment as I turn this over in my head, realizing I wasn't what I thought I was. That instead of reaching for my dreams here in Florence, being free at last,

I was just a decoy: a bright shiny lure flitting through the city, watched in the hope that I might attract something dark.

Pallioti slides the ashtray towards me. Today his face and eyes are made even paler by the severe cut of his suit. He could be a priest himself, I think. A Grand Inquisitor, sitting up here in his office, arranging people in the city below him like pieces on a board, looking down on good and evil. What was it he said to me the day after Billy died? *We live in the picture, but we rarely see it.* Does Pallioti see it, I wonder. Or is that left to God alone? To the bored Jesus looking down on us from his perch at San Miniato?

I could ask him, but it occurs to me I don't even know if Pallioti believes in God. In fact, I don't know anything about him at all. Except that he smokes too much. Finally he stubs his cigarette out, puts a folder on his desk and opens it.

'Marcello Marelli,' he says. 'Aged twenty-five. Born, Mantua.'

'The picture.'

'*Si, certo.*' He nods. Then he does something I've never seen him do before. Ispettore Pallioti reaches into his jacket pocket, and slips on glasses. Maybe they're new. Maybe he's just gotten them, and age is catching up with him the way it catches up with the rest of us mere mortals. He glances at me over the rims.

'The picture,' he says. 'Yes, Marcello would almost certainly have seen it on school trips. The state schools are big on Italy's heritage. I'm sure he went to the ducal palace more than once, and they'd hardly have left out Mantegna.' He sighs and looks back at the papers in front of him.

'Marcello was put into care, made a ward of the state and sent to a state school when he was twelve. His mother was a single parent, a drug addict. Marcello's stepfather abused him, which was why he was removed. His own father is unknown. His mother died of an overdose when he was fifteen. From an early age, Marcello sought solace, possibly sanctuary, in the church. Babinellio thinks he also liked the structure, found it reassuring.' Pallioti glances up at me. 'He was an altar boy,' he says.

I am staring out of the window as I listen, remembering the young man who walked beside me in the dark. One of things he said he wanted was to have a family. How we long to re-create our pasts, if only in dreams, where rage and hurt and damage can't get in our way.

'He did well in school,' Pallioti goes on. 'He was bright. He got a place at the university here in Florence.'

'Is that when he joined Opus?'

They recruit among the vulnerable, Pierangelo told me when I asked him. That's why they like universities. Young people away from home, just starting to find their way in the world. Exchange students. The lonely. Idealists who want to do good but don't know how. There's a joke somewhere in there about showing people *The Way*, but I don't think I'd find it funny. I stub my cigarette out, trying not to feel Marcello's hand in mine.

'Let's just say that Opus Dei is not cooperating,' Pallioti says. 'Your pictures have helped there, the ones with Signora Kalczeska. We believe they'd come by to check up on him, make sure he was still on the "straight and narrow." so to speak. But yes, to answer your question. We think he joined Opus quite soon after he arrived here and moved into one of the Opus houses. He was a young man alone, already religious. Not afraid of hard work and attracted to strict rules, and simple solutions. Opus would have been very attractive to him.'

'Plus he had lousy self-esteem and probably found life terrifying.'

Pallioti nods. 'The victims of sexual abuse usually blame themselves, especially if they were children. According to Babinellio, Marcello would have carried a great deal of rage and guilt. And fear. And, of course, as a child, he saw the dangers of chaos at first hand.'

'Up close and personal.'

The image of the little kid Marcello must have been flashes in front of me as Pallioti raises his eyebrows. 'Nothing,' I shake my head. 'It's just an American saying.'

'The medical examiner found a great deal of old scar tissue, on Marcello's back and thighs.'

My stomach turns cold. I remember standing at the bottom of the ladder in the signora's shop—what? A week ago? And coming face to face with the scar on Marcello's back as his sweatshirt rode up. I assumed it was from his accident. I never even thought of the 'discipline,' of the privilege of mortifying recalcitrant flesh.

Pallioti looks back at the file. 'University didn't go as well as he hoped. He decided at some point to drop out, and he got a place—'

'At the Police Academy.'

The glasses focus on me again. 'How did you know?'

'He told me.'

Pallioti's office has a large half-moon window. Pigeons growl under the eaves and, as we watch, a pair of swallows zoom by, flying in tight, close formation, dipping and looping.

'I met him one night,' I say, watching the tiny birds. 'He walked me home, and we talked about what he wanted to do. He said he had to drop out of the Police Academy because he broke his leg.'

I look back at Pallioti. 'Oh my God, that's it, isn't it?' I remember Marcello talking about pins. And pain. 'He said he was in hospital for a long time. That's the gap. Between me and Caterina, when he started again.'

Pallioti nods. 'We think it's likely that his relationship with Opus declined during that time as well.'

'Why? Because he wasn't living in the house? Because he couldn't fulfil his duties for them? For God's sake, he was in hospital!' This seems crazy, even for Opus. Then I think of another reason. 'Do you think they knew what he did?' I ask. 'To Eleanora and Benedetta? Could they have suspected?'

Opus demands full confession, placing every last thing in your priest's lap. Returning to the status of an innocent. The 'Childhood Before God' idea. Except adults are not children.

Before God or anyone else. No matter what Opus would like. Is it possible that his priest knew what he'd done and told no one? Just pushed him away so the organization wouldn't be tainted?

Pallioti is looking out of the window. 'As I said,' he repeats. 'Opus Dei are declining to cooperate.'

'Can't the cardinal—'

He looks at me, killing the question before I can finish it, and something close to a smile flickers at the corner of his mouth. Of course. That was why the cardinal was so interested in the first place. Opus Dei supports him, he's hardly likely to do anything to alienate them. Like implicating them with a serial killer, for instance. Much less suggest they actually encouraged him, however unwittingly.

'Eleanora Darnelli was a nun,' Pallioti says, reading my mind. 'Of course, her death attracted the cardinal's attention. When Benedetta Lucchese was killed, he became even more concerned.'

I bet he did.

'*Serviam*.' Pallioti repeats the last word Marcello ever said. 'Latin for "I serve." It's also Opus Dei's motto. Babinellio thinks that, to some degree, Marcello may have been doing this to impress Opus. As they pushed him away, he would only have become more frantic. They had been a home to him. Losing his place in it would have been terrifying, given his past, so he would have tried harder and harder to prove himself. Apparently a main tenet of the organization is that its members attempt to bring others to God.'

'Fishing.'

'I'm sorry?' The eyebrows go up again.

'They call it "fishing." I think it's one of the requirements for membership, or at least for good standing. You net other souls for God.' The expression on his face actually makes me laugh. 'Subtlety isn't really one of their strong points,' I add. 'Secrecy, on the other hand...'

Now it's Pallioti who smiles. It transforms his face with

a quick flash of light, and for the first time I wonder how old he is.

'Along with fishing, we believe one of his duties was repairs, replacing the odd roof tile, carpentry, generally care-taking,' he says. 'Opus Dei owns a number of older villas around the city and they take a lot of maintenance. Marcello was good with his hands.'

'So that's how he knew about the House of the Birds?'

'We think so. Opus has been trying to acquire it for some time. At one point they had a survey done, and even volunteered to do some work on it, in an attempt to soften opposition from the owner.'

I was a gardener for a while, he told me, *but that isn't a career.* Not like returning the lost to God. And he would have seen them as lost too, each one of them. Eleanora, a nun leaving the church because of what he would have seen as lust, betraying Christ for sins of the flesh. Benedetta, unmarried, living with a lover and, worse, working actively to get her sister out of Opus Dei. Caterina was a prostitute; that would have been bad enough, and not knowing her, or Rosa, perhaps he saw himself in her son. Ginevra was an ardent defender of women's right to control their own bodies—commit murder, in Marcello's eyes. And Sophie. It wasn't Signora Raguzza's companion who left the grocery bag outside her open door. It was Marcello, who spoke perfectly good English, and who wouldn't have had to stand there long to hear Sophie planning to kidnap children. As for Billy. Well, Billy was Billy. I think of her in her crimson dress, literally the Scarlet Woman. It was the day after I went to Siena that she first mentioned him, said she thought he was cute, and told him so. I remember thinking at the time that a fling with her might be the highlight of his life. Now I cringe at the thought, and remember the expression on his face when she spilled her coins across the floor of the shop and let loose a truly creative catalogue of obscenities. I had thought it was embarrassment, but probably it was rage. Which leaves me. Before he died, Marcello said he never hurt me. Maybe he meant that after I was nice to him he changed his mind.

'He knew all the women,' Pallioti says. He pulls out another cigarette and lights it. 'Or rather,' he adds, 'he knew of them. Opus sent volunteers up to do some maintenance work at Eleanora's convent. Gossip got around. Isabella can't remember, but he may have actually known her, certainly he would have known of her once she left. I gather sheep who leave the fold are publicly shunned. And her sister, who got her out, would be regarded as, at best, lost. At worst, dangerous. Caterina went to the same church he did after he got out of the hospital.'

'And the church did work at the clinic where she was in the methadone programme.'

Pallioti looks up. The picture, I think. The face I thought I recognized as I was leaving. 'If you check,' I say, 'I think you'll find him in a group photo in the conference room.'

He nods and makes a note. 'Ginevra, of course,' he continues, 'was something of a public figure, especially after she threw eggs at the cardinal.'

I understand all this. What I can't understand, though, is how Marcello would have known, two years ago, about Pierangelo and me. The affair would certainly have qualified me for his attentions, and my best guess is that he came across Ty, perhaps in connection with Rinaldo, then somehow made his discovery. Perhaps he saw Piero and me together on the street, or in a bar, anywhere, and recognized me. Florence is a small town that way.

'Both of his past landladies,' Pallioti is saying, 'have told us he was very interested in photography. The most recent even let him set up a dark room in the basement. Unfortunately, we've had to tear her wall down. Marcello did some repair work for her, and made a cache for his souvenirs at the same time. Incidentally, he told her not long ago he needed to photograph buildings because he was thinking of becoming an architect.'

I close my eyes and nod. I have an awful feeling I know which building he was photographing.

'He also had an impressive collection of photos of all the women. Before and after they were killed,' Pallioti adds. 'We found them under his bed.' Neither of us comment on how similar this was to my manila envelope. How Marcello and I were mirroring each other, closing ourselves in our rooms at night and communing with the same dead faces.

Pallioti gets up and goes to the window, leans on the sill with his back to me.

'I am afraid,' he says, 'that the fact he knew you were back in the city was our fault. After the accident he kept in touch with a couple of friends from the academy. He was apparently particularly interested in the newspaper reports of your attack and your husband's murder. He followed it closely. So when your name came up on one of our lists when you re-entered the country, naturally his friend noticed it and mentioned it to him. Marcello was working odd jobs at the time, and the vacancy at the grocery store was a particular stroke of luck. But I'm sure he would have found another way to get close to you if the signora hadn't needed help with her tomatoes. We found a soutane among his clothes,' Pallioti adds. 'We think that after he realized Signora Raguzza received communion at home he sometimes came into the building dressed as a priest.'

The perfect disguise. Like pigeons and showgirls, Billy said, they all look alike. That's how he knew her name too. All he had to do was go through her drawers to find her driver's licence, or her library card. Anthea. He would have done that after he got in with my keys. That would have been easy too. He could have slipped his hand into my bag a hundred times. Or, knowing me, it's entirely possible I did even better and left them on the counter of the grocery store one day when I was in a hurry. Something Pallioti said is bugging me, though.

'He collected clippings on me? Did he do that for all of us?'

'To some extent. But I would have to say you were his favourite. The attack on you, and your husband's murder, apparently fascinated him. He had virtually everything that was written on it.'

'Why?'

Pallioti stubs out his cigarette and looks at me. 'Because,' he says, 'he didn't do it. Marcello was hit by a car on his scooter on the seventeenth of May. On the twenty-fifth, the day you were attacked in the Boboli, he was flat on his back with his leg in traction in the recovery ward of the hospital. He'd been operated on for the second time only the day before, and there is absolutely no possibility that he left his bed. He couldn't even walk for two months.'

I stare at him. 'So,' I say finally. 'Karel Indrizzio. After all.'

He nods. 'Karel Indrizzio after all.'

The silence in the room is thick, heavier than the smoke hanging in a pall above our heads. I feel as if my blood has slowed down, as if it's turned to sludge and no longer moves inside my body. Pallioti is watching me.

'Ty?' I ask. But it's an unfair question. Pallioti can't give me an answer for why he died. It wasn't for God or Grace. It was for nothing more than a wallet. A blue handbag. My husband died because some creep read about murders in the newspaper and saw an easy way to get some euros. And of course Marcello was fascinated by it. Because he was the only one who recognized the attack on us for what it was: a copy of his own work. The exact reverse of what we thought.

'But the mask,' I say. 'I assumed—'

Pallioti takes his glasses off, rubs his hand across his eyes.

'So did I, signora,' he says. 'That was my mistake. I saw what wasn't there.' He looks up at me and smiles. 'For all we know,' Ispettore Pallioti says, 'Karel Indrizzio went to Venice and bought himself a souvenir that fell out of his pocket. On the other hand,' he adds, 'a lot of people use the gardens. So perhaps it was there all along.'

Pallioti walks me down to the lobby of the Questura for the last time. He's quiet, solicitous, as if he's genuinely sorry that he can't wrap up what happened to Ty and me in a neat little bow and hand it over like a present. When he shakes my hand, there's a sadness in his still, pale eyes.

'I know this will sound strange, signora,' he says. 'But it has been a pleasure, making your reacquaintance.'

'For me too,' I say. And I realize with a shock that this is actually true. For a start, I'll miss having someone to sneak cigarettes with.

I watch the straight back of his suit move steadily up the marble staircase, then I push my way out through the revolving doors. The usual late-afternoon crowd is milling in the streets, and as I join them I realize that today is probably the first day since I arrived in Florence two months ago when no one at all is watching me. Walking home towards Pierangelo's, I feel more alone than I have in weeks.

Epilogue

THAT WAS ALMOST a month ago. Now it is late May, and Pierangelo and I are in our third week in the country. Summer is coming. Poppies wash the chalky humps of the Crete Senese and at night the first fireflies pulse and flicker at the edge of the woods.

The house Piero's mother left him sits high on the slope of a line of hills, small mountains really, that look down over a river valley where ducks land in the marshes, their calls echoing back and forth in the evening light. Once it was a fortified farm, part a huge estate, a *fattoria*, that owned as many as thirty or forty farms, and processed the oil and wheat and olives in central stores. Now most of the barns are empty shells, crumbling yellow ruins, or second homes, oases at the end of white dirt roads with bright blue patches of swimming pools and livid squares of sprinkled lawn.

During the war, the partisans controlled these valleys, and in the piazza of every tiny village there is a plaque that bears witness to the names of the dead, lists the shopkeepers, old men, school teachers and wives, pulled out and shot in retribution for

433

every German soldier who met a bullet or a roadside bomb. The killings of Italian civilians for German soldiers usually ran at a rate of about ten to one, but sometimes they soared to twenty, and the bodies were ordered to be left where they fell, rotting under the Tuscan sun.

It's a land of ghosts and barren soil, grey stone, vines, and the gnarled roots of scrub oak and olive. Starlings nest in our deserted barns. Sitting on the terrace, if you are still enough, you can hear the flutter of wings.

The house itself is rectangular, tall and long, the bedrooms, kitchen and dining room on the lower floor and the rooms we live in above, two long interconnected spaces giving on to a loggia, an eyrie that looks out over the river and what is left of the farm buildings, which seem to be disintegrating before our eyes, crumbling back into the soil they rose from. Roofs have fallen in. Wild roses have taken hold along the walls. They claw up to the windows and gutters, their flowers pale scented speckles in the moonlight.

More than once I have watched Pierangelo from the loggia, seen him, when he thought I was asleep or reading, wandering the dirt drive, probing the doorways and the shadowed places, looking, I think, for the ghost of his mother, for some trace of the woman who gave him up as a baby, and whom he never knew. She lived her last years here, and these buildings, this land, is her legacy, all he has, and will ever have, of her. Pierangelo loves it. He calls it a waking dream. But when I first came here, I had nightmares.

I saw Karel Indrizzio standing in the broken doorways of the storage sheds at the bottom of the hill. I smelled acacia in the roses. And in the rustling that moves through the trees when it rains, I heard Marcello, felt his whisper close to my cheek: *Flesh shall pay for the sins of the flesh.*

I've begun to paint again, and we've decided to move the wedding forward. It was Pierangelo's idea. He says Marcello frightened him, made him realize happiness is fragile. Then he laughs and says that maybe it's just his age. Piero turns fifty in a little over a month, and he says the best present I can give him is to marry him. So we'll dispense with the party and relatives, with the white dress and Sicily or Sardinia or Capri. Instead, we'll go to the town hall and, afterwards, we'll come back here, to Monte Lupo.

Most days, Pierangelo commutes to the city and the paper, and I could go with him if I wanted—stay in the apartment, go shopping—but now it is summer, I would rather stay here. I walk, every day, and I like to imagine the paths and deer tracks that cut deep into the forest above the house being used by the partisans, thin young men in worn clothes who slip through the trees. I don't glimpse their ghosts, but I do see deer occasionally, and once even a little black boar. He darts into the path ahead of me and stands with his nose twitching. When he sees me, his tiny eyes squint, his tail goes straight up, and he skittles into the bushes. I start early, as soon as Pierangelo leaves, picking my way along the ridge, watching the line of the river in the valley, and one morning I find the stables. I have heard about them from the woman who comes to clean, picked up whispers in the shop and the local bar. This is where the partisans met.

The buildings stand at the edge of the woodland, above a scrubby field, and I know at once what they are because there's a stone horse's head above the archway where a rusted gate hangs on one hinge.

The walls are the colour of honey. Saplings have grown through the paving stones. Vines and weeds flower and fall. And in the centre there is a huge chestnut tree whose branches spread in a canopy that reaches almost to the roofs. A stone bench, green and furry with moss, circles its trunk, and beside it there's a well. The whispers say traitors' courts were held here, justice meted out, and that collaborators were hanged from these branches. I throw a pebble down into the darkness, hear a whoosh, and then, eventually, a tiny splash.

Six loose boxes, square and dark as monks' cells, ring the yard, and I imagine horses' heads peering over them, their great warm chests pressing against the now rotten wooden doors.

Lavender struggles out of a planter, and when I push the door to a store room, I hear the growl of doves. White ghosts flap out of the shadows and spiral to the peaked roof where they preen and strut.

The place feels as if it has been sleeping here for centuries, and the next day I come back with my paints and sketchbook. I have no idea if the stories are true, if bodies hung from the thick branches or if there are bones in the well, and as my brush moves across the paper, I am no longer sure it matters. Whether the ghosts are visible or invisible, all I know is what I see: that the tree still blossoms, that its branches still throw dappled shade, and that no matter what passed here before, or will come after, the stones are beautiful.